"TELL LAZHENKO TO GET OUT OF THERE. WE NEED A WITNESS. WE NEED AT LEAST ONE PERSON TO LIVE THROUGH THIS, TO TELL US WHAT HAPPENED."

Vellacott looked up at her. "Lazhenko told Moscow to piss off. He's not going to listen to us."

"Just tell him," Caruso said. "For the record."

Vellacott turned back to his console, hit the talk switch. "This is Mission Control–Houston to *Soyuz*. Commander Lazhenko, we repeat. We have determined you must leave the vicinity of space station at once."

Lazhenko's reply was immediate and uncooperative. *"Negative, Houston. Doctor Rey and Rushkin are not yet out."*

Caruso reached her breaking point. She yanked off Vellacott's commset, spoke into the microphone. "Damn it, Yuri! The station isn't going to *move*! It's going to *explode*! The Progress engine has a blocked fuel line! Now get out of there!"

"I understand, Houston," Lazhenko finally answered. *"I leave as soon as Doctor Rey and Rushkin are clear. Soyuz out."*

Caruso threw down the commset in frustration. "We've lost them," she said. "We've lost them all."

FREEFALL

JUDITH & GARFIELD REEVES-STEVENS

POCKET STAR BOOKS

NEW YORK   LONDON   TORONTO   SYDNEY

An *Original* Publication of POCKET BOOKS

A Pocket Star Book published by
POCKET BOOKS, a division of Simon & Schuster, Inc.
1230 Avenue of the Americas, New York, NY 10020

This book is a work of fiction. Names, characters, places and incidents are products of the authors' imagination or are used fictitiously. Any resemblance to actual events or locales or persons, living or dead, is entirely coincidental.

ISBN: 0-7434-0607-9

First Pocket Books paperback edition March 2005

10 9 8 7 6 5 4 3 2 1

POCKET STAR BOOKS and colophon are registered trademarks of Simon & Schuster, Inc.

Designed by Melissa Isriprashad
Cover art and design by Carlos Beltran

Manufactured in the United States of America

For information regarding special discounts for bulk purchases, please contact Simon & Schuster Special Sales at 1-800-456-6798 or business@simonandschuster.com.

For Bill & Liz
with love and appreciation
for their inspiring generosity of spirit
that lifts everyone they touch
into a world where anything is possible

What is history but a fable agreed upon?

—Napoleon Bonaparte

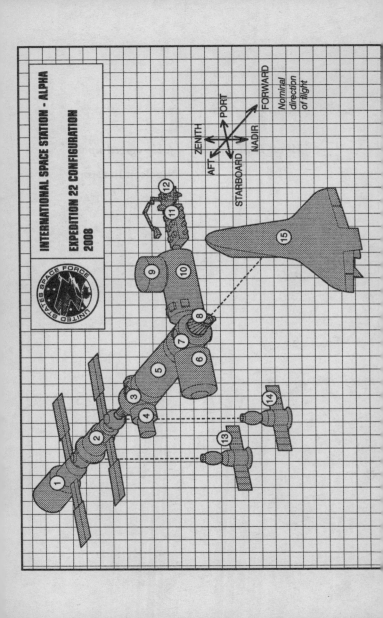

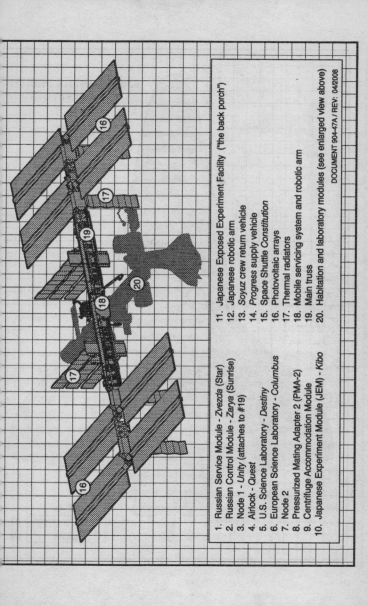

1. Russian Service Module - Zvezda (Star)
2. Russian Control Module - Zarya (Sunrise)
3. Node 1 - *Unity* (attaches to #19)
4. Airlock - *Quest*
5. U.S. Science Laboratory - *Destiny*
6. European Science Laboratory - *Columbus*
7. Node 2
8. Pressurized Mating Adapter 2 (PMA-2)
9. Centrifuge Accommodation Module
10. Japanese Experiment Module (JEM) - *Kibo*

11. Japanese Exposed Experiment Facility ("the back porch")
12. Japanese robotic arm
13. *Soyuz* crew return vehicle
14. *Progress* supply vehicle
15. Space Shuttle *Constitution*
16. Photovoltaic arrays
17. Thermal radiators
18. Mobile servicing system and robotic arm
19. Main truss
20. Habitation and laboratory modules (see enlarged view above)

DOCUMENT 904-47A / REV: 04/2008

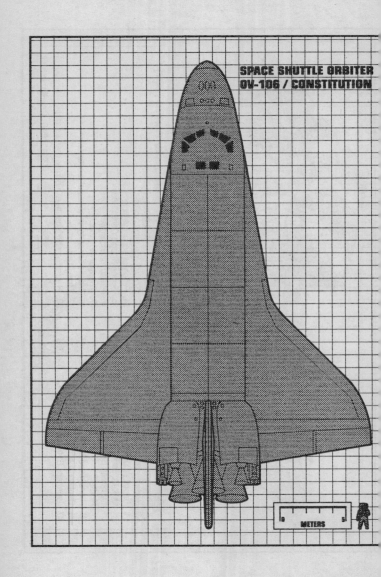

SPACE SHUTTLE ORBITER
OV-106 / CONSTITUTION

METERS

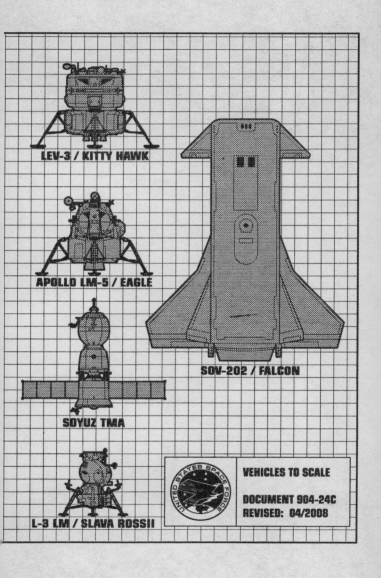

LEV-3 / KITTY HAWK

APOLLO LM-5 / EAGLE

SOYUZ TMA

L-3 LM / SLAVA ROSSII

SOV-202 / FALCON

UNITED STATES SPACE FORCE

VEHICLES TO SCALE

DOCUMENT 904-24C
REVISED: 04/2008

FREEFALL

Prologue

"THEY'RE GOING to get there first."

Air Force Captain Randolph Bailey looked at the attaché case the man from the State Department carried. It didn't belong in the stage-set perfection of the White House library. The honey-oak paneled walls gleamed in the warm glow of the electric candle lights flanking the fireplace, but in that same amber light, the brown leather case was scuffed, its tarnished brass-colored locks dented. Nothing valuable could ever be kept in a case like that.

Which was a lie, of course, Bailey knew. Misdirection. Like everything else in this dark labyrinth of government he had allowed himself to be trapped within. Because if what the man said was true, then that nondescript case carried the ashes of ten billion dollars. Maybe the ashes of democracy.

Bailey self-consciously straightened his suit jacket, uncomfortable with how wrinkled it was. The after-hours summons had come so quickly, he hadn't had time to go home to put on his uniform. He had had to make do with the least crumpled suit rolled up in the trunk of his Mustang, waiting for a trip to the dry cleaners.

"You've seen the report?" Bailey asked. There was no need to say which report.

But the man from the State Department shook his head. As if by habit, he stood to the side of one of the library's two windows, peering out at the floodlit South Lawn as if expecting an attack. An occupational hazard, Bailey decided. The heavy, tied-back green velvet drapes cast a shadow to obscure the man's completely average face, hiding nothing, hiding everything. "It's still being written."

Bailey wasn't surprised. "Twenty-one investigatory panels. Last I heard, between NASA and the contractors, they had more than fifteen hundred people on it."

For just a moment, the man smiled. "Investigatory," he repeated, as if it were a foreign word. His expression became unreadable again, unremarkable, like everything else about him.

Bailey had his own way of dealing with mysteries. "I don't understand," he said bluntly. Like most engineers, he had no patience for intrigue.

The man from the State Department stepped away from the window and smiled again at Bailey. The expression looked genuine, but after two years in D.C., Bailey knew better.

"You will," the man said. He put his case on the seat of a wingback chair near the fireplace, opened it. Bailey saw the extra push the man gave to the tarnished lock on the right, most likely the switch that disarmed the gas canister or flash grenade or whatever other antitheft device protected the case's secrets.

The man took out a thick red folder, closed the case again, locked it. Another habit, Bailey knew. Self-preservation.

The man held out the folder to Bailey. Above the boxed paragraph of fine print detailing the $10,000 fine and mandatory imprisonment for unlawful disclosure of the folder's contents, Bailey saw a single word in heavy black letters, two inches tall.

EXCALIBUR.

He made no move to take the folder. "That's above my pay grade." As a Special Assistant to the President, his security clearance was SECRET, but only for specific, compartmentalized information related to the narrow range of aerospace subjects on which he advised the president. He had been in briefing rooms when ABOVE TOP SECRET folders, carefully closed, had been present on the opposite side of the table. But of the classification levels higher than ABOVE TOP SECRET, Bailey had only heard their code designations in passing, and he had no doubt that those designations, one of which was EXCALIBUR, changed regularly.

The man from the State Department continued to hold the folder out. "You're cleared for this, Captain. You have a need to know."

At any other place, any other time, Bailey would have sought confirmation of such a statement from a ranking officer. But this close to the top of the chain of command, he'd learned that regulations were often subordinated to expediency—even those concerning the proper handling and transmission of classified information.

Still, Bailey glanced back at the double-door entrance to the library. The massive oak doors were still closed, but Bailey knew the stolid Secret Service agents who had escorted him through the East Wing would both be standing in the hall beyond, resolute and unyielding. Until the president was finished with his guests upstairs, no one else would be entering the library. Given the circumstances, it seemed the room was properly secured. Feeling as if he had been asked to disarm a bomb blindfolded, he took the folder.

His first thought was that it was heavier than he'd expected. There was something inside other than ordinary paper.

He slipped his hand under the flap and split the shiny, blue-black paper disk that sealed the folder. Some of the disk's security ink flaked off onto his fingers, shining there like pinpoint beads of black sweat.

Bailey rubbed his fingers together, but the ink flakes, of course, would not rub free. Though there was no visible trace of them against the dark skin on the back of his hand, the flakes had already melted to stain his paler fingertips and palm. Short of the use of caustic chemicals guaranteed to scar, those stains would identify him for at least the next seventy-two hours as a person who had opened an EXCALIBUR document.

He looked inside at the folder's contents and saw the glossy surface of a photographic print. Black and white. At least two dozen, stacked together with an inch-thick sheaf of paper.

Bailey didn't want to see what they pictured. He had come to Washington burning with the pure fire of idealism, an unshakable conviction that the horrors of this decade's first half were firmly in the past. Now, two years later, he spent most of his duty hours fearing for his country, and most of his off-duty hours fearing for his wife and daughters. America, and the world, were that close to the nuclear abyss. Whatever was in these photographs would be the stuff of nightmares.

He pulled out the first one.

It was hideous.

Bailey bit his lip. Four weeks earlier, he had mourned with the rest of the country when disaster had struck at

Cape Kennedy. He doubted he ever would stop mourning. He didn't need to see this.

A human body. No hair, no skin. No facial features. The only recognizable detail a pair of blackened boots. The rest of the body charred black, its husk of skin cracked and flaking like the ink that stained his fingers.

"You really want to show this to the president?" Bailey asked.

The man from the State Department didn't have to answer. There could be no other purpose for this meeting.

Bailey still didn't understand. Wasn't sure he wanted to. "Which one is he?" His voice was suddenly dry, uncertain. "White? Grissom? Chaffee?"

But the man from the State Department reacted to none of the names.

"His name was Valentin Bondarenko."

"Russian." Bailey didn't even make it a question.

"Cosmonaut."

Bailey had heard the rumors, even read the reports of suspected Russian casualties in their space program, dating back to suborbital tragedies as early as 1957. But in his compartmentalized, need-to-know world, he had yet to see any confirmation of those rumors.

He asked the question he knew the man from the State Department was waiting for.

"How is this connected to the Apollo fire?"

"The same thing happened in Baikonur. Six years ago."

"Fire in a capsule?"

"Essentially. It was an isolation exercise. Bondarenko spent ten days in a pressure chamber. On the last day, he swabbed off the adhesive used to keep his medical sensors in place. Tossed the cotton swabs aside. They were soaked in rubbing alcohol. They landed on a hot plate."

Bailey completed the scenario in his mind. With

alcohol-soaked cotton balls as the ignition source, there was only one plausible condition which could lead to the cosmonaut being so totally consumed by flames. "He was in a pure O-two atmosphere. Just like—"

"Just like the Apollo 204 capsule."

Bailey caught his breath. Oxygen wasn't flammable itself, but it was the gas that let everything else burn. "Six years ago?"

"March 23, 1961. Twenty days before Gagarin flew."

"My Lord." Bailey forced himself to flip through the rest of the photographs. Grotesque images of Bondarenko being plastered with salves, being given I.V. fluids through his feet, the only part of his body not charred. "He was alive?"

"For a time."

The one small mercy of the terrible fire at the Cape for Bailey, the one slender straw to be grasped in the dead of night, was that America's Apollo astronauts had succumbed quickly to smoke inhalation when their suits had failed. They had not lingered with the unbearable agony of third-degree burns over ninety-five percent of their bodies as this poor cosmonaut apparently had.

"There were two major similarities," the man from the State Department said. "Pure oxygen atmosphere. No way to open the chamber quickly from the outside."

"And NASA had no idea?" That was the crux of the matter, Bailey knew. On Earth, humans breathed atmosphere that was almost twenty-percent oxygen at an approximate sea-level pressure of fifteen pounds per square inch. In space, to simplify engineering costs, to save mass, and to protect against the shock of sudden decompression from fifteen PSI to the zero PSI of hard vacuum, American astronauts flew in an atmosphere of one-hundred percent oxygen at the much lower pressure of five PSI. Knowing

that a fire such as the one that had killed Bondarenko—
and, it seemed likely, the Apollo 204 astronauts—could
result from such conditions, Bailey couldn't imagine
NASA engineers not taking preventive measures. But the
Mercury and Gemini capsules had flown safely with pure-
oxygen atmospheres. So there had been no impetus to
make changes for the spacecraft of Project Apollo.

"NASA still has no idea," the man from the State
Department said. "Last Thursday and Friday, they had more
meetings at the Cape. The review board released their third
interim report today. Jim Webb phoned the president this
afternoon to discuss it."

Bailey wasn't surprised that James Webb, the chief
administrator of NASA, was dealing directly with the
president on this matter. Like most Americans, the president had absolute faith in the space agency, and given all
the other challenges his administration faced, he appeared
content to let a successful organization continue to run
itself. But the fire in the capsule threatened to change
that. How could it not?

Bailey sensed there was more to what the man from the
State Department was trying to tell him. "Is there something wrong with the interim report?"

"Webb is still defending the pure oxygen atmosphere."

"How can he?" Even unofficially, everything Bailey had
heard leaked from the investigation pointed to the presence
of pure oxygen as being the most significant contributing
factor to the Apollo fire. Especially at the test pressure of
almost seventeen pounds per square inch. Almost a decade
earlier, even the Air Force and the Navy had abandoned
the use of pure O_2 for high-altitude test flights.

"As of two days ago, the board specifically rejects the
idea of changing the use of pure oxygen at five PSI in the
suits and the spacecraft. The only concessions they're will-

ing to make is to re-evaluate the use of a dilutant gas, and to recommend that pressurized oxygen no longer be used in tests and prelaunch operations."

Bailey had so many indignant questions to ask that he didn't know where to begin.

The man waited for none of them. "As far as the interim report's concerned, the board's leaning toward blaming the fire on the presence of combustible materials, deficiencies in the design of firebreaks, and deficiencies in the test's safety protocols."

Bailey finally found his voice. "That's bull. None of those elements mean anything if there's no pure O-two."

The man from the State Department nodded. "See? You do understand."

Bailey tried to work out the logic of the chief administrator's position. He couldn't. "Does the review board have a specific reason for making those determinations?"

"Let me ask *you* a question, Captain. How long do you think it would take to redesign the atmospheric systems for the Apollo capsule and lunar lander?"

"Two years." Bailey stared at the man. "Which puts us on the Moon in '69."

"December of '69," the man said. "Being welcomed by the cosmonauts who'll land in August '68."

"You're saying if NASA concludes the atmospheric mix was wrong, the two-year delay to fix it will stop us from getting to the Moon first?"

"No. That's what you said."

"But is that what Webb's thinking?" Bailey asked.

"The chief administrator of NASA is . . . an honorable man. You won't find anyone who'll support the idea that he's willing to hide the truth and risk the astronauts' lives just to beat the Soviets to the Moon."

The man from the State Department offered Bailey no

clue if he really believed that, or if this odd exchange was simply to engage him in a mock cross-examination, as if he were a lawyer's client being prepped for court.

"Then if not Webb," Bailey said, "someone else at NASA wants to push ahead. A primary contractor. Someone on the review board who has his ear."

The man from the State Department said nothing in reply. Bailey took that silence as an indication of agreement.

"Then why bring this to *me?* Isn't this just the evidence that will convince the review board to redesign the capsule?"

"It is. If they could see it."

Bailey finally understood what was being asked of him. "So you want the president to see these pictures . . . to override whoever's on the review board calling for no redesign, so that . . ." The ultimate conclusion made no sense at all to Bailey. "You want the president to throw the space race?"

"I want no such thing." The man from the State Department folded his hands behind his back. Bailey could see an asymmetrical bulge beneath the man's dark gray suit jacket, beneath his left shoulder. He wondered what sort of clearance a civilian needed to carry a loaded weapon into the White House. "Captain Bailey, at this juncture, there are two ways for America to get to the Moon. One way is to go full speed ahead. Treat our astronauts like experimental animal subjects, and tell ourselves that a twenty-percent fatality rate is an acceptable price to pay for exploration. God knows that is the price the Soviets are paying."

Twenty percent, Bailey thought with shock. That figure could only mean that at least some of the rumors of dead cosmonauts were true.

"The other way," the man continued, "is to redesign and

rebuild the damned Apollo capsule, and send our boys to the Moon the safest way we can."

"Even if it costs us first place?"

"It doesn't have to."

"You know a faster way for us to get to the Moon?"

The man's reply sucked the warmth from the library. "We have the assets in place to ensure that it takes the Soviets longer to get there."

Bailey felt as if the library floor had bucked beneath his feet like a transport plane hitting turbulence. "You can't be serious."

"That is where your need to know ends."

Another small mercy, Bailey thought. Another slender straw.

The man shifted his unreadable gaze to the EXCALIBUR folder. "But what you must know is that just as we have assets within the Soviet space program, they no doubt have assets within ours. Those photographs, that report, could reveal to the Soviets the identity of two of our people."

"Which is why only the president can know what's in here." No one on the review boards could have any knowledge of the file's existence without the possibility of jeopardizing the spies who had passed on its secrets.

The man flashed another half smile. Bailey didn't care. "In an ideal world," the man said. "But for all his talents, the president is not an aeronautical engineer. We need someone to explain to him what he's reading, and seeing. Someone with absolutely no contact with NASA. Some-one—"

"The president can trust."

"Exactly."

For a moment, Bailey almost wanted to laugh. He now had the responsibility of helping guide the president of the United States to a decision that would ensure the safety of

American astronauts going to the Moon. Could there be a more worthwhile, more noble undertaking for an Air Force officer? Yet at the same time, if he succeeded in shaping the president's decision toward the result the man from the State Department wanted, he would also be setting into motion a series of events that would likely endanger innocent victims halfway around the world.

Bailey didn't pretend to know how both goals could be reconciled. It was the nightmare of Washington, of being in a place and time where ultimate, irrevocable decisions could be made. Had to be made.

The man from the State Department cleared his throat, a polite way to bring Bailey's attention back to the present. "Senator Anderson has called for the Senate committee to hold an open hearing Monday, three P.M."

Bailey hefted the folder in his hand. "Can the president be seen to interfere with an open hearing?"

"The Senate serves the president. Once he understands what's at stake, he can make his concerns known to Webb. Webb can make sure that the right questions are asked."

"And the right conclusions reached."

The man from the State Department picked up his attaché case. For a moment, Bailey wondered what other secrets it contained, what other red folders it had carried.

"That's it?" Bailey asked.

"I've done my job, Captain. Now you'll do yours."

The man started toward the library doors.

Bailey held up the folder again. "What about this?"

"Leave it with the president." He looked back at Bailey. "He's cleared for it, too."

Bailey stared at the folder, as if its color came from flames that could scorch the flesh from bones.

The man gave a quick rap on the closed door.

Bailey couldn't help himself. His last question sprang

forth without thought. "Are people really going to die because of this?"

The left-hand door swung open. In the corridor, a Secret Service agent was ready to escort the man away.

But the man held up his hand to the agent, closed the door again, looked back at Bailey. "Captain, what you said earlier, about this being a space race, you're wrong. It's a space war. It always has been."

That was all the answer the man had to give. Bailey knew what happened in war, just like every other American who watched the evening news from the Asian jungles.

The man from the State Department left.

The second Secret Service agent looked in from the corridor. "The president's on his way, sir."

Bailey could hear footsteps in the corridor beyond. Solid, assured. They might as well have been the thunder of falling bombs.

Space war.

Someone would win. Someone would lose.

And innocents, most assuredly, would die.

RED COBRA

T MINUS 10 DAYS

FORTY-ONE YEARS LATER

1

CAPTAIN MITCHELL WEBBER, USN, fell through the night, a shadow on the full Moon. The muted roar of the silenced MC–130E Combat Talon I transport above him was already lost in the biting hiss of icy wind against his helmet. He held his arms close, kept his head down, angled his body for rapid descent.

He punched into the dense cloud layer at 11,000 feet, the transition from clear air marked only by the disappearance of the stars and the streaming rivulets of water on his laser-attenuation goggles. Writhing threads of condensed moisture flashed like pale green lightning in the glow of situational data displayed on the goggles' lenses.

Webber's concentration was absolute, focused on his dropping altitude, the final digits of the readout on his lenses' virtual REDEYE screen a blur. He felt the snap and flutter of his gear and harness straps against his drysuit, but no sense of motion. That would come later, he knew. In the last few seconds.

A voice whispered in his helmet speakers: the communications systems operator of the departing transport plane, transmitting on an encrypted channel. *"Freefall Base to Angel One: Angel Two is flying."*

Freefall was current designation for the Department of Defense's joint foreign-technology retrieval program, run by the U.S. Special Operations Command. Angel Two was Webber's baby-sitter on this mission: Colonel Daniel Varik, USAF Special Forces. Varik's job tonight was to ensure Angel One—Webber—got in and accomplished the primary goal. Getting out again was not a necessary condition of success.

Webber caught the flash of a small red alert square on the computer screen in the upper left of his goggles, next to his Global Positioning Satellite coordinates: 39.37.09 N, 103.42.15 E. A yellow X slid out of the center of two brackets. He was drifting to the west.

Webber adjusted the angle of his fall by extending his right arm and leg, again with no corresponding sense of movement. But the yellow X re-centered in the target and his GPS numbers moved back into an acceptable range, guiding him to a satellite-determined drop zone six inches square. The flashing red alert winked out. Though still plunging blindly through clouds, he was back on the proper free-fall trajectory.

He refocused on his altitude reading, making sure it matched what he'd been told to expect. The base of the cloud cover at target coordinates was 1,500 feet above ground level. The number had come from the transport pilot, just before the green jump light had winked on in the belly of the plane.

He checked his terminal velocity—120 miles per hour. At that speed, his life expectancy after punching the cloud base would be 8.5 seconds. He remained unconcerned. Navy SEALs did not succumb to doubt.

Then Webber broke through the clouds and everything

happened at once. Absolute darkness was replaced by a curving constellation of glittering lights tracing the deep sloping face of the immense Shiyang Dam.

Simultaneously, Webber felt the explosive pop of the automatic-activation device in his main chute as its barometric sensor fired the piston that cut the deployment cord.

An instant later, his viewpoint changed and he was looking at the mountainous horizon against the faint moonglow of the clouds. That meant his main chute had opened and he was now descending vertically.

Webber glanced up to check the inner shell of his black, wing-shaped canopy silhouetted against the pale gray clouds. He confirmed his lines weren't fouled, then looked down, focusing past the REDEYE readout in his goggles.

The layout of what lay below him was exactly as he had memorized during the virtual simulations at Fort Benning: concrete dam, associated hydroelectric-generator outbuildings, and two narrow service roads that wound high into the hills on either side of the installation.

He no longer needed the GPS readouts to find his drop zone.

Webber tugged on his control lines to guide his parafoil to a spot 1,000 feet back from the midpoint of the dam. Ten seconds later, he plunged into the near-freezing, dark water of the Shiyang reservoir. Right on target, deep within enemy territory.

Not that the People's Republic of China *was* America's enemy.

Yet.

The target was one of twelve sites given the code name Red Cobra.

The first of these sites had a history dating back to the

nineties, when China had embarked on a program of building hydroelectric facilities that would dwarf the ambitious construction plans of Chairman Mao and his Great Leap Forward. The gigantic reservoirs were to displace millions of rural Chinese and disrupt vast environmental ecosystems, while priceless archaeological treasures yet to be found would disappear forever. All in the name of modernizing agriculture and efficiently bringing inexpensive, renewable electrical power to the masses.

The agriculture analysts who consulted for the Central Intelligence Agency hadn't thought much of the new Chinese initiative. Their figures indicated the Chinese were building to overcapacity in both irrigation needs and power requirements. Until a low-level civilian analyst in NIMA—the National Imagery and Mapping Agency—stumbled upon a small anomaly.

While reconciling geospatial data of China's Gansu province, which had been radar-mapped from the space shuttle in 1994 with the results of the 2000 Shuttle Radar Topography Mission conducted by NASA for what was then the Defense Mapping Agency, the analyst discovered the topography of an otherwise unremarkable valley had significantly changed.

Instead of its earlier depth of almost nine hundred feet, Xiao Valley was registering a new depth of just under three hundred. The computer-comparison program, which was designed to look for topographical changes indicating new roads and construction that might reveal potential new military targets, automatically flagged this difference for a human analyst to review.

Following standard operating procedure, the analyst checked the coordinates' current state through visual imagery provided by the constellation of Keyhole satellites that monitored China on a twenty-four-hour-a-day basis.

Those images revealed the valley in question was now the reservoir of a large hydroelectric plant constructed sometime between the 1994 and 2000 shuttle missions, in an area where the local population did not appear to be large enough to justify its size.

Seven months after the NIMA analyst had noticed a change in topography, the combined efforts of the CIA, the National Reconnaissance Office, and, finally, the National Security Agency, came to the astonishing though inescapable conclusion that the Chinese had flooded the valley to make it a reservoir, and then had built an underwater installation in it that had escaped satellite detection. The hydroelectric facility was merely a decoy to account for the construction activity associated with the hidden installation.

This sobering discovery led to a thorough review of China's more than 80,000 hydroelectric and reservoir facilities. At twelve of these facilities, signs of other hidden underwater installations were now revealed.

Code-named Red Cobra installations, the twelve sites were subjected to intense, ongoing investigation through orbital imagery, electronic signal intercepts, and, on occasion, on-site observations by clandestine teams of special forces operators.

Overall, the efforts of the American intelligence community were effective in peeling back the layers of secrecy surrounding the twelve Red Cobra targets. Some had been constructed for the assembly of weapons, some for storage of those weapons. Several were linked to high-energy laser- and microwave-weapons research, which explained why considerable power-generation capability had been built in areas where there weren't enough people to use it.

Only Red Cobra 8 had defied explanation.

Then, one month before Mitch Webber and Daniel

Varik stepped into empty air over the center of China, 1,000 miles west of Beijing, satellite images showed Red Cobra 8 was being repurposed. From measurements of the height of the shadows they cast, transport trucks were arriving empty, and leaving full. Employee car and bus traffic diminished. Visible offices no longer remained lit at night.

The conclusion was obvious: Whatever activities had been under way at Red Cobra 8 were reaching an end. If America ever wanted to determine what those activities had been, there would be one last chance for a mission. And if Command's current theory of those activities was correct, there was only one person America could send in.

Mitch Webber.

Even as his momentum drove him deep into the near-freezing waters of the reservoir, Webber took action. His first move was to pull the backup oxygen-supply mouthpiece from his buoyancy-control jacket. Blew into it, cleared it of water, then breathed.

The device worked, buying him time to unlatch his parachute harness and unused emergency chute, then swap his jump helmet and goggles for a full-face diving mask, complete with Divelink transceiver for underwater communication. The instant he tugged on his mask, cleared it, and opened the valve on his LAR-V rebreather, time ceased to be critical for the rest of his transition procedure.

Because of the sophisticated computerized mechanisms in the LAR-V, he could now remain underwater for up to eighteen hours as the rebreather constantly absorbed his exhaled carbon dioxide in a soda-lime powder and replaced it with precisely measured volumes of oxygen. Under current conditions, though, Webber knew the actual limiting factor on the length of his dive was not oxygen, but the operational lifetime of the batteries powering the compact heating element strapped against the small of his back. In the reservoir's frigid water, he needed the heat-pack's warmth that was circulated by his own blood flow through the rest of his body.

Still sinking, Webber calmly drew twin-vane black fins over his dive boots. Then he rolled up his waterlogged parafoil, jump harness, and unused backup chute, clipped lead weights from his harness to the bundle he'd made, and released it, consigning it to the depths of the reservoir.

Lightened, but still hampered by the drag of 120 pounds of equipment, most of it clipped to his dive harness in black, waterproof immersion bags, he took a bearing from his compass, then began to swim for the rendezvous point.

According to the temperature display on his wrist, the reservoir's water was 38° F. That meant he had a maximum exposure time of four hours, although the mission profile called for him and his baby-sitter to undertake less than sixty minutes of diving time.

If they lived that long.

According to the determinations of the DoD's combined intelligence agencies, inside Red Cobra 8 the People's Liberation Army Air Force was developing the long-rumored, fifth-generation Chinese F-20 fighter. The advanced craft was based in part on the Russian MiG-33 Fulcrum airframe, but reportedly with a radical new single engine design that would leave the American Joint Strike Fighter standing still.

Webber and Varik were tasked first with confirming that theory, retrieving whatever plans and images they could, then ensuring those plans and images reached Freefall ana-lysts. They could accomplish their mission either by physi-cally returning the intelligence, or by scanning and digitizing the intelligence in the field, then transmitting it to Special Operations Command by satellite-burst communications. The second scenario did not require either of them to actually leave Chinese territory in order to complete their primary mission. However, a Fulton skyhook extraction team was already in the air, standing by to pluck them both from the ground by means of balloon-borne cables. The United States Air Force had long ago perfected the sound, radar, and flight vector profiles that allowed them to operate individual aircraft over remote areas of China while remaining invisible to China's antiquated air defense system.

There was an additional task in the mission plan, and it was that objective that had brought Webber to this moment. Varik had been selected for the Freefall assignment because he was a trained special forces operator with exceptional skill and success in conducting infiltration/exfiltration missions. But Webber knew he had been selected because he was, in a word, a thief.

His career had begun eighteen years earlier in the Navy, and he had expertly moved from F-14 carrier operations to test pilot. The wider range of aircraft he flew, the more classes of aircraft the Navy trained him to fly, until he had completed foreign-technology familiarization tours at both Wright-Patterson and Groom Lake, popularly known as Area 51. Those postings had given him the opportunity to fly Russian MiGs and a variety of one-of-a-kind experimental and captured craft, only some of which could be called airplanes.

Halfway through his career, Webber received a strong suggestion from his commanding officer to apply for SEAL training as part of a special program to take technical specialists into the field.

In the past, Navy SEALs and special forces operatives of

the other services had been tasked with transporting scientists and engineers to targets within hostile territory, so they could conduct technical evaluations of enemy weapons systems and facilities. Prompted by the alarmingly high fatality rate among those specialists, Special Operations Command created a new program to turn SEALs into expert technicians, and expert technicians into SEALs.

Webber had been one of the first graduates of the program. Subsequently he'd been trained to fly craft he hadn't even suspected existed, from the crewed variant of the Venturestar reusable launch vehicle, to the hypersonic, optical stealth plane code-named Nevada Rain. So far, his training had been put to good use on three occasions, all of which had involved infiltrating enemy territory by water, and leaving at the controls of advanced concept jets. Once, while on detached duty with the Department of Energy's Nuclear Emergency Search Team, he'd even stolen America's own Nevada Rain from Wheeler AFB in Oahu. To Webber's surprise, after six long weeks of debriefing on what was now called the Icefire incident, no charges had been preferred. Instead, he had been presented with an unadorned plaque citing his unnamed contributions to "a significant accomplishment."

Though no one in Freefall Command had seriously thought that he could—or even should—attempt to fly a prototype Chinese F-20 from the Red Cobra 8 facility, the mission plan did allow him the latitude to consider the plane a target of opportunity. The fighter's blueprints and specifications were preferred, particularly if they could be obtained without PLA Air Force personnel realizing they had been compromised, but as a last resort, the DoD was willing to accept delivery of an F-20 and deal with the diplomatic fallout later. The American military establishment had not forgotten how China had dismantled a Navy

EP-3E surveillance plane after a Chinese F-8 fighter had collided with it over the China Sea. Despite the best efforts of the twenty-four crew members to disable and destroy their onboard equipment under perilous conditions, critical technology had been compromised.

The U.S. military continued to look forward to payback, and SOCOMM knew Webber could deliver.

Less than ten minutes after splashdown, navigating by the twin infrared illuminators mounted to the sides of their masks, Webber and Varik reached the top surface of the hidden underwater facility where it joined the dam's inner wall. Exactly as radar imaging had indicated, there was a large water inlet leading into the facility right at that point.

Webber and Varik adjusted their buoyancy-control jackets so they floated at the mouth of the eight-foot diameter pipe, forty feet below the reservoir's surface. The mission planners had been unable to determine the purpose of the pipe, and its appearance offered no additional clues. Webber and Varik would be first to discover its purpose. After a brief exchange of hand signals, they swam into the unknown.

At sixty feet, the pipe turned sharply upward within the dam's wall. As the two men slowly swam up through the pipe, both watched their depth-gauge indicators closely. The rebreathers released no air bubbles by which their rate of ascent could be visually judged.

At an effective depth of less than fifteen feet, the pipe once again curved to the horizontal. Another fifty feet along, Webber and Varik found four large inlets on the pipe's ceiling, each approximately three feet across. Just past the inlets, their infrared illuminators revealed a metal ladder connected to the pipe wall by metal rods.

Webber and Varik reached the ladder, then looked up to

see that it extended into a circular alcove that rose another five feet above the pipe's upper surface. In the ghostly green glow of the REDEYE display, it appeared the alcove was capped by a standard, watertight hatch, complete with large handwheel.

"Depth gauge says that maintenance hatch'll be even with the water level of the reservoir," Varik said. His midwestern twang was mechanically flattened by his Divelink radio's custom voice-recognition chip. It ensured the microphone didn't transmit ambient under-water sound, but sometimes made divers sound like robots. "Best guess: There's a mother of a compartment on the other side of that hatch that's filled with water, and sometimes they have to drain it fast." Then he swam up the ladder, braced his legs and gave the handwheel a twist. Webber could see that it moved easily. A few seconds after that, the water above Webber came alive with a milky blue light that spiked past Varik's dark silhouette as the colonel climbed out through the hatch.

Thirty seconds later, Varik radioed back, "It's clear."

Not knowing what to expect, Webber climbed the ladder, left the water, and sat on the circular edge of the open hatchway's coaming. When he tugged off his mask, he recoiled as a strong smell of chlorine hit him.

When he had wiped his face clear of water, Webber saw that he and Varik were in the bottom of an enormous square-sided enclosure, some forty feet deep, with walls and floor tiled in large, gleaming white ceramic panels. Each of the enclosure's walls had steel ladders, and the three large inlets on its floor corresponded to those in the entry pipe below—apparently emergency drains, as Varik had surmised.

But the enclosure was not as remarkable as what was in it. Overhead and to Webber's right was what appeared to be a giant white cylinder, at least sixty feet long and fifteen feet across. The cylinder was lying on its side in a dry-dock cradle with supports that suspended it ten feet above the enclosure's white floor. Its surface was patterned with a uniform series of perforations, large and numerous enough for the regularly spaced overhead lights on the room's high ceiling to filter through them, like sunlight through a tin can blasted by buckshot.

At first, the object made no sense. But even as Webber was puzzled by it, Varik ignored it. The colonel was already out of his diving gear and unpacking his infiltration equipment. Then, as Webber kicked off his fins and unfastened the cooling vents on his drysuit, the answer was so suddenly obvious, he felt embarrassed it had taken him this long to make sense of his surroundings.

"Varik, this is a neutral buoyancy training pool for microgravity simulation in space. And *that*," Webber said as he pointed up to the bizarre cylinder, "is the Chinese space station."

Varik slung an equipment pack over his shoulder, holstered his Heckler & Koch Mk 23 .45 automatic pistol, then tugged on the headband that held his swingdown infrared eyeviewer. For now, he kept the postage-stamp-size transparent screen folded up against his forehead, out of the way until needed. "That doesn't make sense." He nodded to the closest ladder. "Let's move."

Webber grabbed his own infiltration pack and pulled on his IR viewer headband as he hurried after Varik. "Of course it makes sense. Look at that thing. It's even got a mock-up of a *Shenzhou* capsule."

The *Shenzhou* was China's workhorse crewed-spacecraft. The name meant "Divine Vessel," and the name suited. It was based on the Russian *Soyuz* design, and in full spaceflight configuration with solar arrays spread, the craft did resemble a Christmas tree angel. There was a full-size, perforated-metal replica of one docked at the far end of the space station mock-up.

Varik paused at the ladder, looked back at Webber with a tight expression creasing his lean, lined face. "This is a top secret military facility. The whole world knows China has a space program. They've got astronauts up at their space station right now, same as we do. It's no secret."

"Taikonauts," Webber said. "Chinese astronauts are called taikonauts."

"So I've heard," Varik said. He began to climb. Air Force colonels and Navy captains were of equal rank, but for this mission, Varik had the final word for infiltration procedures. Webber followed in silence.

At floor level, everything Webber saw confirmed his conclusion. There were racks of brightly colored standard SCUBA gear for the safety divers who would accompany the astronaut trainees into the pool. Banks of computer consoles were covered with clear plastic tarps. The Chinese National Space Agency might just have well copied the design of this pool from the Sonny Carter Neutral Buoyancy Lab at the Johnson Space Center in Houston.

But Varik remained uninterested. He headed straight for a set of three double doors beyond the SCUBA racks. There were black rubber mats in front of them, covering the white-tiled floor. Signs with Chinese characters hung on each door.

Varik pointed a pen-size, flexible snakehead camera at the signs, looked at the display screen on the handheld machine-vision translation unit he carried.

" 'Safety station exiting . . . ,' " Varik read as the MVTU scanned the Chinese characters and roughly translated them on its screen. " 'Immersion apparatus removed not through these doors.' 'Synthetic training arenas.' 'Advance productive forces.' " He slapped the MVTU to a silent Velcro patch on his equipment harness. "Synthetic training arenas. We'll go there."

But Webber pointed to the pool. "Isn't that what this is?"

"This room is not part of our mission."

"What mission?" Webber asked. "This facility isn't what SOCOMM thought it was. It's a spaceflight training center—not a military installation. We shouldn't be here. It's a job for the cloak-and-dagger boys."

Without waiting for Webber, or responding to him, Varik opened one door slowly, peered into the corridor beyond. "Let's move," he said, and slipped out.

Webber half expected to hear the stutter of automatic gunfire as a security guard cut Varik down, but he crouched to jam a corner of a black mat into the doorjamb to keep the door from locking, then followed the man anyway, eager to get this fiasco wrapped up quickly. It was one thing to risk his life and the diplomatic relationship between China and America for vital military intelligence that could help maintain peace. It was quite another to risk the same to find out what kind of freeze-dried food Chinese taiko-nauts preferred.

The corridor outside the neutral-buoyancy training room was as wide as a two-lane road, low-ceilinged, and dark. Only a handful of light fixtures were working. But it was easy to see why there were no guards on patrol. The corridor walls were lined with boxes of all sizes, from card-board file cartons to wooden packing crates. Whatever the purpose of the facility, Command was right. It was either shutting down or changing venues.

Varik was already on the other side of the corridor, using picks on the lock of another set of wide doors. Beside those doors was what appeared to be a curved security counter with a neatly built-in computer console.

Webber moved silently to take up position next to Varik, then pointed to the Chinese characters on the sign above the doors. "What's that one say?"

Varik concentrated on his lock picks. "Number One Arena."

Webber's eyes narrowed. There was no possible way Varik could know that. The MVTU he needed to translate Chinese was still attached to his harness. He had not had enough time to use the device, then pack it up in the few seconds he had been alone in the corridor.

Varik had come to this door as if he had already known it would be here.

The lock clicked. Varik pushed the door open and entered. Webber followed him into a small dimly lit anteroom with white adhesive sheets covering the floor, sticky side up. He found that another convincing round of evidence for his conclusion.

"C'mon, Varik. This is to take dust off shoes. We're in clean-room conditions."

The colonel barely looked at Webber. He simply pointed at the adhesive sheet by the inner set of doors. "Then why is there more dirt by those doors than by the one we entered through?"

Webber checked the adhesive panels at both ends of the anteroom, saw that Varik was right. The adhesive was to take dirt off the shoes of people *exiting* this room. But why?

Varik stepped through the inner doors and Webber followed him again, this time into darkness.

Just as Varik did, Webber switched on his infrared flashlight and flipped down his IR viewer. The arm that held the transparent screen two inches in front of his left eye was tipped with a camera lens, its focus designed for infrared. The small wearable computer unit that processed the digital signal from the camera and then created the visual display on the viewer was located on his left shoulder. The small viewer created a pale green image that appeared to float before Webber's left eye, showing him that he and Varik were in a long corridor curving both left and right. The corridor's exterior wall was made of standard concrete block. Its interior wall appeared to be ribbed metal extending upward at least thirty feet. Webber estimated the interior volume of the enclosure it circled had to be at least several hundred feet across. He suspected this section of the facility was built deep within the thick wall of the dam.

"Over there," Varik said. He moved off to the left, to a metal door with rounded corners, raised about two feet above the corridor floor.

Without hesitation, Varik tried the latch handle. The door was unlocked.

There was only one possibility that could account for the colonel's confidence: He already knew what was on the other side of that door.

Varik opened the door, stepped up and through.

Webber matched his action, right behind him, but suddenly stopped. Instead of landing on solid flooring, his feet crunched into coarse sand and gravel.

Webber shone his IR flashlight all around.

In the heart of a sophisticated aerospace installation, he and Varik were standing on a dirt floor strewn with rocks. About one hundred feet away, an object the size of a small cabin stood just at the outside range of Webber's flashlight's IR beam, making most details impossible to see. But not all.

The object was standing on four angled legs. Webber felt the hair on his neck bristle as he fit the last pieces of the puzzle into the overall picture: the *Shenzhou* capsule, the space station mock-up, and now this—a lunar landing vehicle. He kicked at the granulated dirt. He was in a training chamber for lunar taikonauts.

Webber turned, using his flashlight to find Varik by an open electrical cabinet, just as the colonel threw a large rocker switch.

Banks of overhead floodlights suddenly flared into life, duplicating the unshielded brilliance of the sun on the airless Moon.

Webber threw up his arm to shade his eyes, stepped back, bumped into something large and heavy.

He spun around to face a taikonaut who had somehow sneaked up on him from behind. Reflexively, Webber lashed out with a kite blow to the man's chest, only to feel his hand hit empty fabric.

"I think you killed it," Varik said.

Webber flipped up his IR viewer. His attacker was an empty lunar spacesuit hanging on a spring-loaded harness used to simulate lunar gravity.

Varik broke out his camera gear. He handed Webber a Nikon digital camera, little more than a large lens with a pistol grip. "You cover the spacesuits and the scientific gear spread out around the lander. I'll cover the rest." Varik trudged off across the simulated lunar surface, leaving Webber with the empty suit.

For a moment, Webber studied the lander. The topmost part looked familiar—a large, spherical hull studded with a series of small rounded shells, resembling an updated version of the original Apollo mission's lunar module. But the lower half from which the landing legs angled out was unlike anything he had ever seen. What appeared to be outrigger pontoons made from wide curved strips of silvered metal extended from leg to leg. Additional pontoons, if that's what they were, seemed to line the underside of the lander as well.

Varik looked back at Webber. "Ten minutes, Captain. Then we're out." He began to take a series of photographs, turning a half step in a circle after each exposure, creating a panoramic view of the simulated landscape.

Webber switched on his own camera, started photographing the suit, now positive that no one would ever pay attention to the images he took.

More than ever he was convinced that this mission was not what it seemed. No one had expected him to find an advanced concept Chinese fighter in Red Cobra 8. Instead, Colonel Varik had been sent to find the Chinese lunar lander. Which meant, as far as Webber was concerned, both their lives had been put in danger for no useful reason. If this lunar training facility had been shut down, there was a simple explanation—the time for training had ended.

The Chinese were going to the Moon, and they were going sooner than anyone had suspected.

But the question Webber couldn't answer was why the U.S. military considered that to be a threat.

2

SPACE SHUTTLE *CONSTITUTION*

19:47 GMT, THURSDAY, APRIL 3

TWO HUNDRED TWENTY MILES above the Earth, Harper Doyle was the disaster's first casualty.

One of ten crew members working aboard the Space Shuttle *Constitution* and the International Space Station, the shuttle pilot choked to death in agony, his lungs seared by superheated gas from the explosion in the number three avionics bay in the shuttle's mid-deck. Before the smoke from that explosion could be drawn to a combustion detector in the venting system, Doyle had already asphyxiated in his own vomit.

At the time of the initial explosion, Shuttle Commander Vic "Jabba" Hutton was on the *Constitution's* flight deck, listening to his pocket stereo to ease the tedium. He and Mission Specialist Rebecca Oster were reviewing the consumables status report due within the hour at Mission Control–Houston. Their task consisted of little more than reading an Excel spreadsheet on the IBM ThinkPad Velcroed to the orbiter's flight console. Small, pale blue Velcro patches were dotted across every clear surface in the shuttle, adding to its cramped and cluttered feel and giving it the appearance of a vehicle that was perpetually unfinished.

With Bruce Springsteen cranked up to maximum volume, Commander Hutton felt the vibration but missed the metallic pop of the detonation twenty feet below and aft.

Rebecca Oster heard the explosion and looked back behind the commander's position toward the open interdeck access hatch leading to the mid-deck. The movement in microgravity made her thick dark curls bob lazily around her head. "Doyle?" she called out.

Hutton pulled out one of the small ear buds of his stereo. A tinny version of "Born to Run" joined the almost painfully loud background noise of the orbiter's circulating fans and coolant pumps. "What's up?"

"Dunno. Sounded like Doyle blew the wet trash hatch again."

Hutton snorted, not amused by another of his pilot's misadventures. "Tell him to clean it up before any more garbage hits the vents. Again."

Oster slipped her feet from the footstool-style restraining platform that kept her in place before the flight console and pushed off across the small deck to the hatch. On orbit, the shuttle's flight deck seats were removed and stored, so Oster's trajectory was a straight line, expertly calculated to take her headfirst through the interdeck hatch without touching any of its four sides. She had once almost made the U.S. Olympic Women's Diving Team.

Halfway to the hatch, Oster smelled smoke. A heartbeat later, the orbiter's primary fire alarm sounded, and the second explosion was triggered.

The edge of the hatch slammed into Oster's gut and she lost her breath.

Her collision could mean only one thing.

The docked space shuttle was moving.

INTERNATIONAL SPACE STATION

In addition to the three astronauts on *Constitution,* four astronauts and three cosmonauts were aboard the International Space Station. At 21:30 GMT, the station's workday had officially ended, giving the seven-member crew ninety minutes of personal time for an evening meal, exercise, and the review of the next day's schedule. Because the station was technically an international effort, it ran on Greenwich Mean Time, long used by the military under the designation "Zulu."

The departing commander of the twenty-first crew to serve aboard the station, Yuri Lazhenko, and his Science Officer, Bette Norman, were zipped into Lazhenko's sleeping bag in the *Zvezda* Service Module, which served as the crew quarters in the Russian section of the ISS. They were quietly enjoying weightless sex, something at which both had grown adept during the last month of their four-month tour of duty. The excitement of it was only heightened by knowing how NASA officials would be appalled by their flagrant disregard of crew conduct regulations.

Flight Engineer Anatoly Rushkin, the third member of the space station's twenty-first expedition, had sought solitude in the station's emergency return *Soyuz* TMA spacecraft, docked two modules away, beneath a cluster of two Russian research modules and a docking node. He was deep into a Richard Marcinko novel, determined to finish the tattered paperback before leaving the station in three days, grateful for the book's distraction. When his commander had become besotted with the statuesque American science officer, his already miserable life aboard the station had become decidedly worse. He still couldn't believe the beautiful Bette had chosen Lazhenko over him. The man was a Cossack. And married.

Over on the American side, though it was after hours, the three members of the station's new crew, Expedition 22, floated in Destiny—the station's American lab module. They were watching Shuttle Payload Specialist Dr. Corazon Rey deftly operate the station's Canadian-built robot arm.

Cory Rey, herself, was oblivious to her audience: Station Commander Sophia Dante, Flight Engineer Art McArdle, and Brazilian flight physician and science officer, Dr. Hector Lugreb. Too much was riding on what she would or wouldn't accomplish in the remaining eight minutes, thirty seconds of the carefully choreographed robotic-arm transfer sequence.

The maneuver, a dry run for NASA's Mars Sample Return mission still four years and two funding battles away, was Cory's primary reason for being on this flight, the primary reason her employer, TTI Astronautics, had paid for more than a year of her training, and for the Lunar Return Vehicle she was about to open.

After years of watching the Russian Space Agency make millions from aggressively pursuing commercial links with private industry, NASA had finally joined the twenty-first century and underwritten a new business model called the "Enterprise Engine." Now NASA actively sought out commercial partners to develop dual-use technologies that would help the agency carry out its primary mission of exploration, while also allowing it to share in the rewards of for-profit ventures. The technology and procedures developed to recover the lunar samples in the LRV would be the starting point for similar systems used to recover priceless samples from Mars in the years ahead.

Even now, at current collectors' prices, Cory's employer estimated that the Lunar Return Vehicle contained more than a hundred million dollars' worth of lunar rocks and lunar dust, and twenty-five percent of that sum would be NASA's, exclusive of the lump-sum payments made by TTI's advertising partners. Twenty-five million dollars was only a drop in the bucket compared to the five-hundred-million-dollar expense of even a single shuttle mission to the ISS—not counting fixed infrastructure costs—but for the perennially impoverished space agency, the new source of income could someday be significant.

"In on twenty-seven," the flight engineer said beside her. Art "Jester" McArdle was wearing half-frame reading glasses to see the robot arm's position and force-vector readouts displayed on the right-hand flatscreen monitor on Cory's control console. The flight engineer was a good-looking man, forty-five or so, the sort Cory could pick out of a crowded room as a typical Navy aviator, just from his haircut and the way he stood. That McArdle was also a brilliant inorganic chemist specializing in growing nano-structures only confirmed her initial impression of him as the typical Navy overachiever. She knew the type well.

"Almost there," Cory said. She still had a hard time accepting how dozens of seemingly unrelated decisions by the government, NASA, and an upstart aeronautics company had somehow converged to bring her—the holder of a doctorate in oceanography and climatology—to the International Space Station this day, operating the robot arm and looking at a spacecraft from the Moon with the shield-shaped label of Moët & Chandon champagne painted on its side. For the privilege of having the Lunar Return Vehicle festooned with that logo, the French company had paid three million dollars, again with one-quarter of that amount going directly to NASA.

Cory chewed her lower lip, her dark eyes fixed on the target grid that overlay the video signal on the screen of the ThinkPad laptop computer that operated the robot arm's software. The image on that screen came from the miniature camera on the arm's wrist joint, known in NASA's engineering jargon as the Special Purpose Dexterous Manipulator, or SPDM.

"In on eighteen," McArdle read out.

"Got some drift," Cory murmured quietly, both to herself and to Derek Frame, her TTI Astronautics backup operator in the ISS Payload Operations Center, Huntsville, Alabama. The force-feedback loop through her translational hand controller wasn't giving her a confirmation of the arm's unwanted movement, but from the screen on her console, she could see the target grid begin to slide off the gripper handle the arm reached for on the Lunar Return Vehicle.

Cory knew the drift error had to be hardware related because the four-foot-long lunar spacecraft was anchored to the JEM Exposed Facility. That was the rigid platform extending like a back porch from the station's Japanese Experiment Module, called JEM. It was expressly designed for experiments and equipment requiring hard vacuum.

The station's main robot arm was currently attached to the Mobile Transporter that moved along rails on the outside of the central truss that formed the station's spine, running port to starboard, perpendicular to the forward motion of the station's orbital track. Since the Mobile Transporter was also locked into place at one of its ten preset work sites on the truss rails, that left only the arm joints as a possible source of the unwanted movement.

But Cory's skill in remote-control teleoperation had been honed in more dynamic situations than this. As a working oceanographer, she'd already used dual manipulators on robotic submersibles, drilling and retrieving ocean-floor core samples from depths below any a diver could withstand. For those operations, in addition to all the precise movements that were required of her, she had to constantly correct for the deep currents of the sea. So far, improbable though it seemed, working in space was proving to be relatively calmer and simpler.

"Coming back to target," Cory said.

Derek Frame's deep, South-inflected voice reverberated in her earphone. *"Roger that."*

On her laptop screen, the target grid came into alignment once more, and Cory nudged the translational controller forward. More than fifty feet away, outside the Japanese module, the multifingered Special Purpose Dexterous Manipulator did the same.

The moment she finally felt force-feedback pressure against her left thumb and forefinger, Cory squeezed back. One of the telltales on the Lunar Return Vehicle's status board above her laptop flashed green.

"Contact," she said.

"Roger that," Frame replied, confirming that the mechanical fingers had indeed closed on the gripper handle on the lunar spacecraft's sample bay cover. Cory's every move was being monitored by Frame on a duplicate instrument cluster on the ground in Alabama.

"Go for unlock?" Cory asked.

"Go for unlock," Frame agreed.

"Unlocking." Cory kept the fingers of her left hand squeezed tight within the translational controller, then used her right hand to give a sharp twist to her rotational controller.

In space, the mechanical fingers rotated through 360 degrees.

"That's one," Cory said.

She repeated the rotational movement three more times, counting out each one. Then another telltale flashed green. "Sample bay is showing unlock."

Derek Frame's voice faded in a flurry of static. *"Roger that."*

"Go for open?" Cory smiled at the rhythm she and her on-ground backup had fallen into. The two of them had rehearsed this sequence at least two hundred times in the simulators at the Johnson Space Center, and at TTI's White Sands facilities.

"Roger that, Alpha. Go for open."

Cory was amused by Derek's use of "Alpha" because of what it represented: an act of rebellion. During the station's long planning process, it had been called Alpha as a matter of course. But when NASA had decided to be politically correct and change Alpha to "International Space Station," U.S. astronauts had staged a subtle revolt by using the original name as its official radio call sign.

In the soft static that followed Derek Frame's confirmation, Cory also heard faint cheering and applause from her fellow TTI employees in Huntsville, celebrating the near-miraculous restoration of a troubled mission that as of two months ago was feared lost forever. That was how close Cory had come to not being on this flight of the shuttle.

The TTI/Moët & Chandon LRV was the most ambitious privately funded lunar mission to date. Six previous missions had been limited to satellites placed in lunar orbits, photographing and probing the Moon from a distance, usually ending with a deliberate impact into the lunar surface to deposit a time capsule filled with microscopic mementos from people willing to spend up to $5,000 per gram for the privilege.

But four private missions had attempted soft landings on the Moon, and two of those had failed. So four months earlier, when Cory's employer lost all communications with the TTI lander during its descent and landing sequence, it seemed failure had occurred again.

For two lunar days, each four Earth weeks long, TTI operations in White Sands, Nevada, and on Jarvis Island in the Pacific, had struggled in vain to contact the lost probe. But just when TTI's colorful owner, Kai Teller, was prepared to announce the loss of the mission, his Lunar Return Vehicle sent an automated signal announcing it had been loaded with samples by the rover, and had launched itself into lunar orbit.

Teller had then turned what was going to be a sedate news conference into a joyful celebration, proudly praising his programmers who had put enough artificial intelligence in the rover's onboard computers to have it complete its sampling mission without input from the ground. The TTI/Moët & Chandon lunar return mission, he proclaimed, would be the most successful commercial space venture since *Niju*.

One of the two successful soft-landing missions prior to TTI's had resulted in the deployment of a lunar rover by Japan's largest television network, TBS, the Tokyo Broadcasting System. The public's overwhelming reaction to the remarkable rover on the surface of the Moon made the machine the most popular space-mission icon since the beloved little *Sojourner* rover was placed on Mars by the Jet Propulsion Laboratory's Pathfinder spacecraft.

Cory, and hundreds of millions of others, remembered perfectly well the international excitement two years earlier, when the solar-powered, wheeled robot, articulated like a tractor-trailer and about the size of a wheelbarrow, had touched down in the Sea of Tranquility, approximately fifteen miles northeast of *Apollo 11*'s historic first-landing site.

That little rover, dubbed *Niju,* had dutifully made its way across the lunar surface guided by operators on the ground, many of them winners of a contest sponsored by the Japanese network's major advertisers.

Niju, which carried no real scientific instruments other than three high-definition video cameras, had managed to cover just under four miles during the daylight portion of each lunar day, successfully hibernating through the −290°F lunar nights. After almost four months of skirting boulders and craters, it finally came within a mile and a half of Tranquility Base, despite the somewhat embarrassing fact that NASA had no definitive set of lunar coordinates to describe its position.

To the relief of many, *Niju* stopped at the mile-and-a-half limit. The Japanese television network announced that it recognized the historical significance of the landing site, even though the United States continued to refuse to declare any Apollo landing area eligible for protection as a national heritage site.

Whenever the U.S. government did decide to address that inexplicable oversight, UNESCO, the United Nations Educational, Scientific, and Cultural Organization, remained prepared to go further and declare each lunar landing area a World Heritage Site, which would activate a complete set of internationally accepted laws to protect the areas and all equipment left on the Moon. However, UNESCO couldn't act until the USA did. And the USA, for whatever reason, continued to show no intention of doing so.

Despite her government's apparent indifference, Cory, along with just over a billion other television viewers around the world, had been mesmerized by the live broadcast that day, as the Japanese rover's cameras had found the bright reflection of the golden foil of the American lunar lander's descent stage on the stark horizon. Then the rover had moved into position on the slope of a crater, and used its massive telephoto lens to record the scene, at the time, thirty-seven years since Neil Armstrong and Buzz Aldrin had made history.

Cory also remembered watching the debonair Dr. Aldrin on the ABC news special *Return to Tranquility,* which aired the Japanese feed. Aldrin, the lunar module pilot for *Apollo 11,* had not been surprised to see that the American flag he and Armstrong had deployed on the Moon had fallen over, fifty feet from the landing stage of the lunar module. The flag, which had not been specially created for its historical role, but had, instead, been purchased off the shelf from Sears, was bleached white by decades of unfiltered solar radiation. Aldrin told the ABC anchor Peter Jennings that he was certain he had seen the flag fall over in the exhaust from the ascent stage's liftoff, but he had always hoped that he had been mistaken.

Now Cory prepared herself to play her small part in the exploration of the Moon, but hesitated as she heard a hiccup in the raucous drone of the space station's background noise. Reflexively, she looked to Sophia Dante for comment. Space rookies always checked with the veterans for explanation of the dozens of sounds Houston didn't bother to include in simulations. The white-haired commander of Expedition 22 knew them all—she had been on station twice before as a member of a shuttle crew.

"So what was that one?" Cory asked.

"Air pocket," Dante said, straight-faced.

So far the station commander had given Cory the same explanation for all the bumps and shudders of the shuttle launch, up to and including those that occurred on orbit, where air pockets, and air, did not exist.

Nonetheless, Cory found Dante's lack of concern reassuring. Until recently, flying had always been an unnerving experience for Cory, and rocketing up to the space station in the shuttle certainly qualified as the ultimate flight. Fortunately, this time she'd actually been eager for the experience, had even found it thrilling. But only because three years ago, in Antarctica, her involvement in what became known as the Icefire incident had led her to seriously redefine "unnerving" in relation to flying vehicles, when the same terrible event that brought Mitchell Webber back into her life had also taken the life of her adored younger brother, Johnny.

The plaque that Cory had received afterward, from the president of the United States himself, merely cited her unnamed contributions to "a significant accomplishment" with absolutely no mention of what actually had happened to all of them. But Cory's view of everything and everyone had been changed forever. Without that experience, she knew, she could never have accepted the challenge of going into space.

"Opening," Cory said. She pulled back on the translational controller, then began moving the rotational controller through ninety degrees.

On her laptop screen, the target grid appeared stationary. Cory knew that meant the sample-bay cover was moving in synchronization with the robotic fingers gripping it.

Above the laptop, the monitor on the left showed the feed from the video camera mounted on the arm's Mobile Transporter. The monitor's display was aimed to show both the robot arm and the Lunar Return Vehicle locked down on the Japanese module's exterior "porch." To Cory, the shape of the small spacecraft strongly resembled a slightly oversize backyard barbecue propane tank. The thought made her smile as she continued to watch the monitor where the brilliant white robot arm smoothly pulled open the sample-bay cover. Except for the lack of gravity, the entire procedure was running as trouble-free as a simulation.

Until the arm suddenly jerked to the side.

For just an instant, Cory had time to think, *It can't do that.*

Then the American lab module shuddered, and above the incessant, loud background station noise rose the distant warble of a fire alarm.

It was coming from the orbiter.

When the alarm reached the Russian side of the station, one or the other of Commander Lazhenko and Science Officer Norman was upside down in their gray, cocoonlike sleeping bag. In microgravity, without noticeable up and down, all position was relative.

The lovers' struggle to disentangle their interlocking limbs and escape the bag's Velcro tabs was only worsened when the station lurched and drove them both against the wall. The impact snapped loose the sleeping compartment's pull-down writing shelf, spilling Lazhenko's collection of photographs of his infant son and daughter, saved letters, and a swarm of licorice candies from an open bag, creating an instant, annoying, obscuring whirlwind of debris.

Bette Norman, the more agile of the two, spun free of the fabric bag first, naked except for her gold wristwatch and the leather-soled tan wool socks that were the station's standard footwear.

Behind her, the dark-haired Russian, wearing only a red and gray striped crew polo shirt, pushed out of the compartment, but his leg was still caught in the bag and he suddenly pitched toward a wall as the fabric snagged him. As he fought with the last Velcro tab holding him captive, Lazhenko swore in Russian, then called out, "Fire station!"

But Norman, clutching her own blue crew shirt and

matching duty shorts, was already floating toward the hatch leading to the *Zarya* Control Module and its *Soyuz* docking node.

"Bette!" Lazhenko bellowed in disbelief. "Deactivate ventilation!" It was the first crucial step in fighting fire in space. Otherwise, clouds of roiling flames could spread through the air-circulation system as quickly as the wind. *"Then* we secure *Soyuz!"*

Thanks to the depressingly predictable lack of foresight of the American government, NASA's long-promised seven-person Crew Return Vehicle had been canceled, and its supposed replacement, the six-person Crew Exploration Vehicle, was still being designed, and slowly being strangled by cost overruns waiting for funding. Until the CEV was put in service, the station's only lifeboat remained the Russian spacecraft docked two modules away. When the shuttle or a second *Soyuz* wasn't present, the station's crew capacity was restricted to three, the maximum number that could be carried in a single *Soyuz* reentry capsule.

The American science officer glanced back at Lazhenko, but didn't stop. Lazhenko was disconcerted to see full-blown panic in her sky-blue eyes. In his brief, intoxicating experience with her, she'd been like him. Afraid of nothing.

"Bette?"

But Norman's trajectory carried her through the *Zarya's* round hatch and she was gone without a single word.

The Russian station commander stared after her uncomprehendingly. *What would make a trained American astronaut abandon her emergency duties?* But he had no time to seek an answer. He kicked across the module to the environmental control panels and pressed the red master rocker switches that shut off the power to the module's two circulating fans. Next, he manually deactivated the fans' secondary switches so they wouldn't inadvertently start up in the event of a power surge. Then he shut down the zone heaters.

His first task accomplished, Lazhenko spun around headfirst like a swimmer changing directions, and kicked off to the critical-equipment locker. Working as much from schooled instinct as from conscious thought, he pulled out a Russian-designed Personal Breathing Apparatus. The PBA consisted of a mask and attached oxygen-generator cartridge, a long, yellow rubber-covered flashlight, and a backpack fire extinguisher. Though he knew the Russian nitrogen-compound extinguisher could not be used in the non-Russian station modules or in the orbiter, he saw no reason not to be prepared.

Still wrestling with the extinguisher's shoulder straps, Lazhenko pushed off toward the *Zarya* hatch and the *Soyuz*.

Only when the lifeboat was safe could he spare the time to find his pants.

SPACE SHUTTLE *CONSTITUTION*

On *Constitution*'s flight deck, Shuttle Commander Hutton didn't have time to shut down the ventilation system. Protecting the structural integrity of the orbiter and the station came first.

"Houston's got the alarm," Rebecca Oster said sharply. She cupped a hand to her commset, listened. "It's a fire in AV Bay Three."

Hutton heard the edge in Oster's voice. Didn't like it. But understood why it was there. The smell of smoke was strong. The low-pitched warble of the fire alarm drowned out all other sound.

The shuttle commander didn't even have time to pluck his own commset from the console. He rocked back and forth as the deck moved and his restraining platform transferred the motion to him.

"Tell them we just had a second explosion in the payload bay. And give me an eyes-on for the transfer tunnel."

Oster pushed off from the edge of the hatch, floated toward the upper observation windows on the flight deck's ceiling as she relayed Hutton's report to Mission Control.

At the same time, Hutton snapped open the clear plastic covers that protected the fire-suppression switches on the flight console, and for two seconds pressed the ones that glowed red. Their PBIs began flashing to confirm that the built-in Freon-1301 fire extinguishers in the affected avionics bay were discharging.

"Houston says there's nothing in the payload bay that can explode," Oster called back to him.

"Nothing that's supposed to explode," Hutton said. The *Constitution*'s bay held the Leonardo Multipurpose Logistics Module, a large, squat cargo cylinder crammed full of food, water, clothes, personal effects, and scientific payloads, waiting to be offloaded to the station after the lunar sample transfer was completed. Every item packed into the Italian-built supply module was subjected to a twenty-four-step flight-certification process to ensure safety; no runaway chemical reactions allowed.

The fire-suppression indicators now glowed white. The extinguishers were exhausted.

Suddenly, the rhythmic motion in the deck stuttered, redoubled. The orbiter squealed. There was the sound of something brittle snapping.

"Shit," Hutton muttered. He tensed, anticipating the depressurization alarm's blare at any second.

"Another explosion?" Oster had reached the observation windows and saw a cloud of dislodged ice crystals and metallic flakes tumbling just outside. Past the cloud, the vast, improbable assemblage of white cylinders and intricate spans and central truss of the International

Space Station appeared as a surreal, H-shaped kite, twice the length of a U.S. football field, seemingly held aloft by enormous wings of glossy, blue-black photovoltaic arrays.

Those arrays were fluttering.

"Hutton," Oster nervously called out to him. "The transfer tunnel's secure. But the solar arrays . . . they're moving."

"The last explosion set up a vibration," Hutton said tersely. He was already throwing more switches, arming the orbiter's reaction-control thrusters to fire in a series of bursts to quell the flexing of the station's central truss. It was moving like a long fishing pole bouncing on a running man's shoulder.

The shuttle commander's attention swiftly turned to the main status monitor in the center of the console. The display there changed regularly to show analog versions of whatever controls were most critical at any given time.

Right now, the instrument cluster displayed showed the shuttle's orientation was as it should be, tail down to the Earth, nose up to the station.

The main display confirmed the orbiter's main computer was analyzing the readings coming from the onboard laser gyros to calculate a firing sequence to counteract the vibrations—the problem was too complex for any pilot to solve by feel.

That meant Hutton could move to step two on his own emergency pocket checklist.

Immediately, he tugged off his pocket stereo, pressed his commset into his ear, toggled it on.

"Houston, this is *Constitution*. We have a major ONS." ONS meant Off-Nominal Situation. The ultimate NASA euphemism for disaster.

Houston didn't answer.

Hutton looked back at Oster still floating by the upper

windows. She was pressing her own commset tightly against her ear, but she shook her head.

"Cut off," she reported. "We've lost Mission Control."

A new alarm rang out—the one Hutton had been dreading.

The shuttle was depressurizing.

INTERNATIONAL SPACE STATION

Multiple alarms blared as the station's American lab module continued to shake. The three astronauts with Cory all talked at once, to each other and to their commsets.

But Station Commander Dante calmly ticked off orders and procedures as if this were just another simulation—the whole point of her training. In response, Flight Engineer McArdle was already on his way to the orbiter to help with the fire. The station's science officer and flight physician, Dr. Lugreb, was floating at the other end of the module, shutting down its ventilation and heaters.

Dante's last order was to Cory. "Lock down the arm and get back to *Constitution*."

But all Cory could think of was one hundred million dollars' worth of Moon rocks about to be lost in space. On the camera monitor, ten tiny lunar-sample cylinders, each the size of a small thermos bottle, were jumbled together in the Lunar Return Vehicle's sample bay, knocked free by whatever jarring force had dislodged the station's robot arm. She saw a few of the cylinders begin to float free of the small spacecraft.

Disregarding Dante and her order, Cory swung her translational controller back and forth in counter time to the vibrations swaying through the robot arm.

"Doctor Rey, I gave you an order."

Cory punched her left hand forward. Outside the Japanese module; the quick robotic fingers of the station's arm reached out and plucked a tumbling sample cylinder from space.

"Doctor Rey!"

Cory redoubled her efforts, twisting her right hand and angling her left to swing the fingers of the station's arm within reach of the Japanese module's own robotic arm. The smaller Japanese arm wasn't designed for ultra-precise manipulation, but was outfitted with a Sample Retrieval Sleeve resembling a child's Popsicle mold, with a receiving pocket for each sample cylinder. Cory maneuvered the cylinder she had retrieved into one of the sleeve's receiving tubes, pressed the "Accept" control on her console, then released the cylinder and swung the station's arm back to the other errant samples. Her rapid hand and arm movements gave her the feeling she was conducting a vast orchestra.

"Shut the arm down *now*," Dante said sternly. "You are in violation of procedures."

But Cory could not stop now. She had her own personal plans for this mission, and failure wasn't one of them. She reached out remotely and caught another cylinder, all the while berating herself that four had already spun slowly out of reach. *Forty million dollars lost!* "I'm protecting my company's investment, *and* NASA's. Why don't you do *your* job and protect this station?"

Before an astonished Dante could respond to such insubordination, Bette Norman spiraled into the American module. Naked. "What's the status of the LRV?" was the first thing she said as she struggled into her polo shirt. It was inside out.

"Spilling its guts," Cory answered. She didn't have to guess what Norman had been doing. Within ten seconds of floating onto the station, Cory had sensed the sparks between the American science officer and the Russian station commander. "But I'm trying to retrieve as many as—"

All her monitors went dark. All the telltales on her console vanished.

Cory turned her head sharply, regretting the action an instant later as the fluid in her inner ear sloshed into a mini tornado. The module's four hopelessly cluttered white walls spun around her. But she still saw what she'd expected to see. Sophia Dante with her hand on the module's experiment-rack power switch.

"Back to *Constitution*, Doctor," Dante ordered. "Now."

"Derek, are you getting this?" Cory whispered into her commset. Only then did she realize she hadn't heard a word from her TTI backup operator, or anyone else on the ground in Huntsville, since the alarm had sounded. "Now our links are down," she said accusingly to Dante.

The station commander immediately cupped a hand to her own commset, which operated on a different voice loop connecting her to Mission Control. "Houston, this is Alpha. Do you copy?"

No response.

Dante turned to Lugreb. "Doctor, see if McArdle needs any help. But stand by to get back to the *Soyuz* in case we have to evacuate."

In that same moment the module rang as if it had been hit by something outside.

A second later, a new alarm sound rang in Cory's ears.

She'd heard it in simulations, but this was the real thing.

Low pressure.

The shuttle had only been the beginning. Now the station was losing air.

3

YURI LAZHENKO DOVE through the *Zarya* hatchway, caught the edge, and twisted to make a ninety-degree turn into the supply-filled Docking and Storage Module above the *Soyuz* docking node. The maneuver drove the Russian station commander straight into a head-to-head collision with his flight engineer, who was coming the opposite way, out of *Soyuz*.

The two men bounced off each other with a grunt. Rushkin frowned at his commander's lack of pants.

Lazhenko ignored the disapproval. "Is *Soyuz* safe?"

"The seat liners have been changed," Rushkin said stiffly.

Lazhenko nodded. That was the first task undertaken whenever a new crew came aboard the station. The *Soyuz* seat liners custom-fit to the old crew were immediately removed and replaced with a set custom-fit to the new crew. Once the changeover was accomplished, the seat assignments for any evacuation procedure were deemed to be switched as well. "We leave in *Constitution* now," the flight engineer said. "Dante's crew leaves in *Soyuz*."

Lazhenko had no intention of leaving the station. "We haven't had joint evacuation drill yet. So it is more efficient if *we* secure *Soyuz*."

The station's low-pressure alarm sounded.

"It *is* secured," Rushkin said.

"Then let us help our American friends."

"Find your trousers first," Rushkin said, then pushed past his commander, heading for the hatch leading to the station's central Unity node which linked to the American lab module and to *Constitution*.

SPACE SHUTTLE *CONSTITUTION*

"The airlock!" Hutton shouted as the orbiter's depress alarm blared. "Seal the airlock!"

Rebecca Oster knew exactly what her commander feared. "I'm on it!" She pushed against the flight deck ceiling to spin around and head back to the interdeck hatch. This time, she made it through without touching the sides. Only to collide with Harper Doyle.

Oster gasped in surprise, and reflexively shoved the body to the side, feeling her stomach tighten as a thin thread of vomitus slowly arced like the tail of a comet from the pilot's gaping mouth.

But she had no time to do anything else.

The depress alarm wailed unceasingly, issuing forth from the external airlock connected to the hatch in the aft wall of the mid-deck. The airlock itslef was installed in the shuttle's payload bay and connected to the shuttle docking adapter. The docking adapter was attached to the station's Node 2. If the station was imagined as a giant Tinkertoy construction, then nodes could be considered the central connectors which joined each cylindrical module. Node 2 served as a central hub connecting the Japanese module to port, the American lab module aft, and the European

Space Agency Columbus Orbital Facility to starboard. If the station was ever completed in the wake of the schedule delays and funding cutbacks resulting from the loss of the *Columbia* orbiter in 2003, then someday Node 2 would also connect the Centrifuge Accommodation Module to the station's zenith.

From the shuttle's mid-deck, Oster dove into the airlock, knowing the alarm meant the transfer-tunnel connections were being strained by the continuing flexing of the ISS and shuttle. As a weak point, the airlock had to be sealed. She emerged from the hatch into the airlock and then, from the perspective of the shuttle's orientation, looked up and saw uncounted sheets of paper and a variety of small objects whirling about in the upper level of the docking adapter tunnel. Some sheets of paper were flattening against the docking collar seal.

Oster pressed her commset, gave her report. "Hutton, the seal is compromised. We've got a major depress on the station side."

Her commander's voice crackled back to her. *"Close the hatches, both ends."*

"Copy that."

As Oster pushed up toward the open hatch of the Node 2 docking adapter, twenty feet above her, Art McArdle came diving down toward her from the station's American lab module.

"You got a fire?" he shouted.

Oster and McArdle met at the docking adapter hatch. "Fire's out," she said quickly, hoping that was true. Up here, she could hear the high-pitched whistle of escaping air, and from the flight engineer's expression, so could he. "Something exploded in the payload bay," she added. "Started us moving. We've got to seal the tunnel."

McArdle nodded once. "I've got this end."

Oster didn't waste time. In the event of catastrophe, the flight engineer had to go back through the station to the *Soyuz* for evacuation. She had to get back to the shuttle.

She flipped around in the adapter tunnel and kicked back down to the shuttle airlock. The high-pitched whistle of escaping atmosphere had now become a shriek. Papers blew past her, joined by empty food packs that had been improperly stored.

As fear reached out for her, she hit the deck of the airlock too hard, costing her precious seconds to reorient herself. When she next looked up, she saw the square, rounded-corner ISS hatch close, McArdle safe behind it.

But now she felt wind. Air from the shuttle. Streaming past her at an increasing rate.

She kicked wildly, banged her head on the edge of the shuttle airlock hatch, fought her way through the constricted accessway like a swimmer escaping a school of sharks.

Back in the shuttle's mid-deck she grabbed the hatch edge to stop her movement. Her 112 pounds of momentum popped her shoulder.

But she did stop, clinging to the hatch.

It moved beneath her fingers, back and forth.

She heard more creaking. More wind. More alarms.

Oster struggled with the canvas strap that kept the hatch anchored to the mid-deck aft wall. She ripped it free and with the same movement swung the hatch closed.

On her fingers.

She cried out, startled. The hatch hadn't sealed. Her crushed fingers kept it open.

She tried pulling on the hatch with her free hand. But the pressure of the escaping air stopped the hatch from moving.

"Hutton!" she shouted, knowing he couldn't hear her.

Oster braced her feet against the bulkhead, strained. Pulled.

The hatch budged an inch.

It was enough.

Her trapped hand jerked free, spraying a mist of glistening blood drops.

The hatch slammed shut.

She dogged it, tears of pain bubbling from her eyes.

The seal light turned green.

Then the shuttle seemed to drop away from her as a horrendous shriek of metal echoed through the deck. The bulkhead came at her and Oster grabbed the hatch lever to keep from bouncing away.

She knew what had happened this time, too.

Constitution was doing more than moving.

It had torn free of the ISS.

INTERNATIONAL SPACE STATION

Through the porthole in the Node 2 docking-adapter hatch, Art McArdle watched in horror as the shuttle's crew-transfer tunnel beyond blossomed like the casing of a firecracker exploding in slow motion.

Streamers of torn insulation fabric fluttered free like battle flags. Shattered pipes spun end over end. Metal plates slowly rotated away like a deck of cards thrown from a magician's hand.

And past the destruction, *Constitution* fell away from the ISS. Behind the shuttlecraft, the tropically bright blue-and-white of Earth glowed in the brilliant sunlight.

His eyes on the shuttle, McArdle held his breath, knowing what to look for, but he didn't see it.

There was no gout of ice crystals from the shuttle's airlock in its payload bay. Oster had sealed the hatch in time. McArdle let out a sigh.

"Meu Deus . . ." It was Dr. Lugreb. The Brazilian flight surgeon had floated up behind him, to see what he saw.

"They're okay," McArdle said, trying to sound reassuring, but not certain he was succeeding. "Rebecca closed the airlock."

McArdle kept watching the shuttle as it ponderously angled away. Its payload bay doors were open, but appeared undamaged by the debris that trailed from the portion of the destroyed tunnel still linked with its airlock.

"Who else is onboard?" Lugreb asked anxiously.

"Hutton and Doyle, I guess. Rebecca for sure." McArdle paused as he realized the point of Lugreb's question. With only three crew on the shuttle, that left seven crew on the station, four more than could be evacuated. "We'll be fine, Doc. We won't need the *Soyuz.*"

The doctor did not look convinced. He rapidly crossed himself, found the small gold crucifix that floated on a chain around his neck and kissed it. Then his mouth opened in shock.

McArdle turned back to the porthole.

He was just in time to witness the aftermath of the third explosion.

The instant the depress alarm had sounded in the American lab, Commander Dante had kicked over to the module's critical equipment locker. But by the time she'd spun around with the first two PBAs for her crew, Lugreb had disappeared, on his way to assist the already departed McArdle.

Cory grabbed the American-designed, self-sealing breathing mask from Dante, twisted the valve on the air bottle, and pressed the fitting tab to see that the pressurized head straps inflated. Then she shut it off again.

The depress alarm was sounding from the direction of the shuttle.

Dante slapped the second PBA into Bette Norman's hand. "Norman, go find the Russians," Dante ordered. "See if they've got communications."

"Sure thing," Norman said, moving off directly, without bothering to check her breathing mask and air supply.

Dante stared after her for a moment, as if not trusting such quick acquiescence. Then she looked back at Cory. "You're coming with me."

Cory held up her hands in apparent surrender. "No problem."

Dante turned around, dove toward the Node 2 link between the shuttle and the station, with Cory close behind her. But where the station commander headed through the node to join McArdle and Lugreb, Cory pulled up short and turned to her left into the Japanese module. She was gambling Dante would be distracted long enough by whatever was going on that her absence would go unnoticed, at least until she salvaged what she could of her job and TTI's investment.

Though built by JAXA—the Japan Aerospace Exploration Agency—the Japanese Experiment Module looked little different from the American and European-built components of the station. The JEM was fitted with equipment and storage racks whose outer walls curved to fit the cylindrical shape of the module, but whose flat inner surfaces created the standard, four-walled interior. In theory, the walls were supposed to be smooth, with recessed handles and controls. But like every other module on the station, they had been covered with bungee cords and Velcro patches to hold a cluttered assortment of equipment and supplies, from clipboards and pens to fat canvas supply bags that might hold anything from water to clothes. To Cory, the visual effect was similar to swimming into an underwater grotto lined with swaying kelp.

Despite the apparent disarray, Cory knew there was a pattern to it, and she oriented herself to the module's visual references to relative up and down. Though such directions were meaningless in zero gravity, most astronauts felt more comfortable with Earth-based conventions. Thus, throughout the station, module walls facing Earth had been arbitrarily labeled "down."

The command rack for the Japanese module's own exterior robot arm was near the entrance hatch, and as Cory placed her hands on the arm's two controllers, she felt the force-feedback loops confirm that the arm was operational.

With control established, Cory let go of the rotational controller and flicked on the visual monitors. An image of the module's outside "porch" appeared on the video monitor above the laptop that was Velcroed to an angled shelf. On the monitor to the right of the laptop, an image of the arm itself appeared, clearly holding the Sample Retrieval Sleeve.

Cory's next move was to initiate the final stage of the preprogrammed retrieval sequence. All she had to do was enter a four-letter code and the computer-controlled arm would automatically slide the Sample Retrieval Sleeve into the waiting equipment-transfer airlock at the end of the Japanese module, just above the porch.

Cory entered the code and watched the monitor as the arm began its programmed movement. Then she kicked over to the large airlock chamber which protruded from the end wall of the module like an old-fashioned, circular bank vault. Because the final step of any use of a station airlock was to vent atmosphere to space, the equipment-transfer airlocks—too small for an astronaut to use—helped to conserve vital oxygen.

Then Bette Norman floated into the module.

Norman's sudden arrival caught Cory by surprise. As did her first question.

"Did you retrieve the cylinders?" the science officer asked.

Cory held on to the edge of the airlock chamber. "Did you find out if the Russians have a ground loop?"

"Yeah, everything's fine," Norman said. She pushed over to the control console, saw the robotic arm moving on the monitor. "You did get them."

"I got one," Cory said. "There might be a second one in the SPDM. Dante turned off the power before I got a confirm."

"Only one?" Norman looked devastated.

Still holding on to the chamber, Cory looked at Norman with puzzlement. She could think of no explanation for the woman's interest in the sample cylinders. The Moët & Chandon lunar sample return mission wasn't a NASA science project. It was a crass moneymaking scheme for Cory's employer that would also garner huge amounts of free publicity. While the latter had definite appeal to Cory for her own activist reasons, the project had nothing at all to do with the station or its science officer.

"Bette, what's—?"

Cory stopped speaking as she felt a shudder through the chamber.

Because the depressurization siren had stopped, and she could no longer hear the shuttle's distant fire alarm, she had assumed everything was under control. But the station was still rocking, like a suspension bridge swinging.

Norman looked past Cory to the airlock hatch. "Dante wants you in the shuttle. I'll get the cylinder."

"Why should—?"

Another shudder. This time Cory heard a twanging sound, as if steel cables had been cut outside.

Bette Norman surprised her again by kicking straight for the airlock to push Cory aside.

But Cory's training was not limited to oceanography and teleoperation. Without thinking, she seized her attacker's right hand and pinched the soft triangle of flesh between thumb and forefinger. Hard.

Startled by the sharp, intense pain, Norman jerked her hand back at once. The abrupt movement spun her away from the airlock and Cory.

The science officer hit the module's upper wall, colliding with a set of flush-mounted storage cupboards. But she reacted swiftly, regained control, and whirled to confront Cory.

"I want that cylinder," she said.

"Tell me what's going on," Cory countered, confused.

Norman's classic features transformed, freezing into an expression unknown to Cory, whose informal combat training had not prepared her for the face of real battle, the face of a soldier prepared to kill.

"Bette?"

Norman shoved her hand into a pocket on her shorts.

"Bette!"

The science officer now held an indispensable astronaut tool: a Swiss Army knife. Its long blade was unfolding.

"Okay!" Cory said, and shoved herself away from the airlock. "The sample's yours!"

As Cory looped her arm through a padded foot restraint on a side wall, Norman pushed forward, one hand reaching out for the airlock controls.

A deafening bang suddenly thundered in the module.

Cory's foot restraint bucked, which meant the whole module did the same.

And then Bette Norman, with nothing to hang on to, was sucked out of the module with a cry of surprise as a rush of strong wind blew almost loud enough to mask the chorus of every depressurization alarm on the station going off at once.

A gleaming can of polished aluminum, the Leonardo Multipurpose Logistics Module was twenty-one feet long and its diameter matched that of every other major component of the ISS—the largest cylindrical size that could fit within a shuttle's payload bay—fifteen feet.

In the docking adapter used for the shuttle, still clutching his crucifix, Dr. Lugreb was the first to see what happened to the Leonardo module as *Constitution* slowly dropped away from the station. Beside him, Art McArdle was the second. Behind them both, Commander Dante arrived to be the third.

An explosion flashed between the side of the cargo module and the inner wall of the shuttle's payload bay.

The cargo module swung up, some braces damaged, some destroyed.

"*Querida Mãe de Deus,*" Lugreb whispered.

McArdle muttered in disbelief. "It's coming free."

Dante saw what was about to happen. "Get out of there," she urged, as if her orders could cross space to the commander of the shuttle.

They couldn't.

SPACE SHUTTLE *CONSTITUTION*

Hutton was still breathing when the shuttle broke free of the station, so he knew Oster had sealed the airlock hatch. He just didn't know if she had been in the airlock at the time.

"Rebecca!" he shouted. But he couldn't go looking for her. He needed to retask the main computer. Through the forward windows, he could see the station appear to be moving up and away from the shuttle. He couldn't tell if the explosive separation had imparted enough energy to the shuttle to change its orbit, but if the spacecraft was moving lower with open payload doors, it would begin an uncontrolled reentry. Thermal disintegration.

"Still here," Rebecca gasped as she came through the interdeck hatch. She had wrapped her crushed fingers in a bloodstained jacket, the closest thing she could find to first aid as she rushed to the flight deck.

"Good job," Hutton said. He watched the main screen change to bring up the instrument displays he required now. He saw the numbers roll to alert him to the shuttle's change in velocity. He felt a glimmer of hope. He could control this deviation manually, even correct it. "I'm going to translate back to the station. See if you can get Houston, or Dante. Anybody."

"On it," Oster said. Her own voice sounded weak to her. She took a deeper breath, testing the atmosphere. Thin, but still breathable. Hutton sounded confident that he could fly this thing. She decided she'd try to be more confident, too.

She floated to the pilot's station beside Hutton, found Doyle's commset, plugged it in, and prepared to test all the loops.

Another loud crack banged through the flight deck.

"What is it now?" Hutton asked.

The payload station to starboard lit up with warning lights and a chime sounded.

"Leonardo," Oster said.

"Eyes on."

Oster pushed back to the aft observation windows on the back wall of the flight deck. The windows looked into the open payload bay. Her new confidence vanished.

"Oh God . . ."

Hutton turned at the despair in her voice. There was something huge rotating beyond the windows.

He kicked over to her side.

The Leonardo module had partially lifted out of the payload bay, half of its support braces gone, the other half straining, bending, snapping.

"It's going to hit the tail," Oster said.

Hutton didn't care about the tail. He cared about what was to either side of that tail.

The pods holding the OMS engines that were needed to bring the shuttle home.

"But that's not critical, right?" Oster said, her voice rising. "We don't need the tail to fly in space. They can get another shuttle up to us in a month."

Hutton was already diving back to the pilot's station.

In the payload bay, the gleaming supply module rolled like a giant boulder advancing in slow motion.

"We just have to get back to the station, right, Commander?" Oster's tone was pleading. She had spun around to see where he had gone, what he was doing.

Hutton was firing all the hydrazine reaction-control thrusters at a ninety-degree angle to the shuttle's horizontal axis.

"Rebecca, just tell me when we're free of the module," he said.

Oster turned back to the windows to observe the payload bay dropping away from the cargo module. Another few seconds and the enormous, drum-shaped cylinder would slowly tumble past the tail. "Almost . . ." she said. "Almost . . ."

Then the Leonardo module was far enough out of the payload bay that she could see the last bracing strut stretching up to it.

The last bracing strut that refused to break.

Like a giant yo-yo on a string, the Leonardo suddenly began to rebound back toward the shuttle, with all the energy the shuttle had just expended to escape it.

"Commander!" Oster called out. "It's coming back! Get us out of here!"

But all Hutton could think of was the station.

If the shuttle blew up on impact with the module, he had to make sure they were far enough away from the ISS to keep it safe from debris.

"Hutton!"

Hutton fired all the hydrazine thrusters for full reverse along the shuttle's horizontal axis, driving it away from the station.

The Leonardo module now moved on a collision course with the flight deck of the shuttle as Oster shouted, "It's going to hit!"

Hutton fired the forward reaction control thrusters, to make the shuttle's nose swing down, out of the module's way.

Through the aft observation windows the huge module appeared to rise over the flight deck, missing the payload bay's forward wall.

"Missed," Oster gasped.

But Hutton knew it wasn't over.

As the nose of the shuttle pitched away from the station and the serene blue Earth began to slide in front of the forward windows, he felt the shudder as the cargo module's last remaining support brace tugged on the shuttle.

Then the support brace snapped.

Pressed against the aft observation windows, Oster had a

clear view of the cargo module as it finally spun free of the shuttle, as she saw what was going to happen.

"The station . . ."

The shuttle rotated once, then fired thrusters to stop nose up, pointing back at the station Commander Hutton had been trying so hard to protect.

Thin puffs of white vapor flashed from *Constitution*'s aft reaction control thrusters as the shuttle began to move back to the station, now racing the slowly tumbling, gleaming bulk of the Leonardo cargo module.

On the flight deck, Rebecca Oster struggled to bring the shuttle's robotic arm online. But she wasn't a trained operator and the arm had been hit by the Leonardo as the supply module had rolled free of the bay. Nothing she could do could free it.

In the end, there was only one other way to keep the Leonardo from hitting the ISS.

Oster closed her eyes and prayed.

Hutton now guided the shuttle by dead reckoning, tweaking thrusters, to slide ahead of the cargo module, to angle back to block its path.

He would not permit the Leonardo to hit the station.

It hit *Constitution*.

The shuttle's open payload bay doors buckled on impact, groaning horribly.

Hutton fired all the thrusters to impart as much delta vee to the module as possible before—

Just above the forward angle of the space shuttle's stubby wings, the force of the cargo module's strike snapped the shuttle's spine.

The gleaming white craft folded around the silver supply cylinder like a collapsing candy wrapper, a wad of discarded foil.

Then the OMS/RCS fuel tanks ruptured.

Instantly, two immense clouds of monomethyl hydrazine and nitrogen tetroxide erupted. And ignited on contact.

The forward section of the shuttle, where the crew compartment was still intact, whirled violently away from the point of ignition, propelled by the sudden pressure of the explosively expanding gas, centripetal force throwing Hutton against the flight controls, slamming Oster into the forward windows next to him.

The crew compartment spun so rapidly that sunlight strobed through its windows four times a second.

The shuttle's commander struggled to regain the controls. He had to see the station. He had to know if he had succeeded.

Beside him, Oster screamed.

Hutton looked up, ahead.

Constitution's docking adapter node was fifty feet away.

The shuttle's nose rotated once.

The station was twenty feet away.

Hutton caught sight of Lugreb and McArdle behind the station's docking adapter porthole. The doctor was kissing his crucifix.

Good luck, Hutton thought.

The nose of the shuttle rotated for the last time.

INTERNATIONAL SPACE STATION

"Move!" Dante shouted as she kicked back toward the station's American lab module.

Seconds later, the forward compartment of *Constitution* tore into the station's docking adapter, knocking it free, twisting the pressure seal that joined it to the connecting node, twisting the hatch only used for docking.

Lugreb was instantly sucked against the three-inch gap

that popped open along a two-foot stretch of the warped airlock seal.

McArdle grabbed the flight surgeon's hand, braced his feet against the sides of the airlock to pull him free.

Dante grabbed a handhold by the module's airlock, as she too felt herself dragged back by the rush of escaping air. "Get him up here!" she shouted to McArdle, but the growing wind was keeping her from moving through the open hatch leading to the safety of the lab.

She had just swung her free hand to grip the edge of the hatchway when McArdle yanked Lugreb away from the airlock.

But the plump Brazilian doctor had served as a plug of sorts, and with the removal of that plug, the rush of air increased and both McArdle and Lugreb were drawn back to the damaged hatch with just enough force to jar it completely open.

Dante stared aghast as McArdle and Lugreb were blown out the hatch, neither with time or air enough to scream. All around her, pipes and conduits exploded because of the rapidly increasing pressure differential. The adapter and the node were beginning to fill with a morass of swirling debris.

I'm not going to make it, Dante realized. To save the station, what was left of it, she had just enough oxygen in her system to close the lab module's hatch. But not enough to climb through that hatch first.

Thinking only of the station and the very next second, Dante tore at a flimsy air-circulation duct to break it in two where it ran through the hatchway. When the way was clear, she was already short of breath in the vanishing atmosphere. But she forced herself up into the opening.

Just far enough, she told herself. *I just have to reach the hatch and grab the locking lever.* She made it, wrenching the hatch toward herself to snap the Velcro seal of the canvas strap that held the hatch in place. Her final mission accomplished, she relaxed as the pressure of the wind did the rest for her and the hatch blew shut above her. The wind stopped almost at once, no more air escaping. That meant the rest of the station was sealed. Safe.

Her vision already flashing with black stars, Dante looked down to what was left of the docking adapter and saw Bette Norman spinning out of the Japanese module into the web of wires and wreckage. She saw the science officer bounce against the sides of the node, and for a heartbeat, scrabble frantically for a handhold.

But there was nothing Dante could do to help.

She saw Norman's body contort, then go limp as it tumbled out into space.

Alone in the vacuum, in her last seconds of life, Dante was filled with questions she knew she'd never answer. She'd never find out what happened to the shuttle. Or if she'd saved the station.

Or why Norman had been in the Japanese lab.

4

CORY SEALED THE HATCH and gasped for breath. The Japanese module had lost too much air. It was as if she were back in Machu Picchu, 15,000 feet above sea level. She needed her PBA. She found it floating at the module's other end, dove for it.

Working rapidly, she opened the air valve, pressed the fitting tab, and the mask's pressurized straps inflated instantly. The mask slid easily over her head. The moment she'd tugged the mask into position, she took her finger off the tab and the straps deflated again to hold the mask securely in place over her face. Only when she had caught her breath, cradling the mask's air cylinder like a baby's bottle, did she allow herself to think of Bette Norman and her almost certain death.

Whatever the science officer's interest in the lunar-sample cylinders had been, it didn't matter anymore. The only explanation for the force with which Norman had been drawn from the module was a catastrophic depressurization of the station.

But even as she remembered how quickly she had

sealed the hatch, all Cory felt was regret, not guilt. She'd learned the difference, painfully, with Mitchell Webber's guidance, in Antarctica, when her little brother died.

Antarctica had also taught her the importance of preparation in ensuring survival. She looked around the module, taking stock, reviewing the extensive safety training she'd received in the past year, all the procedures she should be following in this situation.

At least, she reassured herself, her oxygen supply was secure. When her current cylinder was exhausted, she knew she could find at least seven more in the module's critical-equipment locker. Because the Japanese module followed the American safety design, she also knew she'd be able to connect her mask to any one of eight oxygen ports to access an even larger emergency air supply. With luck she'd be able to breathe for many hours yet, probably days if the internal oxygen system was intact.

Having established her own immediate survival chances and rating them acceptable, and given that there were no other crew members to aid, Cory quickly moved on to the next steps she'd been trained to take—establishing communications. First with other areas of the station, then with the ground.

She floated to the module's main control rack where she was relieved to discover that the controls were fully labeled in English and Japanese, as well as Russian. The controls for the IAS—Internal Audio Subsystem—were easy to find. She also located the emergency cable with RCA minijacks that let her directly connect the microphone and speaker in her PBA mask to the IAS intercom and phone system.

Counseling herself to remain calm and focused, she plugged one end of the cable into her PBA mask and the other end into the console. Then she flipped on the power and selected the channel for an all-station intercom broad-cast.

"Corazon Rey here. I'm in the JEM. On emergency air. Is there anyone else on the station?"

Heartbeat racing, she waited.

After he had gone through the preflight checklist and con-firmed the status of the *Soyuz,* Yuri Lazhenko found a pair of track pants to wear. Gratifyingly, Rushkin had followed procedures properly and the emergency evacuation space-craft was on its own power, ready to depart at any time.

Lazhenko took a moment to spin around as he tugged on the bright-red pants, then kicked his way up from the *Soyuz* docking module to find and help the others.

By now, Lazhenko was getting used to the shudders that ran through the station. A vibration had been set up that, in time, he knew, would fade. The energy of motion would eventually be converted into the heat of flexing compo-nents, and dampened by the automatic firing of the sta-tion's Russian-built reaction-control thrusters.

But then, just as he passed back through the *Zarya* module, the station lurched as a startling, explosive sound thundered through it.

An instant later, every depress alarm in the station acti-vated.

Lazhenko immediately slapped his hand against the module wall to increase his speed to the central Unity node. Something catastrophic had happened and the first thing any crew member had to do was to secure the undamaged sections of the station.

He slammed into the wall beside the large, square Unity hatch and ripped at the non-regulation eight-inch-diameter, cloth-and-wire tube that kept air circulat-ing through the station in the absence of gravity-driven convection currents. The duct on the Unity side began to flutter away as a wind grew—the station was losing air at an accelerating rate.

His movements almost preprogrammed, Lazhenko moved quickly, without any sense of panic. As station commander and as a cosmonaut, he had trained for this.

He snapped the canvas strap that held the hatch in place and had just begun to swing the hatch closed when Anatoly Rushkin flew toward him from the Unity node. The color of the flight engineer's stricken face matched that of Unity's six antiseptic-white walls.

Despite the still-building force of escaping atmosphere, Lazhenko at once stopped the movement of the hatch, kept it open against the wind, holding out his hand to Rushkin, who grabbed it.

Lazhenko fought the growing outflow of air acting to push his fellow cosmonaut back, pulled Rushkin to safety, to his side. Together, they sealed the hatch.

Then, floating side by side with his commander at the closed hatch, both of them bombarded by the squealing, creaking sounds of the shaking station's walls, Rushkin told Lazhenko what he had seen.

"The shuttle . . . it blew up. I saw . . ." The flight engineer closed his eyes, his eyelids trembling. "Part of it hit the mating adapter . . . tore it loose. The impact . . . it broke the seal on Unity."

Lazhenko reached out for a handhold on the wall, as if that might steady him. The Unity module had been the first U.S.-supplied component to reach orbit. As the station's keystone, centered below the main truss, it linked the forward, Russian half of the station with the larger U.S. and international partners' half.

"Were there survivors?" But Lazhenko knew there was no chance for any. The force of the escaping air he and

Rushkin had just experienced indicated the severity of the depress event.

"I don't know," Rushkin said. "I don't know who was on *Constitution*. Lugreb, McArdle, Dante, I think . . . they were in the adapter." The unasked question hung between them. "I did not see Bette."

Lazhenko turned away abruptly. "See if anyone is transmitting from other modules," he said roughly, then pushed toward the main console. On the other side of Unity were three main lab modules, each with full safe-haven life-support capability: the U.S. module, the Japanese Experiment Module and the European Space Agency's just-installed Columbus Orbital Facility. "I'll contact Mission Control."

When Rushkin plugged his commset in and connected to the IAS, Lazhenko also plugged into the board, but switched to the S-band system. S-band radio provided voice and telemetry transmission channels. The channels were in constant connection with Mission Control through a satellite communications network, no matter where in its orbit the station was.

"Houston, Alpha, do you copy?"

Lazhenko turned the volume control to maximum.

Nothing. Not even static in return.

Lazhenko swore in Russian.

Two hundred and twenty miles from home, he and Rushkin were completely cut off.

Whatever happened next was up to them.

5

ANATOLY RUSHKIN HATED SPACE. All he wanted was to go home. But the ISS flight engineer knew he couldn't, yet. Not until he and his commander knew for certain the fate of their comrades.

After giving his nose a last vigorous scratch, Rushkin reluctantly sealed his flight helmet, knowing that less than thirty seconds later his nose would itch again, and that over the next few hours every other part of his body would join in.

Beside him, about a foot farther back in the tight confines of the *Soyuz* TMA reentry module, Yuri Lazhenko floated against his straps in the center seat, adjusting switches and dials on the control panel, confirming all settings against a thick binder of laminated checklist sheets, written in a unique mixture of Russian and English. It was, Rushkin marveled, as if nothing unusual had happened at all. As if no one had died, let alone Lazhenko's lover.

He opened his own flight binder to prepare for his half of flight prep. Then he heard the commander's voice over his helmet earphones. "You will not reactivate communications."

The order surprised Rushkin. From his position in the right-hand seat, he shifted his shoulders, angling himself so he could look back at Lazhenko through his visor, curious. "I wasn't going to transmit. Only preparing for emergencies."

"Moscow said we will observe complete radio silence. So, we will observe complete radio silence. Go directly to life support."

Rushkin muttered to himself as he flipped through eight pages in his binder until he reached the checklists for setting life-support controls. "Do they *want* the world to think we are all dead?"

For almost an hour after sealing the *Zarya* hatch, he and Lazhenko had tried every communications link the International Space Station had, from emergency voice loops to satellite-service Internet portals, to high-speed Ku-band video channels. Not one was functional. But since each link was independent of the other, his commander did not believe the depress event was responsible for the failure. Lazhenko had pointed out it was improbable that the depress event could equally damage so many individual transmitters and antennae.

"Sabotage?" Rushkin had asked, appalled even by the possibility.

More unsettling yet had been Lazhenko's answer, which had been no answer at all. His only reply had been, "We go to *Soyuz*."

As was usual with each change of station personnel, the custom-molded liners attached to the Kazbek-U seats in the *Soyuz* reentry module had been replaced with new ones cast from the precise biometrics of the Expedition 22 crew, led by Sophia Dante. Fortunately though, the *Sokol* spacesuits used in the *Soyuz* hadn't yet been resized to fit their new wearers through adjustments in the suits' internal drawstrings and straps. That had made suiting-up for the *Soyuz* much faster, since Rushkin's and Lazhenko's suits were still sized to fit them.

As for the seat liners, they would only be an issue if and when the commander made the decision to return to Earth, when he and Rushkin would once again be subjected to gravity. With any luck, the liners would merely be uncomfortable, and not lead to sprained limbs or backs on reentry. Not that either of them would even be aware of a sprained limb or back. After four months in microgravity, it would likely be several days, Rushkin knew, before he and the commander would be able to walk in Earth's gravity again.

As soon as they were strapped into their seats in the *Soyuz,* Lazhenko had switched on the spacecraft's main communications system, set it for Mission Control Center-Moscow, and routinely called for a response, though Rushkin knew neither he nor Lazhenko expected any.

But almost at once, one came back.

Hope had flared in Rushkin.

The reply was from Lazhenko's mission backup, Russian Air Force Colonel Grigory Adamski, telling them to switch to the medical frequency, the one voice loop that was encrypted for privacy.

The instant Lazhenko reacquired Moscow on that frequency, Adamski asked and received answers to several terse questions establishing the condition of the ISS and the possibility of other survivors. But as soon as Lazhenko began asking what telemetry signals Moscow had received about the shuttle's breakup and damage to the station, Adamski interrupted to order strict radio silence until Moscow made contact again over the medical frequency. Then the colonel had broken the connection.

To Rushkin's disgust, Lazhenko had accepted the order without question. "Moscow has their reasons," he'd said. "We will be told when the time is right."

"What if they *wanted* us dead?" the flight engineer asked, not because he thought it was likely, but because he wished to shake Lazhenko. He'd always disliked Lazhenko's tendency to blindly follow his superiors.

"For what possible reason?"

"Construction of the station is almost finished. No more American dollars for Russian Space Agency. So . . . blow it up and get all new contracts to rebuild for Moon-Mars initiative."

Lazhenko was not impressed. "Set the life-support systems."

Rushkin complied with a sigh that momentarily fogged his visor. "Life-support is operational."

Lazhenko closed his binder and slipped it into a webbed pocket on the side of the empty left-hand seat. "Then we are ready."

"We're still going out?" Rushkin was shocked.

Lazhenko twisted around in his seat to look at him directly. "We survived in our modules. With station communications down, there is only one way to know if anyone else survived."

"But Moscow—the colonel said—"

"To maintain radio silence. We will maintain radio silence." Lazhenko turned back to face the flight controls. "And now we will go."

With no communications duties to perform, Rushkin hooked his gloved thumbs into his seat straps to keep his arms from floating free in the cramped cabin, less than six feet across for three cosmonauts. Lazhenko gripped what the Americans referred to as the "unfortunately named" KRUD translational hand controller to the left, and the

KRUO rotational hand controller to the right, and with the gentlest of nudges, the *Soyuz* moved away from the nadir docking port of the *Zarya* module.

If Cory hadn't been wearing her Personal Breathing Apparatus, she might have been laughing.

It was the only sane response to her current situation.

Two hundred and twenty miles above Earth, orbiting at 17,500 miles per hour, in the largest, most sophisticated structure ever built in space, she floated in front of a ten-year-old IBM 760XD laptop waiting for Windows NT to boot so she could fully utilize a radio communications system that was almost a century older.

Technically, she knew the reason why so many of the computer subsystems aboard the station were so hopelessly out of date—NASA's strict testing procedures. Even a short computer program to control the temperature of the hot water in the microgravity shower had to go through more than a year of testing to be certain it would not in any way interfere with the millions of other lines of computer code that were resident on the ISS.

When the station had begun construction in 1998, the onboard flight-certified computer operating system had been Windows 95, and in the interests of strict predictability, it was intended to remain the station's operating system until the ISS reached the end of its mission and was de-orbited, sometime between 2016 and 2020.

The near-obsolete operating system took forever to load on the laptops that served as Personal Computer Stations connected to the ISS local IBM AIX/Windows NT network. But until she had access to the station's online operations manual, Cory knew she didn't have a hope of figuring out how to use the the Japanese module's ham radio system for more than one to nine minutes at a time. That was the range of duration for each line-of-sight communications window with ham stations on the ground as the station flew past them. With none of the station's other communications options working, so far she had made contact with a ham radio operator in Hirakata, Japan, who had been tuned to 145.20 MHz. That was the short-wave frequency already programmed into the module's system for communications with Japanese schools through the ARISS Project—Amateur Radio in the International Space Station. Cory had barely been able to start a conversation with the man, when the signal had faded.

But the Japanese operator spread the word through the amateur radio network, and she had then had brief, but ultimately unproductive conversations with two more civilian operators, in Hawaii and Manitoba. Her breakthrough came when she made contact with Justin Bullicz, a NASA contract employee in Spain.

Bullicz was stationed at the shuttle emergency-landing backup site on the Morón Air Base. He had already been aware of some details of the space disaster, and informed her that NASA was mobilizing ground-based telescopes to take pictures of the station. Within Cory's limited contact window, he had led her through the rapid checklist of her remaining oxygen supplies that had been provided by Houston. He'd also told her how to find the procedures for changing the Japanese lab module's ham radio setup, so she could link to the Amateur Radio Satellite System which would let her stay in longer contact with the ground.

Then that signal faded, too, and Cory was on her own again.

Because NASA had phased out bulky, printed flight manuals on the ISS, the information Bullicz said she required was only available online, from the station's central server. So far, Windows NT had locked up four times as she tried to boot the computer and make a network connection.

But other than not having anyone to talk to, and being at the mercy of an almost decade-behind-the-times operating system, Cory didn't yet feel she was in a hopeless situation. With the extra PBAs in the critical-equipment locker, she had thirty hours of oxygen available to her. Although none of the module's eight emergency oxygen ports were working, for a reason she was unable to determine on her own, she still felt sure that over those thirty hours Mission Control would help her work through whatever mechanical fault had made them inoperative. From her training, she knew the emergency ports would give her several days' worth of additional oxygen. And with the emergency food and water rations in the critical-equipment locker, and the extra flight suit and blankets to help ward off the chill of the module's low atmospheric pressure, she would be in good shape until a rescue party arrived. What a rescue party would entail, she didn't want to think about. But since NASA was an organization that dealt with every possible contingency, Cory was confident that somewhere in their miles of manuals and studies, they had a plan for this situation, too. Especially in the renewed drive for safety following the tragic loss of the shuttle *Columbia*.

The confidence that assessment brought her didn't stop Cory from swearing when the laptop's screen froze for the fifth time.

Her first reaction was to think about slapping the small computer. Hard. It was Velcroed to an angled shelf beside a power outlet and Ethernet port, and made a tempting target. But even after only three days in microgravity, she knew the action would cause more trouble than it was worth. She'd feel better for a second or two, and regret it for much longer as she spun wildly around the lab module.

Instead, she moved on to Plan B. She braced her feet under a restraining loop and unplugged the computer's Ethernet connector. Then she restarted the laptop to see if the problem resided in the ISS network, hoping at the same time that the radio manual might by some wild chance be resident on the laptop's hard drive.

But three long minutes later, after the ThinkPad had finally booted on its own to show an opening screen schematic of the space station's habitable modules, Cory got her answer. The manual she needed was not available.

So much for Plan B.

Cory unhooked her feet from the loop and kicked back across the module to the console with the ham radio unit, which was jammed under a bungee cord to keep it in place. If there was a way to reset the system for extended linkup time through a satellite system, then she'd just have to figure it out, even if it came down to pressing controls at random. Her only other option—and it was completely unacceptable—was to give up and look out the porthole while she waited for her oxygen to run out.

Cory plugged her mask's radio cable back into the console, and turned the RF Gain knob to MAX. Her past experience on ocean-research vessels told her that her best bet for receiving transmissions would be to set the system for maximum and worry about overheating and signal drift later. Then she pressed the Transmit switch on the side of the large gray-plastic box.

Having no idea what amateur radio call signs were in use for the station at this time and frequency, Cory said simply, "This is Corazon Rey on the International Space Station to any Earth station. Mayday, Mayday, Mayday, come back."

She paused to listen, heard nothing, then kept trying. Again and again.

In space, the *Soyuz* TMA resembled a wasp-waisted angel, twenty-four feet long, seven feet across, with solar panel wings that spread thirty-five feet, tip to tip.

On orbit, the craft was composed of three stacked modules. The leading "orbital" module, eight and a half feet long, was an airlock that held, among other systems, the toilet facilities and the hatch that allowed the craft to dock with the ISS.

The middle segment, not quite seven feet long, was the crew cabin and reentry module, with a single observation port and a ventral periscope prism. It was the only part of the craft designed to return to Earth.

The last segment, almost matching the first in length, was the service module, to which the solar panels were attached, and which provided the craft's main propulsion, communications systems, and power supply.

Suggesting to some observers a pinched, sausage-casing stack of modules, the *Soyuz* TMA was the latest version of a craft that had been flying since 1966. It was distinctly different from the aerodynamic U.S. space shuttle, and old-fashioned in comparison to the *Shenzhou,* China's sleek redesign of the *Soyuz*.

In Russian, *Soyuz* means "union," and the first flight of the spacecraft in 1966 took place at the peak of the old Soviet Union's triumphant space program. But the flight, a harbinger of setbacks to come, had ended disastrously when the reentry module's parachutes had failed to deploy, killing the single cosmonaut onboard. That tragedy, and the one that followed in 1971 when three cosmonauts perished in a depressurization event, also during reentry, had led Russian engineers to create an even more robust and reliable version of their space vehicle. By the time orbital construction of the International Space Station began in 1998, more than 220 different individual *Soyuz*-class spacecraft had flown in space.

Like the American Apollo capsule, the *Soyuz* had initially been conceived as a capsule that would take humans to the Moon. Indeed, there were those within the American aerospace industry who maintained that the original *Soyuz* design had been stolen from American plans created by the General Electric Corporation to accompany their bid for the Apollo spacecraft contract in 1961. Whatever its origin, the *Soyuz* was now the vehicle used by the Russian Space Agency to ferry cosmonauts and the occasional paying guest into orbit, and to the ISS. Every six months, a so-called taxi flight would be launched, and the most recent *Soyuz* spacecraft to arrive would remain docked with the station while the crew returned to Earth aboard the last *Soyuz* to visit. The schedule ensured that a fresh lifeboat would always be available for the station's three crew members.

The *Soyuz* design was also the basis for the Russians' automated Progress supply vehicles that serviced the ISS. Unfettered by life-support systems, each uncrewed Progress could ferry more than 5,000 pounds of pressurized cargo, water, and propellant to the station, then serve as a garbage scow to be loaded with waste destined to burn up in the atmosphere on reentry.

On this flight, though, Commander Yuri Lazhenko and Flight Engineer Anatoly Rushkin used their *Soyuz* as a scout vessel to perform a visual inspection of the severely damaged ISS. For a pilot of Lazhenko's experience, the small craft was simple to maneuver around the 356-foot by 290-foot space station. Two separate gyroscopic systems, electronic and infrared, automatically maintained the orientation of the *Soyuz,* so that "down," or nadir, was toward Earth, and "up," or zenith, was toward the station. A third gyroscopic system, used to keep the spacecraft's solar arrays aligned with the sun, wasn't activated for this brief excursion. Lazhenko judged that the *Soyuz's* internal batteries were more than adequate for a few hours of operation.

After undocking, Lazhenko's first maneuver was to drop the *Soyuz* fifty feet down from the station. Then he expertly pitched the craft forward twenty degrees so that he and Rushkin could peer through their cabin's single porthole at the station above them.

Rushkin's stomach tightened as he saw what had happened. "It's finished," he said over his suit radio. For all that he hated the station after his four months aboard it, he felt tears come to his eyes. The ISS was the pinnacle of human achievement in space. It owed its very existence to the pioneering efforts and awe-inspiring bravery of the cosmonauts who had served aboard humanity's first space station, *Salyut 1,* and humanity's best station, up till now, the *Mir.* To Rushkin, and to millions like him around the world, the International Space Station represented the first step into a new future so much better than the recent past, a future fueled by a bright new dream of Russia.

But if the station died, then so did that future, so did that dream.

"What's holding it together?" Lazhenko asked. He had reluctantly decided Rushkin might be correct in his bleak assessment. The station's central truss appeared to have snapped at the P3 segment, so that all four portside solar arrays and the port thermal control panels were disconnected from the habitable center modules.

"Wires and cables," Rushkin said. "See the vapor escaping? There should be more."

Beside him, Lazhenko studied the break point where streams of white gas billowed away, and where ammonia coolant leaked from a ruptured heat transfer conduit, vaporizing in the vacuum.

Rushkin was right. The fact that more liquids weren't escaping suggested that the stresses on the station's wiring, gas, and liquid networks weren't yet strong enough to tear all the pipes and cables apart. Fully 131 separate conduits ran the length of that truss, and some of them were still holding.

A sudden flurry of yellow-white flashes on the Russian half of the station caught Lazhenko's eye. It was as if a small fireworks shell had burst. "RC thrusters are still operational," he said.

The irony was not lost on Rushkin.

With the electricity-powered gyroscopes shut down, the station's computer-controlled thruster system was all that was keeping the station's starboard arrays and the center modules in a stable configuration—despite the deflection forces they had experienced when the shuttle had collided with the mating adapter. But the counterforces the thrusters exerted were no longer being carried along the truss to the portside arrays.

Rushkin studied the apparent bend in the truss at the breakage point. It had changed angle since the first time he had seen it. With each firing of the thrusters, he realized, it would continue to bend even more drastically. Eventually, perhaps in just days, the cumulative effect would be to add so much torque to the station's orientation that the computers would have to have the thrusters fire continuously to compensate, until all fuel was exhausted.

The process would be inexorable. Three, perhaps four days from now, the broken station would start to tumble.

Then, even at this altitude, atmospheric drag would begin to build.

"Six weeks at most," Rushkin said morosely. "Then it burns."

Lazhenko nudged the controls and the *Soyuz* appeared to slide along an invisible rail, moving to port beneath the station to bring the truss breakage into better view. Then he rolled the spacecraft by a few degrees to keep the break point centered in the porthole. "We could cut it free," he said.

"With what?" Rushkin complained. "Our photon torpedoes?"

"The two of us, with tools," Lazhenko said, choosing not to acknowledge his subordinate's faintly disrespectful tone. Even Rushkin, though no admirer of his, was of value if directed properly.

"Us? You're serious?"

"Otherwise, as you said . . ."

"Six weeks, I know." Rushkin sighed, and again his visor fogged before the fan circulating oxygen through his helmet cleared the mist away. What Lazhenko was suggesting was possible, since all the connectors on the rotary joint were designed to be serviceable in space. "But we will need radio contact with Houston. A *lot* of radio contact."

The flight engineer slid away from his seat, his sturdily built body tugging against his seat straps as the *Soyuz* slipped aft below the station. Then, almost in the same movement, his body angled sideways as Lazhenko moved the *Soyuz* back to the center point beneath the space station's central Unity node while also pitching around to keep the spacecraft's porthole aimed at the station.

Not bad for a Cossack, Rushkin thought with grudging admiration. Even he had to admit that flying the *Soyuz* through all three axes of movement at the same time required as much artistry as skill. Yuri Lazhenko *was* the greatest pilot in the Russian Space Agency, even if he was a pig.

Then Rushkin had just enough time to see that the American lab module had been partially wrenched out of position, no longer fully connected to the Unity node, when everything beyond the portal vanished.

For an instant, it seemed to Rushkin that they had suddenly plunged into endless space. Then he realized the station and the *Soyuz* had passed into Earth's shadow and the commander had turned off the main cabin lights. It took a moment, but his view of the station slowly returned as his eyes adjusted to the moonlight that illuminated it.

"Emergency power's still online in the other modules," Lazhenko reported.

Now, Rushkin, too, could see the station's emergency running lights, small pinpoints of brilliance marking key components, shining steadily among the habitable modules and along the starboard photovoltaic arrays. He also saw several observation windows lit from within, which raised an important question.

"Commander, where the portholes are lit up . . . do interior lights work in vacuum?"

As Lazhenko answered, he began moving the *Soyuz* closer to the station. "Lights will work, but batteries will fail. The modules with lights are likely pressurized and sealed."

To Rushkin's surprise, Lazhenko immediately began moving the *Soyuz* closer to the station, in clear defiance of regulations. The ISS operations manual forbade free flight around the station during "night" conditions.

The *Soyuz* bobbed up in front of the station, leading its orbital path like a dolphin skimming ahead of a fast-moving ship.

Lazhenko used his controllers to give the spacecraft another precise nudge, and the porthole aligned with what should have been the Node 2 pressurized mating adapter to which the shuttle had been docked.

Lazhenko reached out and pressed a switch on the flight panel, turning on the docking light.

A heartbeat later, Rushkin closed his eyes, knowing that what he had just seen would stay with him for the rest of his life.

Bette Norman.

Tangled in the tattered remnants of the shuttle's transfer tunnel still attached to the station.

The science officer's polo shirt and shorts were stretched taut over a body swollen to twice its volume by ebullism—the sudden boiling away of subcutaneous blood and moisture beneath the skin. Like the American space shuttles, the ISS was designed to hold a sea-level atmospheric pressure of 14.7 pounds per square inch, and the absolute and instantaneous change from that to hard vacuum was invariably violent.

In all likelihood, Rushkin knew in his sorrow, Lazhenko's lover had mercifully blacked out within seconds of her lungs being emptied of oxygen. She would not have felt the eruptions in the alveoli of her lungs as dissolved gasses literally exploded from her capillaries, exposing liquid blood to boil in vacuum. Her heart, however, would have continued to beat. Had she been rescued and repressurized in the first thirty seconds, her survival would have been more probable than not. Even after two minutes, when her heart finally stopped. At least, according to NASA, which considered astronaut survival possible provided full pressurization and the insertion of a breathing tube to bypass damaged lung tissue was immediately available. From its studies of survivors of vacuum-chamber accidents on Earth, the American space agency had concluded that there appeared to be no long-term neurological effects as a result of explosive decompression, and even the swelling of ebullism eventually subsided.

But Bette Norman had passed far beyond any hope of recovery. Locked in place in her gaping mouth and distended nostrils, dark frozen bubbles of blood were caught like a froth of cooled lava. The obsidian spheres glinted in the docking light, every detail in crisp focus, no atmospheric haze to soften the horrific scene.

"Yuri, I am sorry," Rushkin said. "Truly."

But Lazhenko was an expressionless machine. "When the shuttle hit the adapter, we were able to seal *Zarya*. See the light in that porthole? There could be other survivors who managed to seal the JEM."

Rushkin dragged his gaze away from Norman, to the Japanese Experiment Module, beneath and slightly ahead of the breakage point in the station's truss. The lab module's round observation window was lit.

"We could try SSR," he said tentatively, wondering how far his commander was willing to stretch compliance with his orders. Technically, his suggestion would require breaking Moscow's order to observe strict radio silence, but the Space-to-Space Radio system used on the station, designed for spacewalk and docking communications, had a range of less than five miles.

"First we see if anyone's home," Lazhenko said brusquely. He moved the controllers and the *Soyuz* glided away from Bette Norman's body, even closer to the station.

Whatever the commander was feeling, Rushkin noted, he did not fail to keep the observation window on the JEM in perfect alignment with the single observation port in the *Soyuz* crew cabin.

Rushkin braced himself for impact, but Lazhenko

stopped the *Soyuz* eight feet from the Japanese lab module. The station and the spacecraft were each traveling at 17,500 mph, but in relation to each other, both were still.

As Lazhenko moved a small joystick on the side of the flight console, the circle of illumination from the *Soyuz* docking light slid quickly back and forth over the observation window. In vacuum, there was no beam of light, as there would have been on Earth.

Rushkin felt gooseflesh rise up on his arms. "There!" he said.

A shadow filled the window.

6

VANDENBERG AIR FORCE BASE
17:22 PST, THURSDAY, APRIL 3

THIRTY-TWO HOURS OUT from Red Cobra 8, Mitch Webber was in the belly of an Air Force C-17 Globemaster, heading for his Freefall mission debriefing.

Belted into one of a block of eight stripped-down passenger seats installed in front of the transport plane's main cargo bay, Webber stared out his window, troubled and conflicted. Far below, rising up from California's scrubland, were the red steel and gray concrete monoliths of Vandenberg's space-launch complexes, each sited far enough from the others that it was unlikely, though not impossible, for a single booster explosion to trigger a chain reaction among other rockets poised for takeoff. Where once he would have considered those monoliths symbols of America's scientific prowess and technological might, now he wondered about the integrity of that leadership. His own direct command had lied to him.

The Globemaster's copilot emerged from the cockpit and came down the steps toward him. She was a young Air Force captain with sandy, cropped-short hair, who looked as if she'd just stepped from a recruiting poster. Though

Webber and his seatmate, Varik, wore drab-green flight suits similar to hers, theirs were rumpled from their fourteen-hour flight from Seoul and bore no insignia, names, or rank markings.

Webber prepared himself as the copilot crouched down beside him, her expression somber. She raised her voice to be heard over the heavy drone of the cavernous transport plane's engines.

"Excuse me, Colonel," the copilot said to Varik, before turning to Webber. "Captain, just wanted you to know they're not announcing anything new about the shuttle and the station. Still no word on possible survivors."

"Thank you, Captain." The announcement of the explosions on the space station and the loss of the shuttle had come just ten minutes before he and Varik had boarded the Globemaster in San Diego. There had been no time to learn more on the ground, but the flight crew had been giving him constant updates ever since.

"You're welcome, sir. We'll be landing in ten minutes. They might know more on the ground." The copilot acknowledged Varik again, then returned to the cockpit.

"Tough break," Varik said.

Webber struggled to maintain control of his reactions. For the past thirty-two hours, he'd wanted to confront the colonel about the real purpose of the Freefall mission to Red Cobra 8. He'd abandoned this desire only after concluding that doing so could very likely keep him out of the loop on a permanent basis.

"She hates flying," Webber said, pushing Varik and the mission from his mind, swept once more by his concern for the woman he loved. "She hates jets, anything confined. I still don't know what she's doing up there." *And she probably doesn't either,* he thought. He remembered the day she had told him she was taking the TTI assignment and moving to Houston by herself, and not to Ogden, Utah, with him. It was the day after another of their fiery arguments, so he hadn't taken her seriously.

Unfortunately, in the heat of the moment, Webber had chosen to express that thought aloud, and for the first month Cory was gone, he was certain she'd come to her senses, or that the geniuses at TTI who had hired her would realize their mistake. By the end of the second month, he was damned if he was going to give her the satisfaction of knowing how much he missed her. He cleaned out their rented house in San Diego, shipped her belongings to Houston, and dumped his in storage.

Month three, he was at Hill Air Force Base, deep into training to remotely and simultaneously fly multiple Uncrewed Combat Air Vehicles and deciding for at least the fourth or fifth time in his life that he and Cory Rey were not meant to be together.

"Were you together long?" Varik asked.

That question threw Webber back to the autumn evening when, in the languorous aftermath of a spectacular two-day conflagration, Cory had told him she suspected the attraction and the passion that drew them together like magnets was fueled more by adrenaline than good sense. This time, after their unexpected reunion in Antarctica, they had managed to stay together almost two years. Webber decided that's how long the adrenaline rush of saving the world, or at least a good part of the Pacific Rim, had taken to fade.

But three months ago, when TTI had finally launched their commercial rover to the Moon, Webber had seen a brief news clip of the press conference with the shuttle crew who would be retrieving the lunar rocks from Earth orbit. He had been so convinced that Cory would never get through astronaut training that he had actually been shocked to see her on television in her blue NASA flight suit, as if he'd only then realized how much he'd been counting on her not to make the cut.

But after that first moment of shock, he also remembered thinking, *Good for you, kid.* For someone as stubborn and spoiled and willful as Cory to come up with the focus to endure twelve months of rigorous training, and succeed at it, meant she really could change. He remembered considering whether or not he should give her a call, if only to congratulate her and wish her the best. But he knew that wasn't all he wanted to say to her, and so he had never picked up the phone.

Mitch Webber had few regrets in life. That was one of them. Especially now with Cory caught up in the station disaster, once again in his kind of world, and this time he wasn't there to help her.

Because, given his training and experience, he was one of the few who could. Though Webber had never been in space, he had flown simulators for the crewed variant of the joint NASA/Air Force Venturestar. He had even worked in the National Oceanographic and Atmospheric Administration's Aquarius lab off the Florida Keys, in what NEEMO—NASA Extreme Environment Mission Operations—called a "mission analogue," far more demanding than a mere simulation or training exercise. He'd spent ten days there at a depth of sixty feet, living in an underwater habitat intended to reproduce the experience of living and working on the ISS. The tour had included diving in spacesuits for microgravity simulations of construction and repair activities in space.

Cory's training as a shuttle payload specialist would have been strictly limited to how to respond in an emergency under the guidance of highly trained astronauts. But if the situation on the ISS was as bad as initial reports suggested—

"Webber?" Varik prompted. "You and Doctor Rey? A long time?"

Webber forced himself to the here and now. "Off and on," he said. "We met years ago, lived together for a while, went our separate ways, met up again. Then . . ." He shrugged. "Haven't really talked with her for a year."

"Goes with the territory," Varik said. Then he added, "I almost got married once."

Webber looked more closely at the man. In the six weeks he had known and trained with Colonel Daniel Varik, that admission was the most personal statement the man had made.

"She couldn't take the life." Varik was looking ahead at the closed cockpit door, but Webber suspected he was reliving scenes from his own past as well. The creases of his lean face deepened, lines etched by the pressures of the profession, an unshared life. "You can't blame them."

Webber knew this was the moment when any other person but a soldier would add, "She'll be okay. This will work out. She'll come home." But soldiers understood the world didn't work that way. Things went bad. Good people died for all the wrong reasons. And false hope was crueler than no hope.

Instead, Varik said something odd. "At least Doctor Rey got to go into space, Captain. That's worth something." He spoke as if he were someone who would know.

The Globemaster banked. A long, slow maneuver in such a large plane.

Varik settled back in his seat. "Almost home," he said.

Webber eyed him, puzzled, but left his question, like so many others on this mission, unspoken. Vandenberg was home to the 30th Space Wing of the Air Force Space Command. Varik was Air Force special ops, and they were based in Hurlburt Field, Florida.

To Webber, that meant the colonel had told him yet another lie.

And that only made Webber more determined to learn the truth in the debriefing he and Varik were headed for.

Someone had put him in harm's way for no clear reason, and Webber was looking forward to meeting the officer responsible for that decision, whoever that officer might be.

"First *Challenger.* Then *Columbia.* NASA's always known they were going to lose another shuttle. I'm just surprised it took this long."

Air Force Lieutenant-General Dwight Salyard shrugged as he said those words, but not enough to disturb the perfect creases of his immaculate blue shirt. The personal update he had just been given on the developing ISS situation was far more detailed than what was being reported for public consumption on CNN. Those details were tragic, certainly expensive for the country, but for many reasons they were by no means unexpected. He could see, though, that his reaction wasn't shared by the civilian seated in the wooden chair facing his desk, the man who had briefed him: former NASA Special Administrator for Science Ed Farren.

"You don't agree?" Salyard asked.

Farren frowned, his weathered face crinkling like that of a man twice his seventy years of age. "General, is that how you react when you lose a fighter jet over a combat zone?"

"I haven't been involved with fighters for a goodly number of years, Doctor Farren. But, yes, that is how we react here, because that's the nature of hazardous duty. Losses are expected."

"But not accepted. Not lightly."

Salyard couldn't see the point in arguing, got up from behind his expansive oak desk, and walked across the Air

Force blue industrial carpet to his window, keeping his back to the civilian.

His office was in one of the older administration buildings at the base, dating back to its pre–Air Force days as Camp Cooke. The buildings had been refurbished many times, but lacked the modern glass and steel expansiveness of the base's newest structures. Air Force departments delegated to this building were of two types: relatively unimportant in the grand scheme of things, or intent on seeming so.

Whatever his office lacked in the latest amenities, the general felt the window stretching across the west wall more than made up for them, with its inspiring view of the main runway, and three distant launch complexes. Two of those complexes were hot, one with a Delta II stack, waiting for a civilian weather satellite. The other held an Atlas V, already mated to its classified HAARP payload, also a weather satellite of sorts, though one intended to affect cloud formation rather than report it.

But of even more interest to Salyard was the slow descent and graceful landing of a C-17 transport. He smiled, pleased. Colonel Varik and Captain Webber were on that plane, arriving on schedule for their debriefing.

Salyard checked his reflection in the spotless safety glass, straightened his precisely knotted black tie so it exactly bisected his shirt. The reflection showed a man twenty years younger than Dr. Farren, with a razor-sharp regulation haircut worthy of a new recruit. He turned back to the veteran engineer, eager to get him on his way.

"I do appreciate the personal attention, Doctor Farren. Especially since NASA deemed it important enough to bring you back from retirement for the day. But since there are no critical ongoing Defense Department operations connected with the shuttle program or the ISS, I'm not sure why you have afforded me this honor."

"Recovery," Farren said.

Salyard studied the man, choosing his response carefully. He thought how ideally cast the septuagenarian was for his role of an old-school NASA scientist. Short-sleeved blue shirt buttoned up to the neck. Bolo tie with some sort of irregular slab of polished blue stone at his collar. A white brush cut that contrasted with his sun-creased skin. And clear, clear eyes that belonged to a much younger man. Only the small, almost unnoticeable hearing aids Farren wore betrayed the man's actual vintage.

"Doctor, if I understand correctly, ground-based telescopes have confirmed the break-up of *Constitution*, and infrared imagery shows that no habitable areas remain pressurized in the crew compartment." Salyard waited for Farren to confirm or deny his statement, but the civilian didn't respond, nor did he lose his annoyed frown.

Salyard continued undeterred. "The same telescopes confirm loss of the station's portside solar arrays, and a catastrophic bend or break in the central strut. At present, the only survivor appears to be a shuttle crew member—breathing emergency oxygen in the Japanese lab module and making sporadic contact with the ground. Through an amateur shortwave radio link."

"Doctor Corazon Rey. Payload specialist."

"Since she's cut off from the Russian side of the station and the *Soyuz* lifeboat, I presume she's the one you want to recover."

"Do you leave your men behind?"

Salyard ignored the question. "By all means recover her, Doctor. NASA doesn't need the Air Force's permission."

"We need your help."

Salyard tried to lead his foolish visitor down a different path. "How much oxygen does the payload specialist have?" he asked.

"Thirty hours."

"Best possible time you can get the next shuttle up?"

"Endeavour. Twenty-two days."

"A Russian Progress supply ship?"

"One launched and docked last week, just before *Constitution.* Doctor Rey can't reach it from where she is. The next one will take six weeks to prep."

"What about an ESA Ariane supply module? Or a Japanese H2?"

"Three months and five months respectively," Farren said with impatience. "Both agencies are geared for a much slower tempo of flights. And neither has rescue capability."

Salyard nodded as if genuinely sorry. "As far as I know, none of the civilian tourist operations has a capsule that can reach orbital altitudes, so . . . is any help possible from the Chinese space station?"

Farren's voice sharpened. "They've already sent their regrets that NASA's lack of cooperation with them in the past has resulted in their having no contingency plans. Plus their orbital inclination is all wrong. Their return capsule doesn't have the fuel to change orbits to match the ISS."

"Then it would seem your last hope for a rescue mission is a second crewed *Soyuz* capsule."

Farren gripped the arms of his chair as if preparing to spring from it. "The Russian Space Agency was scheduled to launch a paying guest cosmonaut on a taxi flight in two weeks. They say they can convert the flight to a rescue mission and have it launched in one hundred twenty hours."

"Impressive. How much are they charging?"

For a moment, the civilian's indignation faltered. "You know the Russians well."

"I've had my dealings with them. They've become eager students of capitalism. How much?"

"One hundred million dollars."

"So?"

"The president has authorized the payment from emergency funds."

"Don't kid yourself, Doctor. It'll come out of NASA's budget next year."

"Won't matter, General. Even if the Russians were doing it for free, they're still going to get there ninety hours too late."

Salyard was ready with the counterpoint. "The space station is supposed to have at least three months' emergency oxygen supply onboard at all times."

"It does," Farren agreed grimly. "But like the Progress supply ship, it's not in the same section as Doctor Rey."

Salyard studied the civilian impassively, sensing they had reached a moment of truth. "I wish I could help you."

Farren leaned forward, said what Salyard had hoped he would not.

"I believe you can."

Salyard's back was still to the window. He stayed there, knowing the bright daylight would continue to make it difficult for his visitor to see him clearly. It was always sound strategy to keep one's enemies at a disadvantage. "Doctor, you are going to want to be very careful of what you say next."

The engineer straightened up, squared his shoulders. "General, many years ago, before I joined NASA, my last public-sector position was with Douglas. Working on the Manned Orbiting Laboratory."

Salyard felt relief, none of which he allowed the civilian to see. Farren's data were old, harmless. The MOL project had been the last public gasp of the USAF space program, one of the first practical space stations ever conceived, little more than a long tin can with a two-man Gemini space capsule attached. It had been approved by President

Johnson in 1965, and died in the new budget restraints of 1969, when the government realized they had won the very expensive race to the Moon, but were losing the even more expensive war in Vietnam. "As I recall, that project was canceled almost forty years ago."

"Not the Johnson MOL," Farren said. "The Nixon MOL."

Salyard shook his head as if he didn't understand, when in truth he understood all too well. "You mean Skylab." He tried to anticipate where Farren was going with this, and was unable to. He had not yet grasped his visitor's precise line of attack.

"Skylab was a NASA project."

Salyard nodded. Skylab had been NASA's first real space station. The upper stage of a Saturn V Moon rocket had been modified to become a large home in Earth orbit for three astronauts at a time. It also had made quite a dent in Australia when it had finally fallen to earth.

"But Skylab didn't begin as a NASA project," Farren said.

Salyard felt his face tighten.

"The idea of repurposing Saturn components for a single-module space station . . . that," Farren continued, "was originally an MOL follow-on project. Classified Secret."

"If it is classified Secret, then it's something we shouldn't be discussing."

"It also wasn't the last Air Force space project."

"That isn't news to anyone," Salyard said.

"What I meant to say is, it wasn't the last Air Force *manned* space project."

Salyard caught the emphasis and was certain he knew its significance. He decided his own best response—since he had no intention of being provoked into arresting a former NASA special administrator—was to play along.

"Old news again. Many Air Force astronauts flew on shuttle missions in the eighties."

"I'm not talking about the eighties, General. Or the nineties. I'm talking about the fact that the Air Force had its own astronaut corps in the sixties through the eighties, until *Challenger* blew up. And now apparently doesn't."

Silent, Salyard reassessed all his assumptions about Farren and his purpose in coming here. It was time to find out how much the civilian knew from firsthand information, and how much he was guessing.

"When the shuttle program got back on its feet," Farren said, "there was a shitload of Defense satellites waiting for on-orbit delivery. Until December 2, 1992."

This time, Salyard didn't have to pretend he didn't understand the reference.

"STS-53," the civilian explained condescendingly. "Space Shuttle *Discovery*? An all-military crew? The last Department of Defense shuttle mission. Launched a Lacrosse satellite. Tested a battlefield laser targeting system. A new system to look through clouds. A—"

Salyard interrupted, perplexed. "And all this means . . . ?"

"What this means, General, is that it's a load of bull to believe that after having its own astronaut corps for almost three decades, the Air Force hasn't wanted to send a man back up there in more than fifteen years!"

Salyard took a moment to collect himself, directing his gaze to the framed paintings and posters on the far wall, above the credenza where a mute television showed the latest computer graphic reconstruction of what CNN had been able to piece together of the International Space Station's fate. One of the wall posters depicted a dramatic night launch of a Titan IV, the exhaust cloud glowing like the sun. TAKE THE HIGH GROUND, read its headline. Salyard took the advice now. "I have an appointment to keep,

Doctor. Say what you want to say. Right to the point."

Farren got up from his chair. The easy movement did not look at all like that of a senior citizen. "The United States Air Force has a manned spaceflight capability and—"

"No, sir. We do not," the general said sternly.

The civilian ignored the interruption, kept going. "—NASA is requesting you use that capability to rescue our astronaut."

Salyard started for the door. "Since we've both stated our case, I believe this briefing is over."

"You're going to let Doctor Rey die?"

Salyard put his hand on the brushed stainless steel doorknob. "Despite what you believe, I have no ability to intercede. Thank you for your time."

Farren simply stood where he was.

Salyard waited at the door, his hand still on the door-knob. People in his organization followed a chain of command, and respected it without exception. If the ranking officer said a meeting was over, it was over.

"Something else?" he asked coldly.

"Blue Moon."

Salyard blinked. Felt his hand release its grip on the doorknob. A slow-motion study in self-control.

"Doctor, I want to make myself extremely clear. I don't know what you mean."

But those two words had changed everything.

"General Salyard, if I don't get your assurance that the United States Air Force is going to rescue Doctor Rey—before her oxygen runs out—*and* search for other survivors who might be trapped in the ISS without communications, I'm driving off base and holding a press conference. To announce your decision to deliberately withhold assistance from our astronaut."

Salyard stiffened. "That will not happen," he snapped.

Incredibly, the civilian persisted. "I understand there's a possibility you might decide to keep me here, claiming it's in the national interest. But I guarantee you, if I don't drive off this base, then someone else will be holding that conference in my place."

Salyard faced him in true confusion. It was an open secret that there was no love lost between the Air Force and NASA. At the beginning of the space race, each had barely tolerated the other. And when *Challenger* had exploded, that meager tolerance had turned to open disdain among some of the Air Force's upper echelons. Within the military, NASA was viewed as little more than a commune of space cadets who had no concept of what mastery of the high frontier really meant—survival, and dominance. But the troubled relationship had never descended to this level. "NASA is attempting to *blackmail* the Air Force?"

"I'm retired," Farren said. "NASA has nothing to do with this."

"Then who *do* you represent?" Salyard demanded.

"Will you mount a rescue mission?"

Salyard stalled. "Hypothetical situation. If the Air Force does have a certain manned spaceflight capability, since that capability is unknown to the public, it follows that capability is classified. At the highest level."

"Hypothetically." Farren looked at his watch, and to Salyard, the implication was obvious. The former special administrator from NASA was also on a schedule.

So was Salyard. "That suggests the capability is very expensive—"

The civilian waved a dismissive hand at him. "The blank check the Air Force gets each year for undisclosed, 'black' aerospace projects is larger than NASA's annual budget. And the Air Force does not have to use any portion of those funds to undertake the exploration of the solar system or the universe."

Salyard kept talking through the interruption. "—*and* must serve a vital purpose in the defense of our country."

"And this country's assets. Such as Doctor Rey."

"You're talking about one astronaut, balanced against years of work and hundreds of billions of taxpayer dollars expended to give our country an advantage over our enemies when we need that advantage most. Hypothetically speaking, that is not a zero-sum trade-off."

Farren checked his watch again. "Except that in two hours, the Air Force's manned spaceflight capability will no longer be secret." He began walking toward the door where Salyard stood.

Salyard took a single step forward, as if attempting to physically block the veteran engineer. "*If* that capability existed, your threat to reveal it would most certainly be considered a treasonous act."

Farren stopped, but made it clear that he was not intimidated. "Quite a Catch-22, isn't it, General? You stop me from going out that door, you're confirming that what I say is true, and that will be a strong point to be made at my partner's press conference."

Salyard decided on another tactic, stepped back. "Your partner won't be necessary. I've no reason to hold you here. And you can be sure that when ten or twenty Air Force public information officers give their press conferences to deny your accusations, they will point out that the Air Force did not prevent you from making your absurd claims. Just as we don't go after those crackpots who claim we keep E.T. on ice at Area 51."

Farren glared at Salyard, and the general pressed home his attack.

"How old are you, Doctor Farren? What kind of medications does a man of your age take? Are any of them known to have side effects causing mental confusion?"

Farren was silent. The general smiled. He had the upper hand again.

"No need to answer. The Air Force PIOs will be happy to share that information with the public, so the public can better judge your claims."

Salyard saw his challenger's hands ball into fists at his side.

"What do you know about ancient history, General?"

"Like all history, it's written by the victor. Your point?"

"A thousand years from now, schoolkids are only going to be asked to memorize three names from our time. Hiroshima. Neil Armstrong. And NASA, the organization that made it possible for humanity to leave the Earth. That's all the twentieth century will be remembered for."

Space cadets and dreamers, Salyard thought with contempt. The old fool had not been so difficult to defeat after all. "Fortunately, we are now living in the twenty-first century." He opened the door, ready to resume his day. Varik and Webber would be waiting for him. "Thank you, Doctor Farren."

Farren's shoulders seemed to sag in defeat as if he actually hadn't anticipated the Air Force turning down his request.

"Too much secrecy in this world," the civilian muttered as he passed the general.

"The visitor's parking lot for this complex is down the corridor to the left," Salyard said, unperturbed. As far as he was concerned, secrecy was why there was a world at all. Secrecy was what had allowed the United States to defeat Communist Russia. Secrecy was what would overcome terrorism. And secrecy was what would enable America to amass the defenses she would need when her next great enemy—China—finally awoke.

Farren walked past Salyard's administrative assistant, Sergeant April Tucker, without acknowledgment, and continued to the door that led to the corridor. As soon as his visitor had passed from view, Salyard nodded to his sergeant, then stepped back into his office and picked up his desk phone to report a potential security breach directly to base protective services. When Dr. Edward Farren reached the main gate, he was to be followed by plainclothes personnel in a civilian vehicle. Salyard himself would be taking personal responsibility for informing the office of the Air Force Judge Advocate General of the existence of a possible national security case involving a civilian, and would be requesting permission to proceed with an investigation. *Eventually,* Salyard added to himself.

After he had finished the call on his desk phone, he took a key from his pocket and unlocked the upper right-hand drawer of his desk. In the drawer was a small blue telephone receiver and base, permanently set for full encryption. On that phone, Salyard dialed the Project's phone number of the day from memory.

A pleasant female voice answered, *"Weather services."*

"Salyard for Operations."

A series of familiar clicks sounded as he heard the computers that had analyzed his voiceprint transfer his call to Major Freeman Lowell, Operations Group leader for what was simply called the Project.

The major answered the encrypted call with a terse, *"Operations."*

"General Salyard."

"Lowell here, General."

"I've just been briefed on the ISS situation by Ed Farren. Know him?"

Lowell didn't pause. *"One of the NASA special administrators appointed under O'Keefe. Science, I believe. Office of Human Spaceflight. Retired last administration."*

Salyard carried the blue phoneset to the window as he

talked, peering to the side to find the road leading from the visitors' parking lot. "That's him. He requested the Air Force use what he called its 'manned spaceflight capability' to rescue the surviving astronaut."

"An official NASA request?" Lowell tried to keep his tone neutral, but Salyard could hear his surprise.

"NASA's playing a game, Major. Of course it's an official request, but it's been back-channeled so they can deny it."

"Did he deny it, General?"

"He specifically said he was not here on behalf of NASA."

Lowell jumped to the next step, taking the initiative as all good officers should. *"Where is he now, General?"*

Through his window, the general saw what had to be a ten-year-old silver Mercedes sedan drive slowly away from the lot. *Trust a space cadet not to buy American.* "I've alerted Protective Services. They're going to follow him for now."

"Off the base?"

"He threatened to hold a press conference about Blue Moon."

There was a pause. *"Haven't heard that one for a long time."*

"I don't care what Farren calls it. He said that if I took him into custody, he had a partner who would give the press conference instead. Their claim is going to be that the Air Force has the capability of rescuing the astronaut trapped on the ISS, but chooses not to in order to keep that capability secret."

"Do you know who his partner is?"

"I expect to, once we find out where he's staying, maybe sooner." Salyard was counting on Ed Farren calling his partner from his car. What the civilian wouldn't know was that, as a matter of course, all cell phone conversations originating from or terminating in or near major military bases such as Vandenberg were intercepted and recorded.

Salyard fully expected Farren's partner to be someone at NASA headquarters, maybe the Wicked Witch of the West herself, Chief Administrator Caruso.

By now, Lowell had anticipated the reason for Salyard's call. *"What are your orders, General?"*

"Two," Salyard answered. "First, get Security to pull all available DoD files on Farren, then look for any connection he might have had with the Project. If he's calling it Blue Moon, then that goes back to . . . when?"

"Late seventies, at least, General."

"He might have been with McDonnell Douglas then. That's a good place to start for personnel records. Then do the same check for whoever his partner is, as soon as I get you that name."

"Yes, General. Next?"

"I can't believe a word I hear on CNN, so I need confirmation that the payload specialist is the only one left up there."

"I can confirm that Doctor Rey is the only survivor who's managed to make contact with the ground, General. As for the others . . . other survivors are possible, but without communications, we just can't be sure."

"What was the last communication from our person on-site?"

Salyard could hear Lowell flipping through pages.

"Last contact with Major Norman was approximately one hour before loss of signal. She reported that the transfer was set to proceed as scheduled, and she would intercept as planned."

Salyard didn't like the sound of that. The scheduled time of the transfer of the sample cylinders from the civilian lunar-return vehicle to the station corresponded too closely to the timing of whatever calamity had struck up there. It was entirely possible that Norman's diversion plans had gone awry. It was most unlike her.

"Keep me apprised of the status of the Russians' rescue mission. If they show any sign of getting up there before that survivor's oxygen runs out, we might have to use some influence to slow them down. You understand, Major?"

Lowell was a good officer. He understood the importance of the Project's work, and the need for secrecy. *"Yes, General."*

"Anything else, Major?"

"No, General."

"Then why are you still on the line?"

Salyard grunted approvingly as the phone instantly clicked off. Then he peered out the window again, estimating that the Mercedes should be about to come up on the main gate. He wondered how Farren would feel when he realized he wasn't being taken into custody. Disappointed, perhaps, because it indicated the Air Force was calling his bluff and that he would have to go through with a treasonous act. Or relieved, because he had escaped the drastic measures that might have been employed against him to ensure the most important secrets were kept.

In the end, the general decided neither reaction was of any significance or importance, because Farren hadn't escaped anything. The civilian was only being let loose so he could reveal the others who shared his secret. And as soon as that information came to him, Salyard intended to deal with the old fool by the most efficient and permanent means possible.

There was a war going on. And as the Project's astronaut aboard the ISS—Major Bette Norman—had known, in wars there are always casualties. Military and civilian.

If it was Ed Farren's fate to die in this war, then he wouldn't be the first, or the last. It was merely the price for having chosen the wrong side in the conflict.

NASA.

7

LYNDON B. JOHNSON SPACE CENTER
19:45 CST, THURSDAY, APRIL 3

"OKAY, PEOPLE, we're in pretty good shape."

Tovah Caruso, chief administrator of NASA, stared in disbelief across the cluttered conference table at the stranger who had said those words as she had entered the Action Center in the Mission Operations Wing. "And you are?" she asked.

The lanky young man slowly realized that all fifty people in the crowded room were staring at him. Like everyone else present, he had a picture ID card hanging around his neck, but suddenly his skin was much paler than in his photograph, a striking contrast against his glossy black goatee and carefully trimmed mustache. "Uh, Rick Neale," he said, almost stammering. "OPs Plan." Operations Planner was one of the eleven key flight control positions for the ISS.

Caruso closed the door behind her, leaving her aide in the corridor, and put her oversize coffee travel-mug down on one of the long table's few clear spots. Then she dropped her compact nylon briefcase onto the empty chair that had just been vacated for her and folded her arms. The trim-fitting jacket of her rust-red Tencel pantsuit revealed little of the stresses of the day's travel and Houston heat. Caruso also was trim and compact, twenty years older than Rick Neale, six inches shorter and a good eighty pounds lighter, but right now she still looked as if she could pick the taller youth up with one hand and shotput him through the curtained windows at the back of the room, behind which the translators sat. That was exactly the impression she wanted to make. There was a reason Caruso was the first female chief administrator in the fifty years NASA had been in business. "And your definition of 'good shape' would be?"

Caruso watched Neale swallow hard. No one else in the hot and crowded room was talking. The only sounds were the rush of the overworked air-conditioning vents in the ceiling, and the hum that came from the fifty-inch, touch-sensitive, gas plasma display screen mounted flush in the center of the table. The screen, developed by IBM, had come into use during the 2003 Mars Excursion Rover mission, to enable project participants from the Jet Propulsion Laboratory and around the world to share images and handwritten notes in real time. The so-called MERboards had been so effective they had become an entrenched NASA tool.

Right now, the screen's main window was showing a computer graphic of the ISS derived from ground-based photographs that had been provided by the Air Force's Overwhelmingly Large Telescope Array in an undisclosed Utah location. The still-classified OWL's adaptive optics were routinely used to image and analyze foreign satellites, among other targets, and the enhanced photographs the OWL had given NASA were detailed enough to show a body caught in the wreckage of the space station's Node 2 mating adapter. The images also showed that the Russians' *Soyuz* lifeboat had undocked and was station-keeping near the habitable modules.

Rick Neale began again. "What I mean," he said in a steadier voice, "is that . . . despite what's happened, we can save the three astronauts who survived. And we can save the station."

When the first sign of trouble on *Constitution* had been noted, Caruso had been in a budget-planning meeting at NASA Headquarters in Washington, D.C. By the time ground-based observers were confirming the loss of the shuttle, she was in a motorcade speeding for Dulles and a waiting NASA Gulfstream G-II jet. For the two-and-a-half-hour flight to Houston, she had been on the phones simultaneously to Mission Control–Houston, Mission Control–Moscow, the White House, and U.S. Space Command. As details changed and knowledge increased, nothing had escaped her. But now, in the eight minutes it had taken for her to come from her ground transportation to JSC Building 30 M, which housed the Mission Control Centers for both the shuttle and the ISS, it appeared the situation had changed once again.

"When did we get a confirm on *three* surviving astronauts, Mister Neale?" Caruso asked. She and everyone else in the world knew all about Corazon Rey and her on-again, off-again communications over a ham radio link. That at least one other astronaut had survived could be inferred by the movement of the *Soyuz*. But those facts had indicated only two survivors.

"Lazhenko *and* Rushkin are both in the *Soyuz,* ma'am. Doctor Rey can see them."

"Has she talked to them?"

"SSR is out," a bright-faced young woman at the table volunteered. When Caruso looked inquiringly at her, she added, "Emily Ayers, CATO." Ayers was the Communications and Tracking Officer, responsible for all communications uplink and downlink systems on the U.S. side of the station.

Caruso kept her thoughts to herself. The ISS had nine independent communications options, not counting a standard satellite telephone, space-to-space radio, and the ham radio systems on the Russian side, in the American lab module, and in the JEM, which sheltered Rey at present. That so many of those systems could fail at the same time was unthinkable. Which left only one possible explanation. But this wasn't the time or place to discuss sabotage. Nor were the people in this room the right audience for such a discussion.

"All right, three survivors," Caruso said. She had been up to the station on two of her three shuttle missions. She knew exactly what those three would be feeling right now. "Three seats on the *Soyuz*. Any chance there are other survivors in other modules?"

To have more crew trapped in a dying station than there were rescue facilities was a *Titanic*-like nightmare Caruso did not want to face. But to know for certain that seven more were likely dead was just as terrible a situation. Whatever happened, whatever plan the engineers and managers and flight directors in this room were capable of developing, there would be no good news. Caruso loathed no-win scenarios.

No one in the room answered her question, but Neale leaned across the table to tap the main window on the touch-sensitive plasma screen. The graphic of the station's habitable modules expanded to fill the screen, and he traced his finger along the American lab module. It was obvious it was out of alignment.

"Destiny's been whacked out of . . . uh, it's detached from the Unity node," Neale said. "Anyone who tried to escape into it would . . . wouldn't have made it."

Caruso reached down, pointed to the other side of the screen and the lab module constructed for the European Space Agency. "What about the Columbus module?"

"It's still in its proper configuration," Neale said. "But . . . we don't know if there's anyone in it."

Caruso straightened up. "Here's another question for you, Mister Neale. If Unity's gone, how do we get Doctor Rey out of the JEM and into the *Soyuz*? The Japanese module doesn't having docking capability."

Neale suddenly brightened, turned abruptly away from the display to look with excitement at someone across the room. "Sajit!" he exclaimed. "Show her!"

A gaunt-looking man with white hair feathering brown temples and with gray flecks in his dark beard unrolled an actual paper blueprint over several binders and pads.

"Sajit's the OSO," Neale said. That was the acronym for Operations Support Officer, responsible among other duties for on-orbit maintenance of the station.

"JEM has an airlock," Sajit said quietly. The knuckles of the finger he placed on the lab module's location on the plans were swollen with advanced arthritis.

Caruso shook her head. "It's for equipment transfers. Not large enough for a person."

Sajit looked up with a slight smile. "No, not deep enough. But it *is* large enough for a spacesuit."

Caruso glanced around the room, saw a sea of hopeful smiles—and a great many engineers feeling quite proud of themselves. Obviously this was a strategy that had been thoroughly discussed before she had arrived. "I'm listening."

"Step one," Sajit said, "Doctor Rey opens the exterior hatch of the Japanese module's equipment-transfer airlock. Step two: At the same time, Station Commander Lazhenko and Flight Engineer Rushkin dock their *Soyuz* with the station's Unity airlock, and retrieve an *Orlan* EVA suit."

Caruso could see where this was going, held up her hand. *Orlan* was the Russian word for "eagle." "Why a Russian suit? Why not an EMU?"

"Uh-uh," another engineer at the table said. This one's

wispy and sun-bleached blond hair was tied back in a rough approximation of a longtime surfer's ponytail, but his faded blue eyes shone with intense, focused energy. "Jack Cover, ECLSS." The engineer's responsibility was Environmental Control and Life Support Systems. "The waist connectors on the U.S. suits won't fit through the logistics airlock. But the *Orlan*—"

"Right. Doesn't have connectors," Caruso said. "It's one piece." She remembered her own training over the desolate terrain of Kazakhstan, as a Russian Ilyushin-76 went through a punishing series of parabolic dives, each time creating thirty seconds of microgravity in the cargo hold. In those free-fall conditions, she herself had practiced slipping on the Russian EVA suit. Basically, the backpack life support unit opened like a door, and the cosmonaut wriggled into the complete spacesuit attached to it. Recollecting that experience suggested a number of pertinent questions now.

"Does the backpack and hard torso fit through the airlock?"

The surfer-engineer nodded vigorously. "We just had the backup crew try it out at the training mock-up. The two Russians, they'll have to unpack the suit, take it out of its duffel and off the packing dummy, but it fits."

"How about Doctor Rey getting into it?" Caruso asked. Unlike the U.S. EVA suit that required two astronauts to be properly donned, the *Orlan* was designed to be put on and sealed by an individual astronaut in only three to five minutes. Its backpack door was easily secured and locked by way of a lever mounted on the front chestpiece. But the safety manual called for a second astronaut to confirm that the seal wasn't compromised by excess spacesuit fabric that had to be folded up behind it.

The surfer-engineer deferred to a young Asian woman

in neatly pressed denim overalls and a Houston Rockets T-shirt.

"Michelle Tanaka, EVA, ma'am," she said, identifying herself as the Extravehicular Activity Officer, and thus someone with considerable experience in planning construction spacewalks. "We are facing an imperfect solution with that."

Caruso frowned. "How imperfect?"

"Doctor Rey *can* get a positive pressure seal with the chest lever. But she'll be unable to complete visual inspection."

There was no need for Caruso to ask if Rey had had any training with the Russian suit. Rey had been a shuttle payload specialist. Only the station crew received such training.

"Okay," she said, then took charge swiftly as soon as it became apparent no one in the room had anything more to give her at the moment.

"Tanaka, here's what you do. You find as many *Orlan* training suits as you can dig up around here, and you report to Ellington Field ASAP with a female astronaut for each one." Caruso looked around the room, assessing its resources and their immediate usefulness. "On my authorization. I want the Skytrain on the runway and ready to go by the time the astronauts get there." NASA has acquired the C–9B Skytrain II from the Navy for zero-gravity training flights, replacing the aging KC–135, affectionately known as "The Vomit Comet." "Thirty minutes, no more. Understood?"

Tanaka was already on her feet heading for the door, cell phone in hand. "Yes, ma'am."

"And Tanaka—get a cameraman or video operator or someone onboard to film whoever works out the best technique for securing that suit by herself. If Doctor Rey can hear ham radio signals, there's got to be some way we can use that link to upload digital images to her and show her how to do it."

"Yes, ma'am," Tanaka said, and then she was gone.

"All right, Doctor—" Caruso waited but no last name was immediately forthcoming. "—Sajit. I'm spending a lot of the taxpayers' money because of you right now. What's step three?"

The elderly engineer hesitated, thoughtful. Caruso waited, not pressuring him. "Ah . . . step three, yes. Lazhenko and Rushkin park the *Soyuz* outside the JEM, open the logistics airlock, and—"

Caruso saw another potential problem, interrupted. "Hold on, what are the cosmonauts wearing?"

"Sokols," Neale said promptly. The name meant "falcon" in Russian.

Caruso shook her head. *"Soyuz* pressure suits have to be connected to the spacecraft's oxygen and electrical systems. They're not rated for EVA."

"Apologies, Madam Administrator . . ."

Caruso, and everyone else in the room, looked over to a weary-looking man with deeply shadowed, dark brown eyes and a pronounced five o'clock shadow who stood at the end of the table. His entry into the packed conference room had been unannounced.

"Stepan Ivanovich, RIO. PKA."

"Go ahead," Caruso said. She understood that RIO meant he was the Russian Interface Officer. But she was irrationally annoyed by the man's use of Russian initials for *Rosaviakosmos,* the Russian Aviation and Space Agency. Throughout the ISS project, the Russians always made it a point never to translate acronyms.

"Sokol flight suits are rated for full vacuum," Ivanovich said. "Helmets have full sun visors. For emergency transfer, cosmonaut can connect to sixty-minute life-support unit. But, with Yuri Lazhenko at controls, *Soyuz* can get close enough to kiss JEM. Rushkin will not have to fully emerge

from *Soyuz* hatch to put *Orlan* suit into transfer airlock." Then, as if he were capable of only one thing at a time, the Russian smiled disarmingly.

Caruso automatically returned the smile in kind. "Why doesn't Rushkin trade his *Sokol* for an *Orlan* for the transfer?"

Rick Neale, not Ivanovich, answered her question. "Too many depressurizations, ma'am," Neale said almost apologetically. "The *Soyuz* docking adapter can't reclaim atmosphere. It vents each time it opens. To have the *Soyuz* go back to *Zarya* for Rushkin to change to the *Orlan* there, then to Unity for Doctor Rey's *Orlan*, then to JEM—"

Caruso nodded, already ahead of him, and voiced the conclusion, "And then, presumably, to retrieve Doctor Rey from the damaged Unity module when she depressurizes the JEM. And then to take her back to the *Zarya* so she can change out of the *Orlan* suit, and into a *Sokol* flight suit for the trip home."

"Exactly, Madam Administrator," Ivanovich agreed. "With so many systems offline, we cannot count on Station Commander Lazhenko and Flight Engineer Rushkin being able to recharge their oxygen tanks from station's supply."

Caruso tapped her fingers against her elbow. "You've worked this out?" she asked Neale. "You're confident?" she asked Ivanovich.

Both men said yes, and a chorus of agreement arose from the others in the room, even from the four civilians checkerboarded on the teleconference screen at the end of the table.

"So all we need now is to figure out some way to get this miraculous plan up to the people who have to carry it out."

Ivanovich looked embarrassed. "PKA is confident that we will soon have full voice communications with crew of *Soyuz*."

Caruso shook her head. "Especially now that you have

our hundred-million-dollar commitment to pay for a second flight."

"I do not know nature of technical difficulties our cosmonauts are facing, Madam Administrator."

Caruso didn't believe him, gave him a look that let him know that, then addressed the others in the room and on the screen.

"Okay, the cosmonauts are taken care of. How do we talk to Doctor Rey?"

A broad-shouldered man in a navy blue tracksuit with a large NASA logo raised his hand. "Juan Flores, Ms. Caruso. TOPO."

Flores was the Trajectory Operations Officer, and as if to forestall Caruso from commenting on his choice of clothing, though she had not done so for any others at the table, he quickly offered an explanation anyway, with a gesture to his tracksuit. "I was in the gym when it all went to rat—" Flores paused for a moment, then said, "When the first reports came in."

"As a public servant, I am not unfamiliar with ratshit, Mister Flores," Caruso said dryly. "What were you about to say about getting the message to Doctor Rey?"

A few people chuckled, but Flores ignored them, to continue. "I was about to say that we have NASA and DoD personnel around the world standing by to pick up Doctor Rey as she enters shortwave radio line of sight. They're all networked by instant messaging, so they can relay the sequential information Doctor Rey needs without repetition."

"And that information would be?"

"The settings she needs to make on the radio controls to tie into the amateur radio satellite system."

"That will give us unbroken communications with her?"

"Uh, not exactly."

Caruso's eyes narrowed. "How exactly, Mister Flores?"

Flores responded quickly. "We'll have an approximate thirty-minute window every orbit."

Caruso shook her head and the room went quiet again. "Not acceptable. We're looking at a cosmonaut attempting a novel EVA in the wrong suit, and a payload specialist who's never had any EVA training moving through a torn-apart station to make a transfer into another spacecraft. No way in hell am I allowing that to happen without one hundred percent real-time communications between the *Soyuz* and Doctor Rey and with cosmonauts and astronauts on the ground who have at least some idea of what's involved." She studied each face at the table. "Is that clear?"

As one, the people looking up to her nodded.

Caruso picked up her nylon briefcase. "Then work it out. I'll be in the Ficker." The term meant the FCR—Flight Control Room.

Neale raised his hand again. "Ms. Caruso, don't you want to know how we can use the Progress supply ship to save the station?"

Caruso's chin went up. "Frankly, Mister Neale, I don't give a damn about the station. Job One is bringing our people home. That's why we've got our best and our brightest in this room. As soon as you all tell me how to do that, then, and only then, will I spare time to save the hardware." She looked sharply around the room one last time. "We're NASA. That means we bring our people home."

In the hushed Action Room, the startled group broke into spontaneous applause.

But Caruso was already on her way to the FCR. It was one thing to rally the troops. As NASA administrators before her knew all too well, it was another to actually come through.

"SO, IS THAT Nintendo, PlayStation, or Xbox?"

Webber's comment was directed at what appeared to be a flight simulator—a white, roughly cube-shaped metal construction, two stories tall, supported on seven large hydraulic pistons on the floor of Hangar 27. It was one of the largest simulators he'd seen, and there were few aircraft Webber knew of whose flight decks would require that much volume to replicate.

Walking beside him, still in his rumpled, unmarked flight suit as Webber was, Varik glanced over to see what he was looking at. "More like Atari."

"Atari," Webber repeated.

"As in dates back to the Stone Age. It's a shuttle simulator. From when they thought they might fly shuttles out of here."

Varik's incomplete explanation rankled Webber because the twenty-four-inch-diameter pistons of the simulator sparkled, clean, as if they were in constant use, even though shuttles had never been launched from Vandenberg.

Webber was aware of the California base's long, expensive, and ultimately wasteful association with NASA's Space Transportation System. Billions of taxpayer dollars had been spent to build a launch complex and shuttle support facilities that were never used.

In the '70s, when the space shuttle program had first been proposed, early projections set military payloads as accounting for up to forty percent of all shuttle missions. An old Rockwell hand had told Webber that the Air Force, at its most grandiose stage of planning, envisioned launching twenty missions a year on their own pair of Vandenberg-based shuttles. To date, the most missions in a single year NASA had ever managed at the Florida cape was eight, once in '92, and again in '98.

For the military, the main advantage of flying shuttles from Vandenberg was that spacecraft launched to the south from the base could climb to a polar orbit without passing over inhabited land. Polar orbits permitted monitoring of the entire surface of the Earth and were thus preferable for most surveillance satellites. In contrast, launches from the other side of the country, at the Kennedy Space Center in Florida, were restricted to easterly flight paths, to keep them over the Atlantic in case of disaster.

Technically, Webber knew, shuttles could be launched into near-polar orbits from Kennedy, but the closer an orbit's inclination approached the poles, the more fuel it took to achieve from Kennedy, so the less payload the shuttle could carry. And to reach a true polar orbit from the Atlantic coast launch center would require the government to waive all public safety restrictions and allow the equivalent of a bomb with a lit fuse to fly over the densely populated eastern seaboard. Given that NASA's own MTBF—Mean Time Between Failure—figures predicted that any mission shuttle had one chance in 265 of ending as catastrophically as the last flight of the *Columbia,* Webber didn't think it likely the shuttle would ever be launched over populated areas for any reason. That meant continued military interest in launching shuttles from Vandenberg could not be ruled out.

"Well, someone's still giving that thing a workout," he said. "Check out the pistons."

Varik didn't break stride as they continued heading for a block of offices built against the far wall of the vast hangar. "A couple of contractors on the base use it to try out new instrumentation. Honeywell. TTI. That thing can put the flight deck through a full three-sixty roll."

Webber took another look at the simulator as they passed it. There were no contractor signs or logos on it. It did look large enough to hold a full-size mock-up of an orbiter's partial flight deck, but there wasn't sufficient additional room for the spin mechanisms, which meant the deck would never be able to move through a complete rotation. So the simulator was definitely for something other than the shuttle, but what? And why was Varik holding out on him?

Just before they reached the small block of offices, Webber gave a last, quick glance to the rest of the hangar. From what he could see, it was large enough to hold at least three C-17 Globemasters. But what it actually held today, other than the simulator and the offices, was difficult to judge. Though he could make an educated guess.

Three sections of the hangar had been blocked off by large, white, plasticized-canvas security curtains suspended on chains from ceiling scaffolding. From his own training experience, Webber was able to estimate that one of those sections, smaller than the other two, was just about the right size to hold a satellite component already sealed for delivery to a launch complex. Though each of the other two curtained sections was big enough to hide one or two fighter jets or similarly sized vehicles, it was also possible that together they concealed a single large vehicle. The way the curtains were hung, a crew working on one side of the vehicle wouldn't be able to see what was happening on the other side.

Military efficiency at its finest, Webber thought.

"Welcome to Vandenberg, Captain." Varik was holding open an unfinished wood door with a large, single pane of glass. Through the open doorway, Webber saw walls of gray-painted drywall and rough lumber. Since no security measures were visible, it seemed the enclosure was for the maintenance crew.

Webber paused before entering the complex, unwilling to hold his questions any longer. "Vandenberg's your home base."

"Home?" Varik said, as if he didn't understand the statement.

"You're Special Forces."

"Yeah."

"So shouldn't home be Hurlburt Field in Florida?"

Varik gave him a cryptic look. "For a Navy boy, you know a lot about the Air Force."

Webber shrugged. "Colonel, this mission wasn't—"

Varik held up his hand to interrupt. "Captain, I know what you're going to say, and let me tell you, the best time to say it would be *after* the general's debriefed us."

"The general?" Webber asked. While the United States Special Operations Command had been responsible for logistical planning and execution, the Freefall mission's intelligence goals had been directly overseen by the Defense Intelligence Agency. By all rights, he and Varik should be reporting back to the DIA chief analyst who had sent them into Red Cobra 8.

Varik was all but confirming there *had* been another reason for the Freefall mission than the one Webber had been given.

Varik motioned to Webber to enter the open doorway. "Don't worry, Captain. It'll all make sense."

Webber stepped into a narrow hallway that stretched out before him with windowed doors on either side. As he kept pace with the colonel, he glanced into each empty office he passed. There was no sign of any activity or any working crew. And then, because it had been at least a minute since he'd given thought to Cory, he thought of her again. Somewhere in these offices, there'd be television or a radio.

The ISS was only two hundred and some miles overhead, well within the imaging capabilities of ground-based telescopes. Someone here would have the latest update on the space station. Someone would know if Cory was safe.

Varik stopped at a door not quite at the corridor's end, sharply knocked three times. A male voice from within responded, instructing him to enter.

Varik turned to Webber. "I'll go first and . . . I'll call you in when it's time."

Then he opened the door and shut it behind him, leaving Webber alone in the hall.

Webber resisted both the impulse to put his fist through the door, and to put his ear against it. Despite appearances, this set of offices was apparently secure enough for classified debriefings, so there was little doubt he was being monitored by an unseen camera. He checked his watch and stood at ease, and waited.

It took him four minutes to surreptitiously pinpoint the telltale dark gleam of a hidden camera's observation port in the ceiling. He declined to wave at it. Eight minutes later the door opened again and Varik invited him into a room as cheaply constructed and nondescript as the rest of the office warren. But before Webber could give it greater scrutiny, he instantly snapped to attention to greet the three-star general who stood with Varik.

The lieutenant-general's name badge read SALYARD, and he pumped Webber's hand. "Outstanding work, Captain Webber. In and out of the lion's den, as it were. You've done your country a great service."

Salyard's smile seemed genuine. Varik's expression was neutral.

"At ease," Salyard said, then sat back on the edge of a spindly-legged conference table with a fake, plastic-wood finish on which Webber saw three files, stacked together. The first two were personnel jackets, one dog-eared, one new. His name was on the top file, the dog-eared one. The second jacket looked new and the name FARREN was on its tab. The third file was obscured by the other two.

"I won't bullshit you, Captain," Salyard began. "The purpose of your mission had nothing to do with finding an advanced Chinese fighter."

Webber relaxed slightly. Maybe this would make sense, as Varik had assured him.

Salyard looked over at Varik. "The colonel filled me in. He could tell you had figured that part out. About ten seconds into the mission, he says."

Webber took a chance. "Permission to ask a question, General?"

Salyard nodded. "That's why I'm here, Captain. This is an off-the-record, no-hats conversation. Your country owes you an explanation, and you're going to get it."

"What was the purpose of the mission?"

"We needed to see what was in that lunar training facility."

"The Chinese lunar lander?"

Salyard nodded. "That's just it, Captain. We didn't know it was their lander. We had reason to believe it was a weapons system."

"A weapons system . . . for the Moon?"

Salyard stood up, smoothed down his jacket. "No, not at all. A weapons system designed to be *tested* on the Moon, away from our surveillance satellites."

Webber was curious about how far the general would be willing to go. Further than Colonel Varik, he hoped. "I don't understand."

Salyard's easy manner conveyed the impression the Air Force general had all the time in the world to answer a Navy captain's questions.

"I don't want to stray into compartmentalized areas, Captain, but I think it's safe to say that we all know the next generation of theater tactical weapons will be energy-based. Directed microwaves. High-energy lasers. Particle beams. Straight out of *Star Trek.*"

Webber shot a quick look at Varik, who stood, silent, by the conference table. But the colonel's face remained unreadable and his gaze did not meet Webber's.

"Testing those weapons, in their full-scale versions," the general continued, "is about as noticeable as testing a nuclear warhead. We have satellites that can detect the electromagnetic signature of those tests, and analyze them."

"So . . . ," Webber said, "China wants to test those weapons on the Moon?"

Salyard nodded. "You were in Red Cobra 8. You saw the extent they'll go to, to hide their facilities from us. And they've been talking about going to the Moon for more than a decade. Believe me, their manned spaceflight program has much closer ties to their military than we have with NASA. The Chinese lunar program does represent a perfect blending of civilian and military space initiatives."

Webber thought about the immensity of the Chinese project Salyard was describing. Extremely impressive. Except for one thing.

"But we didn't find a weapons system."

"Which is good news, Captain. A very favorable result. Based on the images that were forwarded to me from your incursion, we've concluded the Chinese are first going to focus on a quick, almost touch-and-go landing on the Moon—a proof-of-concept mission for their spacecraft and technology. So they won't be deploying any weapons for . . . two, perhaps three years, at least."

Webber gave a half smile. "And by then, we'll have surveillance satellites orbiting the Moon."

Salyard lifted his eyebrows. "I couldn't possibly comment on that." And then he returned Webber's smile.

For a moment, it felt to Webber as if the unorthodox debriefing was over. Salyard even turned away from him to the table, to pick up his three files.

But he had one more question.

"General, just before we wrap it up, may I ask why I was chosen for the mission?"

Salyard hesitated with a sigh, then dropped the files back to the table and sat back on the table's edge again, his expression serious.

"Captain . . . there's no easy way to tell you this, but you were the mission's cover."

"Excuse me, General?"

Salyard folded his arms, looked down at the floor. "China has its hooks into us, bad. I don't think there's a branch of the military that isn't infested with their 'little fish' spies. So it is inevitable—*inevitable*—that through their resources in Special Forces Command, they're going to find out that we sent a team to Red Cobra 8."

Webber was struck by the general's dismal assessment of America's operational security in the face of Chinese espionage. But he understood what the general meant. "So you wanted them to think we were going in looking for the fighter, so *they* wouldn't know *we* knew about their plans to test weapons on the Moon."

"Exactly. Everyone connected with the mission, except for Colonel Varik, thought we were going after a jet. And your track record made you the perfect operator for that kind of mission. Even if you had been captured, the cover would have held, because you wouldn't have known anything different from what Special Forces Command knew."

Webber could read between the lines. He knew the general was saying that even if he had been subjected to chemical interrogation and torture, he would have had no secrets to betray because he had been told the same lies the Chinese spies would have discovered.

There was just one flaw in the general's logic. Varik.

"What about the colonel?" Webber asked. "He knew the real purpose of the mission."

Salyard nodded at Varik, as if giving him permission to finally speak.

The colonel reached into his pocket and removed a fifty-cent piece, tossed it to Webber, who caught it in one hand.

Webber recognized the device at once.

He squeezed one edge of the coin and twisted.

The coin split in two to reveal a small, sharp needle hinged into its interior, beside a little hollowed-out, half-Moon section where a fingernail could pry it out. A cover of transparent, soft plastic over the needle kept the drug that coated it fresh. During the cold war, coins like this one were a common component of a pilot's survival gear. Ostensibly intended to provide an easy death when capture and torture appeared inescapable. But every pilot Webber knew who had once carried one, had intended to use it as a weapon of last resort against the enemy, never for themselves.

Webber snapped the coin back together, handed it back to Varik.

"Like they say," the colonel said as he took the coin, "two people can keep a secret if one of them's dead."

Now Webber felt the debriefing really was over. Both he and Varik had been right. He *had* been lied to and used, but at least he'd been told why.

Webber stood back at attention, preparing to be dismissed. "Thank you for your candor, General."

"Thank you for your service, Captain." Salyard picked up the files again, looked at Webber's on top, then added almost as an afterthought, "And I must say I am impressed with your record."

Webber had a standard response to comments like that. "I've been fortunate, General. The Navy has offered me many opportunities."

Salyard pulled a top sheet from Webber's file. "The Navy, the Department of Energy, Department of Homeland Security . . . just about everyone but the Air Force." He gave Webber a sharp look of assessment. "Why'd someone with your talents choose the Navy over the Air Force?"

Webber had a standard reply to that question, too. "The Air Force was my first choice, General, but my parents were married."

Salyard had the grace to smile at the old joke. "Seriously, Captain, if you ever feel you'd like to use your . . . unique talents on a more regular basis, there are a number of opportunities at Vandenberg I think would appeal to you."

Despite himself, Webber couldn't resist asking, "Would

those opportunities have anything to do with that simulator out in the hangar?"

Salyard didn't respond to the question. "You just give me a call anytime, Captain. And thank you, once again."

Webber stood at attention. "Thank you, General."

"That's all, gentlemen. Colonel Varik will take you to Personnel to arrange travel back to Hill."

Then, as an afterthought, he handed the second personnel file in his stack to Varik. "Oh, and Colonel, for that matter we discussed."

"Certainly, General." Varik folded the file in half.

Webber turned to Varik. "I'd like to stop in at the officers' club, first. Check the news."

"Sure thing," Varik said.

"News in particular?" Salyard asked, curious.

"The captain knows one of the astronauts on the station."

Salyard looked at Webber with new interest. "Which one?"

"Cory Rey, payload—"

"Payload specialist on the shuttle," Salyard said. He glanced over at Varik. "I just had a briefing from NASA, and it seems Doctor Rey is safe for the moment, on the station."

"Safe? They know that?"

"Apparently she's been using a ham radio link to talk to the ground. The colonel can help you track down a TV."

Then Salyard added what no soldier would. "I'm sure it will all work out, Captain. NASA's full of good people. They'll get her back."

To Webber, that meant Cory wasn't safe at all, and the general knew it.

9

LYNDON B. JOHNSON SPACE CENTER
ISS FLIGHT CONTROL ROOM
20:05 CST, THURSDAY, APRIL 3

THE FINAL CONSTRUCTION COST of the International Space Station had topped out at sixty-two billion dollars barely 400 percent of its original 1993 estimate, not accounting for the drastic downgrading of size and capabilities it had endured through attrition, overruns, and in the aftermath of the *Columbia* disaster. Fully fifty-four billion of that cost had been paid by the United States, including the money that American taxpayers had loaned to Russia so the Russian Space Agency could supply the components it had promised to build. The other eight billion had come in as welcome dribs and drabs from fourteen other countries, including Japan, Canada, Italy, Brazil, and the European Union.

According to the latest *Fortune* magazine, there were five people on the planet who could match that consortium of countries, and who could have paid for the construction of the station from their own personal holdings. Of those five, two were Americans: William H. Gates II of Microsoft, and Kai Teller of TTI. But of those two, only one had seriously considered it, He had been in ISS Flight Control Room for almost twenty-four hours, ever since *Constitution* had docked with the station and Dr. Corazon Rey had transferred the Moët & Chandon lunar return vehicle from the shuttle's robot arm to the Japanese module's remote manipulator. But twenty-four hours without sleep didn't stop Kai Teller from jumping out of his observer's chair at the Robotics Operations Systems Officer's console the moment he saw NASA Chief Administrator Tovah Caruso stride into the facility.

Caruso saw Teller hurry up the off-center aisle from the second row of consoles and wasn't in the least surprised by his presence. If she had expected anyone to be at the center of a hurricane and look as if he were invigorated by it, Teller was the man who had finally convinced NASA and Congress to become involved in strictly commercial, for-profit space ventures.

Teller was in his early forties, with the dark hair and eyes of a South Sea islander, though Caruso knew his family drew from all of the diverse ethnic groups that had shaped Hawaii. With his tall and slim-hipped frame, he'd always reminded her of an exotic pearl diver. He'd look quite convincing poised at the top of a wind-carved rocky cliff, hair swept back, ready to plunge fearlessly into a far-below sea. Even the man's first name, Kai, meant "ocean." But in the ISS FCR, Teller was more decorously clothed in his signature sun-bleached jeans and white T-shirt. That, Caruso thought, was as close as anyone was getting to the beach here.

Teller held out his hand as he approached. "Tovah," he said. His perfectly controlled smile was worthy of a movie poster, his teeth almost unnatural in their brightness, whiteness.

Caruso took his hand, shook it. "Kai."

Teller's grip tightened for a moment. He was never one to indulge in pointless small talk. "I don't have to tell you that cost is no object."

Small talk wasn't part of Caruso's repertoire, either. She withdrew her hand carefully. "We're going to get her home," she said, not a hint of doubt or equivocation in her tone. "We'll both worry about the bill later."

This time, Teller's smile was the real thing. "Thank you." The charismatic CEO had been up to the station once, too, as a twenty-two million-dollar paying customer of the Russian Space Agency. He knew as well as she did what the survivors on the station would be thinking right now, and how important it was for them to know that nothing stood in the way of their return.

Caruso glanced around what was known as the Blue Flight Control Room, a three-hundred-eighty-five-million-dollar, slightly smaller copy of the space shuttle flight control room next door. It had fifteen Evans Custom 900 series work consoles arranged in five rows, each console with three CRT screens and a large placard identifying its function: THOR, PHALCON, ODIN, ICM . . . incomprehensible to all but the inner priesthood of space travel. Whatever their function, the consoles all faced a main wall with two large video displays. The shuttle flight control room—known as the White FCR—had nineteen consoles, more acronyms, and three large wall displays.

Right now, the center screen in the ISS FCR showed the master telemetry status window, with all traces showing zero values, indicating a total communications failure. A large television screen to the right of the main screens showed a United States Air Force major whom Caruso didn't recognize but felt she should. The major was a striking African-American woman, more than a few pounds over regulation weight, who was carrying on a serious but silent conversation with someone who was obviously on the other end of a videocon link.

"Who's that?" Caruso asked.

Two people answered at once. Teller said, "Space Command." A second voice said, "Cheyenne Mountain." Caruso recognized the second speaker and turned to greet the usually jovial, balding giant of a man: Leo Milankou, ISS Flight Director. The FCR was his kingdom.

"Leo," Caruso said with a quick nod of greeting, "what's Spacecom's involvement?" She prepared herself to hear something shocking about an attempt to blow the ISS out of space. But Milankou's answer wasn't what she expected.

"The Secretary of the Air Force contacted us, put the Milstar–II communications system at NASA's disposal."

Caruso moved to the obvious conclusion. "Milstar can pick up ham radio signals?" There were five Milstar brutes in geosynchronous orbit, Caruso knew—four operational, and one on-orbit spare. Each was the size of a school bus when launched, then spread its immense photovoltaic arrays to unfold like a Japanese robot toy and become almost as large as the shuttle.

The flight director shrugged. "So they tell us."

"They're lying," Teller said smoothly.

Caruso looked between the two men, waiting for an explanation.

Teller had one. "Milstar's a cover, Tovah. It's a basic military radio communications system designed to handle crosslinks and signal processing in space—so the military communications network will survive ground attacks. It handles phone calls, faxes, medium-speed data transmission for all the services, but it's not sensitive to amateur radio signals."

"Then why put it at our disposal?" Caruso asked.

"Obviously, they're using a different satellite system to

pick up Cory's signal. Probably an ELINT spy satellite they don't want to identify, like a second-generation Orion or a Vortex. Those things have fifty-meter antennas that can pick up a short-range signal from a baby monitor." Teller looked pointedly at Milankou, whose countenance remained amiable. "It's all part of the Echelon system."

Caruso recognized Echelon as an old code name for the global network of electronic-signal intercepts created by the National Security Agency. Billions of transmissions each day, from cellular phone calls to encrypted e-mails, were processed through Echelon's hypercomputer "dictionaries," looking for key words and phrases that would automatically send suspect messages to human analysts. "The NSA's probably been picking up Cory's transmissions from the beginning," Teller added.

But Milankou just rolled his eyes. "Haven't you heard? Echelon doesn't exist." The ISS flight director looked back to Caruso. "Space Command says they can make contact with Doctor Rey. At this stage, I'm not inclined to look a gift horse in the mouth."

Caruso looked at Teller. "Neither am I, Leo. I was just in the Action Center. The brain trust there has a pretty good idea for getting Doctor Rey out of JEM and into the *Soyuz*. But it's going to take full communications. Preferably with a video uplink."

Teller regarded her steadily. "I wasn't complaining. Just pointing out that the Air Force was lying to us. They do that, you know."

Caruso didn't take the bait. "Anything else I should know about, Leo?"

"Other than the Russians blackmailing us?"

Caruso had already figured that out for herself. "They must have known their guys and their *Soyuz* were in good shape, but they didn't tell us so we'd have to commit to the hundred-million-dollar rescue flight."

"We can call it off," Milankou said.

But Caruso shook her head. "Too many variables. Is Doctor Rey's transfer going to work? Is the station going to hold together? Are there other survivors we don't know about yet?"

"Merde," Teller said. It appeared he hadn't considered the idea there could be more survivors than could fit in the *Soyuz* for return to Earth.

Caruso raised an eyebrow at him. "Try to keep up with me, Kai. It's why I get the big bucks." She looked back up at the major on the video screen. "How long before we can talk to Doctor Rey?"

Milankou started for the far-left workstation grouping. Three young men were hunched over an Evans console, pointing to a display screen covered with numbers. They were arguing loudly. "I'll check with the comm guys."

Then Caruso was alone with Teller again, in the middle of the busy flight center, in the calm at the center of the storm.

"You do know what's going on, don't you?" Teller asked in a low voice as they both watched the large screens.

Caruso nodded. "It's not an accident."

"Any suspects?"

"NORAD tells me there's a Crisis Action Team in the Pentagon trying to figure that out right now." She glanced sideways at Teller. "How about you?"

Teller kept his eye on the screens, frowned. "Nothing."

But Caruso heard the hesitation, wondered the best way to push him on it, so she could hear his suspicions.

"Spacecom has a full track of the shuttle's flight," Teller said. Caruso realized he was changing the subject, but she also realized she wanted to hear what he had to say.

"Anything useful?"

"*Constitution* was . . . shaken free of the station."

"Didn't decompress?"

"They must have had some warning. It was under control until the end."

Caruso hadn't known that. "If it was under control . . ."

"The cargo module—"

"Leonardo."

"Leonardo. It broke free of the payload bay."

Caruso didn't know how that would be possible, unless . . . "Another not-an-accident."

"Leonardo was on a collision course with the station."

Caruso put the facts together. "Oh, God, Kai . . ."

"They don't know who was at the controls. Probably Doyle. Might even have been Hutton. But—"

"The shuttle deliberately intercepted the Leonardo."

Teller nodded. "The shuttle was safe."

Caruso understood. "But the station wasn't." How could she expect anything else from the people NASA deemed worthy to go into space?

"Whoever was at the controls," she said, "by intercepting the Leonardo module, they saved the station."

"They saved the station," Teller agreed.

Caruso rubbed at her temple. "I just told the brain trust in the Action Center that I didn't care about the hardware. Not until they could tell me how we get the Russians and Doctor Rey home. But . . . suddenly . . . that hardware's worth a lot more than it was."

"Do they really think they can keep the station on orbit?" Teller asked.

"What's left of it. With a Progress burn."

"There goes my plan for buying the salvage rights cheap."

Caruso studied him, unsmiling, though she was not unappreciative of his attempt at humor. His kind wasn't often found in politics, seldom turned up at all inside the Beltway. But NASA had more than its share. The pioneers. The people who never saw boundaries. In Washington, the future was defined as the time between now and the next election. At NASA, teams were already beginning to explore what would be required to launch a hundred-year-long robotic mission to the nearest extrasolar star.

"Something on your mind?" he asked.

She decided to strike. "When I asked you if you had any thoughts about who might be responsible for what's happened up there—"

"I said I didn't know."

"You hesitated, Kai. *Then* you said you didn't know."

Teller hesitated again.

"If you don't tell me what you're thinking," Caruso said, with just an edge of a threat, "I'll have to make speculations of my own."

Teller replied with an equal edge of challenge. "Like what?"

"Like the last thing they were doing on station was retrieving the sample cylinders from your lunar return vehicle. Is that a coincidence?"

Inexplicably, Teller suddenly became defensive, almost angry with her. "That was NASA's LRV as much as it was mine. Dry run for Mars, remember? You guys came up with the transfer protocols. I only paid for it."

"Okay. But . . . you think of anything, I don't care how small—"

"You'll be the first one I tell. Okay?"

"Okay. Good."

"Good."

They held each other's gaze for a moment longer, each trying to see what as-yet-untold secrets were being held back. Then Leo Milankou shambled back toward Caruso.

"Spacecom has isolated Doctor Rey's frequencies and is ready to make contact," the flight director announced.

Caruso's eyes sought the television where the impressive figure of the Spacecom major had been. But she was gone now. Instead there was a blue screen showing the emblem of the United States Space Command: an eagle among four stars, spreading its wings over an Earth orbited by two satellites. Then a small black band appeared at the bottom of the screen, with a time code counting down minutes and seconds.

A voice came over the small speaker on a nearby console, and Caruso instantly connected it with the major she had seen.

"This is U.S. Space Command initiating voice communications with the ISS, at oh-three-twenty-two Zulu. We will acquire voice communications uplink in three minutes . . . mark."

Caruso, Teller, Milankou, and half the other thirty people in the control room stood and stared up at the blue screen, as if hypnotized by its flashing numbers.

"It'll be good to get a firsthand report," Teller murmured.

Caruso nodded, at the same time feeling the full weight of her burden once more. On the one hand, Teller was right, knowing would be good. But on the other, once she had eyewitness confirmation of the fates of the other astronauts, she was the one who would have to step outside and phone their families, and then face the press. Another no-win situation.

Space was full of them.

"Two minutes, thirty seconds."

INTERNATIONAL SPACE STATION

Cory Rey was cold. Her eyes were dry and scratchy. Her throat hurt, her nasal cavities were congested, and even more alarming, if she closed her eyes for more than a moment, or turned her head in the slightest, it was as if she were at the bottom of a spinning cylinder, and an instant later at the top of it about to fall.

She had tried all the tricks Dante and the others had taught her during training. She'd made sure she was aligned with the Japanese lab module's visual references to up and down. She had tightened the foot restraints at the communications console so her feet had to be jammed under it, creating pressure on her soles. Those distractions had worked for a while, but didn't anymore. She hoped her sanity lasted as long as her air.

Her thirty hours of survival on the PBA air cylinders had been whittled away to twenty-six now. She kept telling herself that that was still more than a day. Plenty of time for NASA to figure out something.

They had obviously made sense of her communications attempts, that much she knew. The unseen voices who contacted her now, one after another as the station flew over them, kept relaying to her the information she needed to somehow change the line-of-sight ham radio into something that could take advantage of an amateur satellite repeater.

As soon as she had the radio set up properly, she was going to make someone tell her why it was called "ham," and why the hell something so primitive was on station in the first place. It couldn't even make contact with Lazhenko and Rushkin in the *Soyuz*.

Cory fought down the rising tide of panic within her. She knew part of it was due to her first real bout of vertigo and SMS—Space Motion Sickness—triggered an hour ago by the *Soyuz* docking light that had flashed through the observation window. Until then she'd been one of the lucky one-third of space travelers who somehow escaped microgravity's effects on the inner ear. Even training on NASA's "Vomit Comet" hadn't caused her to use even one of the little white plastic bags thoughtfully jammed into her flight suit pocket. And three days ago, when she had floated out of her acceleration chair on *Constitution*'s mid-deck and experienced real microgravity for the first time, it had felt as natural to her as swimming.

But not now. And not when the docking light had flashed in her peripheral vision. It had caused the Japanese module to magically rise up on end and tumble around her.

Even then she'd struggled to suppress the violent urge to vomit, and kicked over to the window—hoping to see *Constitution*. The *Soyuz* was second best, and after ten minutes of delicate maneuvering, its amazing pilot, Station Commander Lazhenko, had brought his spacecraft close enough to the JEM for her and the two *Soyuz* cosmonauts to communicate with each other by writing on pads of paper and holding the pads up to the portholes.

Despite Rushkin's spelling, Cory had been able to get a mental picture of the space station's condition, and it wasn't good. The *Soyuz,* less than six feet away, had the capability of taking her safely back to Earth. But given all the damage the station had endured, there was no way she could get out of it to join the Russians.

She had only to recall one of her first "chamber rides"—a pressure-chamber session designed to introduce her to the dangers of hypoxia and decompression. The first thing her NASA trainer had told her was that the wonderful movie scene in which the stalwart astronaut transferred from his pod to his spaceship without a helmet just couldn't have happened. Not unless the astronaut had been lucky enough to have a medic on the other side of the airlock, ready to shove a tube into his lungs so air could bypass his pulped throat tissue and bronchial passages.

Once upon a time, her trainer also told her, NASA had considered stocking the ISS and the shuttle fleet with Personal Rescue Enclosure balls—essentially three-foot-diameter beach balls layered with spacesuit materials. The theory was that astronauts trapped as she was now, could be sealed into one of the rescue balls with a one-hour oxygen supply, and then be floated safely through the vacuum by spacesuited rescuers. But all such work had been dropped when NASA realized that a second shuttle could never be prepped for flight fast enough to make a difference in a critical ONS.

Cory made another mental note to herself. When she returned to Earth, she'd have words with whoever was responsible for that decision to do away with the rescue balls. They certainly would offer survival advantages in being able to move from module to module in a crippled space station. And she'd also have similar words with the soulless technical writer or astronaut trainer who'd come up with the chilling ONS acronym—Off-Nominal Situation, indeed. FUS was more like it.

But unlike the unknown technical writer or trainer at least the cosmonauts of the station's Expedition 21 crew were human beings, and one of them, Rushkin, had printed on one sheet of paper the words that she had most needed to see—

NOT LEAVNG W/O U

Cory knew that in twenty-six hours, that sentiment would be moot. But she appreciated knowing that when the end came, if it came, she would not be alone. Two others would be with her, less than six feet away.

Rushkin had also made it easier for her to accept the situation when he had signaled that the *Soyuz* would be moving off to check the other pressurized modules, and he'd held up the cosmonauts' last message.

WILL B BACK

Cory had returned to her ham radio console then, sick, dizzy, tired, and miserable. But comforted.

Then that comfort was trumped when she made her next scheduled radio call, and heard a familiar voice she had never expected to hear again.

"This is U.S. Space Command to Alpha. Alpha, come back."

Cory recognized the voice of reason that had helped to save her once before.

It was Major Bailey.

10

CHEYENNE MOUNTAIN AIR FORCE STATION
SPACE CONTROL CENTER
19:37 MST, THURSDAY, APRIL 3

MAJOR WILHEMINA BAILEY REACHED into space from one thousand seven hundred and fifty feet beneath the surface of Colorado, and thought again, *I love this job*. At her fingertips was a vast control console as complex as any recording studio's mixing board, and through it she had access to the hundreds of billions of dollars of spaceborne assets that kept America—and the world—safe. At least, when they were used correctly.

Three years ago, during what top brass later called the Icefire incident, Bailey had faced a career-defining situation, the kind Air Force instructors loved to discuss in ethics classes at the Academy, and which no graduate ever really wants to experience.

At the height of the crisis, with millions of lives on the line, and the potential for war to erupt between China and the USA, Bailey had been given an order by the general in charge of the National Military Command Center.

Her training had told her she must obey that order. But her instinct told her it was unlawful.

It was the moment and decision all warfighters fear. Shall I be a good soldier? Or shall I be a good human being?

In her moment, Bailey had decided she could be both, and she had shut down all Pentagon communications, isolating it from the world. She'd expected consequences, and she'd been ready for them. But there had been no court-martial. She got a plaque instead—from the president—three months later, when she and her mother and her father and her baby sister, Darlene, from San Diego, had dinner at the White House. The plaque cited her contribution to "a significant accomplishment." The precise contribution was left unspecified. Her father had cried when she shook the president's hand.

That evening, her respect for her commander in chief had soared above its already lofty level when the leader of the most powerful nation in history had listened and laughed and asked probing questions of her father about his time in the White House, working for President Johnson. Once again she heard the stories her father had shared with her as a child and teenager. Stories that began her dream of joining the Air Force.

My threads and connections, Bailey thought, binding together everything and everyone she cared about. There had never been a division between her life and her work.

That thought was still in the major's mind as a welcome call came in for her on her headset. The voice was familiar. It belonged to one of the three other people who had been on the link when Bailey had made her decision to shut down the Pentagon: the enterprising oceanographer and environmental activist now stranded on the ISS.

"Doctor Rey, I am so sorry about the circumstances, but I surely am glad to talk with you again."

Corazon Rey's voice came back over Bailey's headset as

clearly as if she had been calling from only a few miles away in Colorado Springs. *"Let me guess,"* Rey said, with relief and excitement evident, *"you're not transmitting from a ham radio."*

Bailey smiled as she adjusted the settings on her board, then looked across the darkened control room with its glowing screens and whispering technicians to check the station's orbital position on the main, twenty-foot display. "Not exactly, but we won't go into that, if you know what I mean."

The sigh from the voice loop was a reminder to the major that her caller was no stranger to—or fan of—military secrets. *"Does that mean we have longer than seven minutes to talk?"*

Bailey made sure her tone was firm, convincing. "Absolutely. We're with you all the way now, Doctor. You keep your controls set just as they are, and this circuit will remain open." *I hope,* Bailey added to herself, the fervent wish unspoken.

"Thank you, Major. Who else is with us?"

"I have Houston ISS Mission Control standing by, as soon as I lock down your signal." Bailey wanted to wait for the first hand-off of Rey's weak shortwave transmission from a NIAGARA listening post in the Virgin Islands to a SOLITUDE processing center in Menwith Hill, England. If the signal stayed locked, then the ROSETTA computers in Fort Meade, Maryland, would automatically control all other hand-offs around the globe as easily as a civilian wireless phone system traded calls between cells. Dr. Rey's transmissions would then be sent back through the Defense Satellite Communications Network to Cheyenne Mountain for distribution to NASA.

It was a neat trick, thought Bailey. Not that NASA needed to know how it was accomplished.

While she waited for the transmission hand-off, Bailey took the doctor through a checklist of technical readouts to determine the power levels on the Japanese Experiment Module in which she had taken shelter. Bailey was intent on discovering how much longer Rey would be able to transmit, and what her signal drop-off rate would be as the JEM's power inevitably diminished.

The situation turned out to be what the communications team leader at ISS Mission Control had suspected. The JEM was running on batteries, not solar electricity. Bailey knew that meant NASA would have to guide Rey through a selective shutdown of all noncritical systems in the module so that she could maintain heat and radio as long as possible.

"What now?" Rey asked.

Bailey checked the orbital plot. Ninety seconds more and she'd know if the automatic systems would hold the signal. "Almost ready to patch you through, Doctor Rey. I think Houston wants to know the status of the Russians."

"The Soyuz is in good shape, I think. Lazhenko and Rushkin are both on it. We were taking turns holding up written messages. They said they were going to check the other modules. That was . . . oh, maybe ten minutes ago."

Exhaustion muffled Rey's voice now. The elation of hearing a familiar voice was fading. Bailey watched the countdown. One minute. "How're you holding up, Doctor?"

"Where's Captain Kirk when you need him?"

Bailey laughed. She had her opening for the first question she had wanted to ask, the question she had held back because it was personal. But she had to know, and the distraction wasn't such a bad idea for her caller. "How about that other captain?"

This time, she heard a snort over the voice loop.

"Doctor? You still there?"

"Yes. It's just . . . my sinuses feel like they're jammed with cement. Awfully dry up here."

Bailey tweaked the controls, watched a frequency number drift on one of her computer screens at the back of her console. "Ah. I thought you were making a comment about Captain Webber."

"That, too."

Bailey nodded, as if she were in visual communication with Rey, as the last few seconds to hand-off counted down. "You two still seeing each other?" she asked. Until the hand-off, this conversation was just between the two of them, and in Bailey's opinion the doctor and the captain were a match made in heaven. Just like her and Dom.

"If Mitchell wants to see me, Major, all he has to do is look up and here I am. Every ninety minutes."

Oops, Bailey thought. It seemed the on-again, off-again romance between Dr. Rey and Captain Mitch Webber was definitely off again.

On the main screen, the major's displays showed that Rey's transmission was now being received by the SOLI-TUDE antenna array in England.

"One more voice check, Doctor Rey. Do you copy?"

"Yeah, sure, copy that, roger wilco one two three, etcetera."

Bailey smiled to herself as she remembered her caller's penchant for ignoring protocol. "Your signal is locked in, Doctor Rey. I am patching you through to ISS Mission Control, Houston." As a warrior in the chain of command, Bailey had done all she could do for now. As a human being, she knew she hadn't done enough.

But the day wasn't over yet.

LYNDON B. JOHNSON SPACE CENTER
ISS FLIGHT CONTROL ROOM

"Doctor Rey, this is Tovah Caruso. Can you hear me?"

"I sure can. Thanks, Major."

NASA's chief administrator sat back in her chair at the Flight Director's console, with a nod of relief to Kai Teller beside her. As long as communications were maintained, there was a chance Teller's employee could come back.

"Hey, Cory, Kai Teller here. Tovah and I are both in the Blue FCR."

"Hey yourself, boss. I'd better be getting a bonus for this."

"Employee of the month, for sure," Teller said into his commset. "Look, we've got a lot of ground to cover, but the first and most important thing is that Tovah's people have worked out a way to get you on that *Soyuz* and bring you home."

It took a moment for Rey's reply to come back. *"Really?"*

"Really. It's a solid plan. Tovah's going to give you the big picture, then they're going to get some astronauts on the line to talk you through the whole thing. You got that?"

"You made my day."

Caruso leaned forward, ready to toggle on her commset again, but Teller's hand stopped her. She halted in surprise.

"Cory, just before Tovah gets started, how'd the transfer go?"

Caruso studied Teller, puzzled. In all her dealings with him, he had never shown interest in operational procedure. Only in the "big picture," as he always put it. Never details.

Rey seemed to have the same reaction. Her response time was slow once again.

"It didn't go. Whatever happened up here, happened before I got to any of the cylinders. I think most of them spilled."

"No worries," Teller said. "They were only rocks." He nodded at Caruso. "Turning you over to Tovah."

Caruso toggled on her commset to outline NASA's brain trust's plan: The cosmonauts would first cram a spacesuit into the equipment airlock. Once in the suit, Rey was to depressurize the JEM and literally spacewalk from the open hatch of the shattered mating adapter to the *Soyuz.*

"You can handle that, right, Cory?" Teller asked.

"Piece of cake, boss. But this exceeds my job description."

"Automatic promotion from payload specialist to astronaut." Teller looked at Caruso.

"No argument here," Caruso said.

"Deal," Rey answered. *"So how do we get this show on the road?"*

"First," Caruso began, "we're going to need a way to communicate with the Russians. You can probably get them started by holding up a message that says—" Caruso didn't get a chance to finish as Major Bailey cut in.

"Pardon me, Ms. Caruso, Major Bailey back with you. This is my area, if that's all right with you and Mister Teller." Barely waiting for any objection to be raised, none of which materialized from either Caruso or Teller, Bailey continued. *"Doctor Rey, the* Soyuz *does have full communications with Mission Control-Moscow."*

Caruso sat up, startled. She put a hand to her commset microphone, her fingers tightening on it. "What? For how long?"

"That's really not for me to say, ma'am. But I can tell you they're using their secure medical channel."

Beside Caruso, Teller cupped his hand over his own microphone, said in a low voice, "Space Command's been listening to everything the whole time."

Caruso's mood darkened. "At least they're sharing now," she said. "Should help us in the Senate hearings . . ."

"Major," Rey's voice said, *"that secure channel . . . is that something I can use?"*

Caruso and Teller turned to one another simultaneously, questioningly.

"Doctor Rey," Bailey said, *"is there something confidential you'd like to discuss?"*

"Yes. Can you set that up?"

"I can do that, Doctor. Who would you like to speak with?"

"Let's start with you," Rey said.

Caruso's brow furrowed. "Doctor Rey, is this something medical?"

Rey's reply was prompt. *"Yes."*

NASA's chief administrator had no choice. She gave Major Bailey her permission. "Whatever she wants, Major. Just make it fast."

And then Caruso's commset fell silent.

INTERNATIONAL SPACE STATION

"You still there, Doctor?" Major Bailey asked.

Cory scratched around the edge of her PBA. The pressure of its straps combined with the throbbing pain in her sinus cavities was making her head feel twice its size. "Barely. Are we secure?"

"Just you and me."

But Cory had spent enough time dealing with the military to know that, even with someone decent like Wilhemina Bailey, that was highly unlikely. "Are you recording this?"

Bailey paused before answering. *"Uh, that is SOP."*

Cory also knew that in the military, Standard Operating Procedures were for Some Other People. There were always exceptions.

"Major, let's say that I wanted to talk to you about a personal medical condition that has nothing to do with the current mission. Does my need as a civilian for medical privacy give you the authority to turn off the recording for a few minutes?"

Cory could picture Bailey's broad smile as she replied. *"The rules do allow me to do that. For a few minutes. Is that what you're requesting?"*

"I am now," Cory said.

A few seconds later, Bailey spoke again, and this time her voice had an odd, flat sound to it. *"Okay, Doctor Rey, we're now secure and not being recorded. My transmissions are encrypted at source, yours are being encrypted by the satellite network that's picking up your low-power transmission. So to keep anyone else from accidentally listening in, start giving me a test count and begin turning your RF Gain knob toward its minimum setting. I'll let you know if I start to lose you. Copy that?"*

Cory began a slow, careful count from one, turning the knob on the ham radio unit from MAX to MIN. At "fifteen," she had reached the lowest setting and informed the major of that fact.

"That's okay, I've still got a strong channel. What's on your mind?"

What was on Cory's mind was that she was about to admit to Bailey that she had lied to her. And that was definitely something that wouldn't sit well with the major. "I need to talk to Kai Teller over this kind of channel."

"I take it you don't want to discuss a medical issue."

Cory went for broke. "I won't lie to you, Major."

"I think you already have, Doctor."

"I didn't know what else to say," Cory protested. "Look, the guy spent a fortune to get me up here, to send that rover to the Moon and back, and I have proprietary information for him that his competitors could find useful. NASA does allow commercial partners to have corporate secrets, you know."

A distinct pause followed before she heard Bailey's voice again. It held no trace of familiarity or ease. *"Swear to me that what you need to say to Mister Teller has no bearing on what happened to the station and the shuttle."*

If Cory had been ten years old, she would have crossed her fingers. But, instead, she took a deep breath and told the major what she knew Bailey could accept. While that wasn't technically a lie, it wasn't the whole truth, either. Not even she knew that.

"To the best of my knowledge, Major, what I have to discuss with Mister Teller has no bearing on the accident up here. If in some way he thinks it does, then he and I will both share everything we know at once."

There was another long pause, and for a moment, Cory wondered if she had lost contact with Space Command. Then Bailey said, *"We've been through a lot together, Doctor Rey. So I'm going to give you the benefit of the doubt. Five minutes. Secure, and no recordings. But that's it."*

"Thanks, Major. I owe you one."

"You owe me a lot more than one. Stand by . . ."

Cory's laugh of relief fogged up the goggles in her Personal Breathing Apparatus. Despite Bailey's instruction, she couldn't exactly *stand* anywhere.

About a minute later, Bailey came back on the circuit, speaking formally as she connected Space Command with the ISS. Then she added, *"Doctor Rey, I am now switching you over to the secure channel you requested. Are you ready?"*

"Thank you, Major. Yes, I am."

"I'll reconnect in five minutes. Space Command out."

Even as Cory checked her watch to track the time, Teller came on the channel. Her employer sounded worried. *"Cory, Kai Teller here. The major sounds pretty pissed off, so I figure this has to be your idea."*

Cory knew there was no time to waste. "Here's the real story. When everything was going to hell up here, Bette Norman pulled a knife on me to try to get to the samples."

Teller sounded stunned. *"But you said there were no samples."*

Huh? Cory thought, stunned in turn.

"There *are* no samples," she said, upset. Her *life* had been threatened by an *astronaut.* And he was worried about the lunar samples? "But Norman didn't know that. She came charging in after me and pulled a knife on me. So did you find a mother lode of Moon diamonds and forget to tell me about it?"

"Cory, the last time privately owned lunar material was sold at auction, and I'm talking less than a carat of lunar dust, it brought more than four hundred forty thousand dollars. And that's somewhere between twenty to a hundred times more valuable than diamonds."

Cory's pulse fluttered. Teller's response—and numbers—didn't add up. His lunar mission was supposed to return five kilograms of lunar material to the Earth. He'd told her that putting that quantity on the market, with the knowledge of future sample-return missions to come and NASA's eventual plans to establish a permanently crewed base, would drop the collector price to somewhere around twenty dollars per milligram. That price was still enough to make a good profit on a mission costing less than a hundred million dollars, especially with additional income from corporate sponsors like Moët & Chandon. But what did any of that have to do with what lunar dust might have sold for a decade ago?

"Okay," she said carefully. "Then tell me what's on the Moon that's more valuable than Moon dirt."

"Cory, I don't know. Norman might have been confused. Maybe she didn't pull a knife to come after you. Maybe—"

"What do you mean, 'maybe'?! I was there! She wanted the samples and if I was in her way, she was going to stab me!"

"I don't know what to say, Cory. How can I know what was in her mind? I'm sorry."

I'm sorry, too, Cory thought. *Because I don't believe you.* She tried another tactic, to shake him. "Is this something I should tell Caruso?"

"Not right now. Let them focus on getting you down and doing what they can to salvage the station."

Her employer's anxious reply confirmed Cory's suspicion that he did know something that might explain what had nearly happened to her. But he was not about to share it with her, no matter what her situation.

"Okay," she said. "Your call."

"Cory, to be honest, they're looking for a scapegoat, and something like that story about Norman and the samples . . . well, if they think the LRV, or you, were somehow involved in what happened . . . it could set us all back years."

The threat was clear to Cory. But knowledge was power. She decided to hold on to hers as well. "You're the boss."

"Thanks, Cory. We'll straighten everything out when you get back."

"Sure thing. Might as well tell Caruso I'm ready for instructions."

Teller signed off.

Cory floated by the radio unit, waiting.

Then she turned to stare at the equipment-transfer airlock as a startling thought came to her: *What if the airlock already contained a sample cylinder from the LRV?* It would—if the Japanese robotic arm had managed to complete its programmed sequence *before* the station's power systems were disrupted. Maybe she still had a chance to discover first-hand what Norman—and Teller—had considered more valuable than her life.

She checked her watch. She still had two minutes before her five minutes of "privacy" ran out. Cory knew she couldn't do everything she needed to do in two minutes. But she'd have a head start before everyone started wondering why she wasn't responding to the radio.

She unplugged her mask's radio wire from the radio unit, kicked over to the hatch, and grabbed the lever. This time there was no one to stop her going all the way.

She checked the pressure readout to confirm the airlock chamber was sealed and pressurized. It was. All three air-pressure indicators reported a positive, pressurized seal.

Cory floated beside the small hatch, realizing either that meant that the Sample Retrieval Sleeve had been success-fully transferred into the small airlock, or that the airlock had never been opened to admit it. There was only one way to find out what had actually happened.

Feeling breathless, Cory made herself check her watch again. She was coming to the end of her two-minute grace period. Bailey and Houston were going to start question-ing where she was.

What are they going to do, Cory thought, *fire me?* Before she even tried to open the inner door, she pumped the lever that mechanically secured the outer airlock hatch to be sure it was sealed. It was.

Cory unsealed the inner door and cranked its hand-wheel. There was another hissing sound as the pressure equalized between the small airlock and the rest of the module.

When the sound stopped, she pulled the hatch open and reached in for the SRS.

Her hand snapped back, fingers burning. The intensely cold metal of the retrieval sleeve had seared her skin.

Cory scanned the nearby equipment racks, searching in vain for anything she could use for protection. *Nothing.* And she was running out of time.

She took a deep breath, turned off her air cylinder, pulled off the PBA mask, then wriggled out of her blue-and-gray-striped shuttle polo shirt, the movement leaving her spinning slowly beside the open airlock, in her gray track pants and sports bra.

She grabbed a wall restraint to stop her motion, pulled on her mask, restarted the air supply, breathed deeply, and approached the airlock again, this time intending to use her folded polo shirt as a makeshift potholder to pull out the SRS.

All pain and tension lessened when she saw a sample cylinder in position within the metal sleeve.

Still using her shirt protectively, she popped the thermos-size cylinder free of the sleeve, then wedged the cylinder half under a foot restraint on one of the module's walls.

The steel cylinder was designed to be opened by robotic equipment in a mock-up of NASA's proposed Mars Sample Receiving Lab, but Cory knew the manual backup procedure. She reached into a pocket of her track pants to pull out her own NASA-issued Swiss Army knife. She pressed its screwdriver blade against the pressure-relief valve on the cylinder's cap, breaking the perfect vacuum seal created when the cylinder had been opened on the surface of the Moon.

Then she pulled back her PBA mask and gently spit out a blob of saliva that quivered before her, collecting it with her shirt to moisten a section of the fabric. She wrapped the wet section around the cylinder's cap, counting on the intense cold of the metal to freeze the moisture and hold the shirt fabric in place. It did.

With the makeshift grip in place, Cory applied torque to the cap. A few agonizingly long seconds later, the cap started to move.

It took sixteen turns to come free, before Cory, her hand cold and numbed, released the cap to let it spin away.

A gentle cloud of black powder mixed with a few sparkling crystals the size of sand began to float free of the cylinder.

A month ago, Cory thought with a feeling approaching awe, that powder had been on the surface of the Moon, quite probably exactly where it had been deposited billions of years ago.

But Moon dust didn't explain what had almost happened to her.

She gave the cylinder a nudge and a second cloud of dark dust spiraled out, this time accompanied by a handful of rough-textured black stones, no larger than gravel.

Dust and rocks, Cory thought in sudden, angry frustration. *There* had *to be something more.*

She used her shirt to drag the cylinder free of its restraint. Then, instead of shaking the cylinder forward as she would to empty it on Earth, she used the microgravity technique. She pulled the cylinder sharply back from its cloud of lunar dust and stones.

And saw something worth killing for.

Two severed human fingers, shriveled and mummified, each flashing the startling white of bleached bone against blackened, dried flesh.

Now Cory knew what Bette Norman had been so eager to protect and what Kai Teller was so anxious to bring back from the Moon.

Secrets.

WHITE LIGHTNING

T MINUS 7 DAYS

1

CHEYENNE MOUNTAIN AIR FORCE STATION
SPACE CONTROL CENTER
09:15 MST, FRIDAY, APRIL 4

A CONTENTED MOTHER SPIDER in her electromagnetic web, Major Wilhemina Bailey sat at her console with her morning herbal tea assessing the current state of the intricate communications network she'd brought into being the night before.

Right now, almost twenty-four hours since disaster had befallen the International Space Station, that web spun tenuous threads of radio emissions to Cheyenne Mountain, and from there to Mission Control-Houston, Mission Control-Moscow, and the *Soyuz* capsule in orbit with the stricken station high overhead.

Bailey had begun her creation by making good use of the hundred-billion-dollar constellations of America's electronic intelligence satellites and ground-based listening stations. She'd used those constellations to lock onto the pitifully weak ham signals produced by the amateur radio equipment on the space station's Japanese module. Once intercepted and digitally processed to eliminate static and fade, the signals had been sent on to relay satellites in orbits more than 20,000 miles higher than that of the ISS. The relay satellites, in turn, had flashed the signals from one to the other until they could be directed downward to the antennae of the Air Force Space Warfare Center at Shriever AFB, Colorado. There, the signals had been converted to pulses of light and sent twenty-two miles over a land-based fiber-optic network to Bailey's domain, deep beneath Cheyenne Mountain, where they had become electrical signals again and where her technicians and computers had acted quickly to route them through the Defense Satellite Communications Network to Houston and Moscow.

The major was aware that Mission Control–Moscow had their own full communications capability with their *Soyuz* capsule. But, just to avoid any potential misunderstandings, she had ensured that all transmissions to and from the Russian capsule were also captured by her satellites and listening stations and processed along with the ham signals. As yet, Bailey hadn't quite found the time to inform the Russians of her precautionary actions.

She did find time to give her technicians an assignment to complete while she caught a few hours of sleep in the temporary staff quarters two levels up from her processing section. She asked them to kludge together, overnight, a system for transmitting low-resolution black-and-white video images as well, to send to Dr. Rey in the Japanese module.

Specialists from Boeing and Honeywell at ISS Mission Control had begun by taking Rey through extensive circuit checklists to determine what had happened to the station's main communications capabilities. Their best guess at the moment, they reported to Bailey, was that a critical antenna power junction within the station's central Unity module had been damaged, effectively cutting off all send-and-receive functions in the S and Ku bands. Because the

Japanese amateur radio had its own isolated antenna on the outside of the JEM, it was unaffected by whatever had happened in Unity.

Once they'd determined this, the specialists had had Rey connect leads from her ham unit to the module's video-communications link, which Rey had been unable to make work before, to create an improvised setup that was functional. Over that new setup, NASA was now slowly uploading video frames showing her the techniques she had to use to single-handedly don the Russian space-suit in microgravity.

As Bailey slipped on her lightweight commset, with its single earphone and attached slender microphone, she watched as another still video picture appeared scan line by scan line on the leftmost display on her console. Because of the limited bandwidth of the amateur radio receiver, it was taking NASA almost an hour of real time to upload eight minutes of video. And the transmission had to be inter-rupted every time Rey needed to talk to the ground. Which was often.

Bailey saw the red light flash indicating Rey was signal-ing that one of those times was now. She carefully placed her favorite bone-china tea mug in the slide-out plastic holder at the side of her console—a most convenient design feature the Air Force had borrowed from Detroit—then pressed the control that paused the video upload. As soon as the confirmation message appeared on the upload display, she opened the voice channel.

"Spacecom, Alpha, acknowledging."

"Hey, Major, you're back."

Rey sounded more than tired now. Bailey checked NASA's estimate. The doctor had been awake for thirty-six hours.

Bailey knew the importance of being upbeat. "I had to

catch Oprah. It's not as if anything important's going on."

"I can tell you don't work for NASA. The day one of those guys makes a joke when their bosses are listening in is the day the world ends."

Bailey was about to reply when someone else cut into the loop.

"Cory, I heard that. So did the rest of Mission Control." It was Eric Vellacott in Houston, speaking for what Bailey understood to be a team of seven specialists. Vellacott was the veteran astronaut who would be guiding Rey through her spacewalk from the Japanese module to the *Soyuz.*

The rest of the specialist team included a flight surgeon, a skilled Russian/English translator, and the female astronaut who had been videotaped demonstrating the procedure for getting into the Russian *Orlan* suit, along with experts familiar with the suit, the Japanese module, and the damaged docking adapter Rey would have to pass through.

"Just seeing if you're awake down there."

Either Rey had requested a break in the video transmission in order to ask a specific question, or she just needed some human contact. Bailey decided to find out. "How are you doing up there, Doctor?"

"You tell me, Major. Or maybe, Eric. I'm on my second-last bottle of air, so I'm guessing I've got three to four more hours to go. That seem about right?"

Bailey stayed off the circuit, allowing the astronaut to take that question.

"At least four hours," Vellacott confirmed. *"But the good news is that the Russians have retrieved the* Orlan *and Anatoly Rushkin is unpacking it right now."*

"So, how long till I take delivery?"

"Definitely within the hour. Then we're estimating it will take

you about two hours to prep the suit before you put it on. How's that sound?"

"Sounds like I have a one-hour window of air in case anything goes slower than planned."

Rey's voice was tense. *Better tense than afraid,* Bailey thought.

Vellacott's calm voice was determinedly matter-of-fact. *"That's plenty of time, Cory. And Moscow's got a cosmonaut standing by to talk you through the suit preparations. He's got the manual memorized."*

"*Good to know,*" Rey said, but Bailey knew her statement was only words.

Vellacott had sensed the same thing. *"Uh, Cory, to keep the O_2 numbers up, Doctor Benton here would like to remind you that—"*

"*I know,*" Rey interrupted. *"The less I talk the longer the air lasts. I get that a lot."*

"*That's pretty much it,*" Vellacott confirmed.

"*So, I'll just float around up here holding my breath, and you'll let me know when the FedEx truck pulls up outside with the suit."*

"*Sounds like a plan."*

Bailey jumped into the momentary lull. "Doctor, just so you know, we still need about twenty-five minutes to get all of this video up to you. Was there a specific reason you wanted the voice channel?"

"*Major. I was hoping you were back. I do have another private request."*

Bailey sighed. She had already been read the riot act by Tovah Caruso for allowing the doctor to have a private, unrecorded conversation with her employer. And then, when Dr. Rey had not come back on the circuit for almost ten minutes after her talk with Kai Teller, the NASA administrator had come very close to having

Bailey pulled from her post. The saving mitigating factors had been her existing friendship with Dr. Rey, and the doctor's excuse that she'd been delayed by her inability to correctly use one of the self-adhesive toilet bags from the critical-equipment locker. No one on the ground wanted to follow up on that.

But Caruso had made it absolutely clear to Bailey that, in the interests of getting Cory Rey home alive, there were to be no more unmonitored communications.

"Doctor Rey," the major began, trusting she sounded apologetic enough, "NASA has requested that if you have any confidential medical issues you'd like to discuss, you do so with the flight surgeon at Mission Control. Do you have a medical issue?"

"No," Rey said, *"I have a legal issue. I need to know if I can make a verbal update to my will."*

Eric Vellacott was back on the channel. *"Cory, Eric here. Yes, NASA's done this before. You are able to make a verbal codicil to your existing will, provided it's recorded and attested to by a witness who knows you."*

"I knew NASA would have worked it all out," Rey said. *"Major Bailey, you're my designated witness. Would you please set up the private channel again?"*

Bailey shook her head admiringly. It was amazing how much trouble that girl could make for her friends. "Doctor, I'm going to have to have permission from Ms. Caruso."

"Well, get it, okay? Sometime before the suit gets here."

"Major Bailey," Vellacott said, *"I'll get word to the administrator ASAP. Should be back to you in a few minutes."*

"Shall I start the video transmission again, Doctor?"

"As long as you let me know when we can do the will."

"As soon as I hear from NASA," Bailey promised. "Spacecom out."

The major waited a moment to see if Dr. Rey had anything more to say—because she usually did. But when the circuit stayed closed, she tapped the key that restarted the upload. Once again, the current video frame began to grow on the display.

Bailey sighed deeply, put a hand in the small of her back, and arched against it until her spine cracked. Then she reached for her tea, and frowned. Tepid. She glanced around the upper level of the processing facility to see if she might commandeer an airman for a run to the cafeteria, but all her technicians were focused on their own terminals and displays, their work for the moment unrelated to hers. While all of NASA struggled to bring their astronaut home, the business of defending America was continuing undisturbed.

Bailey studied the ugly gray phone at the side of her terminal, the only one of four phones that was specifically for outside calls. *It's not as if I don't know that all of these kids would be afraid to bring me tea, anyway,* she thought. None of the younger airmen on her staff were anything like First Lieutenant Dominic Hubert, the last member of her staff who had done an exemplary job of making sure her cup was always filled. Good thing, because she'd married him.

She thought about giving Dom a call at home, see how the twins were doing. As soon as marriage to his commanding officer had appeared on his horizon, he'd left the service to start his own aerospace consulting business in civilian life. The decision had paid off when Bailey had wanted to return to duty following the birth of their babies. The major smiled as she pictured Dom cradling their squirming double-armful, and then she blinked, startled out of her reverie. The gray phone was buzzing with an incoming call.

Bailey grinned. As always, her husband was zeroing in on her thoughts of him. Dom was good at that, among other things. She reflexively checked her board to be sure there were no alert lights flashing, then picked up the receiver and said, "I was just thinking about you."

The laugh she heard was certainly masculine. But it wasn't Dom's.

"Keeping secrets from your husband, Major?"

Bailey was doubly shocked by another voice from the past.

Captain Webber.

VANDENBERG AIR FORCE BASE

Webber stood at a bank of pay phones outside the officers' mess at Vandenberg, with his back to the dry wind that blew grit in from the scrub surrounding the base's low buildings. He had spent most of Friday night in the officers' club, watching the nonstop coverage of what the networks were calling *Disaster in Space!* Colonel Varik had departed early, but had assigned a young lieutenant to work with Base Services and arrange overnight accommodations in the transient officers' quarters.

Webber had passed another three hours staring at the ceiling in his small room, pretending he was trying to sleep, before he'd given up and headed back to the contractor cafeteria. From a military perspective, at least, the more than sixty aerospace companies that maintained facilities at Vandenberg, and their civilian employees, were well provided for.

It was in the no-frills cafeteria, drinking bad coffee and watching the television monitor that was bolted to the ceiling, that Webber had just caught the most recent NASA press conference. When it was over, he knew whom he had to call.

"Captain Webber," Bailey said warmly, *"I don't know how you got through the switchboard, but I know exactly why you're calling."*

Webber held one hand against his open ear so he could hear the major clearly. Because this was a public call from one military installation to another, he knew the voice line was being monitored at both ends, by Vandenberg and Cheyenne Mountain, and probably at several points along the way. Despite digital transmission, all those intercepts still tended to reduce the volume.

"You've spoken to her." He didn't even have to say Cory's name.

"And how would you know that?"

"I just watched the latest NASA press conference, with the plan to get a spacesuit to her. Someone asked how NASA had been able to tell Cory about the plan over that iffy ham radio hookup, and the NASA PIO said something about the Air Force having provided 'a more robust communications environment.' That means you, Major. Right?"

"'Robust'?" the major chuckled. *"And I'm the first one you think of? It took me and about a hundred other people to put it all together. But you're right. I have spoken with her, and she's doing fine."*

Webber closed his eyes. Why was everyone so insistent on glossing over what had happened, even Bailey? "C'mon, Major. I know Cory can handle herself. But *I* wouldn't be 'fine' in her position."

Bailey was silent for a moment, as if reconsidering what she had first said. *"All right, Captain, the doctor is the same clever, rebellious manipulator she's always been. She's already got me in trouble with the chief administrator. And she's basically got everyone else jumping through hoops in Houston and, best as I can tell, even in Moscow."*

Webber felt a wave of relief. When things were really going bad, Cory went quiet and withdrew. He had only seen the reaction a few times in her, but he knew it was part of Cory's response pattern to high stress. From the major's description, Cory was still fighting, and that's what she had to do to survive. Providing the NASA plan was credible.

"Can she do what they want her to do?"

"Blindfolded, Captain. She's not giving up."

"I know she's not giving up. But I've done some . . . let's just say I've a good idea what they're asking her to do. Is she injured? Space sick? Has she got enough food, water, air supply?"

"She's in good shape. No injuries. Tired but not exhausted."

Webber needed to hear more than general platitudes.

"What aren't you telling me?"

"Well . . . she wants to update her will."

"What?"

"It's covered. NASA says she can make a voice recording as a codicil, provided it's witnessed by someone who knows her. She's asked for me."

"Hold it. Cory said she wanted to update her will?"

"That's what she told me."

"Cory doesn't have a will to update, Major." *That was another thing we used to fight about,* Webber thought. *Hell, we used to fight about everything.* "She hated the whole idea. She was always coming up with excuses not to get one." Not that Cory had ever kept any possessions worth leaving to anyone except Goodwill. They'd fought about that, too.

"If NASA's anything like the Air Force, they hand you a standard will package with your first uniform."

"Except Cory isn't a NASA employee. She works for the company that sent her up there."

"Captain, when was the last time you talked to her?"

Webber couldn't bring himself to say it had been a year, especially if the phone-intercept was live, considering what he'd had to say to convince the station operator to even put his call through to Bailey. "It's been a while. She's been busy. I've been busy."

"*Well, people have a way of changing over 'a while.' Especially if they're going into a high-risk situation.*"

Not Cory, Webber thought, *not that much.* Even if she'd had to make some adjustments to make it through her NASA training. "Maybe," he said. It wasn't important. "Any idea when they're planning to start the transfer?"

"*The last I heard, they were hoping to get the suit to her within the hour. Then she'll have two hours to do whatever it is she has to do to get it ready. And then they start.*"

Webber did the math, didn't like it. "The NASA PIO was fudging the oxygen numbers."

"*She's got an hour safety margin.*"

Webber liked that number even less.

"*Trust me, Captain, I've heard Houston and Moscow go over the whole plan. They're confident. Cory's confident. I think the will update is just her way of covering all the bases. She's going to do this. They're going to bring her home.*" Then Webber heard an electronic chirp over the line. "*I've got traffic, Captain. Have to go.*"

"Thanks, Major. Next time you're talking to Cory, tell her—" But he heard dead air. Bailey had already signed off.

Webber hung up the metal handset and waited for the pay phone's small white screen to tell him how much the call had cost and ask him if he'd like to make another. When it did, he touched No, and the phone spit out his ATM card.

Webber stepped away from the row of phones, squinting into the wind, looking out at the two launch complexes he could see, trying to decide his next course of action. He could go back into the contractor cafeteria, or check to see if the officers' mess had opened yet. Even though he was technically on leave from Hill AFB for three more days, he could even make arrangements to fly out of Vandenberg on the next available flight.

Webber shoved his hands into the pockets of the borrowed green windbreaker he wore over his flight suit, and started to walk along the cracked concrete path leading to the officers' mess.

He had a few days off. He'd call in a few favors. Book a flight out tonight.

Since he couldn't be in space with Cory to help her through the ordeal ahead, Houston was the next best thing.

2

IN THE DARK, HOT, AIRLESS motel room, the audibility of the authoritative voice on the tape was poor quality, but its identity was known to Ed Farren.

Air Force General Dwight Salyard.

"First, get Security to pull all available DoD files on Farren, then look for any connection he might have had with the Project. If he's calling it Blue Moon, then that goes back to . . . when?"

Sweat trickled down the septuagenarian's scalp. He wished the man with the gun would turn on the air conditioning, or the overhead fan, or just get this the hell over with.

There was a pause in the static-marred recording as Salyard listened to the officer he'd called, then the general's voice spoke again.

"He might have been with McDonnell Douglas then. That's a good place to start for personnel records. Then do the same check for whoever his partner is, as soon as I get you that name."

Another pause. Shorter this time.

"I can't believe a word I hear on CNN, so I need confirmation that the payload specialist is the only one left up there."

Another pause. Farren shifted uncomfortably in the cheap plastic chair he was bound to. The duct tape cut into his arms and ankles. His hands and feet were beginning to feel numb.

"Can I have some water?" Farren asked. He squinted to see his captor, who sat in the chair opposite him. But the heavy curtains were drawn and the motel room's only light came from a single, dim bedside lamp across the room. The man's face was shadowed by the dark baseball cap he wore.

"Don't interrupt."

The man with the gun reached out for Farren's right hand and began to bend it back up to the point of breaking.

Farren gasped with shock, startled at the sudden violence. His apprehension increased rapidly as he realized there had been nothing particularly threatening or angry in the man's tone. The words of warning had been uttered as if they were nothing more than a neutral reminder of the rules of whatever terrible game he and his captive were engaged in.

Through his haze of agonizing pain, Farren found it even harder to hear the recording's one-sided conversation as its pitch rose and fell erratically.

"What was the last communication from our person on-site?"

The man released Farren's hand and turned up the volume on the small Philips digital recorder that sat next to Farren's cell phone on the scarred coffee table between them.

Farren's eyes fixed on his cell phone. His bruised wrist throbbed with pain. *Emily was right,* he thought remorsefully. *I should have called her.* But his wife always became so worried about his investigations and the people they upset.

This time, he'd just told her what he usually did: He had a meeting and he'd be away overnight. Emily had stopped insisting on more details a long time ago. He knew their life since retirement was not what she had hoped for.

"Keep me apprised of the status of the Russians' rescue mission. If they show any sign of getting up there before that survivor's oxygen runs out, we might have to use some influence to slow them down. You understand, Major?"

A pause, then Salyard's voice continued. *"Anything else, Major?"*

"That . . . that's almost the end of it," Farren volunteered shakily.

The motel room filled with the hiss of silence on the recording.

"Then why are you still on the line?" General Salyard said.

There was a click, some scraping sounds as a drawer was closed, then nothing further.

Farren's captor switched off the recorder. "Who did you record that for, Doctor?" He pulled back the slide of his .45 to put a cartridge into the chamber, ready to fire. The gun was dark metal, brutal-looking.

"For me," Farren said, rallying. It was time to expose this nasty exercise for the bluff that it was. His captor's movements with his thuggish weapon were so expert and precise that it was certain he was a soldier. But then, Farren had known that the instant the man had pushed his way into his motel room this morning. Soldiers knew how to kill, but they didn't kill retired NASA consultants. This unpleasantness couldn't last much longer.

"Wrong answer," the man said calmly. "We know a man of your education and background wouldn't think he could do this on his own."

"I had to do something," Farren said, indignant. A rush of revitalizing anger swept through him. "I know you bastards can save that woman. The Air Force has been bleeding NASA dry for decades. Taking all our funding. Taking over all our best projects." Those weren't the only reasons he had gone to see General Salyard yesterday, but they were the reasons he believed in most.

"We know your record," the man said. "You're a conspiracy fanatic." He reached into the pocket of his dark blue nylon windbreaker and withdrew a long, black, square-sided object. "Who did you make that recording for?"

I will not be bullied into betraying anyone, Farren thought in sudden fury. *I'll go to more than the media if this man tries to hurt me again.* "I was going to play it in my press conference."

The man began to screw the black object into the barrel of his .45, and Farren realized with horror it was a silencer.

"There was never going to be a press conference," his captor said. "Or you'd have held it right after you made the recording, before we found your hearing-aid bug in the general's office. It was state of the art. Too expensive for a retired NASA engineer."

"I—I—wanted to tell the world." Farren's heartbeat pounded in his ears.

"You had your chance. You didn't act on it."

"The general scared me," Farren said desperately. *If only I'd called Emily . . . told her where I was . . . who I saw . . .*

"That's the first smart thing I've heard you say."

Farren's captor picked up Farren's cell phone from the coffee table. "You people pay cash for these things because you think they're untraceable. You load them with an hour or two of phone calls. Do your business and toss them away, so there's nothing for the police to track."

The man hefted the small device in his hand as if he

were contemplating throwing it. "But we're not the police. Whatever calls you made or took on this phone, all the numbers and the callers' GPS coordinates, they're on a hard drive in Fort Meade, and we are already looking for them."

Farren closed his eyes, felt faint. He tested the strength of the duct tape binding him, knew he'd never break its bonds unaided, no matter how fit he was.

"It might take us a few hours more, but we will find out who sent you to the general's office. Unless . . ."

Farren opened his eyes.

"Unless you give me the name before we find it ourselves. Then I can take you into custody as a 'cooperative witness.' "

Farren cleared his rough, dry throat. "Wh . . . where will you take me . . . as a 'cooperative witness'? "

The man with the gun regarded him steadily. "Back to Vandenberg. You'll be held in custody by Base Protective Services."

"My wife . . ."

"Emily can visit. If you cooperate."

The man slid a hand inside his jacket, pulled out his own cell phone, and put it on the coffee table. The phone was vibrating. It skittered a few inches across the tabletop, stopped for a moment, then moved again.

Farren's captor retrieved the phone, held it up, ready to flip open. "If they give me the name before you do, the deal is off."

"Teller," Farren said, appalled and embarrassed to hear the tremor in his own voice. "Kai Teller." The situation had gone beyond anything he'd ever expected. But there would still be ways he could protest this outrage, once he got out of this room and to the base and talked to Teller's lawyers.

"Teller. TTI Astronautics?"

Farren nodded wearily.

"Teller told you what to say to the general. And then you called him, and you played him the recording."

"Yes, yes!" Farren said with difficulty. "May I have some water now? Please?"

His captor stood up and walked out of the room. Farren heard the sound of running water. When the man came back, he had a glass of water in his hand. He held it to Farren's lips.

Farren drank the cool liquid greedily, almost choked.

The man took the glass away. "Did he tell you about Blue Moon?"

Farren nodded, his eyes on the glass.

The man gave him another sip, then took the glass away again.

"Did you know about Blue Moon before he told you?"

It was easier for Farren to speak now. "No, no, I didn't. I mean, I suspected. We all suspected that . . . I mean, America went to the Moon, and then . . . we *never* went back? That just . . . just never made sense. Can you take the tape off me now?"

"In a moment," his captor said. He flipped open his phone, and Farren suddenly realized the man's phone had stopped buzzing as soon as it was picked up, as if there had been no incoming call, as if he had set it to vibrate himself. It had been a trick to deceive his captive into talking.

Farren sagged back in his chair, barely aware of what the man was doing now. He was an old fool trapped by his own blind arrogance. Emily was right. He would be more cautious in the future.

He watched his captor press two keys on the cell-phone pad, listen for a moment, then say, "It's Varik," pausing as he cocked his head to hold the phone between his shoulder and ear.

He saw the man—Varik—begin to unscrew the silencer

from his gun. The game was over because the battle had been won without a shot.

Then Varik paused as whoever he had called came on the line. "Teller," Varik said. "Farren played him the recording."

Varik listened for a few moments, placing his gun back in one pocket, the silencer in the other. "I understand. I'll be back on base within the hour." Then he closed his cell phone and reached into his jeans pocket. Farren heard the jingle of loose change.

"An hour?" Farren asked. "Vandenberg is only what . . . ten miles away?"

"Nine." Varik checked the silver coin he had taken from his pocket. He stepped around the coffee table, behind Farren's chair.

Farren sighed with relief. As soon as the tape was off, he'd ask to call Emily, tell her how— He frowned as he heard a soft metallic click, felt Varik's hand push his left ear forward, fold it flat. He tried to twist around to see what the man was doing. "What are you—"

Farren felt a pinprick in the crease of his ear.

He died three seconds later.

VANDENBERG AIR FORCE BASE

One hour later, Colonel Daniel Varik was at the three-mile mark of the base jogging course, waiting for the general.

Salyard came to a full stop, breathing deeply in through his nose, exhaling deeply from his mouth, each breath carefully timed and controlled. He felt better for the run. It had helped him to sort through all the variables he faced, to discard the ones that were merely distractions, to focus on the ones that were critical.

Neither officer was in uniform. Varik was still in the jeans, sweatshirt and windbreaker, and blue ball cap he had worn to go to Farren's motel room. Salyard was in running gear.

"The recording?" Salyard asked.

Varik handed him the digital datastick from the Philips recorder. Salyard pushed it down into a pocket of his blue running shorts. "Copies?"

"Not on Farren's end. He had one recorder and a pre-paid cell phone in his room. The receiver for the transmitter he left in your office was in his Mercedes, built into the CD changer in the trunk."

Salyard used a corner of his gray Air Force T-shirt to wipe his face free of the dust and grit the wind had kicked up. "He definitely planned this."

"Teller?" Varik asked.

"A microtransmitter disguised as a hearing aid. A receiver in a CD changer. That isn't the kind of equipment someone throws together overnight."

"So that implies Teller knew the ISS was going to be sabotaged?"

Salyard shook his head. "How could he? That wasn't supposed to happen. Norman was instructed to knock out communications and power for two hours at most. Just long enough to have the two crews evacuate to the shuttle and the *Soyuz,* and give her a chance to check the retrieved sample cylinders. However the major thought she was going to accomplish that, she did it wrong."

"You sure it was her fault?"

The general nodded. That Major Norman had failed was unfortunate, but the conclusion was the only one that fit. As her commanding officer, he had to take full responsibility for what she had done.

He motioned to Varik to join him as he began walking along the dirt path to the gray concrete drinking fountain over the next small rise. He filled the colonel in on the crucial details. They had all the telemetry from the shuttle up to the point its communications failed, and it showed a circuit breaker failing in the avionics bay—as scheduled. Then a secondary power surge had taken out communications the instant the fire alarm sounded.

"That was supposed to draw the shuttle crew from the station," Salyard said. "Houston says the station's communications were knocked out by damage to a single junction in the central Unity node, which is exactly the weak point we identified for Major Norman."

They had reached the drinking fountain.

Salyard pressed the chrome button to let the water run. "But somehow . . . when the major set her plans in motion, everything went out of control."

"If Teller didn't know about the sabotage, then how'd he get Farren in here so quickly?" Varik asked.

Salyard leaned forward to methodically drink the cold water in measured mouthfuls. "Think it through, Daniel. What scenario makes that possible?"

As the general knew he would, Varik found the only possible answer. "He was already planning to send Farren in. For another reason."

Salyard wiped his mouth with the back of his hand. "Exactly. And the ISS situation fell into his lap."

"So what's the other reason for Teller to blackmail the Project?"

"That's what I can't see," Salyard admitted. It was the question that had brought him to the jogging track to think. "First thing I thought was that Teller's a businessman, so he's motivated by opportunities, profit. And he's been hit hard twice this year. TTI lost the Project's nuclear propulsion contract to Lockheed. And, he's got to know by now he's not getting a piece of the kinetic warhead guidance package. So that's at least four hundred million dollars in lost revenue over the next five years.

"But, balanced against that, Teller's still got the full MOL relay upgrade contract, and that'll run ten years at least. So—upset as he might be about what he's lost—by trying to force us to assign him new contracts, he's vulnerable. Because, if he does follow through with his threat to go white with the Project, first thing that'll happen is Congress'll shut everything down to hold years of hearings, and he loses all the contracts he does have."

Varik said nothing as two more joggers ran past them on the path by the fountain. He waited until they were out of hearing range. "You think he's driven by something other than money?"

"I've been through those motives, too," the general said. He began walking back to their rendezvous point on the jogging track. "Is he driven by a misguided desire to pull the veil off the Project? No—he could have done that years ago. Is he working for a foreign power? Maybe the Chinese? No—same argument. By sending in Farren, we know Teller was trying to use the threat of exposing the Project to get something from us. But other than money, I don't know what we have to give him."

Varik strode along, head down, with his hands jammed in his windbreaker pockets. "Farren said he wanted Doctor Rey rescued."

"Doesn't track," Salyard said. "When Teller began planning to send Farren in to plant a bug in my office, Rey wasn't in trouble, and he couldn't possibly know she would be."

"Maybe it is as simple as that," Varik suggested. "All Teller intended Farren to do was to bug your office. The blackmail came later, when he wanted to save his employee."

Salyard had already considered that scenario, too.

"Protective Services say the bug's battery had a maximum operational lifetime of seventy-two hours, and the daily sweep found it within two hours, anyway. And its range was limited to the civilian parking lot. The only purpose that bug could serve was to transmit my immediate reactions to whatever Farren was originally going to say to provoke me."

They were nearing the three-mile mark on the base's jogging track. Salyard began to walk more slowly.

Varik essayed another tactic. "Take the ISS out of the equation. Is there any individual element of the Project that Teller could have exposed? Without exposing all of it, and losing the rest of his contracts."

"It's quantum, Daniel. All or nothing. No middle ground."

The general stopped at the bend in the path as a sergeant led a squad of airmen past them, chanting a running Jodie. The runners repeated each line that the sergeant sang out to them.

"Me and Superman got in a fight,

"I hit him in the head with some Kryptonite

"I hit him so hard I busted his brain

"And now I'm dating Lois Lane."

Salyard looked thoughtful as he watched the squad run by. "What's Kryptonite to Teller?" he asked Varik. "Or, better yet, turn it around. What's Kryptonite to the Project?"

The general's question was rhetorical. He smiled as he put the final piece into position himself. "Teller's lunar sample return mission."

"But how could Teller know that?" Varik asked.

"That's not critical, Daniel. The timing works. Teller had Farren all ready to come in and bug my office, force my hand. And then, because of Norman's ineptitude, the retrieval of Teller's lunar samples on the station occurred at the exact same time as the explosions."

"You're suggesting that Teller sent his rover to the Moon knowing what he was going to find?"

"The Chinese know," Salyard said.

"So Teller *is* working with the Chinese? After all the security checks he has to go through to be one of the Project's contractors?" Varik sounded skeptical.

"No, of course not. But what *is* possible is that Teller had access to the same sources we know the Chinese had access to. They both learned the truth independently. And they're both a threat to the Project."

Varik still looked uncomfortable. "So what's our next move?"

For Salyard, the puzzle was gratifyingly complete. "We're already set to make it. In just eight days we launch, and then ... problem solved."

"And if the Chinese launch in the same window?"

Salyard clapped a hand on Varik's shoulder. "We beat them, Daniel. That much we do know, and that's thanks to you, and Webber. The satellites show the Chinese have nothing on the pad at Jiuquan, and this close to the next launch window, they can't possibly prepare a booster in time. So they're probably planning on next month, which will be a month too late."

"Makes sense."

"I'm extremely confident," Salyard said.

"What do we do about Farren's recording? Teller will have a copy of it."

"Why is it necessary we do anything? It's a bad recording of what may or may not be my voice, carrying on half a conversation. If it is me, then the recording is clearly illegal, and Teller can't risk playing it for anyone. And if it isn't me, then it's of no use at all."

"So we just let Teller twist?"

"And we watch our backs."

"And the lunar samples?"

"I've read the full transcript of what Doctor Rey reported. She confirmed there are no samples. The explosions began before she was able to begin the transfer."

"Then we're safe."

"As long as no one ever finds out what really happened on the station."

"Is that achievable?"

Salyard nodded. "First, we ensure the Russians don't launch their emergency *Soyuz* mission until the station has started tumbling and they can't dock with it. That will rule out any possible salvage attempt. And second, we ensure that Teller's payload specialist doesn't make it back."

"NASA has a plan to get Doctor Rey a spacesuit so she can get on the *Soyuz* that's up there."

"NASA has a plan. So what? We have a better one. Rey won't survive the transfer."

"What about the two Russians up there with her?"

"Nonstarters. The PKA will have them do and say exactly what we tell them."

Varik was silent.

Salyard noticed. "Something you'd like to say, Daniel?"

Varik shrugged. "Something we might not have figured into the game plan."

The general waved a hand, inviting Varik to continue.

"Teller's payload specialist, she's Webber's—"

"Webber's 'friend,' " Salyard interrupted. "Yes, I recall his interest in her. And I have accounted for that."

Now it was Varik's turn to wait for an explanation.

"I've reviewed the captain's record," Salyard said. "I think there's a place for someone of his talents in the Project."

Varik remained noncommittal.

"You don't agree?" Salyard asked.

Varik broke silence. "General, I don't think he's got enough fire in his belly. And if he does end up working for the Project, what happens if he finds out what we did to Rey? Someone like Webber could bring us down."

"Keep your friends close and your enemies closer," the general said. "I want Webber in the Project specifically so he *can* be controlled."

"I don't think he can be, General."

"It's just another quantum scenario, Daniel. All or nothing. Either Webber is controlled, or he's terminated, just like his 'friend.' "

Salyard felt great satisfaction as he dismissed his last two variables.

There would be no more interference with his plans.

The Project was safe. And so were the history books.

3

INTERNATIONAL SPACE STATION
17:11 GMT, FRIDAY, APRIL 4

IF ANATOLY RUSHKIN CLOSED his eyes, he could believe he was back in Star City, at his favorite *banya*. It was in a small and ancient building, older than the Revolution, near the Prophy restaurant and the Star City lake, and it was a favorite of cosmonauts, not the least for the fact that the proprietors brewed their own beer.

The building itself actually held two *banya*s, what the Americans called saunas, rich with the fragrance of smoky wood, each with its own frigid plunge pool. In winter, though, it was much better to make a dash through the snow and leap through an ice-fishing hole into the lake.

Anatoly tried to recapture that delicious shock when the freezing water swept over his overheated skin. The intensity of sensation. The sheer exhilaration of bobbing up from the frozen depths to gulp in pure winter air. The explosion of oils from dried birch branches thrashed against his body.

"Are you still in there?" Commander Lazhenko asked.

The harsh, static-filled crackle in his helmet speakers made Rushkin open his eyes, then frown as he saw that even more beads of sweat had collected on the inside of his visor.

"I believe I am half-melted," Rushkin said. His *Sokol* spacesuit, designed to be worn only in the *Soyuz* capsule, was not intended for strenuous activity. The thirty minutes he had spent in the Unity airlock, laboriously unpacking the *Orlan* EVA suit for Dr. Rey, had taxed his suit's emergency cooling system. Rushkin felt as if he floated in a bubble of sweat, and he had long ago exhausted the half-liter of water that was available to him through a straw in his helmet.

"Then the other half of you is still capable of retrieving the suit," Lazhenko said.

The commander was in the *Soyuz,* for now, fifty feet down from the Unity airlock, beneath the station. When they had arrived, Lazhenko had maneuvered the capsule within three feet of the airlock. That was so Rushkin could tie his safety line to the station without completely leaving the upper module of the *Soyuz*. But then, given the slow undulations that still moved through the station as the twisted port solar arrays conducted their tug of war with the RCS thrusters, Lazhenko had had to quickly back away.

The airlock chamber had been simple to enter because it was already depressurized. Beyond it, the Unity node itself was in hard vacuum.

First, Rushkin had floated through the airlock to shine his flashlight inside the node and see if there were any signs that someone else might have survived in a pressurized module. To aft, his flashlight beam, invisible in vacuum, had found the sealed *Zarya* hatch he and Lazhenko had successfully closed from the other side.

Forward, the hatch to the American lab module was open, and the void beyond was without light. In that well of darkness, Rushkin's flashlight had picked out small bits and pieces of slowly tumbling debris, and the module's far hatch, sealed. The scene itself had told Rushkin its sad story.

Since there were no bodies in the module, the only way its far hatch could have been closed was by someone on the other side. After the shuttle had collided with the docking adapter. Someone who had made the choice to try to save the station, even when there was no chance to save himself, or herself.

Rushkin had tried very hard then not to picture what had to be on the other side of that hatch: the swollen body of Commander Dante, or Dr. Lugreb, or Flight Engineer McArdle. The moment he'd reported his findings to Lazhenko, he'd pushed himself back into the airlock and, scientist though he was, he had closed the hatch between the airlock and Unity so that no dead bodies could float from the darkness to reach out and take him.

Fortunately, the *Orlan* suit had been exactly where it was supposed to be in the airlock storage locker. That was a rare occurrence for the station.

At the changeover between Expeditions 21 and 22, the station's supply database had listed more than 24,000 individual items stowed on board, from rolls of duct tape and individually sealed hygienic towels, to surgical instruments, oxygen generators, and hundreds of spare-part kits for hundreds of devices and subsystems. The most common characteristic shared by those 24,000 items was that very few of them were actually in the location the database specified. Indeed, Rushkin knew that it was one of NASA's dirty little secrets that the main reason most scientific activities on the station fell behind schedule was because of all the time lost searching for critical supplies that were not where they were supposed to be.

Given that deplorable situation, he had felt enormous

relief when he located the lumpy, beige-plastic duffel bag holding the *Orlan,* Velcroed in its proper place in the locker.

But then the real work had begun. The suit had been packed in Baikonur in anticipation that two cosmonauts would be unpacking it in the shirtsleeve environment of the station. Its tabs, tape, and sealed plastic bags were not intended for spacesuited fingers, and it had taken Rushkin more than twenty minutes simply to get the suit out of its duffel bag and remove the plastic torso inside it, in the process creating a perpetual storm of packing foam and plastic spacers that bounced and spun around him.

Once he had the one-piece suit empty and floating like a flattened corpse, Rushkin had then had to pick awkwardly through the duffel bag and its cloud of packing material. There was no other way to be sure he had all of the items on the contents list: gloves, batteries, chemical cartridges for the oxygen system, all interior tubes and wires, and the separately packaged radio components. Then had come the equally exhausting process of gathering up all the smaller items, stuffing them back into the duffel, and resealing it.

As a precaution, Rushkin next tied one end of a safety rope around the spacesuit's leg, looped another section around the duffel, then clipped the other end to his equipment belt. By then, his hands in their minimally insulated gloves—for dexterity—were both aching and freezing, while the rest of him still sweltered. Just trying to look through his helmet visor was like looking out a car's windshield that had no wipers in a thunderstorm.

"Commander Lazhenko," Rushkin finally announced, "I am ready to return to the capsule."

"Anchor yourself at the airlock. I will move in as before."

Rushkin moved slowly to face the open airlock door. With one hand grasping the suit, he used his other to tug himself forward. Ahead, through his smeared visor, he could just make out the welcoming blue glow of reflected earthlight filling the airlock interior. Rushkin's throat tightened. He longed for the day, for the hour, that he would be able to see that blue above him in the sky where it belonged, and not hundreds of miles below.

In a disconcerting instant, the blue light suddenly flared red, then vanished as the station once again moved into the utter black of earth's shadow.

If this were any other EVA transfer, Rushkin knew the onset of a forty-five-minute night would mean it was time to rest. Moving from one spacecraft to another in darkness was something Grandmother NASA did not permit, although construction work was always allowed, of course, provided the floodlights were working.

"Tell me we are not following NASA flight rules," Rushkin said apprehensively. He was in no position to rest at the moment.

The docking light from the *Soyuz* flashed across his visor as Lazhenko closed in. *"It is better to beg forgiveness than ask permission,"* Lazhenko answered. *"Prepare for transfer."*

Rushkin grinned, wearily grateful for miracles. For a Cossack, there was hope for Lazhenko, after all.

Cory Rey floated by the window of the JEM, as if her presence there could draw the *Soyuz* to her faster. From time to time, she looked down to the Earth, and now she saw it was night. She'd given up trying to find recognizable patterns in the loops and whorls of lights below, humanity's fingerprints on the world. From an altitude of just over two hundred miles, one place on Earth seemed pretty much like any other to her, no matter where and when she looked. Her years of seeing the entire planet in space photographs, in which the major landforms were clearly apparent, had led her to expect otherwise. It had been fascinating to discover that her world from space could be so small, and so big, all at the same time.

Now, though, floating in a dying space station, as she breathed her last three hours of oxygen, her thoughts were not so grand or philosophical.

Teller must have known what his LRV was bringing home.

And so had Bette Norman.

Both her employer and the station science officer had been willing to risk not only her life but those of everyone else on the station and the shuttle, because there was no possible way the explosions that destroyed the shuttle and devastated the station had been accidental. Not given their timing—right when she'd first started to use the robotic arm, to begin the retrieval of the LRV sample cylinders. Later, when she had opened the only recovered cylinder herself and seen its grisly contents, the connection between their presence and the disaster had seemed even stronger, more obvious.

But what still was not obvious to Cory, was what to do after she'd placed the remnants of dried flesh and bone in a plastic toilet bag, wrapped them tightly to force out as much air as possible, sealed them with duct tape, then shoved the unnerving package into her sports bra. All that made sense was to keep her discovery to herself until she knew whom she could really trust.

Whatever Teller's motives were for bringing human remains back from the Moon, Cory knew they would be nothing she could support. Not done in secret. And since Bette Norman had been willing to kill to take control of the remains, that ruled out saying anything to Tovah Caruso.

Cory's reasoning led her, reluctantly, to her last option: Major Bailey. The risk was that her story might still disappear into the endless labyrinth of Bailey's chain of command, consumed by the military's autonomic need for secrecy whenever it was faced with something that fell outside of its normal operations. But she saw no other choice. Not given her current communications options and the inordinately high odds that despite all the encouraging talk from the ground, she would not survive the Russians' rescue attempt. The secret of what she had found could not die with her. Not after all the lives it had already cost.

Ironically, Cory thought, the solution to her problem had come, indirectly, from Mitchell Webber. Far away or not, he still couldn't stop telling her what to do. All these thoughts on dying and imminent death had made her recall the pointless arguments the two of them had had about wills.

She heard a thin chime in the low-pressure air of the JEM and looked away from the window to the radio console where a red light was flashing. The video upload was finished. The voice channel was open again.

She kicked over to the controls to plug in her radio link. If she only had three hours left, she was going to make them count.

But to do that she had to convince Major Bailey to let her talk to Mitchell Webber.

CHEYENNE MOUNTAIN AIR FORCE STATION
SPACE CONTROL CENTER

Bailey heard the click that preceded a transmission from the ISS, was relieved she didn't have to wait for Dr. Rey this time.

"Hey, Major—you there?"

Bailey grimaced. The doctor's inability to follow radio protocol was almost certainly deliberate. "Copy that, Alpha," she replied.

"Are we set to go on the will update?"

"Chief Administrator Caruso has given her okay, provided we finish by the time the Russians return with the suit. Is that acceptable?"

"Absolutely. When do we get started?"

Bailey had the radio configuration set up and ready to run at the push of a key on her console. "Right away, Doctor. I'll just confirm with Houston and check the Russians' status." She flipped a small toggle switch. "Houston, do you copy?"

Eric Vellacott was still on duty as Rey's pointman. *"We copy, Spacecom. Rushkin is making the transfer to the Soyuz now. We estimate they'll be back at the JEM within half an hour."*

"Did you get that, Doctor?" Bailey asked.

"Got it. We're already half an hour behind the last schedule NASA gave me. That leaves me with a half-hour window of oxygen."

Vellacott was quick to give assurance. *"No more surprises, Cory. Rushkin is back in the Soyuz and they are moving away from the station to loop back to your module. Can you confirm the JEM airlock is sealed?"*

"You want the same confirmation I gave you an hour ago?"

Bailey decided it was a good time to break in. "Shall we get started, Doctor?"

"I might as well get something done today."

"Houston, this is Spacecom going to secure transmission." Bailey touched the computer key that reset all the communications parameters for her contact with the station. "All right, Doctor, we're good to go."

"Thanks, Major. I've got another surprise for you."

Bailey offered up a small silent prayer for patience. "Doctor Rey, I am under strict orders not to allow you to discuss anything that's not connected to updating your will."

"Who gave you those orders?"

"Chief Administrator Caruso."

"She's a civilian, right? You can ignore whatever she said. Help me out here, Major."

Bailey couldn't help but think she was granting a dying woman's last request. "Go ahead."

"The message I want to pass on, in case I don't get out of this, I want to get it to Mitchell Webber."

"Seriously?" Bailey winced even as the word left her lips. "No, I'm sorry, that's not what I meant to say. I was talking to Captain Webber about an hour ago."

"You're joking!"

Before Bailey could respond, Rey continued. *"Sorry, that's not what I meant to say, either. Is he with you down there?"*

Bailey quickly reviewed what she could remember of her conversation with Captain Webber. "No . . . he didn't say where he was calling from."

"C'mon, Major—you're Space Command. You're not going to let that stop you, are you?"

Bailey wasn't. "Don't go anywhere." She picked up the green phone for internal calls, said, "Outgoing operator."

The voice recognition system transferred her to a human. *"Communications. Sergeant Kohan."*

"Major Bailey. About an hour ago, I received an external call on this line from U.S. Navy Captain Mitchell Webber. I have to talk with the captain again, so I need his contact number."

Bailey heard rapid typing. *"Calling it up now, Major. On your outside line . . . here we go, a call at 10:22. Webber, Mitchell. Identified himself as fiancé to Corazon Rey . . . oh, the woman on the space station."*

Now Bailey knew how Captain Webber had talked his way past the switchboard. "That's the one. Can you reconnect me?"

More typing. *"Sorry, Major. He made the call from a pay phone at . . . here it is . . . Vandenberg AFB."*

Bailey was pleasantly surprised. This wouldn't be difficult at all. She told the sergeant to contact Vandenberg's personnel office, have them locate Captain Webber, and get him to a secure phone at once.

Then she reconnected with Rey. "I've got the captain's location and they're going to get him to a phone ASAP," Bailey said.

"Any idea how long he'll be?"

"Sorry, none."

"Did he say why he called?"

Bailey looked up to the heavens. Were these two ever going to figure it out? "Why do you think he called?"

"I owe him five hundred bucks for shipping my books and CDs to Houston."

"He didn't mention that."

Dead air. Bailey had no intention of changing the topic. The best thing in her life had been finding Dom. And no one in the world would have thought they'd make the pair they did. She had no doubt that someday Dr. Rey and Captain Webber would look back and realize the same thing applied to the two of them. If they would both just smarten up.

"So what's he doing at Vandenberg?"

"He didn't say."

Rey's agitation crackled through Bailey's headset. *"Look, I'm going to start watching this video you sent up to me. When he surfaces, flash me."*

Bailey had to cover all contingencies. "What do you want to do in case Captain Webber can't get to a phone in time?"

"You mean, if he's flying or something?"

"Or something."

"What I have to say won't take long. Give me, let's say, twenty

*minutes from now. If he's not around by then, I'll dump it in your
lap."*

Bailey didn't like the sound of that. What did "I'll dump
it in your lap," have to do with a codicil to a will? "I'll follow your lead, Doctor." Given Rey's situation, Bailey was
not inclined to pry—until she had to.

*"Okay. I'm going to go catch some television. Thanks, Bailey.
Uh, ISS out,"* Rey added at the end, almost sheepishly.

Bailey put the secure channel on standby.

She sat at her console, thoughtful, reviewing the pattern
of Rey's communications. The obvious conclusions troubled her. Something was going on up there that no one
was talking about. Something that involved the doctor's
employer, that neither Rey nor her employer wished to
reveal to NASA.

Bailey rubbed at the back of her neck, trying to figure
out what her duty was in this situation, then realized Rey
had already said it: NASA was a civilian operation. She
straightened up in her chair, uncertain if she should, or
even could, relay her suspicions to anyone outside her
commanding officer. And the last thing she was going to
do was present her commander with an uncertain situation. That was not the Air Force way.

So all she could or should do, Bailey decided, was wait
for more information. Then she'd either see a solution, or
be able to clearly describe a situation requiring a decision
at a higher level. Until then, it didn't matter that she was
the woman who arguably controlled the most powerful
and complex communications network in history, because
Cory Rey had very cleverly reduced her to a status most
ordinary people would find all too familiar, and frustrating.

Major Bailey was waiting for a man to pick up the
phone.

4

INTERNATIONAL SPACE STATION
17:39 GMT, FRIDAY, APRIL 4

ANATOLY RUSHKIN RECONNECTED his suit to the onboard oxygen, electrical, and coolant systems, then tightened the straps that held him against his seat in the *Soyuz* and informed Lazhenko he could begin the flight to the Japanese Experiment Module.

The *Orlan* spacesuit and duffel were in the capsule's forward airlock, and though the *Soyuz* airlock hatch was closed as a precaution against encountering debris, the cosmonauts had not repressurized their craft. They needed to conserve their oxygen for the trip home.

Rushkin felt himself push up against the restraint straps as he saw the ISS fall away through the single porthole. "I wish we had extra PBAs for the American."

Lazhenko was never one to engage in regret. "We did not know we would face this situation. She will have time enough to don the suit."

Rushkin knew that was undoubtedly true, *if* there had been someone else in the JEM to help Rey with the *Orlan*. But on her own, a payload specialist, on her first space flight? Rushkin hoped for the best, but, being Russian, feared the worst.

His helmet speakers crackled and the stern voice of Colonel Grigory Adamski spoke to them from Mission Control-Moscow. *"Commander Lazhenko, telemetry has detected a leak in your main propellant tank."*

Rushkin reacted as if a bomb had exploded under his seat. There was no backup for the capsule's main propellant tank. They could always obtain additional fuel from the emergency tanks on the station's *Zvezda* Service Module, but without a tank to hold that fuel, there was no way to fire the *Soyuz*'s main engine to return to Earth. He leaned forward, using his hands to adjust the position of his helmet as he twisted his head back and forth within, struggling to find the slightest clear angle through the smeared visor that would permit him to read the fuel gauge for himself.

Lazhenko's response indicated no such concern. "Thank you for the caution, Colonel. Onboard readings show propellant at four hundred seventy-one kilos. Unchanged from preliminary flight check."

Adamski replied so quickly that Rushkin wondered if the colonel had been expecting Lazhenko's answer. *"Commander Lazhenko, telemetry has also detected a sporadic circuitry failure in your main console bus. Your onboard readings cannot be trusted."*

"Anatoly," Lazhenko said, "reset fuel system bus. Reset telemetry transmission bus."

"I cannot even see through my visor," Rushkin said plaintively. "We must repressurize the cabin."

Lazhenko sighed, but did not take his attention from manually flying the *Soyuz* to its new position above the JEM Exposed Facility shelf, with the capsule's hatch roughly aligned to the Japanese lab module's airlock. "There is no time for that. We go with our instruments, not your telemetry."

Adamski's tone became more urgent. *"Negative. Mission*

Control now shows you at three hundred twenty kilos of propellant, venting at five kilos per minute, with the rate increasing."

"Anatoly, did you see propellant venting when you were in the station airlock?"

"Not through this visor," Rushkin answered.

"Commander," Adamski said forcefully, *"if you do not begin reentry burn within ten minutes, you will not have enough fuel for return, and your main tank will be too compromised to be recharged from emergency stores. Director Androvich now orders you to withdraw from space station and begin reentry operations checklist at once."*

Rushkin could make out enough detail through the porthole to tell that sections of the ISS were once again nearby, brilliantly white and silver in the docking light. Lazhenko was flawlessly bringing them to their new position.

"We have not recovered all personnel," Lazhenko said evenly.

"If you attempt to proceed with recovery," Adamski replied, *"you will all die."*

Lazhenko's next transmission was as if he had heard nothing from Moscow. "This is *Soyuz* to Mission Control–Houston. We are in position by JEM equipment transfer airlock. Flight Engineer Rushkin is now proceeding to open exterior airlock door and deliver *Orlan.* Do you copy?"

As Rushkin began to untwist the connectors on his restraints, he heard the American astronaut, Eric Vellacott, reply. "Soyuz, *this is Mission Control–Houston. We copy, and will advise Doctor Rey to stand by."*

Adamski's voice overlapped the final words from the American. *"Commander Lazhenko, you have been given a direct order to return at once. You are an officer in the Russian Space Force."*

"That is correct," Lazhenko said quietly. "On the ground, I am an officer. But in space, I am a cosmonaut, and I will not leave a fellow cosmonaut behind." Lazhenko shifted in his seat to look at Rushkin. "Anatoly, do you concur?"

Rushkin wondered who this giant of a man was who had replaced the Cossack he had despised. "I am a cosmonaut as well. I will prepare the airlock for transfer."

Adamski shouted in rage, his voice breaking up in Rushkin's small helmet speakers. *"You will die up there!"*

"Then I save the PKA the price of a funeral. Good-bye, Colonel Adamski. *Soyuz* out."

LYNDON B. JOHNSON SPACE CENTER
ISS FLIGHT CONTROL ROOM

Along with five other members of the ISS team on the floor of the FCR, Tovah Caruso listened in shock as the channel between Mission Control–Moscow and the *Soyuz* was abruptly cut off.

"Leo, what the hell was that all about?" she asked.

The ISS Flight Director gestured with empty hands. "Maybe . . . maybe they *are* venting propellant?"

But Rick Neale, the young Operations Planner who had led the effort to find a way to save Cory Rey and the station, stepped forward to disagree. "They can recharge their tank on the Russian side. Propellant's not a problem."

"They're venting at five kilos a minute," Milankou said, repeating what Adamski had told Lazhenko. "With the rate increasing."

"That's no problem," Neale said. "If they recharge to full capacity, that still gives them at least half an hour to make their burn, before they go below their safety threshold. But it's kind of hard to imagine a pilot like Lazhenko not noticing the thrust coming from a major propellant leak."

"So what's Moscow up to?" Caruso asked. She fixed

Neale with a stern look. "Are you having any trouble at all working with them on the Progress burn?"

"No, ma'am," Neale said earnestly. "Moscow's got all the tracking and orbit data they need. About one hour after the *Soyuz* withdraws to a safe distance, they're going to fire the Progress main engine for twenty-two minutes to take the station up to a three-hundred-forty-mile altitude. Even with tumbling, at that distance it'll be safe from reentry for at least a year."

Caruso chewed her lip, trying to see what she had missed.

Eric Vellacott spoke to her from his chair at his CAP-COM station. "Ms. Caruso, Rushkin is feeding the space-suit into the airlock."

Caruso asked the only question that mattered, the question all of NASA waited to hear answered. "Does that life-support backpack fit through the hatch?" A ground test was one thing, but conditions in space could never be exactly duplicated on earth.

Vellacott toggled on his transmit switch. "*Soyuz,* this is Houston. Administrator Caruso asks if the backpack fits."

Vellacott threw another switch and the labored breathing of Anatoly Rushkin came through Caruso's headset. "*Da! Yes, quite easily.*" More breathing. "*The Orlan is in airlock chamber. I am now pushing through other components in duffel bag.*" The flight engineer was wheezing, as if he had run a marathon, but he uttered no complaint.

There was silence in the flight control room as everyone waited, listening.

"*Everything is in airlock. I am now . . . shutting exterior hatch.*" More breathing, some of it rhythmic. Caruso pictured Rushkin slowly pumping the lever that would mechanically lock the hatch.

"There. JEM airlock sealed. I now return to Soyuz and close its hatch."

Beside Caruso, Rick Neale turned, beaming, to the crowd of observers at the back of the room and raised his thumb to the rest of his planning team from the Action Center. Caruso glanced back to see the whole brain trust clapping and applauding.

Her gaze returned to the main situation screens that still showed no station input. With so much more that could go wrong, it was premature to celebrate. Caruso felt more in sync with the Russians who, by nature, were pessimists.

When it came to the exploration of space, pessimists were usually right.

CHEYENNE MOUNTAIN AIR FORCE STATION
SPACE CONTROL CENTER

Bailey kept flashing the communications alert switch until Rey came on the channel.

"Was that twenty minutes?"

Bailey was pleased to deliver some good news for a change. "The Russians picked up some speed. They've already delivered the suit and sealed the airlock. It's in there and waiting for you."

"Any word from Mitchell?"

"Sorry, no," Bailey said. "Half of Vandenberg is looking for him. He had made arrangements to fly out later tonight, so it's likely he's still somewhere on the base."

"Then you and I have to talk."

But Bailey knew this is where she had to draw the line, even without input from NASA. "Not now, Doctor. Your taxi's outside and the meter's running."

"This is important. I want you to—"

Bailey stopped her. "Doctor Rey, we are now on an open channel."

She heard Rey swear under her breath, then followed that with, *"Sorry, NASA. Look, Major Bailey, I'll go get into that suit now. But before I make the transfer, I have to talk with you."*

Bailey made an instant command decision she knew she'd have to later explain. "Mission Control, this is Spacecom. I am switching to a secure channel for thirty seconds." Then, before Vellacott or Caruso or anyone else in Houston could protest, Bailey cut the circuit and returned to the private configuration already stored in her console computer.

"Doctor, don't say anything. Just listen to me. There's something up with the Russians. Moscow ordered Lazhenko and Rushkin to abandon the station—and you—and start reentry procedures."

"What? Why?"

"I don't know, and from what I could hear them saying in Houston, NASA doesn't know, either. There might be a chance the *Soyuz* is losing propellant. Or there could be something more going wrong with the station. But whatever's going on, trust me, you want to get your skinny butt off that station ASAP." Bailey held her finger over the reset key. "I'm switching back to the open circuit. Don't you dare repeat any of this."

Rey started to object, but Bailey didn't wait for details. "Mission Control, this is Spacecom. We are back online with Alpha."

Vellacott sounded tense, as if he had just been in the middle of a shouting match. *"Doctor Rey, can you proceed to the JEM hatch and check the pressure readings?"*

"Will do. But I have to disconnect from the radio to go that far. The readings are supposed to show vacuum on the other side, right?"

"Copy that," Vellacott confirmed.

Bailey stayed silent as the astronaut began leading Rey

through the procedure that would allow some of her module's low-pressure air to vent into the completely depressurized airlock chamber.

The major knew NASA had calculated that the air pressure in Rey's module had dropped to about five pounds per square inch, about one-third sea level. On the negative side, the air in the module was a mixture of nitrogen and oxygen, and at five pounds per square inch, there was not enough oxygen to support human life.

On the positive side, because the doctor had spent several hours in such a low-pressure environment, breathing pure oxygen from her PBA, she had already gone through the depressurization sequence all ISS spacewalkers were required to complete before beginning an EVA. Otherwise, the consequences for making an immediate transition from the full-pressure, oxygen-nitrogen atmosphere of the station to the low-pressure, pure oxygen environment of a spacesuit were severe: a sudden, debilitating, and eventually crippling case of the bends as compressed nitrogen bubbles expanded in blood and tissue.

As Vellacott had Rey recite the safety procedures intended to ensure the airlock's exterior hatch sealed by Anatoly Rushkin didn't suddenly blow out and depressurize the Japanese module, Bailey's gray phone chimed.

Captain Webber, Bailey thought. *Finally.*

She picked it up at once.

It was Tovah Caruso out for blood.

"Major Bailey—what the hell was that private conversation all about?"

Bailey was ready for her. "I told her about the Russians being ordered to leave her behind."

Caruso was furious. *"That wasn't your call to make."*

"With respect, ma'am, yes it was. That was the information Doctor Rey needed to hear in order to prevent further delays. I used my judgment in relaying that information to her in such a way that no one else on the open circuit could overhear it. She had a need to know."

"I'm having you replaced."

But Rey had already armored Bailey for this move. "Again, with respect, ma'am, if you've noticed, Doctor Rey doesn't trust you people—for whatever reason. So if she balks up there, if she questions orders, if she has any reason at all to believe that what you're telling her is not in her best interest, you've lost her. *And* endangered the lives of two cosmonauts who've just thrown away their careers to do the right thing.

"You still want me off this board, you're welcome to go ahead and try. But every second you waste on that fool's errand is a second you're not trying to get your people home. I suggest you do your job, ma'am, and let me do mine."

Bailey hung up on NASA's chief administrator. It felt good.

VANDENBERG AIR FORCE BASE

Mitch Webber stepped into Salyard's office and stood at attention. "Captain Webber reporting as ordered, General."

Salyard smiled, waved his hand dismissively, rose from behind his desk. "At ease, Captain. It wasn't an order. A request."

Webber took a more relaxed stance. He concealed his surprise. "As you say, General. But in the Navy, a request from the brass is an order from the brass."

"In the Air Force, too," Salyard agreed, motioning for him to sit down in the chair across from Colonel Varik. "In most cases," he added as if imparting an important qualification. Then Salyard sat back on the edge of his desk to face his two guests. "But this isn't most cases."

Webber looked over at the television set on the low credenza at the back of the office, hoping to see if there was anything new from NASA. But the television was switched off, something Webber found unusual in a military commander's office.

He took the seat Salyard indicated, and gave the general his full attention, curious. The fact that Varik was present, though in civilian jeans and sweatshirt, suggested this might be a continuation of yesterday's debriefing. If so, Webber knew all he had to do was answer questions. And if not, then it wasn't worth the effort trying to second-guess the general's intentions. He'd know them soon enough.

Salyard folded his arms, looked out the wide window at the distant launch complexes. "This is one of those conversations that, depending on how things turn out, doesn't necessarily have to have taken place. You understand?"

Webber nodded, focused on the moment, just as he had before stepping from the ramp of an MC-130E over central China. "I've heard about such conversations, General."

Salyard smiled. "Good answer. Because, obviously, you've never had a conversation that didn't take place."

Webber said nothing, certain that Salyard and Varik both would be analyzing every shift of his body, every word he said.

"About an hour ago," Salyard said, "I had a talk with Admiral Kreminic in Washington."

Webber went on high alert. Branimir Kreminic was his commanding officer at Special Operations Command.

"He speaks very highly of you," Salyard continued.

"I can say the same of him, General," Webber said.

"The Admiral said you were doing well at Hill, flying multiple combat uncrewed air vehicles." Salyard leaned forward with an inquisitive expression. "I'm not too clear on what your role in that program is. Developing tactics at this stage?"

Webber instantly understood that the question was a test, and he knew what answer he had to give. What he didn't know was if it would be the answer Salyard was looking for. "That would be something to discuss with the project managers at Hill, General."

Salyard glanced at Varik, nodded thoughtfully, then added almost as an afterthought, "Admiral Kreminic told me he'd be amenable to approving your transfer request, should you make one."

Webber felt a flash of heat on the back of his neck as he realized Salyard's intention for this meeting: The general was going to invite him to join whatever operation he was running out of Vandenberg. All Webber knew about that operation was that Varik was part of it. And that one area of its concern was tracking China's plans to test weapons on the Moon.

Salyard looked at him as if he could read his mind. "You know where this is going." It wasn't a question.

"I can guess, General. I can also see that this might be one of those moments when it pays to be sure there are no false assumptions."

"Fair enough," Salyard agreed. He glanced at Varik again.

Webber had the sudden strong suspicion that whatever offer Salyard was about to make him, the colonel wasn't in favor of it.

"I've read your file, Captain Webber. Your *complete* file. Not the one that follows you from base to base. The one that sits in the vault at Special Ops Command, stamped Secret. The one that explains why you don't have enough service ribbons on your chest, why you don't have the medals you deserve, and why you're not a rear admiral by now."

Webber left all the talking to the general.

"That file tells me you have chosen to work in an area that offers no rewards, except the satisfaction of knowing that your country is safer, and thus the world is safer, because of your sacrifice. Other than a handful of like-minded patriots who serve this nation, no one will ever know your name, or speak of your accomplishments. No fame. No fortune. Only the public obscurity of a naval officer who, on the surface, has accomplished nothing more notable than cashing his paycheck for eighteen years.

"So, today," the general concluded, "I'm putting an offer on the table."

Salyard paused, as if waiting for Webber to respond.

Webber did. "Is there anything you can tell me about that offer, General?"

"Just what I've told you, Captain. I've read your complete record. I know the things you've done in the past. I can guess the things that interest you, that keep you in this profession of ours."

The general sat back, waiting.

Webber let thirty seconds elapse. It was clear they were discussing his joining an operation or a project so secret that not even its potential recruits had a need to know its purpose. But still, there were some practical matters he had to consider.

"If this conversation turns out to actually have taken place," he said cautiously, "in general terms, what might the next step be?"

Salyard studied him, then appeared to decide he could provide a small amount of additional information. "The paperwork is simple." He turned to take a thin file folder, completely unremarkable, from his desk. Webber had no doubt that his own name was already printed on whatever document was inside. "There's a security form to be signed. Admiral Kreminic is prepared to issue transfer orders for detached duty."

Webber tested the opportunity that was being offered. He didn't like Varik. He didn't know if Vandenberg would end up being his home base, as well, or if he'd suddenly find himself on assignment back in Antarctica for the next five years. There was only one reason that would inspire him to go the next step with Salyard: the huge flight simulator in Hangar 27. He'd be in the loop.

But still he hesitated, thinking of his reactions over the past twenty-four hours, after hearing about Cory and the station. "I have some personal matters I need to attend to."

"Seven days?" Salyard suggested. "Get squared away at Hill, then take the R and R you're due."

Seven days, Webber thought. Time enough to see Cory when she returned, if he wanted. If she wanted. Or to attend a memorial service.

As quickly as that, he realized he'd made his decision, and that Salyard and Varik knew it, too. He stood because he thought it was the thing to do. "General Salyard, I accept your offer."

For an instant, Salyard's briefly flashed grin reminded Webber of the tales about hapless innocents signing contracts only to realize they had sold their souls to the devil. He put the image aside. Dwight Salyard was a general in the United States Air Force. Hardly a refuge for devils or dishonor.

Salyard shook Webber's hand with both of his. "Great things will come of this, Captain." He handed Webber the file folder and pen. "The first step."

Webber opened the folder to find a single sheet of paper with a standard Department of Defense security oath stating the undersigned acknowledged that violation of any applicable rule, regulation, or order prescribed or otherwise

issued by the Project relating to the safeguarding or security of Restricted Data or other classified or sensitive information would be subject to a civil penalty not to exceed
$100,000 for each such violation, and confinement in a
military prison for a term not longer than life.

" 'The Project,' " Webber said as he signed and dated
the form.

Salyard didn't check the signed document, merely
closed the file and put it behind him on the desk. " 'The
Project.' Makes it easier to carry on some conversations
under less than secure circumstances." He was about to say
something else when his phone rang.

Salyard excused himself, answered the phone. "Yes,
Sergeant?" Salyard listened, looked at Webber, then at Varik.
"No. No, not for a few hours at least. Yes. He should be
available then. Very good." He replaced the receiver, looked
at Webber. "Captain, how'd you like a closer look at that
simulator you noticed?"

The promptness of the invitation was a surprise to
Webber. He checked his watch with regret. "I'm catching an
Air National Guard transport to Ellington Field at seven."

"Houston?" Salyard asked.

Webber nodded, then caught himself. "Yes, General. I
have some friends at Johnson. I thought I'd be closer to . . .
everything that's happening up there."

"You're a lot closer than you were five minutes ago,"
Salyard said. " 'The Project'—since 1998, it's been the sixth
branch of this country's military."

The general put his hand solidly on Webber's shoulder,
welcoming him into the fold.

"Congratulations, Captain Webber, you've just joined
the United States Space Force."

5

CORY REY FELT like Houdini in reverse as she prepared to wriggle into a straitjacket, not out of it, although the one-size-fits-all design of the Russian *Orlan* spacesuit made perfect sense. The *Orlan* could be left on the station and used by whichever crew member happened to need it for a given task. Adjustments to the length of the arms and legs were made simply by tightening or releasing a simple system of cords inside the suit. The technique was much more basic than the modular mix-and-match system of the American suits with their separate arms and legs.

Cory decided that, viewed from the front, the *Orlan* looked exactly as anyone would expect a spacesuit to look—a bulky, white jumpsuit with a large helmet, an American flag patch on the left shoulder, a Russian tricolor on the right, and prominent blue identification bands running down the arms and ringing the elbows and knees.

The back of the suit, however, was unique because its backpack, containing the suit's oxygen supply, carbon-dioxide scrubber, batteries, water-cooling system pump and heat exchanger, and voice radio and telemetry units, was not a separate unit. Instead, it was hinged like a cupboard door, opening and closing on a rectangular frame to which the rest of the suit was permanently attached. A tunnel of spacesuit fabric emerged from that frame like the cuff on a sleeve, and it was that extra fabric that would have to be carefully folded away before the backpack could close.

In principle, Cory knew putting on the suit was no different from stepping through a door to slide into a pair of overalls. But in microgravity, with oxygen running out and a space station coming apart all around her, she was having difficulty with the principle.

"How're you doing, Doctor?" Bailey asked. The major had been checking in every five minutes since Cory had retrieved the suit from the ELM, where Anatoly Rushkin had left it for her.

"Almost ready to get into this thing," Cory said, exhausted, but oddly, no longer tired, nor overwhelmed by her aching sinuses and the irritating blobs of mucus that bubbled out from her stuffed nose behind the mask, or by her scratchy eyes, now so dry her eyelids sometimes were caught in midblink. It seemed that contemplating impending acts of madness was *the* way to stay awake and keep alert.

"Mission Control reports you're at twenty minutes on your PBA."

"Copy that," Cory said as she wrapped a Velcro strap around the left boot of the *Orlan,* binding it in place with its toe looped under a foot restraint. NASA's experiments on the C-9B Skytrain II airplane had revealed one of the secrets for getting into this suit without advance practice. If the *Orlan* was tied in place, there'd be something for the astronaut—*and that's me now,* Cory thought—to push and pull against.

She took a moment to check the position of her last

oxygen cylinder on the wraparound Velcro belt at the waist of her gray track pants. The cylinder was held in place by a holster of cloth straps attached to the belt. Eric Vellacott's team had kindly warned her that switching from her PBA air supply to that of the *Orlan* was going to be the most dangerous part of getting into the Russian suit.

At some point in getting into the Russian suit, she was going to have to take off her PBA *before* she could close the *Orlan's* backpack. The Russian suit's oxygen would be flowing, but in the low pressure of the JEM, she wouldn't be able to count on being able to breathe enough of it until she got the backpack sealed. According to Eric Vellacott, the best time an astronaut had clocked for this maneuver on the Skytrain was forty-eight seconds.

Great, Cory thought. Given the other optimistic time-lines NASA had been feeding her today, that probably meant she'd have to hold her breath twice as long. *Like a minute and a half.* She'd never managed that in her life, even during her SCUBA certification dives. Then again, even the record time was suspect to Cory, because she knew, as Vellacott had to, that the Vomit Comet could only create microgravity conditions for about thirty seconds, not forty-eight.

Cory took stock again. With both boots of the empty Russian suit strapped down now, the frame of its backpack "doorway" wedged under an experiment rack to hold it in place, and the separately packaged backpack components installed and confirmed operational, she had completed all the preparation NASA had advised. Houston's step-by-step instructions had made this part of the process, at least, simple and straightforward.

But Bailey had still not answered her inquiry about what had happened to the cosmonaut in Moscow, the expert who was supposed to have talked her through the

Orlan suit procedures. Neither had Bailey been forthcoming when Cory had asked why she wasn't hearing from Vellacott as often. For some as-yet-unspecified reason it seemed Major Bailey at Cheyenne Mountain, Colorado, was now her sole intermediary with ground, replacing Eric Vellacott at Mission Control–Houston.

But those answers had to wait. She had less than fifteen minutes of PBA oxygen remaining and the inevitable could not be delayed any longer. The *Orlan* suit held an eight-hour supply, and could recharge from the *Soyuz* and from stores in the Russian half of the station.

Cory untangled the gray-blue jumpsuit she had shoved behind a bungee cord on one of the module walls. It was the *Orlan* water-cooling garment, and she had to put it on before she got into the suit. Without it, her own body heat would cook her in the sealed spacesuit.

"Hey, there, Major," Cory said. "The *Orlan*'s tied into position and I am now putting on my sexy Russian lingerie."

"Copy that," Bailey answered. *"You're at fifteen minutes."*

"Got it," Cory said. She wriggled out of her gray track pants, polo shirt, and NASA-issued underpants, so clad only in her gray sports bra she could pull on what NASA delicately called a MAG, for Maximum Absorption Garment, and what she called a bulky, crinkly diaper. *So much for the dignity of space travel,* Cory thought as she used adhesive strips to seal the MAG in place to prevent leakage.

Then she fought her way into the slippery chintzlike fabric of the cooling garment, shuddering as she felt its sewn-in network of thin, soft plastic tubes grab her like the coils of freezing snakes.

Her final step before attempting the spacesuit itself was to quickly take off her PBA mask, just for the few seconds it took her to tug the cloth cap holding the

Orlan's radio earphones and two small microphones over her short hair. The eccentric headgear made Cory think of an old-fashioned baby's bonnet, elastic chin strap and all. She knew the American astronauts still referred to the low-tech solution for keeping their commsets in place as "Snoopy Caps," for the comic-strip beagle who had become the unofficial mascot of the Apollo Moon program.

As she slipped her PBA mask back on, Cory had to pull back the cloth edges of the Russian cap so her mask could again make a tight seal against her skin. Then she floated beside the *Orlan* suit, trying not to think about the approaching moment of truth.

The suit's hollow arms waved disconcertingly back and forth like seaweed in slow currents as Cory connected the feeder tubes from her gray-blue cooling garment to the cooling tubes in the *Orlan*'s open backpack. She pressed the orange activation switch and heard a whirring sound as the water pump started. A few moments later, she felt the cooling garment's plastic pipes shift and gurgle against her skin as water pumped into them, forcing air bubbles out. It was like wearing a Jacuzzi.

"That's it, Major," Cory reported to her ground control. "The cooling system is on. No visible leaks. Time to crawl inside."

"Copy that," Bailey acknowledged.

The moment of truth was now.

Cory took a long deep breath. The flight surgeon had suggested she hyperventilate just before she took off her PBA for good. She'd be helping to load additional oxygen into her blood and extending the length of time she could hold her breath. The trick, the flight surgeon told her, was not to hyperventilate too much, because she'd also be loading her blood with additional carbon dioxide, and that would *reduce* the length of time she could hold her breath. NASA hadn't been able to define "too much" for Cory. The best counsel the flight surgeon had for her was "Stop just before you feel dizzy." Not so helpful.

She paused. There was one more question ground control had yet to answer.

"So, this is it, Major," Cory said. "Any good news?"

"Sorry, Doctor. They can't locate him."

"Then do we still have our deal?" Her secret was not dying with her. One way or another, someone on the ground was going to learn what had come back from the Moon, and how important it had been to someone.

"Doctor," Bailey countered, *"you have less than ten minutes of oxygen remaining, and Houston reminds you that that figure is just a best-guess estimate."*

Cory floated, staring at the open back of the Russian spacesuit that was going to either save her or entomb her. She held firm. "What I want will take less than one minute, Major. I need to do this, and you're the only one who can help me."

"All right, Doctor. One minute. Mission Control-Houston, this is Spacecom switching to a secure channel with Alpha for sixty seconds."

The sharp edge in the major's voice told Cory that Bailey felt she'd been blackmailed.

"The clock is ticking, Doctor."

"Are you recording this?"

"As you requested. You now have fifty-five seconds."

For the last two hours, while her body had dutifully followed orders, Cory's mind had been endlessly rehearsing her statement, and now the words tumbled from her in a rush.

"My name is Corazon Annunciata Rey. On April 3, onboard the International Space Station, just prior to whatever led to its current critical ONS, I retrieved one sample cylinder from the TTI lunar return vehicle.

"On April 4, I was able to recover the sample cylinder from the equipment transfer airlock of the JEM. I broke the pressure seal on the cylinder and manually unscrewed the cap. Inside, among approximately five hundred grams of what appeared to be lunar stones and regolith, I also found two human fingers, desiccated—"

"What?!" Bailey interrupted.

"Don't stop me!—almost mummified in appearance, with exposed bones showing what appear to be cut marks below the midjoint. There is no possibility of these remains having originated within the ISS. I clearly observed them as they came out of the lunar sample cylinder. The fingers are now sealed in plastic and I will take them with me in the *Orlan* spacesuit as I attempt to board the *Soyuz* piloted by Yuri Lazhenko.

"It is my belief that Science Officer Bette Norman was aware of the possibility of the remains being present in the sample cylinder, because she attempted to use violence against me to reach the cylinder before I could. She was prevented from doing so by a major depress event which likely resulted in her death."

Cory paused, oddly at peace now that she had finally shared her discovery. "That's it, Major Bailey."

"Doctor . . . are you certain that's what you found?" Bailey sounded bewildered.

Cory touched her chest, felt the hard package she carried inside her sports bra, inside the liquid-coolant garment. "I've got them right here, Major. They're flesh and bone, no question."

"But . . . no one's ever died on the Moon."

"No one we know of." Cory took another deep breath, and whether it was her imagination or not, the flow of oxygen into her PBA didn't seem as strong as it once was.

"And why would Major Norman—"

Cory hurried on. "I haven't time for this. If something happens to me, you have to get this recording to Mitchell."

"Doctor, I don't know if—"

Cory had rehearsed her next speech, also, anticipating, dreading, this reaction from the major. She raised her voice to full volume to drown out any more interruptions. "Major Bailey! This has nothing at all to do with the military! You do not have to share this with your commander! It's a personal communication about a private business project which I am asking you to give to a friend. And that is all!"

"Switching back to open channel."

"Major! At least talk to him—before you do anything! Promise me!"

"Mission Control-Houston, this is Spacecom returning to—"

"Please! Before you make your decision! Talk to Mitchell!"

"All right—I will. This is Spacecom returning to an open channel."

Cory's voice dropped to normal levels. "I'm disconnecting from the radio now, so next time you all hear from me, I'll be using the suit's SSR."

"Doctor?"

"Still here, Major Bailey." Cory had her hand on the radio wire plugged into the side of her PBA.

"Best way to straighten this out is to get down here and tell the man yourself."

"Copy that," Cory said. Then she pulled the plug, and she was on her own.

LYNDON B. JOHNSON SPACE CENTER
ISS FLIGHT CONTROL ROOM

Tovah Caruso checked to be sure her commset "Push-To-Talk" button was off, then turned to Eric Vellacott, sitting beside her at his CAPCOM console. "Is Rey losing it?" Caruso asked.

Vellacott flicked off his PTT button as well. "Don't know her well enough to say, Ms. Caruso. But she's sharp. Driven. Definitely not a quitter. All good qualities in her current situation."

"What about that last bit? Shouting at the major? What was that about?"

"Something to do with her will update?"

Caruso didn't enjoy being outside the loop. Especially a loop involving Major Bailey. "I don't think so. Whatever they talked about on that secure loop, it requires some kind of decision from Bailey. And the major didn't want to make it. And who's this 'Mitchell' Bailey's supposed to discuss her decision with?"

Vellacott shrugged. "Just from what the two of them have been saying over the open circuit, I'd guess Cory's talking about an old boyfriend. They've been trying to track him down at Vandenberg, get him on the phone."

"Vandenberg," Caruso said as she rubbed the back of her neck where a tension headache was building slowly. "Just what we need in the mix. The damned Air Force."

She looked up at the main situation boards. The right screen showed the ISS was currently over Italy. With luck, that meant Rey would be sealed in her suit and ready for her spacewalk to the *Soyuz* when the station moved back into daylight. But then, when had luck been a part of anything today?

Caruso took off her commset and stood up. "I'm going

to find out if Teller has any idea what's going through her head."

Vellacott nodded. "I'll send someone for you as soon as the Russians report her SSR is operating."

"Much appreciated," Caruso said. But with everything else that had gone wrong, she wasn't counting on Rey's Space-to-Space Radio working, either.

Caruso then headed for the entrance. As she walked up the aisle between the Evans consoles, she glanced over the knot of civilians in the far corner—pool reporters. *The vultures are out,* she thought. The routine shuttle mission to swap ISS crews now had the distinction of being the first NASA mission since *Apollo 11* to have continuous media coverage. Her agency's space program was no longer the defining dream for a country looking to the future, it had become the latest ten-minute distraction for a populace raised on disaster films and eager for a sequel to *Columbia*.

Her dark thoughts mingling with prayers for those in peril in outer space, Caruso reached the doors just as Kai Teller entered, and put out a hand to detain her.

For once, the man looked his age. "Tovah, did you know Ed Farren?"

It took Caruso a moment to place the name. "Oh, sure. Old Human Space Flight guy. We still use him on committees and . . ." She looked at Teller. He'd used past tense.

"I just got a call. He's dead."

"Sorry to hear that," Caruso said. "He was getting up there, wasn't he? I mean, he was old."

Teller nodded. "But he was in terrific shape. He worked for me. Consulting."

"So what happened?" Teller was clearly devastated by the news. Caruso wondered why his reaction was so strong.

Teller moved nearer to her, dropped his voice even though no one was close enough to overhear them. "The police say it looks like a heart attack, but . . . listen, Tovah, this is probably something I should have told you before."

Caruso bristled. More suppressed data. She was getting really tired of this. "What now?"

"Ed . . . came to me a few days ago . . . said, well, it was a pretty wild story. He didn't have a lot to back it up . . ."

"And?" Caruso prompted.

"He thought there was a chance this mission might be sabotaged."

Caruso exploded in fury. "I could have you arrested for withholding vital information from me." She saw several staffers look up from their consoles, curious, then look down quickly, as if trying to avoid her eye, and anger.

"Tovah," Teller said indignantly. "Ed was a genuine conspiracy nut. He was always talking about the Air Force stealing the best projects from NASA, hiding technological breakthroughs."

"That's no secret, Kai. It's a fact." For decades NASA had seen some of its most promising areas of research suddenly disappear into black holes, assigned to military labs that promptly stopped publishing results. Only occasionally did the technology find its way back to NASA, as with the heatshields protecting the Mercury, Gemini, and Apollo capsules. Those shields were originally developed to protect nuclear warheads once planned to be launched through space. Even the venerable Hubble Space Telescope was a modified version of a Keyhole surveillance satellite. More often than not, however, the street was one-way.

"Whatever. But I believe Ed Farren was murdered. Because he knew something and he wouldn't shut up about it."

"Something about this." Caruso looked back at the main display screens and then at Teller. "Dammit, Kai," she said. "I'm going to have to report this."

Teller nodded vigorously. "But I want you to. I mean, local police, they find a man in his seventies dead in his motel-room bed, they're going to say heart attack and let it go. We have to have a full autopsy, Tovah. Tox screen. The works."

Caruso stared at Teller. "Hold it right there. Local police? Motel room? Where was Farren?"

"He was at a motel near Vandenberg." Teller stopped when he saw Caruso's startled reaction. "Is that important?"

"Just a coincidence," she said, wondering if that was true. Rey and Farren were both on TTI's payroll. And both had gotten into trouble. "A friend of Doctor Rey's is based at Vandenberg. She's been trying to get hold of him."

"Captain Mitch Webber?"

"Mitch—Mitchell. Yeah, that's the name. You know him?"

"His name came up in Cory's background check. But he's Navy. I think he's based in San Diego."

Caruso turned around looking for Vellacott, saw him leaning back in his chair, staring up at the main screens, no indication of talking with anyone. She turned back to Teller. "Any idea what your consultant was doing at Vandenberg?"

"Ed's got friends all through aerospace. He was probably talking to someone on the base."

Caruso went back to the beginning. "So who would want to sabotage the ISS?"

"Our country has enemies," Teller replied as if the answer were obvious.

Caruso wanted to put the whole confusing matter to rest as quickly as possible. She still had Rey—and Major Bailey—to worry about. "All right. I'm going to take this to the FBI. Get them to take jurisdiction over the investigation into Ed Farren's death. But I warn you, Kai, it's going to go public fast. We'll both be called on the carpet. And you in particular had better have a good excuse for not coming forward with Farren's suspicions. No matter how crazy they were."

"I understand," Teller said. "That's *if* the FBI finds something."

But NASA's chief administrator knew it wouldn't be that simple. "Even if they don't, the very fact that someone mentioned the 'S' word is going to light a fire under the media."

Teller shrugged. "The price we pay for a free society."

"Spoken like a man with a publicist, a private jet, and an estate half the size of Maui."

Teller didn't respond to her sarcasm, he was looking at something behind her.

Caruso turned to the front of the room, to see the telemetry screen on the right flashing with numbers. Some of the onboard sensors on the station were beginning to transmit data again.

She left Teller standing at the entrance as she headed back toward Vellacott's console. "Is that from the station?" she called out.

An engineer answered from the ODIN console— Onboard Data, Interfaces, and Networks. "Space commander's relaying telemetry from the Progress, Ms. Caruso. Moscow's powering it up."

Caruso took her chair again, slipped on her commset. The Progress was the uncrewed Russian supply capsule docked with the station. In addition to the craft's being used to ferry supplies up to the station and take waste away for burning in the atmosphere, its engine was used to periodically lift the station's orbit. Later today, if all went according to Rick Neale's plan, it would do exactly that, to keep the station from experiencing a fiery reentry in the weeks ahead.

"Aren't the Russians jumping the gun?" Caruso asked with a frown. It wasn't like *Rosaviakosmos* to be ahead of schedule on anything.

Rick Neale was at the tracking and orbit console behind her, reading the telemetry on his own screen. "The Progress burn is set for 16:40 this afternoon. But they're heating the fuel lines and they've started the fuel-tank mixers." Something in the young engineer's voice caught Caruso's attention. Uncertainty.

She looked back at him. "What's the significance of that?"

"Um, Progress operations calls for mixing the hydrogen slurry and heating the engine components twenty-two minutes before firing the main engine."

Caruso's eyes widened. Immediately, she stood up and scanned the room for Stepan Ivanovich, the Russian Interface Officer from the PKA. She didn't see him. "They're not thinking of firing Progress in twenty-two minutes, are they?"

Eric Vellacott understood her urgency.

"They *can't* fire before Doctor Rey gets out of there," he said. "That'd take her out of reach of the *Soyuz*. It could even ram the station *into* the *Soyuz*."

"Holy shit, ma'am," Neale suddenly exclaimed and pointed up to the telemetry board. "They've started their countdown."

Caruso hit the talk button on her commset. "Major Bailey, this is Caruso. I want Mission Control-Moscow and I want them now!"

6

CORY REY WAS out of time. And air. The last few breaths she had tried and failed to draw from her PBA had only served to make the mask tighter. Her last bottle of oxygen was finished, and she wasn't yet in position to close the backpack of her Russian spacesuit. There was only one thing left to do, and she did it as fast as she could.

She twisted the pressure regulator valve in the top-right corner of the suit's open frame and heard the instant hiss of the oxygen that streamed into the suit's helmet, its flow propelled by a tiny fan.

Holding on to the *Orlan's* frame with both hands, she swung her feet up and into the short tunnel of spacesuit fabric attached to it, and then pushed into the suit's legs until her feet reached halfway down. She stopped there, now sitting on the edge of the suit's open frame, as if she were perched on a window ledge.

With no time to hyperventilate as she'd been advised to, Cory yanked off her PBA mask and, holding on to the frame again, she pulled herself forward to shove her face into the fabric entrance tunnel, past and under its bunched-up edges, pushing into the suit's upper body, up and inside the helmet, as far as possible. Then she breathed in as deeply as she could.

No air at all passed into Cory's straining lungs.

It took several panicked breaths before she realized she wasn't blacking out. Somehow she was drawing in enough pure oxygen to keep herself alive.

Now she could attempt something even more impossible.

Awkwardly stuffed within the unsealed suit, her arms at her sides, and her face still up in the helmet so she could breathe, Cory put one hand to her waist and ripped off the Velcro belt that held her empty oxygen cylinder in place. Then she used both her hands to push the belt and cylinder and her discarded PBA mask from the front of her body around to her back, out the entrance-tunnel's fabric sleeve.

Success. But the maneuver was only half over. Because her suit was still unsealed.

Cory took several deep breaths from the helmet, holding in as much oxygen as she could, then half-turned in the frame so she could pull on the elastic cords that were supposed to gather and fold the entry tunnel's excess fabric and drag it inside the suit. In NASA's video demonstration, the procedure had looked like turning a pillowcase inside-out while still inside the pillow.

For once, it was good to be five foot two. The hard torso of the *Orlan* spacesuit had been built to accommodate large Russian men. Cory was able to turn almost completely around in it. She even managed to keep her arm and hand from getting caught in the fabric tail, while feeling around to confirm that it had folded properly. The whole point was to keep any fabric from overhanging the frame. If it did, she knew, the backpack might not close.

With the fabric tunnel finally tucked up behind her, Cory turned around so she could look out through the suit's visor. She paused to take a few more deep breaths, and found breathing getting easier. Even though the suit's backpack was still open, the air pressure inside the *Orlan* was now slightly higher than the air pressure of the module.

She was ready for the hard stuff.

Cory pulled her arms up her sides and shoved her hands into the spacesuit's arms. Because she'd locked down the spacesuit's boots under foot restraints, she was now able to rock back and forth in the restraints, stopping only when both her hands were in their respective gloves.

Next she pulled with her left hand and pushed with her right arm to turn her upper body and the suit's torso ninety degrees to release the edge of the backpack from the experiment rack where she'd wedged it in place. The moment it bobbed free, Cory put her right hand on the suit's red chest lever and began to pump it. After ten pumps, the lever locked, signaling that the backpack had closed as much as it was going to.

Without a second pair of eyes to check the seal on her back, Cory knew she had no way of knowing if a stray corner of fabric had left a potentially fatal crack from which her oxygen could escape. All she could do was continue on the course she'd set. So she turned the pressure control beside the red lever to inflate the silicone gasket in the *Orlan*'s backpack frame and, she hoped, form an airtight seal.

Cory tensed, then relaxed as she felt a small compressor in her backpack thump rapidly, then slow, then stop. Her suit was on and sealed—most likely.

"How about that," she said aloud, savoring her one small step toward survival, trying not to think about the giant leap to come. Her voice sounded flat and weak in the odd confines of the helmet. She raised her left arm to find the forearm panel that held her radio controls and switched on her short-range, Space-to-Space Radio transceiver.

"This is Cory Rey to anyone out there, believe it or not, I am in the—"

"Doctor Rey! This is Anatoly! I am directly outside JEM hatch! You must come out at once!"

Cory's brief feeling of accomplishment and safety vanished. "Why? What's happened now?"

"The Progress engine is going to fire in nine minutes! To lift station to higher orbit!"

"With us on it?" Cory asked, incredulous. "What are they thinking?"

"No one knows, Doctor. Communication circuits to Mission Control-Moscow are down. Beyond even Major Bailey's wizardry. If we do not leave station within nine minutes, we will never leave."

In space, Yuri Lazhenko steadfastly held his capsule's position thirty feet out from the farthest extent of the mangled ruins that stretched from the Node 2 mating adapter and trapped the hideously distended body of Bette Norman.

Lazhenko was certain Moscow had intended the same ugly fate for Dr. Rey, though he didn't know why. There was no other reason for Moscow's transparently false story of the propellant leak, except to provide an excuse for him and his flight engineer to leave the American to die alone.

Once again they have misjudged me, Lazhenko thought. The knowledge that maniacs in Moscow had decided to murder Rey, and were now willing to sacrifice two of their own cosmonauts to do so, only fed his desire to save her life, return to Earth, and expose the entire sorry scheme.

"The Progress countdown is now T minus eight minutes," Major Bailey's voice announced.

Lazhenko knew he was the only one who could hear reports from the ground now. Inside the station, Rushkin would only be able to pick up SSR signals from the *Soyuz*—and from Rey's spacesuit, when and if it became operational. "Anatoly. Eight minutes."

Rushkin's breathless reply was curt. *"Understood."* Lazhenko knew why. The *Soyuz* capsule could begin to move away from the station as late as fifteen seconds before the Progress engine fired. Even that brief time was enough to get out of the station's way as its speed increased and its orbit rose.

But Rushkin was now far back in Node 2, waiting for the American to depressurize the Japanese module so she could open its hatch. Lazhenko had estimated it would take Rushkin and Rey no less than ten minutes to safely move past the debris and wreckage of Node 2 and the mating adapter, then make their way to the *Soyuz*. They no longer had that much time, but Lazhenko could not admit defeat. He had already disconnected his umbilicals and attached his emergency-transfer life-support unit, strapping the Kevlar-covered knapsack-size package to his chest. He twisted his restraint lock, then floated from his seat, pushing himself into the orbital module with its open airlock hatch.

He looked back to the mating adapter fifty feet away. Bette Norman floated at the twenty-foot mark, the farthest extent of the debris extending from the station. His gaze resolutely swept past the swollen corpse, following the white line of the safety rope running from the airlock of the *Soyuz* to a handhold on the mating adapter. He focused only on the new mission he set for himself.

"Anatoly," Lazhenko radioed. "I am coming to disconnect your safety line from the mating adapter. When the time comes, I will tow you both from the wreckage."

"No!" Rushkin radioed back. *"You must not leave the controls of the capsule! The station is still flexing!"*

Lazhenko knew that was true. What was almost a standing wave was passing along the unbroken section of the truss now, causing the station to undulate once every ninety seconds, caught as it was between opposing forces: the broken section of truss holding the port solar arrays, and the reaction control system thrusters that kept firing in a vain attempt to stabilize the remainder of the station. But Lazhenko had been watching and timing the movements, and had noted that they were always up and down in relation to the direction of the station's orbit. The *Soyuz* was unlikely to be hit where it was now.

"It is our only chance," Lazhenko radioed to Rushkin. Then he clipped his safety line to the line Rushkin had already set in place, and pulled himself into space.

Rushkin floated in the dark confines of Node 2. To his left was the sealed hatch that led to the American lab. To his right, the morass of tangled wreckage between the Node and the ruined mating adapter. Behind him, the open hatch to the Columbus Orbital Facility, and Sophia Dante, her bloated body grotesquely held in place by a hand that had ballooned beneath a foot restraint, perhaps the last action the brave commander had taken to keep herself from being blown into space.

But like Lazhenko, Rushkin was focused on his latest mission, and chose only to see the hatch directly before him that led to the Japanese Experiment Module. Behind that hatch, Dr. Rey was alive and in the *Orlan* suit. But the hatch wouldn't open because the pressure sensors read that Node 2 was in vacuum.

"No use," Rey radioed from within the module.

Rushkin knew the American had been trying to manually disconnect the hatch's locks. *"Anatoly, you've got to get going."*

"We have plenty of time," Rushkin lied grimly as he studied the bulkhead surrounding the hatch, and picked out the access panel most likely to cover the pressure sensors. "Get ready to try again. When I say."

He unclipped his safety line and held up the large, stainless steel carabiner clip like a hammer. Next he grabbed a restraint, locked his arm, then rapped the clip against the panel, to pop it loose. Behind it were two tiny switching circuits connected to two small, sealed pressure chambers.

Rushkin grinned with relief, snapped the clip back to his equipment belt, then extended two fingers to press against the chambers' diaphragms. "I have now pressurized node," he radioed to Rey. "Try hatch again."

A moment later came her excited reply: *"It's working!"*

Rushkin held himself in position, continuing to make the sensors read the pressure of his fingers as the atmospheric pressure in the node.

The hatch lever began to move. Rey was unsealing it. *"Anatoly, your line is now free."*

Rushkin turned as much as he could to look to his right and saw Lazhenko's silhouette outside the docking adapter. "Yuri, get back to *Soyuz!*" he radioed to his commander.

But Lazhenko had set his own plan in motion. *"Get through as much of the wreckage as you can. But when the time comes, I will tow you both from the station."*

Rushkin swore, then shouted, "You're only making things worse!" With his safety line disconnected from its tie-down point, it was now free to float and snag on any one of the hundreds of pipes and filaments trailing from the mating adapter. As well as adding to the danger he and the American already faced together, the commander had just endangered himself.

"Major Bailey says we are at six minutes. I will see you in the capsule." Then Lazhenko tugged on the rope and turned back to his spacecraft.

"It's open!" Rushkin heard Rey exclaim. *"Coming through."*

Rushkin pushed back from the hatchway as Rey appeared, moving awkwardly, but moving. He kicked forward to grab her hand, no time to waste. "Quickly, let me check seal." He gave the American's arm a tug to make her spin around, and she loudly protested the dizzying movement. But his quick inspection showed him that her backpack was properly closed.

"Well done, Doctor. You are cosmonaut now."

"A very dizzy cosmonaut," Rey said. "Oh, God . . . Sophia . . ."

Rushkin saw her expression, knew where she was looking. "It is Commander Dante," he said. "And you must prepare yourself. Bette Norman is . . . outside, caught in wreckage."

Rey nodded, tight-faced. "I'm all right. What do we have to do?"

Rushkin pushed the American upright so she floated at his side, then took Rey's own safety line clip and put it in her hand. "First, we move from node to docking adapter."

He saw Cory stare past him at the jungle of debris they'd have to clear. "Then we put our clips on safety line leading to *Soyuz,* and we join Commander Lazhenko. Two hours later, we are in Kazakhstan, drinking vodka in little bar I know in Arkalyk where we land."

"Okay, but drinks are on me," Rey said faintly. "Who goes first?"

"I do." Rushkin began to ease forward, cautiously

brushing stiff wiring conduits and splintered coolant pipes to the side, methodically checking that no splinters or sharp shards bristled from anything he was about to touch.

"*Anatoly,*" Lazhenko said over the SSR, "*five minutes.*"

"Was that Commander Lazhenko?" Rey asked.

"Can you not hear him on suit radio?"

"Just barely. Did he say five minutes?"

"*Da.*" His commander's idea had been good, not bad, Rushkin realized. He and Rey would never be able to move fast enough through the ruined section of the station to reach the *Soyuz* in time. Their only hope was Lazhenko's being able to tow them from the station. Without damaging their suits too badly. Or tangling the safety line.

"Then shouldn't we be moving faster?"

"Stay close behind." Rushkin waded into the wreckage as if it were nothing more dangerous than tall grass. He ripped, pushed, tore, and twisted it. Then felt a sharp pain in his left hand, and gasped out loud.

"What is it? What happened?" Rey called out to him.

Out of her line of sight, Rushkin held his left hand in front of his visor and saw the sharp curl of metal that had punctured the thin layers of his glove—just beside the metal plate protecting his palm. The pain he felt told him the cold shard had pierced his flesh. "Nothing," he said, hoping the shard itself would seal the puncture in his glove. *I have to keep moving,* Rushkin told himself. No matter what he had said to the American, she was not a cosmonaut. Her survival was his responsibility now.

Rushkin reached forward again. Seeing too late that the curl of metal was also entangled in a thin filament of wire. Seeing that filament now tug the metal free. Hearing the hiss of escaping air as his pressure regulators automatically increased the flow of oxygen, making up for what was being lost through the hole in his punctured glove.

"Four minutes," Lazhenko radioed.

Rey's voice was right behind him. "Are you sure you're all right?"

Rushkin knew the American would not have seen what just happened. His being in front of her was probably interfering with her suit's radio reception, as well. He heard his regulators slow the flow of oxygen, and looked down to see a small black bead appear on the edge of his glove. Then he laughed out loud. His own blood had been drawn into the puncture, where it had frozen. His suit was sealed again.

"Everything is fine," Rushkin said joyfully. "We keep moving! Not much farther!"

He was going to get the American off the station. All was not lost.

LYNDON B. JOHNSON SPACE CENTER
ISS FLIGHT CONTROL ROOM

Tovah Caruso was on her feet, and so were the rest of the staff in the Blue Flight Control Room. What had begun as a disaster and developed into a tragedy had become a surreal nightmare wildly and senselessly careening out of control.

In four minutes, the Russian supply capsule was going to fire its main engine, supposedly to lift the ISS to a higher, safer orbit. Under normal operations, Houston had no direct access to Russian telemetry, but Major Bailey had provided a realtime feed. The information it provided was unnerving. The same telemetry that carried the countdown data for the Progress now showed a pressure blockage in one of the four propellant lines that fed the supply craft's main engine, as if that one fuel line had deliberately not been heated. When that engine ignited, it was going to explode like a bomb and take what little remained of the station with it.

And Moscow was refusing to communicate with Houston.

Caruso stalked back to the desk where Stepan Ivanovich had been installed. The interface officer from *Rosaviakosmos* was on the phone, speaking rapidly in frantic Russian, his Palm Pilot switched on before him. Then he abruptly sputtered into silence and slammed down the receiver. "I am sorry, Madam Chief Administrator, but I am unable to reach Mission Control through normal phone channels."

"Then call your embassy in Washington," Caruso ordered, unbelieving. "Call anybody. But you get me through to those idiots in Moscow *now!*"

"But . . ." Ivanovich looked up at the main board. ". . . four minutes . . . how?"

Knowing he was right made Caruso even angrier. She pointed a finger at the pale-skinned Russian as if she were brandishing a weapon. "I'm holding you personally responsible for those three lives. You! Personally!" And then, because she knew there was no real way she could punish Ivanovich, Caruso whirled around and marched back to Eric Vellacott at CAPCOM.

"How did this happen?" she said as she stared up at the displays. "Why did this happen?"

Kai Teller approached, put a hand on her shoulder. "Whatever it takes, Tovah, you know that . . ."

Caruso shook off his hand. "If I find out you could have stopped this . . ."

"Three minutes," Vellacott announced.

"One more time," Caruso said. "Tell Lazhenko to get out of there. We need a witness. We need at least one person to live through this, to tell us what happened."

Vellacott looked up at her. "Lazhenko told Moscow to piss off. He's not going to listen to us."

"Just tell him," Caruso said. "For the record."

Vellacott turned back to his console, hit the PTT switch. "This is Mission Control-Houston to *Soyuz*. Commander Lazhenko, we repeat. We have determined you must leave the vicinity of space station at once."

Lazhenko's reply was immediate and uncooperative. *"Negative, Houston. Doctor Rey and Rushkin are not yet out. There is time to tow them from station before it moves."*

Caruso reached her breaking point. She yanked off Vellacott's commset, spoke into the microphone. "Damn it, Yuri! The station isn't going to *move!* It's going to *explode!* The Progress engine has a blocked fuel line! Now get out of there!"

"Two minutes," a tentative voice announced from another console.

"I understand, Houston," Lazhenko finally answered. *"I leave as soon as Doctor Rey and Rushkin are clear.* Soyuz out."

Caruso threw down the commset in frustration. "We've lost them," she said. "We've lost them all."

INTERNATIONAL SPACE STATION

Cory's spacesuit fought her every inch of the way. Each movement she made was a struggle against the pressure of oxygen at five pounds per square inch that inflated the *Orlan*, forcing its arms and legs into fixed position, turning her into a Thanksgiving Day parade balloon. And since her body floated inside the suit, there was little in the way of friction to help her hold her own position.

"Two minutes," Lazhenko radioed them.

Despite the maddening battle with her suit, Cory knew she'd made progress. She was closer to the docking adapter and open space because the transmission from the *Soyuz* was steadily increasing in strength. But the realization brought no joy. She and Rushkin were only halfway through the adapter debris. There was no way they could exit the station, let alone cross to the *Soyuz*, before the Progress fired, or exploded, or whatever it was rigged to do. Not in two minutes.

Even so, she heard Lazhenko's voice again, urging them on. *"Move as quickly as you can. I am moving* Soyuz *to adapter."*

Rushkin, floating just in front of her, answered for them both, without stopping his attempts to clear the way. "Yuri, don't be idiot. If *Soyuz* gets fouled in debris, then you are lost, too."

"We are not lost yet. Move!"

Rushkin suddenly pushed farther ahead, then halted, twisting, swearing in Russian as he realized he was unable to continue forward. Behind him, Cory saw what had snagged him: a large cable, caught under the leading edge of his helmet neck-ring.

"I see it! Hold still!" she commanded. She strained to push one arm forward to grab Rushkin's boot, then pulled herself up his back until she reached the cable. She tugged it free of the metal ring.

"Okay, you can move now."

But instead, Rushkin rotated until he was facing her, visor to visor. He grabbed for her belt and shoved her toward the remains of the docking adapter. "You go first now. Grab hold of line."

The sudden movement swirled the fluid in Cory's ears and all at once she was falling and flying and spinning toward the gleaming white *Soyuz* hanging fifty feet away. Eyes wide, she spread her arms and made a grab for a jumbled coil of safety line to the side, and snagged a loop, just as she passed out of the adapter, into space. But her body kept moving in accordance with Newton's law—remaining in motion until another force could act on her. A splintered pipe slid past her. Cory held on to the line with one hand and with the other reached out, caught the pipe, and managed to pivot around her shoulder joint as her hand stopped still and her body didn't, until she faced back the way she had come, swaying at the end of the pipe, but no longer moving away from the station.

Cory's heart beat wildly until she saw Rushkin finally appear in the adapter, pulling a tangle of wires off his arm. She heard his voice in her helmet as he looked out at her and waved.

"Attach your clip to safety line. So Yuri can tow you."

Only then did Cory realize that she'd dragged the entire safety line with her. Leaving none for Rushkin. On any other station spacewalk, she thought, horrified, there would be a simple solution to his dilemma. All spacewalking astronauts wore EVA Rescue—Simplified Aid for SAFERS—small nitrogen jets capable of propelling astronauts in all directions. The SAFERs were extra security in case a spacewalker's safety line became disconnected. But Rushkin's suit had not been intended for spacewalks, and hers had no built-in SAFERs. The only way she and Rushkin could move in space was by the force of their own muscles.

Cory had her answer. She would crawl along the pipe.

"I'm bringing the line to you!" she called to Rushkin.

"No!" Rushkin waved wildly at her. *"Go with Yuri! Look! Behind you!"*

Cory had to pull herself closer to the pipe so she could rotate sideways and look behind her, to see what Rushkin saw. The *Soyuz*. Moving toward her, small flashes silently flaring from its RCS thrusters.

Then she heard Lazhenko. *"Anatoly, push away from station. Hard as you can. I'll retrieve you after Doctor Rey."*

"No, Yuri!" Rushkin shouted back. *"Take her with you! Now! You cannot outfly explosion of Progress. But I can beat countdown!"*

Cory rotated away from the *Soyuz,* to look at Rushkin, not understanding what he meant. Until he pushed himself off the mating adapter and disappeared beneath it, rapidly moving from one handhold to another.

Rushkin was going for the Progress.

Her cry and Lazhenko's overlapped. "Rushkin!" *"Anatoly! Where are you going?"*

"I am going where we should have gone in first place."

"Anatoly . . . I could have saved you . . ."

"I know, Commander. But I am only one who can save station."

Then Cory heard another voice, a faint one, over Lazhenko's radio. *"One minute."* And then, Lazhenko, a second afterward.

"Doctor Rey, please look behind you."

Cory rotated again, and for a moment, against the blinding sun, she saw an angel, wings outspread, sweeping in to save her.

But it was the *Soyuz*.

Anatoly Rushkin was her angel.

Anatoly Rushkin was dreaming of Moscow and the heat of the *banya* and the thrill of the frigid water and stopping the Progress from firing as he flew across the bottom of the American lab, moving effortlessly, no longer bothered by the throbbing pain in his left hand. Before him, at the end of the module, was the cylinder of the Pressurized Mating

Adapter 3, descending at a ninety-degree angle from the Unity node.

As Rushkin reached Adapter 3, he smoothly braked himself with his arms, then found the adapter's first hand-hold and pulled himself to it, simultaneously switching his notion of relative up and down. Rushkin smiled. Now the curving surface of the adapter was beneath him, and the immense blue and white swirl of the Pacific was directly ahead, sunlight sparkling from that distant ocean as if from the surface of the most perfect diamond. It took him less than ten seconds to fly across the adapter's length, grabbing the last handhold to stop himself from continuing into an endless fall to his home. *That will come later,* he thought calmly.

For a few seconds, Rushkin remained there, dangling from the edge of the adapter, his target in sight: the Progress supply ship, docked to the bottom of the adapter, directly beneath the center point of the station where its thrust could be equally applied.

He had only seconds to do his job.

But he was a flight engineer in the PKA. Seconds were all he needed.

Cory stretched out her hand and caught the slender hand-hold at the edge of the open airlock on the nose of the *Soyuz.* "I have it," she told Lazhenko. Her first EVA was over. But she did not feel safe. Too much had happened. And still could.

"Clip on to it, then climb in."

Cory released the tow line that was her last connection to the station, took her clip from her belt, and attached it to the handhold that was her new lifeline. Then she pulled herself into the open airlock.

"I see you, Doctor Rey."

Cory looked into the *Soyuz*, saw Lazhenko raise a hand to her in the reentry module. *"Ten seconds. Hold on, please."*

She floated in the rest of the way. Saw a fat pipe that followed the curved wall of the orbital module. Got a grip on it.

Whatever happens next, she thought. *At least I'm not alone. But Rushkin—*

The *Soyuz* began to move.

Rushkin felt euphoric as he flew down the outside of the Progress, recognizing every inch of it, knowing exactly what he was looking for. He caught hold of the port solar panel, then swung like a monkey to hang by one arm from the flared skirt of the service module surrounding the bell of its main rocket engine. The electrical supply line to the ignition chamber was painted red, impossible to miss in the bright light reflecting directly up from the Earth below.

Rushkin reached in beside the bell of the engine. "Let's see you blow it up now, you Cossacks!" He pushed down and twisted the thick connector till he felt it click, then yanked on the wire bundle and it popped free of its pin receptor, designed only to withstand the vibrations of the engine, not human intervention.

Rushkin gazed at the disconnected cable with just enough time to celebrate his triumph and glory in what he had done. He had saved the station.

Then the countdown reached zero.

The Progress engine attempted to fire.

Cory pulled herself to the edge of the open airlock to stare out at the receding station as Mission Control's countdown whispered in her ear. The *Soyuz* was on the starboard side of the station, where Lazhenko had moved the reentry module to avoid any forward spray of debris.

A brilliant white form floated at the lowest part of the Progress spacecraft, the lowest part of the station. Cory blinked. *Rushkin!*

She called out to Lazhenko, sure that he could see him too, through the *Soyuz* porthole. "Do you see him? What's he doing?"

"Anatoly is attempting to disconnect main-engine power line. To prevent ignition." There was pride in Lazhenko's voice. And resignation.

Cory watched without comprehension as a gout of white vapor sprayed explosively from the Progress and swept Rushkin away from the service module an instant before the Progress silently exploded in a puff of what looked like white steam.

"What happened?" she asked, confused. There'd been no flash, no concussion, and, it seemed to her, no damage to the station.

"Oxidizer line ruptured . . . but without hydrazine . . . did not ignite." Lazhenko's voice broke, choked.

"Does that mean we can save—"

Lazhenko interrupted her, his grief raw and unconcealed. *"Anatoly is gone. Oxidizer . . . it will eat through spacesuit in seconds. He is hero now."*

Rushkin had sacrificed himself. For her. Cory felt sick. *This is what it's really like to be in Mitchell's world,* she thought. In Antarctica, she'd only been a passenger.

Then Lazhenko's shout filled her helmet. *"Doctor Rey, look at station!"*

As Cory clung to the opening of the *Soyuz* airlock, from her vantage point it seemed the entire massive structure was bending, as if caught in some unusual optical distortion.

"Force of venting gas . . . it added more stress to truss!"

Then she saw the cause of Lazhenko's excitement. And

what Rushkin's sacrifice had bought. The vast wings of the
port solar arrays, which had been partially disconnected,
changing the balance of the station and forcing the station-
keeping thrusters into near constant operation, had broken
free! The Progress depressurization had added just enough
momentum to the station to sever the final connecting
pipes and conduits that held the damaged section in place.
The array, gleaming blue-black in the sunlight, was drifting
away from the station now, an enormous leaf of metal
slowly tumbling as if caught in a gust of wind. On the rest
of the station, the RCS thrusters had stopped firing.

"It's stable!" Lazhenko was laughing, crying. *"He did save
the station! . . . Anatoly . . . Anatoly . . ."*

Cory slowly swung the *Soyuz* airlock hatch shut. On
Hutton, Doyle, and Oster. McArdle, Lugreb, and Dante.
Norman.

And Anatoly Rushkin.

If she survived, and if Major Bailey ever found him, she
had another secret to share with Mitchell Webber.

She understood him better now.

7

MITCH WEBBER LOOKED through the forward view-port of the Space Operations Vehicle to see the Earth, 24,000 miles away, a perfect blue shimmering sphere. But the intricately detailed illusion was false, a digital image created by the simulator's holographic projectors and his liquid-crystal goggles.

"Closing at five hundred meters," a voice from the seat beside him said. "You'll want to bring it down to twenty." The voice belonged to Colonel Daniel Varik, his SOV copilot.

Webber turned his attention back to his main pilot's display screen, pulled back slightly on both hand controllers, and watched his velocity drop relative to target. The SOV simulator controls were smooth and intuitive for a pilot of his experience. *If the machine they simulated were real,* he thought, *it would be magnificent.*

"You're sliding in just under the mark, Captain . . . watch the pitch and even her out. . . ."

Webber's helicopter instincts urged him to use his feet for this final stage, using pedals to keep the SOV aligned with its target in all six degrees of movement. But, incredibly, the craft he was piloting in this simulated mission required input from only two hand controllers, and Webber felt the wide, low-ceilinged cabin shift around him in response to his manipulation of those controls.

"Almost . . . almost . . . ," Varik said.

Webber saw the target box on the main display flash green and he locked the controls. *Dead-on,* he thought, pleased with himself.

"Not bad," Varik said. "Let's check the target."

Webber grinned. "If it's still there. I've crashed into it twice."

"Everyone crashes at the beginning," Varik admitted. "This thing is one big mother. Takes some getting used to." He tightened his restraints. "Do a one-eighty and you'll see the prize in the Cracker Jack box."

A one-eighty roll in a simulator, Webber marveled to himself. He'd been in many fighter simulators capable of full rotation for upset training, but none had ever been this large.

A full eight feet across and fifteen feet deep, the SOV flight cabin had four permanently installed seats up front. There was room to add four more in the rear, the final number dependent on individual-mission requirements for personnel and payload.

Webber was intrigued that, unlike most other flight decks, this one was not tapered toward the front. The slope of its low ceiling, only five feet above the deck, began just above the side-by-side pilot's and copilot's seats to merge into the viewport. And that viewport was wide, almost six feet across and four feet deep.

Although Webber could see that the viewport was inset approximately eight inches from the exterior surface of the vehicle, there seemed to be no other clues to the outer configuration of the SOV.

Then he amended his observation. There was a crude, wedge-shaped outline of the simulated craft on one of the status-display screens.

Dedicated monitors filled the two curved horseshoe-shaped consoles scooped out before his and Varik's pilot and copilot stations. The screens were in a cleanly organized palette of colors relating to function: Flight displays were green; life-support, blue; communications, purple; electrical subsystems, yellow; and weapons, red.

When Webber had first taken the pilot's seat in the simulator and noticed the red screens, the first thing he'd said was, "Isn't there a treaty outlawing weapons in space?"

"The SOV doesn't carry anything like that," Varik said. "Outer Space Treaty of 1967, Article Four, prohibits weapons of mass destruction in space." The colonel continued to look straight ahead as he added, "Same article authorizes the use of 'any equipment or facility required for the peaceful exploration of space.' Sometimes, you have to use weapons to maintain the peace."

Webber tightened his own restraints without further response. He'd heard this kind of reasoning before. It was clear the legality of arming a spacecraft had been examined, and appropriate loopholes had been found. When the time was right, Varik, or someone, would tell him what weapons the SOV would carry.

He locked his translational controller and gave a small twist to the rotational. At once, the SOV cabin began to rotate left to right, and the distant Earth arced convincingly past the viewport.

When the cabin was completely upside down, the roll stopped, and Webber glanced down, or up, through the viewport to see what appeared to be a large satellite, apparently fifty feet away, with two narrow solar panels affixed like a pair of wings. On its opposite side was a large mesh antenna, circular, with struts like an open umbrella, perhaps thirty feet across.

"Communications satellite," Webber said admiringly. The quality of the simulated view was impressive.

"Look closer," Varik said.

Webber studied the satellite's blocky components, looking for unique detail. Some components were wrapped in gold foil, others painted white. Then he saw a splash of color: a red rectangle with a gold star in its upper left corner, surrounded by smaller flecks of gold representing smaller stars.

Webber refined his assessment. "A *Chinese* communications satellite."

"Apstar Six," Varik said. "Launched two years ago, in geosynchronous orbit more or less over New Guinea. About half its circuits handle civilian television and telecommunication traffic for China. The rest of the circuits are for a backup PLA military network." The colonel pointed to the satellite. "Now look to the left of the flag, around seven o'clock."

Webber complied but found nothing of note. "All I see is a . . . I don't know, a heat exchanger? The blue box."

"That blue box has a two-pound shaped charge that will shred the inside of the satellite without cracking its case and releasing debris."

Webber forced his neck to move against the pressure of gravity, so he could look over at Varik.

Varik was smiling, the rare expression animating his usually impassive face. "China ever decides to move against Taiwan, the PLA's going to find it's suddenly without any communications capability better than a walkie-talkie. I attached that charge to that satellite myself."

The satellite was real? Webber looked around the simulator's flight cabin. "This thing's operational?"

Varik nodded. "Spin us around."

Webber rolled the cabin again to bring them right side up. *There's a chance I could fly in space someday!* he thought. "How long?" he asked, hoping this time the colonel could and would be more forthcoming. And Varik was.

"The Space Operations Vehicle had its first flight three years ago, which is when Salyard made me my offer. But, the Air Force—since '98, the Space Force—we've been in space since the end of Apollo, beginning with modified Apollo-type command and service modules from Rockwell. Back then, we were just a smaller operation within the Air Force: Project White Lightning."

Webber tried not to laugh, but couldn't help himself. The project name was clearly some general's idea of a joke. "White Lightning. As in moonshine?"

Either oblivious or immune to humor, intentional or otherwise, the colonel ignored Webber's reaction and question. "Anyway, when the shuttle program started, we tried to switch over to that, but . . . after *Challenger,* we needed a more dependable system. So in '92, with Project Constant Star, we began launching two-man, lifting-body vehicles, miniature shuttles, right from Vandenberg."

"No one's noticed these launches?" Webber said, having trouble believing what he'd just heard. Almost everyone in the aerospace community, himself included, had heard the rumors of classified Apollo follow-on missions into Earth orbit back in the seventies, as well as those of the military's Manned Orbiting Laboratory that came after NASA's Skylab space station. But Varik had just *confirmed* those rumors. *And* revealed the existence of a *second* crewed spaceflight program in operation beyond NASA's.

"All the time, Captain," Varik said. "We don't hide them. This is Vandenberg. We call them secret DoD satellite launches. They go into polar orbits just like spy satellites.

And after they reach orbit, they disappear, just like spy satellites. If we sometimes set off an explosion in the original orbital track where ground-based stations pick it up, we issue a press release saying a DoD satellite failed to reach orbit or malfunctioned. There're enough launches and enough missing satellites to provide all the cover we need. It's a regular traffic jam up there."

Now Webber was back on more familiar ground: The orbit of the Chinese satellite didn't fit the colonel's story. Once again he wasn't being told everything. "That Chinese satellite wasn't in a polar orbit. Not if it was geosynchronous."

But Varik had a good answer ready. "This isn't our only launch facility. And for changing orbits . . . give us enough fuel and we can go anywhere."

Webber tried a different question. He patted the arm of his pilot's seat. "Does this thing carry enough fuel?"

"Not at launch. But the Space Force runs on the Air Force model."

"You've prepositioned fuel in space." Webber's response was not a question.

"Captain, this country has a fully functioning, military, manned spaceflight capability," Varik said with cool pride. "We use it to gather intelligence on foreign satellites, and to place neutralizing devices on potential enemy satellites. We are able to repair and upgrade our own defense satellites much more quickly and efficiently than any shuttle crew. And should any space-based adversary attempt to threaten our country or our country's interests, I guarantee you they will cease to be space-based within hours, without any indication of action on our part. Space is the ultimate high ground of the twenty-first century, and we own it."

Webber's gut reaction was anything but cool. *Cory.* "Does the Space Force have the capability of sending a rescue mission to the ISS?" he asked.

Varik nodded, as if unsurprised by the question, almost as if he had been expecting it. "Since the first ISS component launched, we've had a contingency rescue/resupply mission capable of launch within eighteen hours of a critical ONS. There's a rescue crew on the pad right now, in one of these SOVs. That mission's holding at T minus three hours until we learn whether the Russian effort to get a suit to Doctor Rey was successful. If there had been more survivors than could be carried on the *Soyuz*—"

"I understand," Webber said, his quick hope crushed, hating to hear the rest.

The colonel continued anyway, "—we would have put our crew onboard and continued with the launch. But there's nothing we can do now that the *Soyuz* can't. We're just waiting to find out if we're really necessary."

Webber nodded. The only good news was that, for the first time, he felt he could be at home in his new branch of service. The colonel had just told him that the Force had developed a rescue capacity and was ready to use it—as a last resort. It was the honorable thing to do. From his own experience with secret military projects, Webber knew that it would require an extraordinary decision on the part of the Pentagon to reveal the existence of something like the U.S. Space Force merely to save one civilian astronaut.

"So," he made himself ask Varik, "how many of these SOVs are there?" It was time to get a sense of where he might fit into flight assignments.

"We have two operational. The *Falcon* and the *Eagle*. A third one's going to be delivered next year. Plus, we still have two of the two-man lifting bodies. But they're just for quick missions in low Earth orbit. They haven't flown since Iraq."

Webber saw no reason not to be blunt. "How many pilots do you have?"

"Enough," Varik said, his second smile broader than

the last one. "We do a lot of cross-training. Everyone who launches in one of these has enough training to bring it home on automated systems. But for rendezvous with foreign satellites, and for repair and upgrade missions to our own, we use specialists. I don't have a hand in flight assignments, but my best guess is you'll get the fourth chair position for a routine maintenance flight within the year. Specialist pilot takes about another year past that."

Webber gave a silent whistle. In space within a year, flying in space within two. "At NASA, it takes six to eight years to make pilot. That's why I never applied."

"Their loss," Varik said. "With us, on average, everyone in the astronaut pool gets at least one flight a year. And that number's going up."

"Amazing," Webber said quietly.

"I know the feeling, Captain."

"What's that?"

"Good news, and no one to share it with."

Webber merely nodded, suddenly feeling exposed. That had been exactly what he had been thinking. He was going to experience something that only a handful of humans would ever share in his lifetime—a handful that now included Cory—but who knew if she'd even survive today, let alone be talking to him a year from now. "This has been outstanding, Colonel. Thank you for arranging a sneak preview."

He checked his watch. He was due to leave for Houston within the hour.

Varik slipped off the large, tinted liquid-crystal shutter goggles he wore. "Usually the simulator's going twenty-four, seven. But with the . . . rescue crew on standby, we have a lot of downtime."

Webber took off his own set of goggles. The bright light

in the cabin made him squint, but as he once more looked out through the viewport, he saw a thick screen of translucent mesh about ten feet away, and on it a circular blue smear of flickering light where the Earth used to be. The simulator's holographic projection system was the best he'd ever seen.

Varik leaned forward to shut down the simulator controls, and at the same time spoke into his commset. "This is SOV to Central. We're done here. Shutting down."

Webber heard a hiss in his commset speaker. They had flown the simulated mission under radio silence, which Varik had told him was of critical importance for any flight near a communications satellite, where radio channels could bleed into one another. Now the simulator technician who had filled in for the voice of Space Force Central Command came on.

"Copy that, SOV. Leave the shutdown for now. We have General Salyard out here for Captain Webber."

Webber glanced questioningly at Varik, who was in the midst of unfastening his restraints. "Watch your head," Varik advised. It wasn't clear if the colonel was referring to departing the simulator or talking to the general. But all that concerned Webber now was that only bad news would have brought Salyard out to him so soon after they'd last spoken. *What if he's here because of Cory?*

Though Webber had seen death, had dealt death, had escaped death by seconds and by inches, the cold equations of his profession still could not shield him from its impact when it was so personal.

He shrugged off his chest restraints and got to his feet. Being careful to keep crouched over, he made his decision about which of the two ways into the SOV flight cabin to take—the round airlock in the deck at the back of the cabin, or the square hatch in the ceiling, midway.

The ceiling hatch was what they'd used to enter, so Webber located the folded-down ladder there, opened the hatch, and climbed out.

A white-jumpsuited simulator technician on a catwalk, ten feet away from the hull of the cabin, swung a cable-suspended walkway over to him. Webber waited until he saw the technician make sure the hooks on the end of the walkway were locked into the restraining bolts by the hatch. Then he crossed the walkway, his footsteps clanging on its metal surface. As he stepped off onto the catwalk, he heard Varik's boots hit the walkway behind him.

The catwalk ended on an upper level of the huge containment room where a door stood open. With Varik still following, Webber entered the harshly lit, computer-filled control room, and saw General Salyard. The general's lips were pursed.

"Colonel. Captain. There appears to have been another explosion on the ISS. From what we can gather, the Russians tried to use the Progress supply ship to boost the station's orbit and . . . the Progress exploded. We believe the *Soyuz* capsule was hit by debris and . . . we have lost contact."

Varik asked the question that Webber could not. "No survivors?"

Salyard's eyes moved to Webber. "I'm sorry, Captain."

Webber's first response, in no way betrayed by his expression, was the double gut-punch of overpowering loss, and guilt. Over the past hour, Cory had been alone up there in the real world, trapped, facing death in a way she was never meant to, while, down here, he'd been in a fantasy world, playing with a fifty-million-dollar video game, lost in visions of his own space adventure. His call to Bailey, his arrangements to get to Houston, to somehow greet Cory on her return and let her know how the prospect of losing her had made everything clear to him—all of it useless. He'd been useless.

Salyard checked his watch. "In about thirty minutes, whatever's left up there will be passing over an OWL site, and we'll be taking high-resolution images. But for now, all that space surveillance radar tracking is showing is a debris cloud with nothing large enough to be an intact module."

"Thank you, General. I appreciate being told in person."

"We look after our own, Captain. If you need extra personal time, you take it."

Webber shook his head. The mission continued. *But then,* he thought, *it had to.* "No, General. Seven days should be fine. Thank you again."

"Captain, can I call for transport to the field? For your flight?" It was Varik trying to be helpful.

Webber shook his head again, overwhelmed by dark thoughts of balance in the universe. Two possibilities, one gained, one lost. Going into space himself. Cory ending up there, alone. Neither possibility anything he'd ever dreamed might happen.

"Not necessary. I won't be going to Houston. I'll get a flight back to Hill."

"I'll have my sergeant handle the details," Salyard said. "Anything else we can do?"

Webber fought to keep his voice even and unemotional. "I could use a phone."

"Certainly," the general said. "The old contractors' offices downstairs, where we met. You'll find one there."

Varik opened the door and Webber left.

He wanted to find out if Bailey knew more. And why she hadn't called him first.

8

LYNDON B. JOHNSON SPACE CENTER
ISS FLIGHT CONTROL ROOM
13:50 CST, FRIDAY, APRIL 4

IN THE LAST FEW SECONDS, the only sound in the Blue Flight Control Room was the subdued voice of the Public Affairs Officer at the back, reciting the countdown. All those in the crowded room, including Chief Administrator Caruso and the other NASA staff, Kai Teller of TTI, and Stepan Ivanovich of the Russian Aviation and Space Agency, stared helplessly at the display screen showing Russian telemetry by way of Space Command. There was no way to interrupt the countdown because Mission Control-Moscow remained out of touch. Ignition of the Progress spacecraft's main engine would occur. And without video from the station, there was no way to make sense of the garbled voice communications coming from the *Soyuz*. No way to know the positions of Cory Rey and Anatoly Rushkin, nor if Yuri Lazhenko had moved the *Soyuz* out of harm's way.

Caruso suspected he hadn't. Lazhenko was a pilot. He would not balk at the last second, give up his mission. Neither had her husband. The last time she'd heard Phil's voice was on the flight data recorder tape, calmly describing the techniques he was using to regain control of the X-32B Joint Strike Fighter prototype he was testing. His voice had never faltered, stopped only at the instant his aircraft plowed into the Nevada desert. Yuri Lazhenko was no different. The best astronauts never were. It was Caruso's belief that the character traits NASA sought so avidly in potential space travelers were the very same ones that made the chosen few such single-minded, self-directed, pains-in-the-ass. And yet, when everything that could go wrong did go wrong, those same qualities also made them heroes.

"... five ... four ..."

Caruso blinked as a group of numbers suddenly disappeared on the telemetry screen. "What the hell ... ?" A chorus of other voices from the floor told her others shared her surprise.

"... two ... one ..."

Now all the telemetry numbers winked out as Spacecom's satellites lost contact with the Progress.

"That's it," Teller said, but Caruso was not so willing to concede defeat. Not when there was an unanswered question.

"Someone—anyone," she said to the room at large. "Why was that first block of numbers blanked out at five seconds?"

"Uh, that was in the electrical bus subgrouping . . ." Caruso turned in the direction of the voice, saw a stocky, dark-haired woman at the ODIN console, checking a page in a binder manual.

"According to this . . . ," the woman said, "it was the main-ignition, circuit-status indicator."

"What would make the numbers go out?" Caruso asked.

"If the circuit went dead, Ms. Caruso."

Caruso had a sudden flash of insight. She turned to Ivanovich. "Rushkin's a flight engineer. Would he know how to physically disable the Progress engine?"

The Russian liaison officer looked pained. "Madam Chief Administrator, even I would not know where to begin to do such a thing. Perhaps Anatoly Rushkin could, but . . . all telemetry stopped at zero. I do not think he could disable entire spacecraft."

Caruso hit the transmit switch on her commset. "Major Bailey, are you picking up anything from the *Soyuz?*"

"Negative, Houston. We lost the carrier at ignition. No signals at all from the station or the Soyuz." Bailey cleared her throat. *"We have just received a new radar return from Kaena Point."*

"Go ahead," Caruso said, but she braced herself for bad news. Kaena Point was a military radar station on Oahu, Hawaii. Normally, it functioned as part of the Western Test Range, tracking test firings of Minuteman missiles and other military rockets over the Pacific. But when no tests were scheduled, it supported Spacecom's Space Surveillance Center, located in Major Bailey's own Cheyenne Mountain. Kaena was also one of the most accurate ground-based radars capable of tracking orbital objects, and it had been tracking the ISS on each pass it made over the Pacific since the first sign of trouble on the station.

"Kaena Point confirms a sudden debris cloud occupying space station's orbital position. They make out no hard contact with anything large enough to be an intact module or the Soyuz. *The debris cloud is spreading out along the orbital path, consistent with the release of gas and propellant, and consistent with critical failure of all station components."*

Bailey's news left little room for hope. "When will we have our next chance at visual imagery?" Caruso asked.

"Approximately twenty-five minutes. The de—what remains of the station should be passing within range of the CONUS OWL facility at that time."

"Thank you, Major Bailey." There was nothing more for Caruso to do or say at Mission Control. The shuttle, the station, and ten irreplaceable lives were no longer anyone's mission.

Caruso carefully replaced her commset on the console. "I have to call the president," she said to Teller and Ivanovich.

"Tovah, I'm so sorry," Teller said.

Ivanovich just turned away from them, seemingly too overcome to speak.

It was a toss-up, Caruso thought wearily, which of the three of them, herself, Teller, and Ivanovich, looked worse. "You know what I'm afraid of?" she asked Teller.

He shook his head.

"That we didn't just lose the station. That we just lost NASA. The shuttle, the station . . . what's that worth? Sixty-five billion dollars? Losing *Columbia* put us on the brink, and now we've gone into the abyss. How many politicians do you think will be willing to vote us money again?"

Teller's response was unexpected. "You know what I'm afraid of?" he asked in a low voice. "Whoever it is who gets the *next* sixty-five billion dollars. Because that's who gains if NASA's put out of business."

Caruso's eyes widened. She knew exactly what Teller was suggesting, but the idea was unthinkable. That, after years of watching for enemies from without, America had been blindsided by enemies from within.

"I want to know whatever it is you know," she demanded. "No holding back this time."

"I haven't got anything definite yet," Teller began, then stopped as he saw the suspicion on Caruso's face. "Tovah, I swear I've just been putting the pieces together. Did you tell the FBI about Farren?"

She nodded slowly. She had found a minute to make that call. But now a disturbing thought was gaining ground within her that Teller could be manipulating her. That there was something he did not want to share with her. *But why? And what?*

"Then let's see what they turn up. With the station gone—conveniently along with all the witnesses—Ed might be the smoking gun we need."

"The smoking gun we need for what?"

Teller's eyes locked on hers. "Let me put it this way, Tovah. If someone *has* just declared war on NASA, will you fight back?"

Caruso felt her neck stiffen painfully as her mind filled with all the responses she could give Teller, none of them permissible or advisable. *Because,* she thought, *if NASA's biggest rival, biggest enemy has somehow done this, I am going to personally see to it that it is blown out of space, and turned back into the branch of the Army that spawned it in 1947.*

Caruso stalked out of the FCR, ready to bring down the United States Air Force.

CHEYENNE MOUNTAIN AIR FORCE STATION
SPACE CONTROL CENTER

Major Bailey picked up the gray phone when it rang. There was only one outside caller the switchboard would put through now.

"Captain, where are you?"

Webber's answer was unexpected. *"Vandenberg."*

"You must have been down a silo, then," Bailey said. "I've had half the base looking for you for hours."

"No one told me that, Major. I was in a training session."

Bailey believed the best way to deal with bad news was

head-on. "Captain, I know this won't be easy, but you were the only person she wanted to talk to."

"She said that?"

Bailey's throat tightened as she heard the open anguish in Webber's voice. "She had a message for you, and just for you. And when we couldn't track you down, she . . . she told it to me." Bailey hurried on before Webber could respond. She had no intention of repeating—on a monitored line—the doctor's startling account of discovery and assault. "Captain, is there any way you can get out here?"

"Colorado Springs?"

"Yeah," Bailey said, grateful that the captain was quick-witted like her darling husband. Webber had not asked about the message. "You can stay at the house, see the kids. Dom would love to see you again. And we could talk."

"Yeah. I've got a couple of days' leave. I could be out tomorrow."

"Tomorrow would be good," Bailey said briskly. Even through their weak connection, she heard Webber's flat tone of despair.

Bailey couldn't keep her voice from softening, despite whoever might be listening to them. "She never gave up, Captain. Had the suit on. From what we could hear from the *Soyuz,* she got out of the lab module. She just . . . they all just ran out of time."

Webber was silent for a moment before asking her something else she couldn't answer, but this time because she didn't know. *"What about the Progress? Any idea what made it explode?"*

"Not even I can get through to Moscow, Captain. I don't know if they screwed up, if there was another malfunction . . . no one knows. It's an unforgiving environment and—" Bailey broke off. "Just a moment, Captain."

A flashing red light and a low warning tone from the

command center's PA system sent Bailey's gaze to the main board as a new, flickering orbital track suddenly appeared over the Pacific. *Scratch that,* she thought in alarm. It was a *sub*orbital track.

"Major?" Webber said. *"You have to go?"*

Bailey stared at the origin point of the track. "Captain, stay on the line, would you?" She put the receiver down, brought up additional screens on her console, looking for more information.

She looked up as a fresh-faced young technician ran up to her station with a printout.

"It's debris from the station, Major. Reentering over the Pacific. Going to hit someplace inland . . ." The technician read the coordinates off the sheet. "Approximately one one eight degrees west, three-fiver north. Developing."

Bailey swiftly typed the longitude and latitude into her keyboard, saw the ETEM map come up on her rightmost screen. "I want better resolution, Lieutenant," Bailey said sharply. "And you take another look at what's on the screen. That track is clean, no wobble."

The rattled technician looked at the screen, panic-stricken. Clearly, she didn't know what Bailey meant. So Bailey told her. "It's not debris, Lieutenant. That's a controlled reentry track."

The young woman's mouth dropped open in surprise. "The *Soyuz?*"

"Either that, or we're under attack by Martians. Get me a precise impact point, *now,* Lieutenant. That track's not going to deviate."

"Yes, Major." The lieutenant almost flew back to her workstation.

Bailey picked up the gray receiver. "You still there, Captain?"

"Yes. What is it?"

"Are you still on Freefall reserve?"

Webber hesitated. *"Yes . . ."*

"Well then get your butt out to an assembly point." Bailey checked the time readout. "U.S. Space Command is calling a continental Freefall Alert, and Vandenberg is the staging base for the team closest to the impact zone."

"Something from the station?" Webber asked, as if he were afraid to know the answer. But his voice was no longer despondent.

"It's the *Soyuz*. Someone's coming home, Captain Webber. You hurry, you can be the first to say hello."

MOJAVE DESERT

In the last fifteen minutes of the one-hour night flight from Vandenberg, the Sikorsky KH-60R helicopter carrying the Freefall recovery team switched over to hushed flight mode as it descended to five hundred feet, flying at 130 mph.

In hushed mode, the KH-60R burned thirty percent more fuel, and so could not carry the weapons and armor of its combat variants. But fuel cost was not critical for the specialized, low-observability surveillance and recovery missions for which the Star Hawk had been designed. From the ground, the Star Hawk's overhead passage mimicked the sound of the evening desert breeze.

Outfitted with five rotor blades instead of the usual four, the KH variant of the Hawk model used its extra blade to reduce individual blade-loading by twenty percent, allowing each blade to use a smaller—and thus less noisy—angle of attack. The Star Hawk's extra blade also permitted the helo's engine to run at a slower—and quieter—speed, since the entire blade assembly could move more slowly as well.

The extra-blade advantages were only the first of several

engineering techniques responsible for dropping the Star Hawk's acoustical signature from the 86 decibels of a Special Operations MH-60K Pave Hawk, to a remarkable 60 decibels, scarcely louder than the sound of normal conversation. The other techniques included an engine compartment constructed from a honeycombed carbon-fiber material that successfully deadened multiple-frequency noise, and dynamic antinoise generators that worked like pilots' sound-deadening earphones to flatten any additional noise escaping from the helo's soundproofed exhaust.

Within the sound-insulated crew and passenger compartment, the Star Hawk's noise-reduction properties were even more remarkable. Mitch Webber did not need to wear headphones and a mike to talk with the helo's flight crew of three or with the others in his Freefall team.

Like Webber, the other Freefall personnel onboard were military, all selected as local-reserve Freefall recovery specialists. Freefall Red Team was one of twenty-eight first-response teams based at American military installations around the world. Freefall's specific mission was to be first on-site whenever U.S. aerospace hardware returned to Earth in a foreign location. And, also, whenever foreign aerospace hardware returned to Earth in CONUS—the continental United States—or other American areas of interest. A version of Freefall had been operational three years before the official beginning of the space age: October 4, 1957—the launch of the world's first artificial satellite, *Sputnik,* which marked a technological achievement by the Soviet Union that had been feared by America for a decade. In the years since, the specialized operation had gone by many different code names: Moondust, Blowfly, Longshot, and Skyfall, among others.

Each member of the current Freefall team on this mission, including Webber, was outfitted in a standard drab-green Air Force jumpsuit with no insignia or names, though two of the team carried role-specific equipment. The small aluminum briefcase braced between Captain Paulsen Mack's boots contained the sensitive detectors and sniffers that the safety officer would be using to scan the retrieval site for radiation and toxic chemicals. The team linguist, Lieutenant Rayne Fujito, fluent in both Mandarin and Russian, carried a Machine Vision Translation Unit at least twice the size of the one used by Colonel Daniel Varik in Red Cobra 8. The model was new to Webber.

Major Josef Grego, the propulsion engineer, a quiet man who also commanded the range safety department at Vandenberg, and Webber, serving as the airframe and flight-control engineer, were Red Team's retrieved-vehicle experts. And Master Sergeant Rak Summerall, at least four inches taller than Webber's own five feet, eleven inches, was the security guard—what Webber thought of as Red Team's muscle. The sergeant's task would be to secure the impact zone, a broad responsibility that included everything from diverting civilians to digging a diversion-trench for any leaking substances.

As a Freefall reservist, Webber had participated in five recovery alerts with similar teams. Two alerts had been false alarms: Whatever had been tracked as heading for an impact had burned up in the atmosphere. Of Webber's three subsequent outings, the first ended with the recovery of a long-lost weather satellite launched in the eighties, which had failed to reach its intended orbit and had apparently collided with another piece of space debris ten years later. That piece of space junk eventually came to rest in a smoking hole outside a gas station in Warren County, Ohio. Since the recovered object was not a vehicle, Webber had had no tasks to perform. He'd spent the rest of the mission listening to the local team talk about other, more interesting recoveries. Some of the tales had been quite unusual.

He had been of more use on the Freefall team that retrieved a MiG-25 Foxbat from a small airfield near Coyame, Mexico, where mechanical failure had forced the jet down. Having been purchased by a Mexican drug lord who intended to use it against a rival's smuggling operations, the Russian jet had been flown from Brazil. The last word Webber had on the case, the Justice Department was still trying to figure out how the Foxbat had turned up in Brazil in the first place. The sophisticated jet was now at Groom Lake, Nevada.

His last and most recent Freefall mission had been undeniably intriguing. Though requiring even less of his talents than the weather-satellite mission, it had offered considerably more mystery than the Foxbat mission. Webber's Freefall team had been scrambled from San Diego in response to an alert from the Space Surveillance Center in Cheyenne Mountain, and flown into the Chocolate Mountains near the California–Arizona border. Then, just as they saw what appeared to be an incandescent ball of fire apparently stuck to the side of a cliff, they were surrounded by three other helicopters, and were recalled.

As was usual for those in his line of work, when he later heard the rumors about what had happened that day, he never discussed them, and even tried not to think about them. At least, not until the day someone of a higher rank raised the topic.

But Webber knew that this, his sixth Freefall mission, was one for the record books. And so did the rest of his team. Spacecom had confirmed the suborbital track and velocity of the reentering object as consistent with the *Soyuz* capsule from the International Space Station. For the first time in all their experience, a Freefall mission was a rescue mission. And though Webber knew he should concentrate only on probabilities and what the next moment might bring, he could only think of possibilities.

Since the *Soyuz* was not programmed for automatic entry, the assumption was that at least one survivor was onboard, likely Station Commander Yuri Lazhenko. Spacecom had also advised Freefall Red Team of another outside chance, that Lazhenko had succeeded in retrieving his flight engineer, Anatoly Rushkin, and, even more remote, one of the shuttle's payload specialists, Dr. Corazon Rey.

A voice rang out in the near-silence of the passenger compartment. "We got it," the copilot shouted out from the flight deck.

Webber pressed his face against the dark window beside him, saw only the barest suggestion of the desert floor flashing by in waning moonlight.

"And we've got company," the copilot added.

Webber knew the flight crew were using Forward Looking Infrared viewers so, for them, the *Soyuz* reentry module, superheated by its fiery plunge through the atmosphere, would be like a highway flare against the cooler desert floor. He got to his feet, braced one hand against the high ceiling, and stared ahead through the flight deck windows. But he still saw only darkness.

He moved forward to look beyond the pilots' bulky helmets at the FLIR display, one of four computer screens in their console. On that screen he saw a bright-green, gumdrop shape that he recognized—a *Soyuz* reentry module, seemingly intact and undeformed.

Then Webber saw something that made him go on alert: four ghostly figures to one side of the module. Whoever was down there, at least one of them had not arrived from space. The *Soyuz* could only carry three passengers.

The Sikorsky KH-60R slowed for landing.

Webber turned around and went back to his team. "Sergeant Summerall, we have at least one civilian down there. Possibly four."

"Understood, sir," the sergeant said. He unhooked a large flashlight from his belt, and checked the position of the holster holding his nonlethal stun-dart gun. "I'm good to go."

"Brace for touchdown," the pilot said.

The helicopter rocked to a stop and Summerall was up at once, sliding open the starboard hatch to jump out into darkness. The chill desert air flowed past Webber's face as he sprinted through a deeply shadowed landscape after Summerall, both of them heading for the charred and blackened reentry module fifty feet away, haloed by the brilliant spotlight from the KH-60R.

As he ran, Webber could see smoke curling out from beneath the capsule, where four solid-fuel retrorockets had fired in the last five feet of its descent. A deep furrow in the sandy soil told him that the module had been dragged about twenty feet while its parachute collapsed slowly. The Spacecom estimates had put touchdown at least twenty minutes earlier.

He stopped in front of the spacecraft, and directed the beam of his flashlight along and up the thick, orange parachute cords that trailed from its large round open hatch. The hatch was offset from the blunt nose of the *Soyuz* capsule. Billowing parachute fabric swelled in the rising wind, and appeared to stretch for hundreds of feet. There was no sign of fouling.

He swung his flashlight beam to one side of the capsule, where Summerall had cornered his four targets. Four denim-clad teenagers, two girls and two boys, their dirt bikes on the ground behind them, beside a pile of nylon backpacks, were silhouetted against the low mesquite bushes and the thick and twisted skeletal forms of the desert's Joshua trees. All four stared past Summerall in shocked amazement at the smoking reentry module.

"Step away from the spacecraft," Summerall said as he moved to put his substantial frame between the campers and the *Soyuz* capsule.

"Spacecraft?!" one of the boys exclaimed. He turned to the girl beside him. "See? I told you! Silent black helicopters! UFO recovery! This is just like the *X-Files!*"

"Are there aliens inside that thing?" the second girl asked Captain Mack in wonder as she watched him aim the metal probe of a gamma particle detector at the module.

"Don't you kids watch any news?" the safety officer asked with irritation. "It's the lifeboat from the space station."

"Ladies and gentlemen, please. Step away," Summerall repeated firmly, walking toward the teenagers with arms outspread, as if intending to sweep them up.

"Like, did something happen to the space station?" the second boy asked as they all stumbled backward into their dirt bikes.

"Don't you get it?" the other girl whispered. "It's a UFO cover-up. They're just saying that."

With a sympathetic glance to Summerall, Webber dismissed the civilians from his mind and moved quickly around the spacecraft, checking its other, unlit side with his flashlight. The crew hatch on top wasn't open. *Not so good,* Webber thought.

He located the porthole, approached it, ignoring the heat that radiated from the module's blackened skin, its temperature hot enough to burn. Acrid smoke from the rockets stung his eyes. He peered in through the porthole, saw lights on the flight controls, knew that meant some form of internal power was still working. His flashlight beam fell on two cosmonauts in spacesuits, and a third empty seat. Neither cosmonaut was moving.

"We got two!" Webber shouted. "Let's get the hatch off!"

Major Grego was beside him in moments with his hands in linked position, ready to boost the long-limbed Lieutenant Fujito to the top of the *Soyuz* capsule. The linguist carefully braced herself against the craft's hot skin, then used the cuff of her flight suit sleeve to rub carbon off the crew hatch.

Webber waited, intent, as the backlit Fujito reached for something on the top of the module, gave a powerful tug, then jumped down and shouted, "Clear!" as she retreated from the craft. Five seconds later, a loud pop sounded and the top hatch swung up on one side, more smoke wisping away from the charges that had blown it open.

In the same instant, Webber tossed his flashlight aside and leapt up on the module, giving no thought to the searing heat as he gripped the edge of the open hatch and scrambled up the rough-textured insulation that had protected the module from the ten-thousand-degree heat of reentry. He reached for the hatch cover and threw it back, then squeezed through the narrow opening, barely a yard across, and dropped into the capsule, feet first, to land on the empty seat. The module interior smelled like burnt rubber and scorched metal.

Webber turned first to the cosmonaut in the left-hand seat, knowing that was where a passenger would sit, farthest from the controls. He cracked the seal on the cosmonaut's helmet, then flipped back the helmet.

It was Yuri Lazhenko. The cosmonaut's eyes were closed. His mouth was open.

"It's Lazhenko!" Webber shouted. He reached into the helmet, slapped the Russian's face as best he could. "Lazhenko!"

The cosmonaut groaned.

"He's alive!" Webber twisted around to the pilot's seat, to the figure whose spacesuit was bulkier than Lazhenko's, cracked the seal on the suit's visor and slid it open. A flash-light beam stabbed through the porthole and lit the small, heart-shaped face within the shadows.

Webber lost the ability to speak and breathe as Cory's dark eyes opened, blinked, looked up at him.

"Mitchell? It's about bloody time," she murmured.

Webber knew better than to argue with her.

MAJOR WILHEMINA BAILEY WAS accustomed in her line of work to making decisions and being part of actions that literally could and had shaped the future of her country and the world. But she wasn't accustomed to seeing the results of those decisions and actions debated on television. Which they had been *ad nauseam*. Only now, five days after the whole mess began, was television getting back to its normal round of soaps and sitcoms and what it passed off as reality.

Full media coverage of *Disaster in Space!* had begun within an hour of the first news reports about trouble with the shuttle and the station. By the time of NASA's announcement of the loss of another shuttle, every network in America had been on twenty-four-hour duty, with countless freelance experts and almost-experts and network news analysts relentlessly parsing the possible fate of the shuttle and station crews. Then had come reports of the Russian station crew's final race against time to save Dr. Rey, a valiant effort that ended catastrophically with the explosion of the Russian supply ship, and the all-but-certain loss of the last survivors from the station.

The mob of anchors and reporters and talk show hosts solemnly delivered their summaries and eulogies and were moving on to newer, fresher stories when the *Soyuz* capsule made its unexpected appearance, suggesting at least one and, NASA revealed, possibly more survivors had escaped from orbit. The cooling story was red-hot again, and this time the frenzied mob had visuals.

A new set of ground-based telephoto images made available by the Air Force to NASA, and by NASA in turn to the media, showed the ISS as it actually was: intact and stable, though missing its port solar arrays. Some overexuberant reporters even called the space station's survival a miracle, somehow forgetting that eight people had died.

Despite all the intense talk and scrutiny, the media and the public did not learn that the ISS photo images' resolution had been deliberately downgraded to conceal the actual imaging capabilities of the U.S. Air Force. They learned only that radar signals, no longer obscured by the clouds of vaporized rocket fuel and oxidizer that had dispersed from the station's vicinity, confirmed that the station was as the Air Force's OWL photo images showed it to be. The station's port solar arrays had been located slowly tumbling in a lower orbit and were expected to burn up on reentry within the next week.

With those revelations, the world's attention now shifted, focusing avidly on endlessly repeated dramatic night shots of the Freefall retrieval of the *Soyuz* from the Mojave Desert, and the subsequent medevac helo-airlift of the two station survivors: the Russian *Soyuz* pilot Yuri Lazhenko and the American payload specialist, Corazon Rey. But that attention faded with the media's growing realization that ready access to the survivors would not be forthcoming. Then, just as it seemed the spotlight would sweep on again, yet another space-related story arrived. With even better footage.

Mission Control–Moscow was ablaze. Three enormous satellite dish antennae had collapsed in the heat from a spectacular transformer fire. For more than a day, fire trucks and helicopters dumped water onto Russia's Flight Control Center compound in the small town of Korolyov outside Moscow, in a desperate and ultimately successful attempt to save the facility's main buildings, including Mission Control. Even so, *Rosaviakosmos* reluctantly informed NASA it would be several weeks before they could restore their communications capabilities.

The timing of this PKA admission had sparked Bailey's interest, coming as it did just as the ISS crisis was winding down and America got back to business as usual.

She'd been reviewing Spacecom's timeline of the events in space, which had been created as an aid for the upcoming investigations and inquiries. In backup data collected for that breakdown, she'd discovered something worthy of her interest.

Infrared satellite surveillance of the region outside of Moscow clearly showed that the transformer fire at the Russian space compound had begun almost an hour *after* Mission Control–Moscow had stopped responding to outside attempts at communications, and almost thirty minutes *after* the space station had been presumed lost.

To Bailey, it was a classic example of a fire set after the fact to hide evidence. But what evidence? And for what reason? She'd resolved to run the issue to ground as soon as she was back at the Mountain. Then she'd gone home for a rare two-day break to pamper her babies, her husband, *and* herself.

That's what she was doing right now, stretched out in

Dom's ratty old green-leather recliner, bare feet resting on the polished walnut coffee table. She was relaxing in their cozily carpeted family room with its picture-window view out back of Pike's Peak, snow-capped and sunlit. She had snuggled into a thick red sweater that her mother had knit, her favorite jeans, and was breathing in the aromatic fumes of a mug of herbal tea she held in one hand while her other used the television remote to surf through all the news channels. She was content to let her peaceful home work its magic on her, releasing the tension of the past crazy week, enjoying the extra hour of sun, courtesy of the start of daylight savings time. Of course, Bailey knew, it was only peaceful at the moment because she was alone. Dom and the twins were napping in the master bedroom.

Then she heard the sound of a car's engine out in the cul-de-sac in front of the house. Traffic was a rarity on their rustic dead-end street. A few years from now, she thought with a smile, her babies would be out there doing wheelies on their tricycles and bicycles.

The car engine stopped. Bailey put her mug on the thick stack of unread newspapers by her chair. Her guests had arrived. She slid out of the recliner, and walked quickly down the cold, tiled hallway that led to the front door, hoping they'd notice her taped sign, warning against use of the doorbell. She opened the front door just as Mitch Webber opened the screen door to knock. He also wore jeans, along with a beat-up, brown leather jacket.

"Captain," she said, sweeping his tall frame into a bear hug.

"Mitch," he said in a voice muffled by her heavy sweater. "We're both off duty." Stepping back, he held the screen door open for his companion, who was awkwardly making her way up the flagstone walk, leaning heavily on the aluminum crutch under her right arm.

Dr. Rey was paler than Bailey had ever seen her, with violet smudges under both eyes. Bailey was afraid to hug her, she looked so small and fragile in her heather-gray slacks and pullover. "What happened to you, Doctor?"

"I didn't fit the seat," Rey said gamely. "And I'm off-duty, too, Major. So it's 'Cory' and—?"

Bailey beamed, "Willie." She reached out to Rey, who held out her left arm and managed a half-hug, wincing.

"Sorry, wrenched my back when the parachute opened."

As Bailey ushered her guests into her small living room, she realized that both were empty-handed. That wasn't the arrangement they had made. "Where're your things?"

"In the car," Webber said. He was helping Rey to Bailey's latest pride and joy, her new three-seater sofa of candy-apple red velvet. Down-filled, decadent, and, almost as important in a house with babies, washable. "I'll bring them in later."

"I can do it," Rey protested and pulled her arm away from Webber. Unassisted, she sat down with some difficulty on the very edge of the soft sofa, leaning forward to keep her back straight.

Bailey sighed. *Kids.* Little or big they were all the same. They needed someone more mature to supervise them. She plucked a few extra cushions from the back of the sofa and tucked them firmly behind Rey before she could protest again. Then she walked back to the open front door, to pull it shut. Through the screen door, she saw an oversize black SUV parked by the curb. Another vehicle, a dusty green sedan, apparently lost, slowly turned around in the cul-de-sac and drove off down the street, only to stop five houses away.

"You give up on Volvos?" Bailey asked Webber as she returned to the living room. Neither she nor Rey had been able to fathom why a man who had been a test pilot, who still undertook all manner of hazardous duty, chose to drive a brown Volvo station wagon on his own time.

Webber was sitting on the arm of the sofa, on the end farthest from Cory. "Hertz at the airport only had two, and they're both rented."

Rey shot Bailey a glance. "Must be a test pilots' convention in town."

That teeter-totter had only two seats and Bailey wasn't getting on to play. "What can I get you two?" she asked.

She saw Webber and Rey look at each other simultaneously, as if able to communicate by thought alone.

"Don't look at me," Rey said to Webber. "This is your idea."

Webber looked indignant. "My idea?"

"Tea? Coffee? Beer? Wine?" Bailey asked as she waited to see who would take charge. If no one did, and very soon, she would.

But Webber stepped up.

"Thanks, maybe later," he said. "Right now . . ." He dug into his jacket pocket, pulled out a small package wrapped in clear plastic and gray duct tape. "I think we'd better settle this."

"What's that?" Bailey asked. Then she realized she knew the answer. "Oh." She looked at Rey. *"That."* She plunked herself down in the wooden rocking chair she'd placed at right angles to the sofa. Her bare feet sank into the thick fibers of the black flokati-style rug. The dramatic red and black color scheme of the room had been her idea. It went beautifully with Georgia O'Keeffe's equally dramatic red poppies over the fireplace. Dom had given her the print for Valentine's Day this year, to mark their anniversary.

"Them, actually," Rey said. She held up her hand to make a peace sign. "Two."

Webber warily regarded the package he held, as if it

might somehow leap from his hand. "She shoved them into my flight suit before they took her to Vandenberg." He looked over at Rey as he spoke to Bailey. "I actually opened it before I saw her again."

"I told you not to," Rey said.

"Well, I did." Webber turned back to face Bailey. "And apparently you know all about them, too. So here we are."

It seemed to Bailey that there were more sparks than usual between Webber and Rey. But so far, no one was confiding much to her. "To do what?" she asked, rocking slightly in her chair.

Rey shifted uncomfortably against Bailey's pile of cushions, grimacing. "The Boy Scout thinks I've stolen from my employer and should give them back."

"Technically," Bailey said mildly, "the Boy Scout might be right."

But diplomacy didn't count for much today. Both her guests took offense at her statement.

"Right?" Rey said.

"Technically?" Webber said.

"It all depends where . . . *they* come from," Bailey continued, still rocking gently back and forth in her nursing chair.

Rey's chin lifted. Her pale cheeks reddened. "Willie, they come from the Moon. I saw them come out of the sample cylinder myself."

"In that case," Bailey said, "they *can't* belong to your employer."

Rey gave a triumphant look to Webber who frowned, confused.

"International law," Bailey explained. "Anything left on the Moon belongs to the government that left it, regardless of who might retrieve it. So, those . . . things . . . are the property of the United States government, which has transferred ownership of all space artifacts to the Smithsonian Institution. Or they belong to the Russian government. Since those are the only two countries that have put vehicles on the Moon, those are your only two choices."

"Except," Webber said, "Russia never sent humans to the Moon. And Japan landed their television rover."

Bailey had had three days to think about this bizarre situation. She dug her toes into the rug to put a stop to the movement of her chair. "True. But before Russia put their first cosmonaut into space, they launched a lot of animals. They even flew turtles around the Moon at least a year before Armstrong landed. Wouldn't surprise me if they sent monkeys or some kind of ape to the Moon and never talked about it. *Nor,*" she added before either Webber or Rey could interrupt, "would it surprise me, *if* those things do turn out to be human, to find out they're from some kind of experiment left by the Apollo missions."

"Apollo astronauts left human body parts on the Moon?" Webber asked in disbelief.

"Off the record," Bailey said, "NASA's flown bodies and body parts on the shuttle. They deny it, but it's true. They've tried conducting medical procedures on that plane that dips and dives to create zero-gravity, but they can only do that for half a minute at a time. Apparently, when you're operating on rabbits and mice, or dissecting human corpses, thirty seconds doesn't cut it. And when the DoD was running its own shuttle missions, a lot of that stuff went on. So why not during Apollo?"

Webber's surprisingly quick loss of combativeness told Bailey the captain also knew something about military missions in space.

Rey's slumping posture reflected her dejection. "So my fingers might not be from some long-lost lunar astronaut?"

Bailey began slowly rocking again as she skirted the edge of her security oath. "Off the record, I've heard stories about some long-lost cosmonauts, back in the early sixties. Now I'm not confirming . . . or denying . . . those stories, but they do date from the days when the old Soviet Union would only announce a space mission *after* it had been successfully launched. But as for going to the Moon?" Bailey paused, then shook her head. "I haven't even heard *rumors* of anything but the Apollo missions. So, if those things are from the Moon, my money's on them being part of a scientific experiment package either left by Apollo astronauts, or by one of the Russian landers."

"Is there any way we can find out, one way or another?" Webber asked.

"*Without* spilling everything to the Pentagon," Rey added.

"Yeah, there's a way to find out," Bailey said. "I'll go get Dom." She stood up from her chair.

Rey looked up at her, surprised. "You told him?"

Bailey rolled her eyes. "Cory, we're married. We share everything that isn't restricted information." She looked sternly at the two seated on opposite sides of her lovely red sofa. "Sharing is a good thing."

Then she left them, to see if Dom agreed with her.

Unlike his wife, Dominic Hubert was convinced it was very possible an American astronaut had died on the Moon. Because, he maintained, the pieces didn't add up.

"Which pieces?" Webber forced himself to ask. He was squeezed rather uncomfortably into the small eating nook in the Bailey-Hubert kitchen, Cory beside him on the cushioned pine bench. The major and her civilian husband sat on stools facing them. Behind the parents, pushed off against one wall, Webber counted two painted-wood highchairs, one yellow and one green. Cory's package occupied the seat of honor: direct center on the rustic pine table.

Webber only half-listened as Bailey's husband launched into a recitation of the number of command modules and service modules and lunar modules that had been built for the Apollo project.

"Originally, there were supposed to be ten Apollo landings," Hubert said as he leaned forward in his excitement, the bright red shock of his no-longer-regulation-length hair almost standing on end. "Eleven through twenty, and that's not counting the Apollo Extension Systems missions, or the Apollo Applications Programs that were supposed to come next to set up long-duration outposts.

Webber caught the smile of indulgent affection that Bailey bestowed on her ardent husband. There was not a hint of judgment in her attitude. Webber wished that he and Cory could be as easy. *As if that'll ever happen,* he thought. Even if he could make the case for a cease-fire, there was no guarantee that Cory could or would accept one. Their chances depended on what they'd both gone through this past year. And what that had told them about their true feelings for each other. *If I ever get a chance to tell her.*

"So," Bailey's husband continued, "in the mid-sixties— before any of the so-called budget cuts that were supposedly responsible for ending the Moon program—NASA ordered enough hardware for the next ten years. I mean, it took years to build those things, so they had to fill the pipeline. But once the pipeline was filled?" Hubert's fingers mimicked the action of scissors. "The government started trimming NASA's budget. So—the story goes—they started cutting missions."

Cory nodded. "Cutting the budgets of successful programs does seem to be the American way." She had her hands wrapped around a blue earthenware mug. Coffee. Strong and black. None of the major's calming tea for her.

Webber did not respond to the meaningful look Cory gave him as she added, "At least when the Republicans are in power."

He looked at Bailey in mute appeal. She knew, as well as he did, that finding Democrats in the upper levels of the military, especially among those whose job it was to take action, was like Diogenes' search for an honest man in Athens.

But intervention was unnecessary. Bailey's husband let the moment pass.

"Forget anything you've read, the Apollo cuts weren't a political decision. I mean, they didn't just cut the missions that were scheduled for the end of the program, Apollos Eighteen through Twenty. They cut from the *middle*. Apollos Fifteen, Sixteen, and Seventeen."

"But, those missions flew," Cory said. "I saw *From the Earth to the Moon*. Eleven was the first, then Twelve. Then Thirteen didn't land. But Fourteen through Seventeen did."

The aeronautical engineer's enthusiasm for his argument was reflected in the flush that blotched his freckled cheeks. "NASA took the missions at the end, and renumbered them so they looked like the cut missions in the middle. Think of that! Three missions, already in the middle of the building pipeline, and all the hardware, it just . . . vanished from the production line."

Webber said nothing. Until a week ago, he'd have jumped in and debated the point. But Varik's impromptu briefing in the SOV simulator had given him a good idea where some of that missing hardware had ended up.

"But one of those capsules flew, honey." Bailey patted her husband's hand. "The Apollo–*Soyuz* flight. Remember?

First joint American–Russian mission in space." The major held up her tea mug, questioningly. "More coffee, anyone?"

Webber shook his head, so did Cory. Hubert declined as well. But he was in agreement with the major's statement.

"Sure," Hubert said, "and three more Apollo command and service modules carried Skylab crews into orbit and back. That's fifteen that publicly flew with astronauts aboard. But then," he paused dramatically, "you gotta check the NASA official figures. They say North American Rockwell built fifteen command modules. And that's just plain impossible. What about the modules used for testing? What about flight spares? What about Apollo 204, the one that had the fire on the launch pad?"

Hubert sat back, triumphant, as he voiced his own conclusion. "My best guess is that Rockwell built between twenty-five to thirty of those command modules, with anywhere between five and eight sent directly to the Air Force for classified missions."

The whole topic was beginning to make Webber uncomfortable. He knew Hubert had once worked in Cheyenne Mountain with Bailey, before the two married.

Before her husband could say more, Bailey added what Webber was thinking. "Of course, the only reason Dom can say all this is because he's a civilian."

"Understand, none of this I learned while I was in the Air Force," Hubert said, making it a point of professional pride. "There are a lot of people in the public sector of the aerospace industry who've been tearing apart the old space program records. Just try to reconcile the earnings records of the major contractors with the public orders they received from NASA. They don't come close to matching. Rockwell, Douglas, all those companies? Turns out they've been building things for years that nobody's got a look at.

And I'm not just talking spy satellites and missile components."

Webber was more than ready for a change of subject. He tapped the wooden tabletop, indicating the plastic-wrapped package in the center. "So, Dom, you're saying those *might* come from an American astronaut who died on a classified mission to the Moon?"

"I'm saying it's a possibility." The civilian engineer gave a nod to his wife. "It's also possible they're from some medical experiment left by one of the public Apollo flights, or the Russian landers. The way I see it, Captain, it gives us three questions to check out. First of all, *are* those remains human? Second, *have* they been on the Moon? And third, since when?"

Webber had four more days before he had to report to General Salyard. "How long do you think it'll take you to answer those three questions?" he asked, curious.

"I just have to make a phone call." Hubert looked at Cory. "If Cory's willing to expand the circle, that is."

Webber sympathized with Bailey as she gave her husband an anxious look. Cory's schemes usually had the same effect on him.

"Oh, I'm willing," Cory said. "As long as we're talking about going to a civilian. But I'm adding two more questions to the list." She put a hand on top of the plastic package. "I want to know how Kai Teller knew to send his rover to where these things were on the Moon. And what he hoped to accomplish by bringing them back."

"I'll make the call," Dom said.

10

UNIVERSITY OF COLORADO AT COLORADO SPRINGS
DEPARTMENT OF PHYSICS AND ENERGY SCIENCE
20:47 MDT, TUESDAY, APRIL 8

"THE MOON HAS *no* magnetic field," Tripurasundari Shiourie said as she gestured gracefully with a bottle of hydrochloric acid, tracing an imaginary magnetic field around an imaginary Moon.

Webber concealed his growing restlessness, forced himself to sit quietly on the worn stool in the basement lab of the Royceman Energy Science physics lab, in front of a laptop computer whose screen displayed a magnified, polarized, and unidentifiable image. He, and the rest of Cory's former circle of four, had spent the last half hour watching Shiourie sweep back and forth through her lab, switching on humming machines, cutting, electrifying, and spending an inordinate amount of time aiming a macroscopic video camera at a brightly lit sliver of bone she had carefully planed from what she referred to as "Cory's objects."

"That's what makes this so very easy," the physics professor continued. She lowered a slender glass tube into the bottle of acid, let it dip just below the surface of the clear liquid, then deftly placed the tip of her bare finger over the open top and lifted it out again.

"How easy?" Cory asked.

"You will all want to keep watching . . ."

Webber sighed inwardly while the physics professor hunched over the camera and the laptop screen went dark as the shadow of her hand blocked the lights that illuminated the bone sample.

"This will now be the moment of truth," Shiourie said. With absolute precision, she lifted her fingertip from the glass tube just long enough for a single drop of acid to fall on the bone. She discarded the tube into a thick-walled metal container the size of a wastebasket, then stood back and flashed a brilliant smile at her audience.

There was no doubt that Hubert's friend and expert was a skilled performance artist. But she also possessed a quick intelligence that made Webber wonder if the physics professor had agreed to carry out this procedure to humor Bailey's husband, or because she also believed in his wild theories.

"How long is this moment going to be?" Bailey asked.

Shiourie checked the delicate gold bracelet-watch she wore on an equally delicate wrist. The small diamonds sparkling on her watch face were a match for the considerably larger stones in her stud earrings. Webber decided that unless physics professors were paid exceptionally well in Colorado, Shiourie had other sources of income. Her expensively coiffed dark hair swept back from well-tended, dark-brown skin, and her pleated camel trousers and precisely-tailored navy blazer were uncommon on a casual campus that favored jeans and plaid flannel.

Shiourie raised an eyebrow. "Five minutes should do it." Then she smiled slyly at Bailey. "So, tell me, Major, what do you know about Roswell today?"

Hubert laughed as his wife shook her head. "Same as any day, Sunny. Nothing."

Professor Shiourie shared her joke with Webber and Cory. "I am always asking Wilhemina that. And she is always answering, 'Nothing.' But someday, when she says, 'I cannot talk about it,' that is the day I will know that the topic has come up at her work."

Shiourie turned to Webber. "You're in the Air Force, too, I can see."

Bailey gave him an apologetic look. Hubert just looked interested.

Great, Webber thought. *Now it's my turn.* "Navy."

"Ah, but still you are an aviator."

Webber nodded. "When they let me."

"You have the look." She tilted her head to one side, considering him carefully. "Have you ever seen a UFO?"

"Nothing I couldn't explain," Webber said smoothly. He saw Bailey suppress a smile.

Shiourie pursed her lips as if she had caught him in a lie. "Very well, Navy pilot, what is it you know about Roswell?"

"It's in New Mexico." Webber caught Cory's eye, but she just looked at him innocently, as if she didn't understand how much he hated this kind of thing.

"No, no," Shiourie said. She glanced at her watch again, keeping track of the time. "The crashed alien spacecraft. The retrieval of alien life-forms. The source of the laser and fiber optics and even Velcro—all from reverse-engineered alien technology."

Webber soldiered on. "Other than knowing Velcro was inspired by thistles, I don't know anything about Roswell."

"Pity. The Navy was involved," Shiourie said.

"In recovering aliens and UFOs?" Cory asked. Webber was relieved to hear the clear skepticism in her voice.

"Oh, that is not what I was saying, Doctor. You have

to pay close attention. I said, the Navy was involved in Roswell. The UFO crash story, that is just that—a story."

Webber noted the nod of agreement Bailey's husband gave his friend. "So . . . which camp are you in?" he asked, intrigued by Shiourie's sudden and apparent reversal. "Believer, or nonbeliever?"

The professor regarded Webber with pity, as if he were one of her slower students. "Precision in language is a lost art. Are there UFOs? That is, objects that fly that are unidentifiable? Of course. Does it follow that a UFO is therefore an alien craft? Absolutely not. Did a UFO crash at Roswell on or about July 7, 1947? Without question. Was it an alien spacecraft? Alas, no. It was exactly what the Air Force said it was in those two preposterous reports they published in the nineties." She looked at Bailey. "No offense."

"Then why call them preposterous if you think they're accurate?" Cory asked.

"Because," Shiourie said, "those reports still covered up the *true* events of Roswell."

"And those events are?"

"Sir Arthur Conan Doyle. *Silver Blaze.* What was the curious incident that Sherlock Holmes identified as the clue that solved the crime?" Shiourie's smile was knowing.

Cory only had herself to blame, Webber thought. This obviously was the price of the after-hours favor called in by Bailey's husband. But did he have to pay it, too? Surely the professor would have to get back to whatever test she was running on the bone sliver soon.

No one could remember the story.

"The night of the murder, the stable dog *didn't* bark," Shiourie said triumphantly. "That told Sherlock the horse thief was known to the dog. Therefore, the absence of evidence was evidence of the crime."

Bailey and her husband had both been quiet for some time. *Because,* Webber thought wearily, *they've heard all this junk before. Cory's fresh meat.*

"I don't see the connection," Cory said, frowning, not content to leave well enough alone. "No dogs barked at Roswell?"

Shiourie clapped her hands together in pleasure. "That is it, exactly! There was the official Army Air Corps press release about the capture of a flying disk! Reporters and curiosity seekers came from all over. The switchboard overloaded with calls from as far away as England and France. And in the meantime, a top-secret balloon experiment had fallen into a farmer's field and the Army needed to hush it up. Why? To keep any foreign agents in the area from finding out what the purpose of the experiment was. So . . . public confusion. A classified cover-up. And yet? Even with all that going on, the official base records for the Roswell Army Airfield show nothing unusual going on, *nothing* during that entire period. No personnel recalled or dispatched to handle the balloon retrieval. Not even to provide extra security for the base. Now how can that be possible unless . . . the official records have been purged, altered, or outright replaced. Which therefore indicates, very strongly, something unusual *did* go on."

"Is there a point to this, Professor?" Webber asked. Favor or not, this was getting painful.

But Shiourie took his question seriously. "There is," she said gravely. "The modern folklore of crashed saucer stories was created from an astounding convergence of coincidence."

Webber gave up, for Cory's sake. The bone-sliver test couldn't last forever. "And that coincidence was?" he asked dutifully.

"Three," Shiourie said. "There were three coincidences. The first was the crash of a Project Mogul balloon train. The balloon carried a sophisticated microphone system developed by the Army. They were hoping it would hear the acoustic effects of the Soviets' atmospheric atomic-bomb tests. The second was the Army's flying-saucer press release. Someone was hoping it would divert attention from the crashed balloon. It didn't. The third was what really happened at Roswell in that last week of June 1947."

Shiourie paused. "Wilhemina, I am not crossing the line into official government secrets?"

Bailey waved her hands. "You're on your own here, Sunny. I've never heard anything official, so I can't comment."

All Webber wanted was for the conversation to end, so naturally Cory prolonged it. "Okay, I'll go for it," she said. "What really did happen at Roswell?"

Webber leaned back on his stool, resting his back against the ledge of a lab table as Professor Shiourie began her explanation, slim arms folded and hugged tightly to her chest.

"Oh, it was very tragic, Doctor. Roswell Army Airfield was the home base for the 509th Bomb Group. The first and, at the time, the only bomber group armed with atomic weapons." Shiourie glanced over at Webber. "That was why there were foreign agents in the vicinity, and why the Army was so serious about hiding the nature of the Mogul balloon project. But it was the atomic bombs that led to tragedy. The military establishment knew they were the future of warfare, and a bitter political fight was being waged between the Army and Navy as to which branch would take control of them."

The rambling conversation that had filled the time required to test Cory's samples now had Webber's full attention. He had studied the history of nuclear weapons at the Naval Academy and knew about the early rivalry between the Army and the Navy. Hubert's friend had those facts right, at least.

Shiourie noticed his reaction. She nodded, serious. "You know the truth of what I am saying. The fight followed two strategies, as these fights often do. The Army and the Navy each described their own strengths. To prove they were the better service to control the bomb. And they also stopped at nothing to describe the other's shortcomings."

All trace of Shiourie's previous light bantering was gone. "On the night of June 27, a team of Navy commandos, what used to be called 'Naked Warriors,' the forerunners of today's SEALs—" The physics professor stopped for a moment as Cory pointed a finger at Webber.

"A pilot *and* a SEAL," Shiourie said. "Most unusual, but then you will find this doubly interesting, Captain. The Navy commandos were on a tactical assessment mission. To test the Army's security arrangements at the airfield. A training exercise, planned ahead of time in Washington. But no one told the soldiers at Roswell.

"All twelve Navy commandos were killed that night, along with twenty soldiers. Another eight wounded. Some of the commandos managed to get a bomber started and rolled it to the end of the runway. Soldiers tore it to pieces with 50-caliber, jeep-mounted machine guns. A wing fuel tank exploded. An atomic bomb casing cracked when the bomber's wheels collapsed. Can you imagine?"

Webber understood he was representing the Navy in this room, so he did his best not to be rude. "I know training missions sometimes go awry, Professor. But a defensive exercise like the one you're describing would never reach the operational stage. Not without the commander of the base knowing about it."

"Oh, I think he did know about it," Shiourie said. "And he chose not to acknowledge it. And his plan to humiliate the Navy commandos went very badly out of control. American soldiers killing American sailors. An atomic bomb damaged, a bomber lost, because of interservice rivalry and incompetence. What would the American people think? Even worse, what would the Soviets think about America's ability to control her atomic weapons? Can you think of a better reason for a cover-up? To alter base records? A better explanation for why six months of historically important communications logs between the Pentagon and Roswell Air Field were destroyed? A better reason why so many people in Roswell remember that *something* happened at the base around then, yet don't know the details?

"And five days later," Shiourie continued, "when the burned and mutilated bodies of the soldiers and sailors were flown out under cover of darkness . . . when men in radiation suits had recovered the cracked bomb, and the damaged bomber was cut up and shipped out so its fate would never be reflected in the records . . . just by coincidence, the balloon crashed, the press release came out, the attention of the world focused on Roswell for all the wrong reasons . . . and a legend was born."

"If you know all this," Webber asked, "why doesn't everyone?"

"It is not exciting, is it?" Shiourie said with a little shrug. "No little green men. No fantastic flying machines. Just thirty-two innocent young men whose lives were wasted by the incompetence and arrogance of the old men who commanded them. But the old men weren't stupid. The evidence disappeared. The Navy and Army each got an atomic bomb program. And now, sixty years later, there's no one left, no one to remember, and no one to care."

Webber looked over at the computer screen. He hated being the scapegoat for simpleminded civilians who saw only the flaws of the military. Who never seemed to understand that the military saw those flaws, too, and was constantly working to better itself. If he had the time and the diplomacy, he'd be only too glad to explain to Hubert's friend that the situation she'd described would be as abhorrent to the military structure as it was to her.

But he didn't have the time and he was all out of diplomacy. He wanted to leave here with Cory and he wanted to leave soon. He just had to think of a way not to appear rude.

"Is that what's supposed to happen?" he asked, pointing to the screen. At least five minutes had passed since Professor Shiourie had dropped hydrochloric acid onto the sliver of bone from Cory's sample.

At the beginning of the experiment, under the bright lights and through a polarizing filter, the transparently thin sliver had appeared like a pattern of silvery yellow foam squeezed between two sheets of glass. But now, the foam pattern had turned muddy brown-black, and was crisscrossed by what appeared to be a vaguely fan-shaped pattern of silvery lines.

The physicist reached to the small tray in which the sample rested, and moved the sample back and forth within the tray. As she did so, the view on the laptop screen changed. To Webber, it now appeared as if all the lines were converging on a single point, somewhere outside the body of the sample.

"Do you know what we are looking at here?" Professor Shiourie asked her audience.

"Don't be a pain, Sunny," Bailey said. "You gave us the sermon, now give us our supper."

Shiourie was not offended by Bailey's rebuke. Her playfulness regained, she smiled and wagged a finger at the major. "The acid broke down the bone matrix. Except where the matrix had been altered by the passage of high-speed radiation particles."

Webber straightened up, relieved. The major was finally taking control of the situation, having obviously been down this road before with her husband and his friend.

Shiourie turned to Cory. "When you were in space, Doctor, I am very sure you saw these particles. When you closed your eyes?"

Cory nodded. "Once or twice a minute, trying to sleep, I'd see these things that looked like meteor trails just flash across my vision. But . . . my eyes would be closed."

"Still, those trails were caused by the gamma particles whizzing through your head, triggering the rods and cones in your retina. You saw more of them over the South Atlantic, is that not right?"

Cory hesitated. "I . . . I can't be sure. I never really knew where I was. But I remember someone, I guess it was Commander Dante, she said she could tell when the station was over the South Atlantic because of all the light trails she saw."

"The South Atlantic Anomaly," Shiourie said with a nod. "It is a weak point in the Earth's magnetic field. The magnetic field protects the surface of the Earth from high-energy particles coming from the sun, collects them and carries them to the poles where they become the northern lights and the aurora australis." She pointed a professorial finger at Webber. "But what was it I said about the Moon?"

Webber automatically answered as if he were back in training. "It has no magnetic field."

"So, anything on the surface of the Moon is exposed to hard radiation. And by examining the extent of that exposure, we can estimate how long it has been exposed."

Webber slid forward, off his stool. "You're saying that those fingers *have* been on the Moon."

"I am a scientist, Captain Webber. All I can say is that the sample of bone I have just examined shows radiation damage, and that damage is consistent with having been exposed to the sun somewhere outside the protection of Earth's magnetic field." Shiourie used a pair of tongs to pick up the blackened husk of the finger from which she had sliced the sample. "To confirm that that location was the Moon, I would suggest conducting a spectroscopic analysis of the dust on this object. Lunar dust is quite distinctive, easy to identify."

"Is that a test you can do?" Cory asked.

"The university does have the equipment. But I would have to think of a worthy excuse to use it on something like this." The professor smiled apologetically as she contemplated the fingers. "It is not in my department."

"What is your department?" Webber asked.

"High-energy physics. At this university, I teach plasma physics and introductory nuclear energy production. At the Air Force Academy, I teach space-based engineering principles related to high-energy physics."

"Weapons design?" he asked.

Shiourie lifted one eyebrow. "As I hope Major Bailey will someday say to me, I cannot discuss it."

Webber understood. "You teach at the Academy."

"Which is why I know a pilot when I see one. And why I can only discuss my . . . unusual hobby with trusted friends and fellow conspirators."

The last thing Webber wanted or needed was to be lumped in with the conspiracists and UFO nuts who were attracted to the Air Force like sharks to blood. He turned to Cory.

"These results good enough for you?" he asked.

"I saw where they came from, remember? You're the one who needed evidence."

"If I can interrupt here," Hubert tactfully intervened, "it would be helpful to run the spectroscopic analysis for confirmation." He turned to Shiourie. "Sunny, what if we brushed off some of the dark particles on the finger? You could say they were recovered from an Apollo mission patch or artifact sold at auction. They're a legal source of lunar dust."

Shiourie liked the suggestion. "A few micrograms of dust would be easier to explain than a human body part." She began searching through a wall-mounted metal cabinet.

"And then what?" Webber asked Cory, because someone had to. "So you prove the fingers have been on the Moon. Then what do you do?"

Cory looked at him as if he were particularly stupid. "Then we find out *how* they got to the Moon, Mitchell."

Webber addressed his next questions to Bailey and to the professor, in the hopes that they would be more open to reason. "And what if those fingers got to the Moon because of a restricted military operation? What do you two propose to do then? Break operational security?"

Bailey looked pained and Shiourie appeared not to have heard the question. The professor held one of the fingers with tongs above a small plastic specimen bag, and used what appeared to be a large, soft, painter's brush to dislodge the dust that covered it.

But Cory locked in on Webber like a Sidewinder missile. "Mitchell, do you know something about these things we don't?"

Webber ditched what he had been about to say, because Cory was right. Although he didn't know for a fact that the Air Force—or the Space Force—had sent a classified mission to the Moon, he *was* able to make more than an informed guess. And that meant there was nothing more he could say about the subject. "I don't want to talk about it."

Cory's eyes narrowed. "I've seen that expression before. You don't want to talk about it because you *can't* talk about it."

"Professor Shiourie, I think we need to be on our way now," Bailey said. "Dom and I told the baby-sitter we'd be home by eleven."

Shiourie used the tongs to drop the dusted finger into the new metal sample case she had provided, no larger than a small pen case, filled with a sterile plastic packing material. Then she handed the case to Cory. "It has been a pleasure to meet you, Doctor Rey. I will have the dust at the spectroscopy lab tomorrow morning. And I will have no difficulty finding a student or two to run the analysis. They will be quite excited by the opportunity."

Webber detected a hint of apology, a hint of understanding in Shiourie's nod to him. "It has been a pleasure to meet you as well, Captain. Good flying."

Webber picked up his leather jacket from the lab bench behind him, then handed Cory her crutch for the walk up the stairs from the basement.

Outside, the evening air was cool and mountain crisp, and Webber pulled his jacket tighter. A three-quarter Moon and a handful of stars shone through the orange haze of campus lights that bathed the smooth green expanse of the university commons.

Completely from habit, Webber scanned the immediate area for any signs of trouble. Which meant he was the first to see the two men in the shadowed lane beside the Royceman Building, and the dark car with fogged windows just behind them, parked precisely halfway between two streetlamps, in minimum illumination.

Webber put his hand on Hubert's shoulder, speaking quietly to him and to Bailey. "Get ready to help Cory back into the building. Jam the door any way you can."

He had no time to respond to Cory's automatic protest when one of the men began to run toward them, shouting. "Corazon Rey!"

"Inside now! Everyone!" Webber ordered as he stepped off the wide concrete pathway to confront the running man skidding to a stop before him.

"Identify yourself," Webber said.

"Out of the way," the man answered, shifting to bypass him.

Webber went into blocking stance. "I said, identify yourself."

This time the man's response was to reach into his suit jacket.

That was enough for Webber. He grabbed the man's wrist and wrenched the man's empty hand up and away from the jacket as he drove his knee into the man's groin, dropping him instantly.

Then the second man charged him, shouting, a .38 revolver already drawn. "On the ground! On the ground now!"

Webber reached down, yanked open the jacket of the man he'd neutralized and found another .38 in a shoulder holster. So used to fighting other soldiers, he took no time to stop to consider why the guns were present. Instead he leapt to his feet, aiming the .38 at the second man in a two-handed grip, shouting the same command. "Down! Down! Down!"

He felt a weak blow against his legs. Without looking, Webber slammed the .38 against the side of the first man's head, to neutralize him more effectively.

By then, the second man was on him, swinging his own

gun at Webber's head. But Webber absorbed the force of the charge and used it to throw his attacker off balance and roll him to land facedown on the grass. Then he jumped on the second man's back, heard his target's breath explode from him, leaned down to twist the man's head around, and as he did so, saw blood streaming from his nose. Webber jammed the barrel of the .38 against the man's temple.

"Identify yourself!" he repeated. His own breath was slow and even.

The second man spat out a clotted clump of blood. "FBI, asshole. We're here to talk to Doctor Rey. But *you! You're* under arrest!"

Webber shoved the gun into the back of his jeans, slid a hand into the man's jacket, found a billfold, pulled it out and flipped it open.

The silver badge inside was regulation.

Webber straightened up, pulled the gun from his back waistband, snapped its cylinder out and shook loose its cartridges. Then he dropped the gun on the grass.

As the bleeding FBI agent staggered to his feet and pulled a pair of handcuffs from his belt, Webber shot a glance back at the main entrance doors of the Royceman Building. Through the door windows he saw Bailey's husband, but no Bailey. And no Cory.

If Cory had been straight with him, Webber reasoned, then only three people besides herself and him knew about the recovered lunar samples: Bailey, Hubert, and Professor Shiourie. So why was the FBI pursuing Cory so aggressively?

Or more to the point, Webber thought, *what else is Cory keeping from me?*

11

"**THE FBI FINALLY CAME** to talk to me," Tovah Caruso said. "Turns out you were right."

Kai Teller looked up at her from under the wing of his sleek and costly corporate jet, an eight-passenger, four-crew Gulfstream V, white and silver with TTI's dynamic ellipse logo outlined in blue on its tail. Caruso and the industrialist were standing on the tarmac of Ellington Field—once an Army Air Corps station, then an Air Force base, now a commercial airport for the city of Houston, primarily serving the National Guard, NASA, and private industry.

Five hundred yards away, a 737 cargo jet in UPS brown and gold began its taxi for takeoff. Teller had to raise his voice to a shout to be heard over the growl of its idling. "About what?"

Caruso waited as Teller ducked out from under the wing. His annoying question required no answer. He knew very well what she wanted to talk to him about, and why she'd driven all the way out here by herself, away from NASA and prying ears. She brushed her hair from her forehead though the gusting wind blew it back again, the scent of jet fuel and diesel exhaust evoking bittersweet memories for her.

"Ed Farren," she said.

Teller used what looked to be a starched linen cloth to wipe oil from his hands, then nodded over at the open passenger hatch of his plane. There was no one on the fold-down staircase, or anyone else nearby. Still, he leaned closer as he asked a one-word question. "Murdered?"

"As it turns out, very professionally."

Teller remained silent while the UPS jet's engines built up power, then punched down the runway.

"Connected?" he asked then. He didn't say to what. He didn't have to.

But Caruso wasn't here to answer his questions. She expected him to answer hers. "Kai, they're treating *me* like a suspect."

"That's ridiculous."

Caruso's crisp khaki slacks flattened against her legs as the wind strengthened. "No, it's not. You remember what happened to senior staff after *Columbia*. Congress is going to want a scapegoat. Any day now, the White House is going to suspend me. They'll keep me on the payroll for the first hearings, but my career's history." Her right eye teared up and she reflexively blinked as windblown grit slipped beneath her contact lens. She put a hand to hold her eyelid closed before her eye could spasm, nodded toward the metal staircase. "Can we go inside?"

Teller gestured to the hatch, at once solicitous. "Of course."

Inside the luxuriously appointed plane, he slid back the cherrywood shelf that covered the bar sink in the galley alcove of the main cabin. Then he turned on the water for her and disappeared into the head to finish cleaning his hands.

Caruso popped the errant lens from her eye, rummaged through her small olive Coach bag for her lens case, remembering how on both her trips to the ISS, she had taken three backup pairs of contacts with her, but had never lost even a single lens. She wondered if Cory Rey, in turn, had discovered the great secret of space travel: that it was often as mundane as it was astounding.

Her host was back by the time she'd replaced her lens and repaired her smeared eye makeup. "Just thinking about it, Tovah, I really don't believe you're in danger."

Teller bent down to slide out a cupboard drawer below the sink, from which he plucked a large, ribbed-plastic bottle of designer water. "Remember how the ISS started out? It was *Space Station Freedom,* the cherry on Ronald Reagan's Star Wars space defense initiative. Bush the First got the funding through Congress by a single vote." He waved the bottle at her. Caruso nodded.

"And," Teller said as he slid open another cupboard to remove two cut-crystal Steuben tumblers, "let's not forget that every president since has been cutting the balls off the thing because none of them's had the guts to stand up and pull a Kennedy and say we belong in space because we damn well *belong* in space." He filled the glasses from the bottle. "Face it. The vision for space exploration, the Moon–Mars initiative, it's all political window-dresssing that will never be funded. Just once, I'd like to hear a president come out and say that as a species we're explorers, and exploring space will elevate our spirit and take the limits off a future we can't begin to imagine. And leave it at that."

He passed a tumbler to her. "Sorry for the lecture. But my point is the station's too big, too old, and too expensive for one person to be responsible for it. They won't come after you."

"I'm already in their sights," Caruso said. She took a sip of welcome cool water. The cut-crystal vessel felt heavy, expensive. *Nothing but the best for Kai,* she thought. He hadn't changed at all. "Not because I'm responsible for the station being there. But because I might be responsible for having lost it."

Teller took a last swallow from his own glass. "It's not lost," he said. He held up the water bottle, questioningly.

Caruso shook her head. "In eighteen days we launch *Endeavour* over the review board's objections. If it can dock, it's going to boost the station's orbit, and then the crew's basically going to shut the station down and put it in mothballs. By the best estimates we've got, it'll take at least three more survey missions before we know how to even begin to start repairs. It'll be years before there's a permanent crew onboard again. And with the shuttle fleet slated to stop flying in two years ..."

Teller regarded her earnestly. "But the station's not *lost,* Tovah. And NASA *will* repair it. And it *will* have a crew again. And then we will send astronauts back to the Moon. How many European ships sank trying to find a passage to China before Columbus reached the shores of North America? That's the other thing I hate about politicians being involved in the space program. None of them has the guts to face a real challenge."

He poured himself more water, drank it quickly, wiped his mouth with the back of his hand. "Remember what President Kennedy said? 'We choose to go to the Moon and do these other things, not because they are easy, but because they are *hard.*'" He set the empty tumbler back on the bar counter with a grimace of disgust. "God ... congressmen and senators. Tell them something's going to take longer than the next election to accomplish and they're all moral cowards."

Caruso regarded him, perplexed, trying to decide why Teller was being so uncharacteristically obtuse. "That debate's over, Kai. No one cares about the future. Washington just saw sixty-five billion dollars get sucked into a black hole and they're going to want someone to pay for that."

"So, why you, Tovah?" Teller moved away from the counter, dropped into a wide, dove-gray leather passenger seat, then pressed a control that swung him around to face the seat behind him. "Come on, sit down," he told her.

Exasperated, Caruso plunked her glass down on the counter and took the chair across from him. "Because of you, of course."

A flash of temper darkened Teller's handsome face. "Go on."

"Ed Farren," Caruso said again, feeling quite resentful herself. How much longer would it take the man to realize what was really going on? "First you told me he came to you, saying someone might be out to sabotage the station. Then you came to me, and said maybe he was murdered because of what he was saying. Well, he *was* murdered, Kai. By someone who injected him with a lethal muscle relaxant—one drop, behind his ear. That's a place no one would look, without a reason."

"Connect the dots, Tovah."

"You and me."

Teller's fixed expression was unreadable. "We were over long before we began our professional relationship."

"Try looking at it the way the FBI does, right now," Caruso said. "The way the Senate investigators will, all too soon. You and I had a personal relationship. Now we have a professional one. Worth several tens of millions of dollars to NASA, and three times that amount to TTI."

"Excuse me," Teller said, "but I lost everything on the

Caruso nodded. "Lazhenko's family is already in the U.S. embassy in Moscow. He's at Walter Reed demanding refugee status for everyone. And the FBI's saying it all tracks. Someone was out to get the station, one way or another. Plan A was one or two small explosions that might never be traced. Plan B? Blow up the Progress."

"My God, Tovah . . ."

Caruso studied Teller's stricken face. "So, tell me, *do* you have enemies in Russia?"

He shook his head. "I don't even warrant enemies in the United States. TTI's what's considered a specialty player. Contracts for small, niche components the big boys don't want. Not a lot of competition. And all my competitors are doing better than I am this year, I assure you. How can the Feds think *any* of this is true?"

"All that matters is that they do," Caruso said crossly. Her eye still hurt. She wondered if she'd scratched her cornea. *Great,* she thought. *I'll be wearing an eyepatch at the hearings. That'll do wonders for my public image.*

"I'll talk to the FBI, tell them anything I can, that might help."

"First, tell *me,*" Caruso said. "Because I'm the one they're coming for. What, exactly, did Ed Farren tell you he suspected?"

Teller rubbed at his forehead. "Okay. Just before the *Constitution* launched, the day before, in fact, Ed called me, said we had to meet in person. We were both at Kennedy. I liked the guy, for God's sake. We had a beer at the Rusty Pelican in Cocoa Beach."

Caruso nodded. She knew the place. A canal-front industry dive with sawdust on a wood-plank floor, red checkerboard plastic tablecloths, and five televisions hanging from the ceiling tuned to NASA TV instead of ESPN.

"Ed was worried," Teller continued. "He'd heard that

someone might have built a small explosive device and packaged it to look like on-orbit rations."

"For the ISS?"

Teller nodded. "Part of the shipment in the Leonardo module that was going up."

Now it was Caruso's turn to feel shaken. "Who did Farren hear that from?" All food supplies for the station and the shuttle went through extensive quality-control procedures during preparation. But once packaged, they were probably subjected to the least amount of scrutiny of any item to fly into space. More stringent guidelines were in place only for the more obviously dangerous cargo components, such as electrical equipment, computers, and anything pressurized.

It wasn't as if NASA hadn't known for a long time that replacing food packages was the easiest way to smuggle something into orbit. But no one had ever come up with what the motives for smuggling to the station would be. The astronauts were already allowed to take almost anything of a personal nature they wanted, within their weight restrictions,.

"Wouldn't say or didn't know," Teller answered. "But I think Ed knew someone who works at the company making the packaging material, the bags and trays. They'd had a theft. Apparently, some of the food packs had been found discarded, contaminated by plastic-explosive residue."

"Found by who?" Caruso demanded sharply. "And why'd Farren tell you and not the FBI?"

"C'mon, Tovah, you know what this business is like. Who would have listened to him? There're a hundred Ed Farren's out there, all certain there's some vast secret about space travel they need to expose. If I came to you about every story I'd heard, you wouldn't listen to me if I told you the sky was blue."

"But Farren thought you were different. He thought you'd believe him."

Teller sighed. "Poor bastard. I didn't. We've already talked about this, Tovah. I thought Ed was just being Ed. The old guy was always on about some conspiracy or other. If it wasn't the Air Force withholding technology from you or threatening researchers who wouldn't agree to cover up their work, it was the Army or the Coast Guard, or whatever. A few years back he even raised a stink about the Navy sitting on a technique for generating unlimited power in space with tethered satellites. When he finally got some people to write about it, he claimed he was being followed and his phone was being tapped."

"But then we lost *Constitution*," Caruso said, feeling sick that the entire tragedy might have been prevented.

"Well, that was different, wasn't it," Teller said. "It was too much of a coincidence for me. Ed's story about an explosive on the Leonardo. The Leonardo still in the shuttle's payload bay when the shuttle exploded. I had to tell someone."

"Did Farren tell you *anything* about *why* someone might want to blow up the shuttle or the station?"

Teller shook his head. "Nothing. I asked him that myself. But he didn't know. Seemed to think it was another attack against the country. Didn't need any more reason than that."

Caruso rested her head against the high seatback, overwhelmed by the enormity of what still remained unknown about what had happened. "Too bad this flying yacht of yours doesn't just take off. Tahiti sounds about right."

Teller's glance was considering. "I'm going to the Cape right now to wrap up the sponsorship issues. But I'm heading back to Maui in a few days." He made it sound like an invitation.

Caruso hesitated, remembering the rarity of experience that Kai's life offered as standard fare. But she shook her head. "That's just what the FBI would like to see. The co-conspirators making a break for it."

"We're not co-conspirators. We're friends."

Caruso slid forward in her chair. "Only if you promise to visit me in prison." She paused, knowing her next question would seem odd to Teller, because it puzzled her as well. "Kai, there was a name the FBI mentioned. They wondered if it had any connection to Farren." But before she could say more, the plane shifted and she heard quick footsteps on the passenger staircase.

An athletic young man in a well-tailored blue uniform ducked through the hatch and smiled at her. "Hello, ma'am." He nodded to Teller. "Mister Teller, there's something on the news might be of interest. It just came on in the pilot's lounge."

"Sure," Teller said. His employee raised a soft-hued tapestry panel on a forward bulkhead to reveal a widescreen plasma television, then adjusted the controls beside it and the screen came to life. First, with static, then with an open-vested and shirt-sleeved reporter standing in the middle of desert scrub, speaking into a handheld microphone. Below the reporter, a title bar read FOX NEWS LIVE. Inset in the upper left-hand corner was a photograph of an aircraft very familiar to Caruso. A Boeing KC-135, the class NASA used to use to create short periods of simulated microgravity, for astronaut training.

In the distance, behind the newscaster, she saw a thin column of black smoke rising into blue sky, where helicopters circled.

"There's been a crash," Caruso said.

The pilot turned up the sound.

". . . first crash of a plane flying this type of mission,

Christine," the reporter was saying over the drone of the overhead helicopters.

A woman's voice came on. "But do we know if any astronauts were onboard?"

Caruso leaned forward in alarm. "Where is that?"

"I believe it's in California, ma'am," Teller's pilot said. "A training mission out of Vandenberg."

Caruso's immediate relief was followed swiftly by guilt. "Those poor people." The smoke obviously meant a pilot and copilot had died, along with a flight engineer and however many technicians and specialists had been onboard conducting their studies and experiments.

Teller turned to Caruso. "Air Force pilots. Not astronauts. So at least it's not bad news for NASA."

"We still don't have a list of casualties, Christine," the reporter said onscreen. "But we do know that NASA no longer uses this type of aircraft for weightlessness training. Since this flight originated from the Vandenberg Air Force Base, we don't expect to learn that any NASA astronauts or astronaut trainees were involved. Apparently, the Air Force flies these 'zero-g' missions to test equipment that might someday go into space."

When the on-screen reporter began repeating himself, Teller told the young pilot to kill the sound, then asked him to step outside the jet again. His employee made a quick exit without complaint or question.

"So, should I call the FBI?" Teller asked Caruso. "Or will you let them know they can call me?"

Caruso stood up. The cabin was high-ceilinged enough that she didn't have to worry about banging her head. "Personally, I'd wait until they came calling."

"Okay. But I suppose I shouldn't be in any hurry to get to Maui. Wouldn't want the Feds to think I'm on the lam."

"Speaking of which—that name I was asking you about?"

"The one the FBI mentioned?" Teller stood up and began stretching his back.

"That's it. Varik. Daniel Varik. Did Farren ever mention him?"

"A friend? Coworker? Or fellow traveler along the road to conspiracy?"

"Just a name."

"Sorry, it doesn't make a connection."

"I should go." She held out her hand, Teller took it, surprised her by kissing the back of it.

"Tovah, I know you're not in real trouble," he told her, still holding on to her hand. "But keep in the back of your head, whatever happens, there's always a place for you in TTI."

Caruso pulled her hand away. The man was incorrigible. "Me? With a specialty player and builder of niche components?"

"I *am* going to build another LRV," Teller said. "If NASA doesn't get back to the Moon fast, then it's going to belong to private enterprise. Let the Japanese send all the television rovers they want. I intend to start mining."

"We'll talk," Caruso promised him. She put a hand on the open hatch, before stepping out onto the staircase. "But, Kai, really, if there are any enemies you should watch out for . . . watch out for them."

"No enemies."

It was either a statement of fact or a call to action. Caruso wondered how long it would take the FBI to tell her which.

Ten minutes later, Tovah Caruso pulled her white, rented, Lincoln Town Car off to the side of Dixie Farm Road and waited for the black Crown Victoria that had been following her to pull up behind.

When the driver came up to her window, she already had the digital transmitter out of her inside jacket pocket, and she was slowly peeling back the thin strip of adhesive tape that held the microphone beneath her right collar-bone.

"You got that?" she asked, still not able to believe that she had agreed to tape her conversation with Teller. She handed him the listening gear.

"We got it," the FBI agent said. "What was his reaction to Daniel Varik?"

"He didn't recognize the name. I'm sure of it."

She glanced up at the plain-featured man in his plain dark suit who stood on the gravel shoulder beside her car door. She found him studying her as if he knew something she didn't, and was this close to telling her.

"It's not Kai," she said. "It can't be."

"Someone's responsible for what happened up there," the FBI agent said. Then he gravely thanked her for her cooperation, said he'd be in touch, and walked back to his car. He drove off in a cloud of dust and gravel.

Caruso discovered she was trembling, in no condition yet to drive. She closed her eyes to collect herself, only to see again the column of smoke from the crash site of the Air Force KC-135. More destruction, just like the shuttle and the station.

And NASA's future.

12

WITH THE EXCEPTION of the electromagnetic ghosts of its flight crew, little else remained of the Air Force KC-135 beyond a gaping hole in the earth, around which fluttered a handful of small white flags on thin wire stakes, marking the sites where a pitiful few body parts had been recovered. On either side of the hole, smoke still drifted upward from misshapen mounds of scorched metal, the only evidence of the four Pratt and Whitney turbofan engines that had carried the aircraft aloft, and then had driven it into the desert floor, at a speed exceeding 600 mph.

Sixty miles from Vandenberg and the Pacific, General Salyard stood in the shade of the large mess tent being used to shelter five long metal tables. On those gleaming stainless-steel surfaces, classified wreckage was painstakingly being sorted by airmen wearing white decontamination overalls, breathing masks, and thick rubber gloves.

The most recognizable objects were large sections of near-indestructible Kevlar fabric from the outer layer of the Expeditionary Mobility Suits that had been onboard the plane. Some smaller shards and twisted splinters could be identified as belonging to the suits' polycarbonate helmets and Distributed Life-Support Components. But of the four brave men who had been wearing them, there was almost nothing.

With the necessary detachment of a commander on a battlefield strewn with his dead, Salyard turned away from the tables, to contemplate the barren foothills of the Sierra Madre Mountains and the blackened pit that had been gouged in the dry earth so early this morning. In the general's hand was the palm-size digital player containing the final words spoken by the KC-135 pilot, captured by his aircraft's Flight Data Satellite Relay Transmitter.

Development of the new satellite system had been pioneered by the Air Force as an adjunct to the traditional "black box" flight data recorders in use on most planes. Those physical, solid-state recorders captured cockpit voice recordings and up to 700 different flight profile and engineering parameters. The new FDSAT transmitters could handle only 88 key flight parameters plus cockpit voices, but the system's chief advantage was that all FDR data and voice recordings were continuously uploaded to a satellite communications network instead of being kept on the plane. That meant critical data could be downloaded and made available within minutes of a crash instead of days, immediately aiding rescue workers and investigators and, more significantly, providing instant evidence of whether or not an act of terrorism had been committed.

The KC-135's standard crash-survivable memory units had been installed in the tail, and housed in a titanium cylinder that could endure impacts up to 3,400 gs, and fires of 2,000° F. Salyard knew there would be more complete details—perhaps even definitive answers—in that cylinder, though it could take a week or more to excavate, clean, and reconnect it for data recovery. In battle, waiting a week for crucial intelligence was waiting a week too long. The stripped-down, real-time satellite recording had told him what he needed to know, when he needed to know it— right now.

Salyard turned to the man who now stood beside him, Colonel Daniel Varik. "You've listened to this?"

"No, General. I brought it straight from data relay. Your eyes only."

Salyard walked out from the tent and into the relentless midday sun, away from anyone who might inadvertently overhear what he had to say. Two MH–60 Pave Hawk helicopters thundered past overhead, patrolling the crash site, keeping television news helos at bay.

Salyard gave Varik the small player. "When you get a chance. The pilot and copilot fought the controls till the end. But it wasn't an accident."

The dry inland wind shifted and brought the stench of charred earth to them. Neither Salyard nor Varik reacted.

"From what the pilot says on the recording," Salyard continued, "they had an autopilot override error. It engaged by itself, took them into a dive, then didn't let them disengage and pull up."

"The autopilot should have disengaged the moment the ground-proximity alert went off."

"Should have," Salyard agreed, sure he knew the reason for the failure. "The autopilot system is manufactured by Boeing. But at Vandenberg, the cockpit electronics maintenance contract was awarded to TTI."

In the distance, airmen in bright yellow biohazard suits picked through the unrecognizable remnants of the plane. Two HH–60G Pave Hawk rescue helicopters remained parked nearby, ready to transport recovery personnel and critical wreckage components back to base as needed.

"You're saying Teller did this?" Varik asked, as if the idea was impossible.

"His new countermove, taking out the entire primary crew of the *Falcon,* five days before launch. No question." When Salyard had first been alerted that this plane had gone down, a profound calm had enveloped him, and he still felt its influence. "The war is no longer being fought in shadow."

"So he *does* know everything?"

"Along with us, and the Chinese." Even now, Salyard could see the ebb and flow of that three-way battle laid out before him, a flowchart of inevitable confrontation and decisive escalation. "And Teller played it out perfectly. Almost a year after we had finally located Site One, we discovered our data had been compromised by the Chinese. And while we were focused on what Beijing was planning to do in response, Teller launched his rover to the Moon, perilously close to the target coordinates, but not directly to them. At the time, we couldn't be sure of his motives, so we probed his defenses with a subtle countermove, and shut down communications to his LRV."

"But it didn't stop him," Varik said. "He was expecting we'd do that."

"Which told us what we needed to know, Daniel. The fact that Teller had anticipated losing contact with his rover and had had it programmed to complete the mission on its own was proof he knew exactly where that rover was landing and what it would find there. In detail."

Warrior to warrior, Salyard could appreciate his enemy's tactics. From that appreciation, he knew, would come knowledge. And from that knowledge, victory. It was the only acceptable end goal of his flowchart of battle.

"The samples came back to the station," Salyard said,

"because he had outmaneuvered us. So we countered with an interception, which didn't play out the way we had planned, but was still effective. Then . . ." The general stopped in midsentence, as he suddenly saw the hidden pattern in Teller's plan.

"My God." Salyard was overcome with the realization that the Project was now exposed to attack from an unsuspected, but lethal direction. He shared his reasoning with his trusted subordinate. "What happened on the station, that's what triggered Teller's next countermove—sending Farren to act as if he wanted to blackmail us."

"But Farren told you he was there on orders from NASA," Varik said. "And he was trying to blackmail us."

"No, he wasn't." Salyard's thoughts spun in all directions, tracking Teller's wheels within wheels. "I *assumed* Farren was seeing me on NASA's behalf. It was just the kind of ploy Tovah Caruso would try. I was wrong, but Farren's connection to NASA was key to Teller's plan. He chose Farren to deliver a message to us, knowing that I'd assume NASA was attempting to reveal the Project. The old man was a decoy. A feint. And I reacted as predicted."

In his tan-and-brown desert camouflage battle dress uniform, like Varik, Salyard stood motionless, just another element within the lifeless landscape that surrounded them. This far from the searchers in the pit, all that moved were the helicopters circling on their ceaseless patrol.

Varik broke the silence. "General, what if we had responded to Farren's threat as he intended? What if the Project *had* launched a rescue mission?"

"Teller knew we would never expose ourselves for the sake of a single civilian. It didn't matter what Farren threatened to do."

"Then I'm lost. Why did Teller send Farren in if there was no chance Farren would succeed?"

To Salyard, it was unnerving how completely he had allowed himself to be drawn in by Teller's misdirection. "Teller *wanted* me to eliminate Farren. He was counting on it."

"A deliberate sacrifice? For what gain?"

"So if the time came, he could use Farren's *death* as a weapon against me."

"If that's true, then Teller was taking a risk. Farren was an old man. The police report said his death was the result of a heart attack."

"The police," Salyard agreed. "That's where it would start. And if the samples had made their way back to Teller, that's where it would have ended. But if I were Teller, when I saw that the station had been destroyed, I'd have known who was responsible for keeping my samples from me. So to strike back, I'd have asked someone highly placed to take another look at Farren's death. A closer look."

The general did not deceive himself. The stakes had been increased again. "Daniel, I guarantee you, right at this moment the FBI is taking that closer look into Farren's death. By now, they've probably determined he wasn't killed by a heart attack. And the last place he visited was my office."

"General, that might have been Teller's plan, but the station wasn't destroyed."

"Only because of Russian incompetence," Salyard said. For more than ten years, the Russian space program had been bankrupt, dependent on the largesse of the American government, which funneled taxpayer dollars to the PKA through NASA. But NASA dollars came with stringent conditions, and little opportunity was available for transferring those funds to purposes not specifically related to the ISS. It had been the United States Air Force that had smoothed the gray areas, with money from its classified budget that received only the most cursory oversight and was easily diverted.

Unbeknownst to those without a need to know, the USAF paid and was still paying for luxurious country *dacha*s, new American cars, vacations on the Black Sea, wide-screen televisions, laptop computers . . . all the inducements necessary to keep Russian space scientists and engineers content to remain in Russia, and not look for new horizons in China or the Middle East.

In return, the Air Force—and Salyard's Space Force— received the fruits of Russia's decades of brute-force engineering expertise. And that included secrets of kerosene-burning rockets that outperformed the overdesigned liquid-fueled motors favored by NASA, as well as remarkable ionized-gas generators that created plasma screens around any aircraft to reduce aerodynamic drag *and* render them invisible to radar.

But the best return on such Air Force investment had always been obedience, abroad and at home. The few remaining, operational, Russian surveillance satellites that passed over targets of interest to an enemy of America, could be counted on to malfunction. Microchip components of various weapons systems destined for non-NATO governments had dormant computer viruses and backdoor access to the programming code burned into them, so a single software command could downgrade or shut those systems down. And if the Air Force needed a Progress supply ship to blow up while docked with the ISS, even at the cost of two cosmonauts' lives, there were enough Flight Control Center engineers and technicians on the payroll to arrange such an accident without ever alerting suspicion in the managers of the Russian Space Agency.

But those bought-and-paid-for engineers and technicians had failed, and Salyard wanted to know why.

Four days ago, for almost an hour, his victory had been certain. Radar confirmed the station had been destroyed with no survivors, ending any chance of samples returning from Site One. He himself had given the sad news to Captain Webber.

Then the news had changed. High-resolution images from the OWL facility delivered to his office had shown two-thirds of the station intact. And, at almost the same time, he'd received the NORAD report of the *Soyuz* capsule reentering.

Varik interrupted Salyard's review of his changing battlefront. "General? I don't think we have anything to be concerned about when it comes to the FBI. Whatever the incident or condition that caused Teller to send Farren to you, the station is as good as destroyed. And most important, no samples came back with the woman and the Russian."

"As far as we know, Colonel." Salyard knew that Varik had not heard the recording of Rey's conversation with her employer, reporting her inability to retrieve the samples from the LRV. Though he hoped that report was accurate, he had no way of verifying it. There was still the matter of the unrecorded, private conversations Rey had had with her high-level contact at Spacecom.

Salyard continued with the information he felt was more appropriate for his subordinate. "But I've had Air Force Intelligence put out the word to all facilities capable of identifying lunar material. If Doctor Rey or the Russian did manage to bring something from the station, and Teller intends to make use of it in some way, the first thing he'll have to do is authenticate it. Most of the spectroscopy labs that can do that kind of analysis depend on government contracts. If any of them are asked to authenticate lunar material, rest assured we'll hear about it before Teller does. And when that happens, I've given orders to have Doctor Rey immediately brought in for questioning."

"And then?" Varik asked.

"And then we'll take appropriate action against Teller, and against Rey." Salyard checked his watch. "So much for the enemy. What's our condition?"

Varik was ready with his report, even though he must have known that it would not be well received. "Rodriguez and Bowden are flying in from White Sands. In separate jets."

"So that's our mission specialist and SOV pilot." Salyard frowned as he realized Varik had not volunteered the status of the rest of the backup crew. "What about a commander and pilot for the *Kitty Hawk?*"

Varik squared his shoulders. "We have no properly trained individuals available for those slots, General. We don't have the depth of personnel."

Salyard knew the staffing situation was tight. And he was all too aware that he personally had eliminated the possibility of a preflight total loss of crew from the contingency plans. At most, the Project could have fielded two replacements for the *Falcon*'s crew, and because of cross-training, all positions could have been filled. But to have lost all four in a routine training mission was a scenario he had not anticipated.

Someday, when the Space Force was publicly known, they would have no trouble attracting pilots. But as long as it was a restricted operation, finding pilots with the qualifications for spaceflight and who hadn't already joined NASA would remain a challenge. And to face that challenge, sometimes difficult decisions were called for.

Salyard knew this was one of those times. He made the hard choice.

"The Chinese have nothing on the pad, so we're safe in concluding they are at least three weeks from launch." Salyard knew it would take China that long to prep, test, and fuel. "So we are on hold. I want the *Falcon* kept on the pad, but we will go on the next window, next month."

"What if the Chinese roll out their booster today?"

"Then we will launch early, and cope with the lighting conditions at the site as best we can."

Varik looked uncomfortable at having to ask another question. "And what should I do about crew selection, General?"

"Congratulations, Colonel Varik, you are now the commander of the *Falcon*'s mission. And Captain Webber is the *Kitty Hawk* pilot. Get in touch with him, let him know his furlough's over and he's to report to Vandenberg ASAP."

It was a moment before Varik could respond, and Salyard knew why. The colonel would be pleased by his selection as commander, and furious at Webber's selection as pilot. "General, with respect, Captain Webber hasn't—"

"I know what you're going to say, and there's no need. Webber is a phenomenally skilled pilot with considerable space-related training. He could probably land the *Kitty Hawk* today if we needed him to. And if you lock him up in the simulator for the next month, I have no doubt you will make him into the pilot we need."

"Understood, General."

Salyard knew Varik would accept his orders, but he could see his subordinate was not happy with them.

"Daniel, keep in mind, if the *Falcon*'s mission fails, the Space Force is out of business, and so is the United States. Teller knows that. That's why he's pushed us." Salyard looked up as the two Pave Hawks circled past. In that moment, he knew what he had to do—jump to the end of the flowchart, bypassing *all* intermediate stages. "And that's why I am now directing you to eliminate Kai Teller."

Varik appeared to choose his next words carefully. "That will . . . entail some risk."

"Not as much risk as our losing," Salyard said. "This war ends now. And *I* am the one who will end it."

Varik had his orders.

Teller was a dead man.

13

COLORADO SPRINGS FEDERAL BUILDING
08:31 MDT, WEDNESDAY, APRIL 9

"I'M STILL MAD at you," Cory Rey said.

Webber opened the passenger door of his rented Toyota Land Cruiser. "Tell me something I don't already know." He kept out of her way as she hoisted herself into the high passenger seat, lifting her crutch in after her. "It's your fault," she said quietly, then shut the door before he could do it for her.

Webber walked around the huge SUV to the driver's side. Whenever he took to civilian roads, he wanted as much armor around him as possible. He took enough risks in his work. No need to add to them unnecessarily.

He opened his door, got in, and started the engine, but then just couldn't help himself. *"How* is it my fault?"

"You attacked two FBI agents, Rambo."

"I defended myself and my friends from two unidentified men with guns who charged us from the shadows."

"And the Feds bought that excuse?"

Webber waved to the blue sky beyond the parking lot of the tall, isolated building housing the Colorado Springs field office of the FBI. "We're out, aren't we? The sun is shining. It's a brand-new day."

He glanced to the side, saw Cory regarding him almost sadly.

"What?" he asked.

"When did you get so sarcastic all of a sudden?"

"Must be the company I keep."

"Mitchell, we haven't even talked to each other for more than a year."

Webber wanted to punch the roof, hit the steering wheel, get out of the car and walk away—do anything except say what he knew he had to say. "Cory . . . when I heard what was happening up on the station . . . I was worried for you. I . . . I should have called . . . not let a year go by."

"More than a year," Cory corrected.

But Webber didn't argue. "However long. I'm sorry."

"I thought you never wanted to see me again," she said. "When my boxes arrived from San Diego, and there was no note. Nothing but the damn invoice from the movers. I thought that was your 'Dear John' letter to me."

Webber shook his head. Maybe at the time, that had been his intention. But if so, he regretted it now. "No. It wasn't."

Cory, as always, seemed to have the ability to look right through him. "Or else, it was, and it's taken this long for you to come to your senses."

"Maybe," Webber half admitted, wanting the conversation to move on.

"Want to go check into a cheap motel?" Cory asked.

"Cory . . ."

Cory shrugged with a grin, letting him know he had taken the bait again. "Or, we could always get a coffee at Starbucks."

"Coffee." Webber threw the Cruiser into reverse, turned to back out of the parking space the FBI had thoughtfully provided for the car when they had impounded it.

"You're such a Boy Scout, Mitchell."

"I thought I was Rambo."

"It's that odd mix I find so captivating."

Webber wove the Cruiser through the maze of parking barricades protecting the building, then turned out onto Rood Avenue, heading for a stretch of stores he had seen last night when the FBI had brought him in, separately from Cory. Bailey and Hubert had been allowed to go straight home.

He checked awnings and store signs to left and right. There was bound to be a coffee shop among them. "The Feds treated you okay?" he asked.

"The ones who tried to interrogate me were good little government robots. They kept asking the same questions, over and over."

"Did you answer any of them?" Webber asked, though he was pretty sure he knew what her answer to that one would be.

"What do you think? Did you?"

"They only wanted to teach me a lesson," Webber said. "They knew they were wrong for not identifying themselves. But that didn't mean they couldn't try to make me sweat a little."

"You? Good luck."

"Yeah, well, when dawn came, I promised I wouldn't beat up any more FBI agents, and they promised not to arrest me."

"That was it for the whole night?"

Webber scanned ahead, looking for a likely spot for a coffee shop or restaurant. "They asked my name, ran my ID. Asked what I was doing at the university—"

"You didn't tell them, did you?" Cory asked with real concern.

"Visiting a friend of a friend. That's all I said. They didn't think it was all that unusual that the hero of the space station disaster might want to meet a physics professor. Go figure."

"They called me a 'hero'?"

"Aren't you?"

The sharp edge that was so often in Cory's tone disappeared. "Anatoly Rushkin is a hero. Sophia Dante. Whoever was at the controls of the *Constitution*. I was just payload."

"Not true," Webber said. But he tabled his protest as he saw a green and black Starbucks sign, looked for a parking space that could take his behemoth of a vehicle. Cory was feeling down right now, that's why her self-assessment was so bleak. Besides, arguing wouldn't take them anywhere near where he hoped they'd go this time. "So what sort of questions did they try to get you to answer?"

"All over the map. There's one." Cory pointed to an open spot with a meter.

"Too small," Webber said, and kept driving. "What was all over the map?"

"It's obvious the FBI think whatever happened to the station was sabotage, and I got the feeling they're trying to figure out if it was directed at the station, the shuttle, or someone onboard."

Webber put on the blinker to turn onto a residential street and circle back to check parking again. The brown Taurus behind him hit its brakes with a screech, but the driver didn't honk. He had been following too close.

Webber made the turn, checking to be sure the Taurus didn't. Everything was making him suspicious this morning. "The FBI actually thinks someone would go to all the trouble of blowing up the space station to get one person?"

"Crazy, huh? Sounds like something only the government would do."

Webber declined to rise to the bait, saw a free spot between the driveways of two houses, pulled in. Then he remembered Cory's crutch. "Is this too far to walk?"

"I can crawl," Cory said.

Webber was about to open his door, when he decided there were a few questions he had to ask that might be best asked in private. "Did they ask anything about the . . . the remains from the Moon?"

Cory seemed to understand the reason for not leaving the car. "Every once in a while they said something about the sample cylinders. But I think they were hung up on the fact that the first explosion happened just when I opened the LRV, as if there might be some link."

"Could there be?"

"You know, I've been thinking about that. It makes no sense that someone would set a bomb to destroy the shuttle and the station the moment I retrieved the samples. But you know what does make sense?"

Webber had forgotten how compelling Cory could be when her mind was at work. He had missed that, too, more than he had realized. "What?" he asked, playing his role as sounding board.

"If the explosion was intended to be a diversion."

"Why does that make sense?"

"I was up there because I had spent a year training to use all the robotic manipulator systems, troubleshoot them, repair them on site if I had to. But once I retrieved the sample cylinders and put them into the retrieval sleeve, everything past that point was an automated sequence anyone could follow through with. My part of the job was over. So, if someone wanted to get those samples for themselves, that was the earliest moment they could get them."

Cory's scenario made real sense to Webber. "You do the work. Then the unknown party creates a diversion . . ."

"If there's a fire, a little depressurization, everyone scrambles back to the shuttle and the *Soyuz* . . ."

"And the unknown party . . . what? Steals the lunar samples and smuggles them back to Earth? That doesn't work, does it?"

"It does if the unknown party—or, in this case, Major Norman—only wanted part of the samples. The fingers."

Webber remembered Cory telling him that the station's science officer had drawn a Swiss Army knife on her, determined to get to the samples before Cory could. At the time, he had thought the most likely reason for Norman's action was her desire to save scientifically important cargo. But if Cory's speculation was right . . .

"You think Bette Norman knew the fingers were going to be in the samples?"

Cory tapped her finger against the padded top of her crutch. "At the very least, she knew there was something important in the samples she had been ordered to retrieve. But even if she didn't know exactly what she was after, whoever she was working for did."

"But the diversion went wrong," Webber pointed out, "and destroyed the shuttle and the station."

"Actually, it gets even worse than that."

"I'm listening," Webber said, both fascinated and appalled by what Cory was spelling out.

"Let's say the first explosions were a diversion gone wrong. You know about Lazhenko and wanting asylum for himself and his family?"

"I was at the landing site, Cory. He used my phone."

"Oh, right. Anyway, Lazhenko's convinced that the controllers in Moscow deliberately tried to blow up the station and kill the rest of us."

"So, it wasn't just a diversion. It's a cover-up?"

"Technically," Cory said, "it's a cover-up of the diversion gone wrong. Whoever wanted the remains from the Moon couldn't get them, so they decided no one could get them."

Webber felt the hair on his arms prickle as he drew the final conclusion. He started the Cruiser's engine again.

"Aren't we having coffee?" Cory asked.

Webber put on the blinker, checked for traffic as he started to pull away from the curb. "Not now."

Cory frowned. "And we're not going to a cheap motel, are we?"

"Back to the FBI," Webber said.

"What?!" Cory made a grab for the steering wheel.

Webber hit the brakes, half out of his parking spot, turned urgently to Cory. "Don't you get it? Someone blew up the space station and the shuttle to stop those remains from coming back to Earth—*and you brought them back to Earth!*"

Cory seemed to wilt before him.

"They're not going to stop, Cory," Webber said. "If you're right, you and Lazhenko are in as much danger right now as you ever were up there. So I'm taking you back to the FBI, and I want you to tell them everything. That's the only way I can keep you safe."

Cory rallied enough to protest. "Now you're the one who doesn't get it, Mitchell. If you ask yourself who has the ability to destroy the space station, one of the usual suspects has to be the government. We *can't* go back to the FBI."

"Cory, you need protection!"

Cory reached out and tried to twist the key out of the ignition. "I do not need to be protected by people who might be trying to kill me!"

The keys wouldn't come out while the Cruiser was in Drive. But Webber put a hand over Cory's to pull it away from the key and keep the Cruiser running. "Cory, the government has better ways to kill you than by blowing up their own space station!"

"That's what I'm afraid of!"

And then the Cruiser clanged and lurched as a car drove into its side, sending Webber against the steering wheel and slamming Cory against her passenger door.

"You still with me?" Webber gasped, the wind knocked out of him.

Cory nodded, more startled than hurt. She pointed out Webber's window and Webber turned to see a clean-cut young man in a black windbreaker rushing around from the driver's side of the tan Taurus that was wedged into the rear panel of the Cruiser.

Immediately, Webber realized what had happened. The Cruiser had been half out of its parking spot and the driver of the Taurus had obviously not been paying attention and—

"Don't kill him or anything," Cory said quickly. "It was an accident."

But Webber already knew it wasn't. The brown Taurus was the same car that had almost hit him when he had turned onto this street. The same car that had then driven on as he had watched it.

"Everyone okay?" the driver shouted through Webber's window.

"Stay in the car," Webber hissed at Cory. "That car was following us."

"Oh, shit," Cory said. She scrabbled for her crutch.

Webber was already opening his door as the man, stepping out of the way, began sliding his hand behind his back.

Webber was a move ahead. He shoved the door open as hard as he could and sent the driver flying.

An instant later, Webber heard the crash of glass and Cory's cry and turned to see the driver's accomplice reach through Cory's shattered window, unlock her door, and yank her out.

Webber sprang out of the Cruiser only to freeze in place as the driver, half-lying, half-sitting on the road, trained a .45 on him. Webber recognized the model. An H&K Mk 23. The same one he used.

"Close the door," the driver said as he got to his feet.

"Mitchell . . . ," Cory called in a strangled gasp. The second man was dragging her to the Taurus, his arm locked in a stranglehold around her neck, keeping her off balance, unable to employ any move that Webber had taught her.

"Don't even think about it," the driver warned Webber. "Close the door."

Webber closed his car door behind him, keeping his eyes locked on the driver's eyes, assessing his intent.

"Turn around," the driver said.

"Mitchell!"

The second man was now pushing Cory into the Taurus, behind a security screen that divided the backseat from the front. The moment the second man slammed the brown car's door, Webber saw Cory struggling to open the door on the other side. But she couldn't.

Webber faced the driver and his gun. "You're not FBI."

"Turn around," the driver repeated. This time, he raised his weapon to make his point more emphatically.

Webber turned around.

"Hands on the car," the driver said.

Webber put his hands on the side of his SUV. His right hand fit almost perfectly into the gap between the Land Cruiser's windshield and its radio antenna. He waited for the driver to start to pat him down, knowing that a half second after the driver's hand touched him, the driver would be out of the game.

But the driver didn't touch him.

Webber tried to look over his shoulder to be sure the driver was still there. He was. "Aren't you going to search me?" Webber asked.

"That won't be necessary. Now turn around."

Webber turned slowly, understanding that the little charade he had just participated in was for the benefit of any observers in the nearby houses. Almost one-third of the population of Colorado Springs was connected to the military. They would know what proper procedures were. Webber had no doubt that the driver planned to shoot him, and all that any witnesses would be able to recall was that the driver had behaved just like a real policeman.

"Who are you working for?" Webber demanded as he stepped back against the car. Now his left hand found the base of the Cruiser's antenna. It wouldn't be as clean or as easy, but in Webber's mind, the driver was still going to be just as dead.

"Colorado State Patrol," the driver said. "I've got a badge and everything."

Cory yelled something muffled from the Taurus. Webber deliberately did not react, but the driver's eyes shifted, for just an instant.

An instant was all it took for Webber to snap the antenna and thrust it forward like a spear to puncture the driver's eye.

Even as his eyeball popped and his mouth opened in a gasp of pain, the driver fired his gun.

But by then, Webber had already started the left-handed blocking sweep that thrust the driver's arm aside so the bullet missed its mark. At the same time, Webber pivoted in with his right hand, palm coming up precisely to catch the driver's chin, applying maximum force to make his head snap sideways, not quite breaking his neck but pinching the nerves severely enough to make him collapse in spasms.

Webber followed the driver down, grasping the H&K .45 and rolling forward to come up in a crouch, aiming that gun at the second man who held a matching H&K .45 against the car window separating him from Cory.

"I'll kill her," the second man threatened with conviction.

At this range, Webber knew he couldn't miss and didn't hesitate. He tapped the man one inch above the bridge of his nose, instantly pulping his brain tissue, with the supersonic shockwave of the bullet's impact traveling even faster than the nervous system's ability to send a final twitch to the finger on the trigger.

As if his bones and muscles had liquefied along with his brain, the second man went limp, collapsed.

Webber knelt beside the moaning, coughing driver, found a badge case identifying him as a criminal investigator for the Colorado State Patrol, but he carried no other identification. As Webber finished his quick search, he became aware of Cory's rhythmic pounding on the door of the Taurus.

He also heard sirens. The neighbors had seen enough.

Webber rushed to the Taurus, called out to Cory to back away, then used the H&K's pistol grip to shatter the back window. When the door still didn't open, he reached in and pulled her out. Wishing he could just hoist her over his shoulder, instead he put an arm around her waist, half-dragged her back to the Cruiser, and almost tossed her in.

"How could you shoot him?" Cory said, shocked. "He had a gun on me! He could have killed me!"

Webber was already in the driver's seat, slamming the still-idling Cruiser back into Drive as the sirens grew closer.

"If he had been ordered to kill you, he'd never have taken you from the car. His orders were to take you to someone."

"Who?!" Cory asked.

The Cruiser's tires squealed as Webber hit the gas. "Good question," he said grimly. "Why don't we find out?"

14

KAI TELLER STEPPED DOWN from his Gulfstream V into the heart of the enemy: the runway known as the Skid Strip in the center of the Cape Canaveral Air Force Station at the Kennedy Space Center.

He paused for a moment to relish the tang of the Atlantic, so much a part of the heavy, humid air of Florida, its rich scent a reminder of his past triumphs at Kennedy. Remarkable though those memories were, it was only days before they'd be eclipsed by his greatest coup yet—complete control of America's space program.

As his three-member flight crew exited behind him, heading for the jet's aft storage compartment and his luggage, Teller stood in the shade of his plane, directly opposite the single-story building on the far side of the runway. Technically, the small airport facility was part of Patrick Air Force Base and a Department of Defense installation. But historically, as the site of NASA's earliest manned spaceflights, Cape Canaveral Air Force Station was an integral part of the Kennedy Space Center, just across the Banana River.

More than forty years after the successes of the Mercury and Gemini programs, it was from this small station that NASA's expendable vehicle launches still took place— robotic missions to Mars and the other planets, satellites for the Earth, probes to chase comets and asteroids. Only the space shuttle launched from the grounds of Kennedy proper. But to the general public, the two sites were one and the same, all under the informal name, the Cape.

Though Teller knew better, he often maintained that particular confusion in his conversations, knowing how much it annoyed the "blue suits" of the Air Force.

Today, Air Force station traffic was light, and standard. Parked to the left of the station's small Landing Aids Control Building, Teller counted eight of NASA's thirty-plane fleet of Northrup T-38 jets assigned to the astronaut corps, their large clear canopies gaping wide like alligator jaws. The two-seater, twin-engined planes were both a training necessity and a much-appreciated perk, in that the T-38s were essentially a private jet service for astronaut pilots, allowing them to keep up their flight hours and maintain their flying edge.

To the right of the control center were two Pave Hawk rescue helicopters, being worked on by Air Force maintenance crews. Their presence was also unremarkable. With so many thousands of tons of explosive propellants in the immediate area, rapid-response rescue services were essential.

Next to the Pave Hawks, another craft was being refueled: a NASA Gulfstream, similar to the one that had taken Tovah Caruso to Houston. This one, Teller guessed, had most likely delivered other senior NASA functionaries to Kennedy in preparation for their appearances before the multiple boards of inquiry already being arranged. Most likely, those functionaries were also preparing to drive their knives into their chief administrator's back.

Despite his words of comfort to her a few hours ago in Houston, Teller suspected Caruso would be out of NASA even faster than she feared. Not that he cared. He no longer needed her. Like Ed Farren, another of his pawns in a much bigger game, Caruso had been useful to draw the enemy out into the open, leaving it vulnerable to counterattack. But she was no longer necessary. He was finally ready to mount that attack.

Part of what had inspired him to reach for this, his greatest victory, was, Teller knew, a consequence of his being born on Maui, a small volcanic island surrounded by a limitless ocean. He had been tantalized throughout his childhood by the knowledge that other, greater, stranger lands surrounded even that. The metaphor of Earth for Maui, and space for the ocean was too obvious to deny.

But even more important were those long-ago mornings when his father had awakened him well before dawn, then led him to the rail of the dew-damp, timbered balcony of their home to stare out to the northwest and watch the stars disappear as distant clouds flared red and the sky turned incandescent, as if the Earth had reversed its rotation and the sun was about to emerge on the wrong side of the world.

Nuclear tests, his father had told him, and young Kai had had no intellectual grasp of the meaning of those words. But his heart had been seized by something more primal when his father explained that the light that could banish night was created by something that scientists had built and exploded just over five hundred miles away, something no larger than the Teller family's Volkswagen Beetle.

To Kai Teller the child, all those words of explanation had blended into one stirring, soaring, compelling concept:

Science was magic. He had spent the rest of his life attempting to recapture that magic and control it himself.

Three years ago, for ten incredible days, he had done exactly that. He'd ridden the fire of a Proton rocket and voyaged where fewer than a thousand humans had ever gone—into space. On the third night, long after his father's death, he had watched the endless darkness in exhilarated anticipation as the pilot of his *Soyuz* spacecraft docked with the half-built International Space Station. Then he'd left the cramped capsule itself and floated into a permanent outpost in space, knowing in that moment—his true birth—that he was touching the future.

His five days on the station had cost him twenty-two million dollars, the whole amount paid to the Russian Aviation and Space Agency. But he'd have sold everything he owned to spend even one day beyond the Earth, in the limitless ocean of space.

Someday, Teller knew, it was inevitable that more people would live in space, and on the Moon, some even within his lifetime. After that, more would live and work on Mars, and on the ships that sailed the void between the three worlds. As for reaching the stars—so distant from Earth that even the space probes of the 1970s and '80s would have to travel for millennia more to reach the closest one—well, that goal was merely a matter of engineering. Just as the technology of the year 2000 had surpassed that of the year 1900, it wasn't difficult to predict that the technology of 2100 would amaze the people living now, and that the technology of 2200 and 2300 would likely approach the limits of current comprehension. Farther into the future than that, and the famous observation by Arthur C. Clarke would certainly prove true: Any sufficiently advanced technology is indistinguishable from magic.

Humans belong in space, Teller thought. *And on other worlds.* His father had died too soon, too soon to see his own son take one of humanity's first steps off the home world. And the same thing was going to happen to him, Teller knew. He'd die before humanity took the next step: its grand exodus to the interplanetary—perhaps interstellar—destiny that was inescapable.

But thanks to him, at least that day was going to arrive sooner and not later for the generations still to come.

He'd devoted his whole life to making space travel a reality for every child who dreamed. His company was focused completely on the development of new capabilities that could make space travel safer, more affordable, and more routine for everyone. Everything he did was in furtherance of that goal. Nothing—no one—had a right to obstruct or prevent the achievement of something of such importance to the future of humanity. Not even General Dwight Salyard and the United States Space Force.

Simply destroying the USSF had never been a rational option, though. Too many valuable resources wasted. Far better to bring them under the control of someone who could properly exploit them.

Teller saw a familiar, heavyset figure begin to cross the runway, coming from the control building. It was Derek Frame, flight systems manager of TTI's Lunar Return Vehicle program. By rights, it was Frame who should have been TTI's payload specialist on the most recent shuttle flight, instead of serving as Cory Rey's backup. But the Alabaman, who had spent the past twenty years of his life in front of a computer screen, was ten years too old and fifty pounds too heavy for NASA to have approved him for flight training. Good as he was, Cory Rey had turned out to be better. But though Frame had not been able to demonstrate his abilities on the ISS last week, in less than three weeks, Teller would be giving him his chance to perform even more momentous work, not in Earth orbit, but on the Moon.

Frame was wearing a faded Reyn Spooner shirt with a riot of orange and green parrots and tropical blossoms over a sorry, wrinkled pair of khaki pants. Sweat trickled down his flushed cheeks into wild tufts of salt-and-pepper sideburns that did little to narrow his round and multichinned face. But his wide smile as he hurried toward the shade of his employer's plane told Teller that the news was good. Nonetheless, Teller still could not relax.

His plan to bring Salyard under his control required two elements to be unassailable. One element was already in place, and might be enough to make the general blink. *But without the second—*

"Doctor Rey brought back samples," Frame wheezed, speaking as quietly as he could, so that Teller's flight crew wouldn't hear him.

A wave of elation swept through Teller. Now Salyard would have no choice but to submit. Still, the stakes were high enough that Frame's high spirits could not be accepted as proof.

"How do we know?" he asked.

Frame raised his eyebrows comically. "Salyard told us." He grinned. "The general had a good idea, put out the word that any lab with a Raman spectroscopy setup that had previously done lunar calibrations—"

"Of course," Teller interrupted. Rey would want proof that what she had surreptitiously retrieved from the LRV had actually come from the Moon.

Undeterred, Frame jumped ahead in his story. "So he got a hit. The physics lab at the University of Colorado at Colorado Springs."

"Air Force territory." The implications were troubling

to Teller. The Air Force Academy was located outside Colorado Springs, and so was Cheyenne Mountain AFS.

"Doctor Rey *is* there," Frame confirmed.

Teller glanced to the side, but his well-trained flight crew was staying together by the plane's tail, well out of earshot. "Do we know why she's there?" he asked Frame.

"Nope. But she's obviously not working for Salyard, otherwise—"

"Otherwise he wouldn't have asked labs to be on the alert," Teller agreed. "And you know this because . . . ?"

"It's direct from Sergeant Tucker," Frame whispered.

Teller looked forward to the day the general discovered that his own personal assistant had been on the TTI payroll for a year. Next to his trip to the station, Teller considered Sergeant April Tucker the best investment he had ever made.

"Was she able to tell us what kind of samples were being tested?"

"A few particles of dust," Frame said. "The cover story is that the dust is from an Apollo astronaut patch a collector wants to sell. Legitimate, but private."

Teller took a moment to consider the cover story. "That doesn't sound like Rey. She doesn't tend to think that far ahead." It was one of the reasons he'd sought her out as his payload specialist. As an activist-slash-scientist, Rey was committed, idealistic to a fault, and from what he had heard from classified sources about her involvement in the Icefire incident, more than capable of taking on anything NASA could throw at her.

In his first meetings with Rey, he had also detected that her almost automatic dislike of big business and government conveniently blinded her to some of the subtler actions and strategies undertaken by those institutions to ensure their own survival. That flaw had suggested to him that he could welcome her into TTI without fearing she would immediately sniff out the true purpose of his LRV mission. And, if she ever did discover why he'd committed a hundred million dollars of his company's resources to what was on the surface little more than a high-profile publicity stunt, he'd be able to count on her distrust of the government in general and the military in particular to sway her to his side of the argument. Her predictability had reminded him of Caruso, who was also reliably anti–Air Force. Teller welcomed predictability. It equated with malleability.

"You think Cory's in business with someone?" Frame asked.

Teller nodded. "Someone she must have told about the samples." *Now that* is *troublesome,* he thought. While he was confident he could predict Rey's actions, how someone else might respond was an X factor.

"You know," Frame said reassuringly, "she might just have come back with rocks and regolith."

"Then she'd have no reason to hide the news from me," Teller said.

Frame wiped his glistening forehead with the short sleeve of his shirt. "She could have wanted to sell the samples on her own."

"Not her. She's honest to a fault."

"How can she be if she's hiding the samples from you?"

"She's only keeping them from me because she thinks I'm keeping something from her. Which, of course, I am."

"Meaning what? That it's not just rocks and regolith?" Frame was practically panting in the heat, obviously longing to return to air conditioning.

Teller waved for his crew to join him. "Meaning we have to assume Rey has at least some of the artifacts the rover was programmed to recover. The dust she wanted tested . . . she probably brushed it off one of them."

"So where does this put us?"

"Still one step ahead of the general," Teller said, breaking off his talk with Frame to instruct his crew to go to the control building and complete the jet's check-in, that he'd follow shortly.

"Salyard'll be after her, too," Frame cautioned as he and Teller watched the TTI crew enter the control building.

Teller stepped out of the shade of his plane. "That could be a win-win situation."

Frame stared at him, all aversion to the heat and sunshine apparently forgotten. "You're joking."

But Teller had already thought through the two possible outcomes of the game. "Number one, any effort Salyard expends on Rey is effort he can't expend against TTI. So that helps us right away. Two, if he does take her in, she won't tell him anything, just on general principle. She'll raise such an unholy furor that . . ." Teller pictured the collision between the general and the activist, unable to imagine a more perfect example of the irresistible force meeting the immovable object.

"You know how Salyard operates," Frame said, worried. "Whatever she knows, he's going to know. It's just a matter of when."

"Well, that's part of the win-win equation, isn't it? Salyard already knows that I know what's on the Moon. Since he's not an idiot, he'll also suspect I moved against his primary crew in retaliation for his move against Farren."

Teller started off in the direction of his crew and the Air Force station control building.

Frame hurried along beside him, breathing heavily. "But . . . you wanted Farren dead."

"You're still missing the point," Teller said. "I wanted Farren killed on Salyard's orders. That way, I was able to use

Caruso to start an FBI investigation into Farren's murder that goes directly to Salyard's doorstep."

Frame stopped abruptly, looked confused. "How does *that* give us a double win with Cory?"

They were halfway across the runway. Teller halted, tried to make it simple. "Look, Salyard's a bureaucrat more than he's a soldier. He'll protect his turf before he'll try to fulfill his mission. Which is exactly why he shouldn't be in the position he's in. With the FBI on the prowl, and a primary crew to replace, he's going to pull back to his bunker till he can launch his mission. While he's trying to ride out the storm, he'll be frantic to clean up loose ends, and Rey is the biggest one he'll have in hand. He'll waste time and resources on her, only to discover that she's not in possession of the samples—"

"How do you know that?" Frame asked.

"Frame, someone crafted the cover story of where the lunar dust came from. That means Rey has at least one person helping her. Probably more. They're the ones who'll know where the samples are—"

"So Salyard will end up getting them."

"No," Teller said, tiring of the constant interruptions, but realizing they were the price he had to pay for keeping someone of Frame's still-useful abilities on his team. "We'll get them first, because we have the information now. Okay?"

"But what about Cory?" Frame asked.

"What about her?" Teller started walking toward the control building again and Frame fell into step beside him. "She's served her purpose to us. When she's served her purpose for Salyard, he'll take care of her the way he took care of Farren." He shot a sideways glance at Frame to gauge his reaction, hoping the man was not going soft on him. "Which means Salyard saves us the trouble of eliminating

Rey ourselves. One more thing we can hold over the general when the negotiations begin."

Frame had no more questions. "One more launch window," he said.

"Twenty-eight days at most," Teller agreed. *Until Salyard is my puppet,* he thought, as he pushed open the glass door that led into the air-conditioned refuge of the control building, leaving behind the steamy Florida air, hot sun, and the Air Force helicopter-maintenance crewman with the twenty-two-inch supercardioid shotgun microphone, already transmitting a recording of his runway conversation back to Vandenberg AFB, and General Salyard.

15

"**HERE'S THE DUMB THING,**" Cory Rey told Webber in the quiet darkness of the odd 1970s-themed—*No, make that 1970s-built,* she corrected herself—motel room that had become their hiding ground. Her back was propped up against one of the arms of the vivid orange couch, her legs stretched out full-length on its fuzzy-wool cushions, her aluminum crutch on the gold shag rug beside her. "Four days ago, I thought I was going to die in space. Three days ago, I thought I was going to die coming back to Earth. Last night, the FBI questioned me about a murder, and this morning I nearly got kidnapped by two maniacs you say are probably special ops soldiers. . . ."

"I'm waiting for the dumb part," Webber said. He was across from her, hunched forward on an ugly brown bean-bag chair, flipping through channels on the silent television, alert for any mention of the shooting off Rood Avenue, five hours ago. So far, there had been nothing. The Air Force *owned* Colorado Springs.

"I feel safe with you." Cory couldn't believe she was actually admitting this to Webber. Her insane desire to confess could only mean she was finally losing self-control. *What will I say next?* she thought despairingly. She held her breath, but Webber didn't push his luck.

"Good," he told her. "But you're not safe enough yet."

"Just what kind of danger do you think we're in?" Cory heard the waver in her own voice. *I'm falling apart! What's wrong with me?* She had difficulty concentrating on Webber's answer.

"Cory, those men had guns. They weren't going to kill you right away, but they were definitely planning to kill me."

"But *why?*"

"Come on." Webber looked at her in surprise, clearly wondering why she'd even asked the question. "Because of what you brought back."

"But no one knows I brought back anything!" Cory struggled to free herself from the grip of her strange emotional state, to think again as she always did. "Except for you and Bailey, and Dom."

"And Dom's friend, Doctor, uh . . ." Webber hesitated as if he couldn't remember the physics professor's name.

Webber was no linguist. Cory smiled for the first time in days. "Tripurasundari Shiourie," she said.

"Sunny," Webber said.

Cory's smile faded. "You think she's working for whoever sent the special ops guys after us?"

"I don't know. She's an incomplete part of the equation."

"Equation?" Cory said. "Another shuttle lost. The station all but ruined. Eight astronauts dead. Thugs with guns coming after us. And you've put all of that into a balanced equation with neat rows of numbers? Talk about a dumb thing."

She saw the muscles in Webber's jaw flex, but he kept

his temper. "Everything that's happened *is* part of a pattern. If we can identify that pattern, determine its cause, then we can determine its goal. If we know the goal, then we can act to prevent it. Thinking of these events as an equation to be solved helps me identify, analyze, and predict."

Cory sighed. She'd antagonized him, and he was right to object. This wasn't the time or place. "Mitchell, I'm sorry." She resolved to be more helpful. "There's another incomplete part you left out."

Webber waited for her explanation.

"Up there, when . . ." Cory swallowed the lump that suddenly constricted her throat. ". . . when I thought there was a chance I might not make it back, and I asked Bailey to find you . . . so I could tell you what I'd found . . ."

Webber nodded, waiting for her to get to the point. Cory herself had no idea why she was finding it so hard to do just that. All she could think was, *Great! Another souvenir of being in Mitchell's world—post-traumatic stress.*

". . . and then when Bailey couldn't find you . . ."

"I know all this, Cory. You gave her the message, instead of me."

"But here's the thing. Bailey and I were supposed to be talking on a private, encrypted channel. No recording. But maybe . . . I don't know . . . could someone else have heard us?"

Webber's thoughtful expression told her that her speculation wasn't likely, but that he was keeping an open mind. "The major's good at what she does, but we'll have to ask if that's a possibility."

There was a knock at the door. Cory went rigid. No longer sure what to expect anymore, she looked at once to Webber.

He held his finger to his lips. Then, in one swift silent

motion, he was out of his chair and on his feet, moving to one side of the door.

The knock repeated, same rhythm as before, but this time with two extra raps at the end.

"It's them," Webber said, and put his eye to the door's security lens.

"A secret code?" Cory whispered. And then was infuriated with herself as Webber unhooked the brass door chain without bothering to answer her. Why would he? Of course a code made sense in their present situation.

Webber opened the door for Major Bailey and her husband. Bailey was still in civilian clothes. Both she and Hubert were wearing logo-free baseball caps and matching dark-blue jackets. Hubert was holding two white plastic bags of groceries. Bailey handed Webber a set of keys.

"We got you a black Intrepid," she said. "Around back by the ice machine."

It was like living in a spy movie, Cory marveled.

Bailey turned to her as if she had read her mind. "People are trying to hurt you—being cautious is a good idea. Dom, honey, those can go right in the kitchen."

Bailey's husband walked over to the room's small kitchenette corner and set the two bags down on its fake wood-grain counter, next to the avocado-green range. The erratic humming and buzzing of the matching, half-size, avocado-green refrigerator sounded like an electrical transformer approaching failure.

"We didn't see any sign of anyone following us from the house," Hubert said as he unpacked soup cans and bread rolls from the grocery bags. "We rented the cars from two different lots."

"Did you do a last-minute switch?" Webber asked. He had followed Hubert into the kitchenette and now was ripping open a bag of red and green apples.

"Just like you said," Bailey confirmed. She described how, at each car rental lot, she and Hubert had filled out the paperwork, stepped out to pick up the car they had rented, then gone back to the counter to request a last-minute change to another car already on the lot. Then, while Bailey had waited to have her paperwork redone, Hubert had watched the new car. The procedure had been the same at the second lot. Only this time, Bailey had watched the new car while Hubert had returned to the counter for the revised paperwork. As Webber had explained, the procedure meant they could be reasonably certain the cars they'd rented were free of listening devices or GPS trackers.

"How about helicopters?" Webber selected a large red apple, bit into it.

"You're serious?" Cory asked.

Webber nodded, swallowed. "If you have any other suggestions," he said around another bite of his apple, "this would be the time to make them. You don't want to go to the FBI. The police are out of the question. And NASA reports to the same government the FBI does. No mystery where that leaves us."

"Up a stinking creek," Hubert said. He took off his ball cap and rubbed the top of his head, making his violently red hair bristle like an unruly mop. "Sunny's dropped out of sight."

"Dr. Shiourie?" Webber said, cheek bulging with apple, not stumbling at all in pronouncing the physicist's name.

Cory swung her legs off the couch in sudden alarm. "Where're the fingers?" Last night, when Webber and the FBI had come back into the physics building, she'd slipped the sample case containing them to Hubert. He'd promised to give them back to Shiourie for safekeeping.

"Safe and sound." Hubert slipped a hand between one

of the paper grocery sacks inside a plastic bag, and retrieved the small metal case. "I never got the chance to give this to Sunny, so I hid it in her lab. When I couldn't get through to her this morning, I went back for them."

"Any idea what happened to her?" Webber asked as Hubert took the sample case over to Cory, who immediately opened and just as quickly shut it. The fingers were still inside.

Hubert cast an inquiring glance back at his wife, still by the door. Bailey shrugged, arms folded across her chest, "Go ahead, Mulder, you're the conspiracy expert."

Hubert reacted as if his wife's statement was fact. "If all this *is* about the samples, then there's only one thing that connects them to Sunny." He pulled out a high barstool from the kitchenette to sit on and face his audience. "And," he added, before Cory could respond, "it's not just that we went to see her. That's not enough. Otherwise Willie and I would have gone missing, too."

"So what's the tie-in?" Bailey asked her husband.

"Sunny was trying to arrange spectroscopic analysis of the lunar dust. Her university has the right kind of Raman spectrograph to do it quickly, and Sunny said they've had experience doing calibration analyses of lunar meteorites and Apollo samples. She told me she thought there'd be fewer than fifty facilities in the country that could say the same."

"Someone set a trap for her," Webber said. As punctuation, he lofted his apple core into the wastebasket across the room.

"That's what I'd do," Hubert agreed.

"Well, I don't get it," Cory said. She was feeling left out in all the military coziness.

Hubert took pity on her. "All it would take is fifty phone calls to fifty labs, asking to be notified if anyone came in with a sample they wanted tested to see if it came from the Moon."

Cory's eyes narrowed. "Guess who has the influence to make those fifty calls and be confident the labs will call back."

Hubert nodded slowly, admitting the undeniable. "A branch of the government."

"Listen to both of you," Webber said. "The government can't be responsible for every evil in the land. How could any government agency contact fifty independent, civilian labs, and ask for information that's none of their business?"

In the silence that followed, it was Bailey, not Cory, who laughed first, Hubert who became the peacemaker.

"Actually, you raise a good point," Hubert said to Webber, "but there's a good explanation." He looked around at his three listeners. "NASA has a tough reputation for going after people who try to sell Moon rocks from the Apollo missions. There *are* a handful of rocks that are in legitimate private hands: the ones that started out as gifts President Nixon gave foreign dignitaries, and all the little chips that were presented to key people in the space program. Over the years, some of those ended up being sold legitimately in estate sales. But some lunar rocks have also gone missing from labs and museums strictly by theft. When they show up on the collectors' market, NASA and the FBI always hammer whoever's trying to sell them. So, any facility equipped to do a quick, calibrated analysis of potential lunar material has probably *already* been contacted by the FBI several times in other cases. Any request like that would be strictly business as usual."

"But you're still saying it's the government," Webber argued.

Cory intervened on Hubert's side. "Mitchell, aren't

you the one who said our 'kidnappers' were special ops
soldiers?"

Webber sighed. "I said they had probably *been* special
ops. Past tense, Cory. People leave the service every day.
They get other jobs that require the skills they've learned at
government expense. I didn't say they were *working* for the
government. *You* did."

Bailey pulled off her jacket, tossed it on the couch, and
walked past them all to the small kitchenette. "I think we
should all take a break to eat something, and regroup." She
pushed up her sweater sleeves.

The major's practical suggestion appealed to everyone.
Dinner was the diner's choice of soup, apples, and ham-
and-cheese-bun sandwiches. Bailey remembered that
Cory was a vegetarian, and made a plain cheese bun for
her. The simple homey activity lessened the tension in the
room.

"Is this what they call going to the mattresses?" Cory
picked up a second cheese bun from the plate Bailey had
put beside her on the couch.

"Only if we were going to hit back," Hubert said. His
legs splayed awkwardly to either side of the brown beanbag
chair.

"Can't we?"

"Who's the enemy, Cory?" Webber asked, mouth full
again. Bailey had allocated Cory's ham to Webber, and he
was making short work of it, sitting on the rug with his
back to the couch. *All those hard muscles,* Cory thought, *eating their heads off.* And then just as quickly she tried to think
of something else.

"Why do we have to know who the enemy is before
fighting back?" she asked in return.

Webber licked his fingers and wiped them on his jeans.
"This is going to be good. You want us to go up against the

FBI and NASA just on general principle? Figure out the details later?"

"No," Cory said indignantly. "I say we go to CNN or *60 Minutes*. Tell a reporter everything, let the news media sort it out."

Webber shook his head. "Cory, right now, there's nothing to sort out. Let's say you're right. There's some awful secret the government's hiding and they're using illegal methods to keep it hidden."

"That sounds about right," Cory muttered.

"Sometimes," Webber persevered, "there's a reason the government needs to keep a secret. This might be one of those times. And if you start talking to reporters without knowing where your statements will lead, you might be causing irreparable harm to this country's interests."

"Get serious," Cory said.

"Then how's this," Webber tried. "You go shooting off about some wild conspiracy and nothing comes of it, what happens to *your* reputation and career? Right now, you're an opinionated activist. What happens if you become a whacked-out crackpot?" Faster than Cory could come up with any objections, Webber added, "Even Professor Shiourie knows better than to talk in public about her interest in UFOs."

"And that's because Sunny knows it's too dangerous, Cory." Hubert helpfully jumped into the fray. "The moment you go to the media, you'll be alerting whoever's behind this—government or not—to the fact that you don't know who it is you're facing. That gives them the advantage. They'll be able to cover their tracks while the media investigate. That pretty much guarantees the media won't find anything. And that'll leave you out in the cold in a week or two or three, with no protection, and no one to turn to next."

Cory looked in appeal at Bailey, who just smiled and kept out of it. "So this is what this country's come to? Even the free press is ineffectual?"

"You're just figuring that out now?" Webber said.

"Don't start, Mitchell." They had had this debate too many times before.

"All right, I won't," he conceded. "But no media contact until we know who we're up against. And before we go any further, there is something we have to do to guarantee your safety."

"I'm all for that," Cory said. "So?"

"Choose a side," he told her.

Cory didn't have a clue what he meant, but suspected that Bailey and her husband did. The two of them had picked up the empty plates and were taking them into the kitchen, leaving Cory and Webber to talk on their own. "I beg your pardon?"

"We know that at least two different parties are after those samples."

Cory knew no such thing. "Name them."

"Teller Technologies for one," Webber said. "They launched their lunar rover, then sent you up to the station to recover whatever it brought back."

Webber was right. She still wasn't thinking properly. "Okay, but other than the flowers he sent to my hospital room, I haven't seen or even heard from Kai Teller yet."

"That's probably a good sign," Webber said. "I think we can assume that your boss didn't try to blow up the station to prevent his own samples from coming back. So it's unlikely he sent those two pros after you today." He gave her a measured look. "The guy's got resources. Corporate security."

"Oh, no," Cory said emphatically. "I see where you're heading and no way am I going for that ride."

That's when Bailey cut in, dish towel in hand. "Hang on, Cory, it makes sense to me. Teller must have known what his LRV was going to bring back from the Moon. If you tell him you have what he wants, given the fortune he must have already spent, you could ask whatever you want in exchange for it."

"Blackmail? That makes more sense?"

"Cory . . ." Webber said. "You're looking for a fight again."

"You're the soldier."

"Naval aviator."

"Whatever. You're the one whose job it is to kill people."

Webber finally lost his temper. "It is my job to know how to kill people so effectively that no one in their right mind would dare provoke me. That's defense, Cory. That's what the military's mission is. By knowing how to wage war better than anyone else, we prevent war."

Cory covered her ears with her hands. "And I wondered why this last year was so peaceful." She glared at him. "Because you weren't talking to me."

"Kids!" Bailey said warningly.

Cory and Webber glared at Bailey for a change. Hubert disappeared behind the open cupboard doors as Cory heard the sound of dishes clattering.

"Is the tantrum over?" Bailey asked. No one answered. "I'll take that as a yes. Now, let's get back to Mitch's point, because he was making a good one."

Cory was beginning to get the feeling she was being railroaded. "You—both of you," she said to Webber and Bailey, "want me to go to Kai, give him the samples, and ask for protection?"

"Safe harbor," Webber said. "You might even learn something from him. Like who else wants those things."

Cory called out to Bailey's husband for support. "Dom, do you hear what's happening here?"

Hubert reappeared as he shut the kitchen cupboard doors. "They're giving you good advice?"

"No sale," Cory said. "A Navy captain and an Air Force major are both telling me to avoid the government." She turned to Webber. "How come you're not saying, Let's go talk to someone at the Pentagon?" Then she looked at Bailey. "And you, Willie, you haven't once suggested I tell my story to anyone at Space Command. You'd think they'd at least be interested in something affecting the space station."

Cory sat back on the couch and folded her arms across her chest. "So why *are* you two telling me to go to a civilian for protection?"

Webber and Bailey exchanged glances, as something unspoken passed between them.

"Until we know what's going on," Webber began carefully, "the civilian option appears to be the safest."

Cory looked from Webber to Bailey, but both their faces bore the same deliberately calibrated neutral expression. She knew that stonewalling expression only too well. It meant neither one was going to argue with her.

"Mitchell," she said, "remember when I asked you how they managed to keep that invisible airplane secret for so long?"

"What invisible airplane?" Hubert asked with sudden interest.

"Alleged invisible airplane," Webber said icily.

"Dom," Bailey warned.

"Sorry," Hubert replied, then sat back in silence.

"Alleged," Cory muttered. "Anyway, when I asked, you got that same blank expression on your face. No confirmation. No denial. Like all the other times I strayed into some precious military secret of yours, that's how you responded." She glanced back at Hubert. "Does Willie do that to you?"

Hubert gave her a blank look, no confirmation, no denial.

"Thanks a lot," Cory said. "You'd think if the military wanted you people to keep secrets, they'd at least teach you how to tell a lie."

She turned back to Webber and Bailey. "As soon as I see that face, Mitchell, I know you're holding back. And right now, I know that you—and you, Willie—you both know something about something in the military that's connected to what's going on, and because of what you know, you don't want me going anywhere near any branch of the government."

"If, by some wild stretch of the imagination, you're right," Webber said, "doesn't that suggest that going to Teller makes even more sense, because the advice the major and I are giving you is based on fact, not suspicion?"

Cory sat back on the couch, picked up a cushion and hugged it to her. "You do know something, you bastard. And you're not telling. So much for Willie's lecture on sharing."

Cory saw Webber's cheeks flush and she knew if it weren't for the presence of Bailey and Hubert, the decibel level in the hotel room would take a sudden rise as Webber substituted volume for logic.

But once again, Bailey stepped in to take control. "Captain Webber, why don't we go check out the car?"

Webber didn't take his eyes off Cory as he stood up. "Good idea."

Bailey gave her husband's wild hair a little ruffle. "I won't be long." Then she and Webber stepped outside.

"Do you know what they're going to talk about?" Cory demanded of Hubert.

"Even if I did," he said, "I probably couldn't say."

Dominic Hubert was one in a million, Cory thought. Bailey's husband didn't even look perturbed. "Don't you ever get sick of so many secrets?" she asked.

"Not the ones that serve their purpose," Hubert said comfortably.

Cory hugged her cushion closer. "Right now, the secrets worrying me are the ones that might get me killed."

Hubert's smile was full of sympathy. "Then you can bet those are the secrets they're talking about."

Without exchanging a word, Webber and Bailey both headed to the back of the hotel where they could walk the grounds in darkness, well away from the lights of the empty parking lot. A wide tract of grass stretched from the gravel edge of the parking lot to a dark wall of tall pine trees. It was late enough that only the occasional distant rush of a car on the road out front spoiled the silence of the night. And only when Webber and Bailey were in the protection of the shadows and the silence, did their conversation resume, each voice almost a whisper.

"There's something you should know I haven't told Cory," Webber said.

"Personal or professional?" Bailey asked.

"Professional. I took a new assignment this week. I was supposed to have some furlough coming to me, but that went by the boards. I have to report ASAP. Be on a plane by noon tomorrow."

"So we need to get the doctor squared away before then."

"If we can."

They walked in silence, until Webber asked, "Okay, who wants to go first?"

"I don't think the judges at our courts-martial will

care," Bailey answered curtly. But at least she was smiling as she spoke.

Webber looked up at the sky past the jagged wall of trees, but the stars were obscured by low clouds and the pale glow of distant city lights. So he kept his eyes on nothing as he cautiously chose his words, trying to keep from coughing in the chilled, crisp air. "Then I'll go. I am . . . aware of certain operations within the Air Force, related to space, which make me suspect that any return of unusual samples from the Moon would be . . . of intense interest to . . . certain parties within the Air Force."

"How intense?" Bailey asked. Webber noted that the major didn't seem concerned about framing their conversation in such a way that they could testify about it later. Everything was going to be on the table.

"I can't believe they'd use deadly force," Webber said, still speaking quietly, "so I don't think the Air Force would be connected with the thugs who came after Cory and me this morning. But if the Air Force does take her for questioning, I could see her being slapped with a nondisclosure order. And she is utterly incapable of complying with something like that. Which means federal prison." He glanced at Bailey, a silhouette beside him. "Your turn."

"To be blunt, I'm not as certain about deadly force."

Webber reacted as if to gunfire. "What?"

Bailey seemed pained by what she decided to say next. "Look, what I'm going to say isn't a breach of operational security because . . . well, it's not official, and it's nothing I learned at work. It's a story my father told me. He worked for President Johnson, you know."

Webber did know. He had met Colonel Randolph Bailey, U.S. Air Force, retired, several years ago. A remarkable man who was extremely proud of his daughters.

"It was back in the sixties," Bailey said. "Dad was a captain at the time. And he was a White House 'special assistant,' which in his case meant he helped brief the president on aerospace issues."

"You're following a family tradition."

"I like to think so," Bailey agreed, but Webber heard her wistful tone. Whatever the major was about to tell him, he knew it was something that upset her. "Anyway, most of the time my father said he was just a front man for the Joint Chiefs. They'd prepare all these dense reports on why they needed this bomber and that fighter and . . . well, Dad was from Texas, he could cut through the crap and give the president the straight goods. Johnson liked people who got to the point." Bailey gave a forced laugh. "So I suppose that's what I should do about now.

"Anyway, my father had his office at the Pentagon, and usually all his meetings with the president were set up in advance. But this one time he told me about . . ." Bailey stopped walking and in the darkness Webber could see her turn to him. "Do you remember the Apollo fire?"

"When the three astronauts were killed in a ground test. Nineteen sixty-seven?"

"That's it," Bailey said. "January."

"I know of it," Webber said, "but I was still in diapers. I don't think it made much of an impression at the time."

"I don't remember it either," Bailey admitted. "But my father always said it was a horrible time for the country. The astronauts were heroes."

"Still are."

"Still are," the major agreed. She returned to her story. "There was such pressure coming from the whole space race thing with the Russians, so when those poor astronauts burned to death . . . it was as if everyone in the country knew them, and as if everyone in the country felt the

Moon slip from their grasp. At least, that's the way my dad tells it."

"I can understand."

"Anyway, they had all sorts of hearings trying to figure out what went wrong, just like the ones they've got scheduled for the space station."

"It was oxygen, wasn't it?" Webber asked. "That's what caused the fire in the Apollo capsule. A pure oxygen atmosphere."

"That was a primary contributing factor," Bailey said. "But there were all sorts of other deficiencies in the Apollo command module design that made everything worse. Improper fireproofing and insulation. The hatch was pretty much impossible to open quickly in an emergency. But that oxygen atmosphere . . . They called my father into the White House on a weekend and this man, Dad never knew who he was, just some man from the State Department . . . this man showed him some photographs."

"Of the astronauts?"

"Of a *cosmonaut*. A dead cosmonaut. I forget his name, but . . . he had died on the ground, in a fire in a test chamber filled with a pure oxygen atmosphere."

"Just like our guys?"

"Just like our guys. My father said those photographs were the worst thing he had ever seen. Burns to ninety-five percent of the man's body, but he hung on for hours." Bailey shivered. "That accident happened about three weeks before Yuri Gagarin became the first human in space, and it was never reported. Group photos of the cosmonauts were retouched to make it seem as if the one who'd died had never existed. And the truly tragic thing was—"

Webber could see it coming. "If NASA had known

about it, then they might have rethought using pure-oxygen atmospheres in their capsules."

"And the part that would drive Cory up the wall is that the intelligence community *did* know about it."

Again Webber was surprised. "So, at the height of the Cold War, we had agents in the Soviet space program?"

"So my father says. And this is all aboveboard because the whole story about the cosmonaut and the fire that killed him, that all came out in the nineties, after *glasnost*. But at the time, even though the intelligence community knew what had happened, they couldn't tell NASA because—"

"The Soviets had their own people in our space program, and word would get back to Moscow about *our* spies."

"Which is why the man from the State Department showed the photos to Dad. There was so much political bullshit going on that the first report was going to ignore the danger of an all-oxygen atmosphere."

"But they ended up redesigning the entire command module, didn't they?" Webber asked. "And they changed the atmosphere."

"Atmosphere *and* pressure. In part, because of my father. The people in intelligence couldn't tell NASA what they knew, but they could tell my father, and he could tell Johnson, and Johnson could tell the NASA administrator that the preliminary report was unacceptable. The capsule couldn't just be modified. It had to be completely redesigned from the ground up. And it was."

Webber took a deep breath of the damp Colorado evening air. He could smell the grass and the nearby pine trees. The image of fishing in a mountain stream came to him. He drove it from his mind.

"Not that this isn't fascinating stuff, Major, but what's the tie to Cory and deadly force?"

"One of the reasons the investigatory committees were dragging their feet over redesigning the capsule was the delay it would cause. Apollo had been scheduled to put astronauts on the Moon in 1968. At the time, they thought that a redesign would push that off to December 1969."

Webber thought he saw the connection. "They thought the Russians were going to beat them."

"Dad said that when he met with the man from State, the best estimates had the Russians landing in the summer of 1968."

An idea suddenly struck Webber with such force that he rocked on his feet. "Major, do you think there's any chance those fingers are from a *Russian* cosmonaut? Is it possible they *did* land in '68?"

"And didn't tell anybody?" Bailey shook her head. "Come on, Captain. Even if they did manage to keep it a secret in 1968, and I don't know why they would, there's still no reason for it to be a secret today. There would've been thousands of people involved, and not even my dear sweet Dom who goes to *X-Files* conventions would believe all those people could keep a secret. Besides," she added, "there's a very good reason why the Russians' Moon program failed."

"And that is?"

"We sabotaged it."

Webber regarded her in amazement. He wondered what else the major had been keeping to herself. "Your father told you that?"

"More or less. He didn't have direct knowledge of any operation in particular. But he remembers what the man from State told him that night. He said there were two ways for America to get to the Moon. One way was to continue on with the command module exactly as it was, treat the astronauts like experimental animals, and keep launching till a crew survived the trip to the Moon and back. The other way was . . ." Bailey hesitated.

"Sabotage?" Webber asked.

"My father didn't know for sure, but lots of Russian boosters blew up back then."

Webber jammed his hands into the pockets of his leather jacket. It was getting cold. "How about that. There's even a secret history for the space race. Good thing Cory isn't hearing this."

"That was another thing the man from State told my father. He said it wasn't a space race at all. It was a space war. And always had been."

Bailey's trying to warn me, Webber thought. *But could she really be suggesting that a confrontation from the sixties was still going on today? If so, between which parties? And for what purpose?*

Webber explored the possibilities, and didn't like the implications. The events in space, the mystery surrounding Cory's lunar samples—what if they did have something to do with an undeclared and secret war in space?

Whatever was going on, Webber knew he had to do all he could to keep Cory out of the crossfire, and he had to do it by noon tomorrow.

16

"**WHY WOULD THE** United States Air Force want to sabotage the space station?"

Tovah Caruso stared across her immaculate desktop, past the exceptionally detailed model of the Space Shuttle *Constitution,* at the unsmiling gray presence of FBI Special Agent Raymond Hong. She resented wasting one of her final days on such a specious theory.

"Why would you ask me that?"

Caruso felt removed from this bizarre conversation, not only because of its ridiculous subject, but because NASA was slipping away from her. In her present position, each letter, each phone call and decision, felt like her last.

"You don't believe it's possible?" Hong asked. His voice was a monotone, as devoid of color as his conservative black suit, and he was watching her as if he expected her to suddenly confess that she personally had destroyed the shuttle and the station.

"Where's the sense of it?" she asked, annoyed. "NASA's budget doesn't affect the Air Force's expenditures." She ticked off her points with increasing irritation. "Whenever one of our research programs intersects with defense work, the Air Force always wins the jurisdictional fight. The Air Force has on-orbit observational platforms with capabilities far more sophisticated than anything the station could do. The Air Force also has the authority to take control of the shuttle fleet whenever it determines the security of the country is at risk. And," she added with a touch of bitterness, "the military in general takes great delight in using NASA as a smokescreen. We're considered a defense agency, and every year we're forced to publicly spend parts of our budget on research the Air Force and the Navy have already completed and surpassed. Why? So our supposed enemies will conclude America's capabilities are less advanced than they really are.

"NASA's a poor cousin to the military, Mister Hong. And as much as they dislike us, we're useful to them. So, since we provide an advantage to the Air Force, and represent no threat, without a motive, how can there be a crime?"

"Just so we're clear, Ms. Caruso, you agree there *has* been a crime?"

Caruso sighed. Hong was not only irritating, he was implacable. She supposed it went with his job. But he was right. She nodded, reluctantly.

There had indeed been a crime. The chain of mechanical failures indicated in the last seconds of telemetry from the shuttle and the station defied even the most generous definitions of coincidence. Simultaneous malfunctions in the shuttle avionics bay, in the payload bay, in the station's communications systems—*all* of the communications systems—clearly indicated a precise and premeditated plan, not an accident.

"Here's something to consider, though," she told her interrogator. "In Houston, there's a tiger team analyzing the sequence of component failures on the shuttle and the station, and they came up with an interesting observation. Not evidence, but it might suggest a different direction to investigate."

"Has this observation made it into a report?" Hong asked sharply. His own annoyance finally brought some color to his voice.

"It will by the end of the day," Caruso said, hoping to placate him. It seemed Mr. Hong was a man who wanted all the facts under his control, and no one else's.

"Here's the situation," she said. "The original flight plan for the resupply portion of *Constitution*'s mission to the station called for the Leonardo module to be docked with the station the day after arrival. That's standard procedure, so at least the supplies are available for the station crew in the event of a shuttle emergency undock, or emergency deorbit."

"Why was that flight plan not followed?" Hong asked. The FBI agent's question was an accusation.

Caruso answered calmly. "Commander Dante changed the order of events so the Lunar Return Vehicle transfer could be handled as one operation instead of two."

"I don't understand." Hong made that statement sound as if he thought she was deliberately trying to mislead him.

Caruso refused to be bullied. "The LRV mission was a practice run for a Mars Sample Return mission. Because of the strong possibility that Martian regolith and—"

"Regolith?" Hong interrupted. "I don't know that term."

"It's basically dirt, Mister Hong. On Earth, we'd call it soil which, technically, is a combination of finely eroded or decomposed minerals, and biological material. On the Moon, however, there's never been biological activity, so the regolith's only the fine, decomposed minerals. But from the results of the ESA's Mars Express orbiter and our own Mars Exploration Rovers . . ."

Seeing the look on Hong's face, Caruso realized she was losing him. "Bottom line: We want to avoid the extremely remote possibility of infecting Earth with potential Martian bacteria. So, one of the new, critical-science missions for the space station is to serve as the Martian receiving laboratory. The station will be where all samples from Mars will undergo preliminary tests for bio-logical activity before being transferred to Earth."

Caruso stopped, looked at him questioningly, but Hong merely said, "Continue."

"So," Caruso said, picking up her account of the lunar sample recovery procedure that had preceded the loss of the shuttle, "instead of returning to Earth, the LRV returned to Earth orbit. Two days after launch, *Constitution* rendezvoused with the LRV and retrieved it with the robot arm. Then, when *Constitution* docked with the station, the LRV was transferred from the shuttle's robot arm to the station's arm. At that point, once the shuttle arm was free, the crew was supposed to have attached the Leonardo module to the mating adapter."

"Supposed to," Hong repeated. "Why didn't they, Ms. Caruso?"

"There was some concern about the integrity of the lockdown of the LRV. Rather than commit to an unscheduled and thus hazardous spacewalk to check it, Commander Dante asked for permission to continue the recovery of the sample cylinders from the LRV before moving the Leonardo, and the flight managers approved."

"And this change was important. Why?"

Bluntness was obviously an asset in the FBI, Caruso thought. "Because, according to the tiger team in Houston, the way the timing on the malfunctions works out, if the

Leonardo module had been transferred on schedule, we wouldn't have lost the shuttle, and there would have been no subsequent structural damage to the station."

"What would have happened instead?"

"The shuttle and the station would have lost communications with the ground. The explosion in the Leonardo module would have caused a small depress event—"

"Depress event?"

"Depressurization. We would have lost atmosphere—oxygen—through the supply module, but that could have been dealt with simply by sealing the docking hatch."

"What would have been the end result of this hypothetical chain of events?"

Hong's impersonal persistence angered Caruso. Millions of people had been affected by what had happened. The labor of thousands had been lost. Eight astronauts had died. "I don't know what the end state would have been, Mister Hong. But within ten minutes of the first malfunction on the shuttle, we would have had ten lives secured: seven crew on *Constitution,* and three in the *Soyuz.* What happened after that would have been dependent on whatever decisions Hutton and Dante made. My guess is that both would have elected to remain on orbit to assess the damage, and then carry out repairs."

"Could repairs have been carried out?" Hong asked.

"Most of them, certainly. Communications would have remained spotty for the station, but everything else . . . more an inconvenience than an attempt at destruction."

Hong sat back in his chair, looked out the rain-streaked window. Caruso didn't bother with the view. On a good day, she could see the Capitol dome to the east, the White House to the west. But rain clouds were low today, and the view was as dour and unappealing as Special Agent Hong.

"Here's another question for you to consider," Hong

said at last. "Assuming the loss of the shuttle and the extensive structural damage to the station were unintended consequences of a criminal act intended to inflict less injury, then why would the United States Air Force want to *inconvenience* the shuttle and station?"

"What is all this about, Agent Hong? Why the Air Force? Inconvenience or destruction, there's still no motive."

Hong regarded her with more interest. "We will step back then, if it makes it easier for you to address the situation, Ms. Caruso. If not the Air Force, then who else would have a motive to inconvenience NASA?"

Caruso was beginning to regret she had turned down Teller's invitation to Maui. "Off the record?"

Hong was silent but Caruso spoke more for herself than for his report. *It's not as if I'll lose my job,* she thought. *That's already taken care of.*

"First," Caruso said, "the Russians. Maybe they figured they could shake us down for more money. Like that hundred million dollars for the unneeded rescue mission."

"I understand that mission was canceled when Doctor Rey and Commander Lazhenko returned."

"Damn right."

"Who else?" Hong asked.

Caruso shrugged. "Disgruntled employees? Maybe, but . . . most of the people who work at NASA, on the hardware, on the missions, even in clerical support, they're not in it because they think it's their meal ticket or their 'job.' They're like soldiers in a war. There's a lot of idealism here. People are very aware they're working on things that are bigger than any one person. Granted, there are a lot of people constantly upset with the government bureaucracy of this place, but not with what we're trying to accomplish overall. I can't imagine anyone who's made the effort to work at NASA, to then turn around and try to damage one of our projects like that. Unless . . ."

"Unless?"

"There *is* a lot of pressure. I suppose someone could snap."

Hong frowned, as if he were a teacher who had discovered his pupil had cheated on an exam. "When people 'snap,' Ms. Caruso, they tend to carry out a quick and decisive act of violence. What happened to the shuttle and the station, as you've described it, seems too time-consuming and methodical to fit that profile. Who else?"

"Another guess. A . . . disgruntled contractor, maybe?"

"Someone who could profit from the repairs that would be required?"

"Scratch that last one," Caruso said. Hong's question had pointed to a flaw in her reasoning. If the repairs were merely an inconvenience, and the majority of them could be made on orbit, then at most NASA would be looking at a few million dollars' worth of spare parts, spread among several contractors. So again there was no motive.

"Who else?"

"Martians?" Caruso volunteered halfheartedly.

Hong's steady gaze did not falter, and for a moment Caruso contemplated the fascinating idea that somewhere in the bowels of the FBI building or the Pentagon, the scenario already existed in which the destruction of the shuttle was the opening salvo in a war with aliens.

"Who else?" Hong asked.

Caruso abandoned her entertaining fantasy and surrendered to reality. "Your turn, Agent Hong." And was astonished when Hong took her at her word.

The FBI agent reached down to take something from the black briefcase at his feet, then placed a personnel sheet on her desktop. The color photo in the upper right corner showed a tough, lean, military type with short, almost Marine-style hair.

"Daniel Varik," Hong said. "Colonel, U.S. Air Force."

Completely confused now, Caruso picked up the sheet, scanned the information printed on it. Varik was the name the FBI had told her to mention to Teller when she had taped her conversation with him. Teller had had no reaction she had noticed, but obviously this Varik was someone the FBI associated with the crime.

"You think this fellow Varik did something to the station?" she asked, puzzled. From what she could make out of the military jargon and acronyms on the personnel sheet, the man had had an unremarkable, by-the-books career.

"Not the station. We believe Daniel Varik murdered Edward Farren."

Caruso handed back the sheet as if it had suddenly become something unclean. "Why?"

"Why did he do it? Or why do we think he's the murderer?"

"Both."

The taciturn FBI agent became almost loquacious, and Caruso began to wonder why she was being honored with so much information. Especially now, when she was on her way out. The FBI would know that.

"Varik was recorded by three hidden surveillance cameras on the morning Farren was murdered. One in a parking lot across from Farren's hotel. One in an ATM. And one monitoring a side entrance to the hotel from an exterior light fixture. We have tape of him arriving, disabling two exposed cameras, moving along a corridor toward Farren's room, and then returning, thirty-two minutes later. The time corresponds with Farren's time of death. The identification is positive."

Caruso stared at the photo of Varik, as if the image might come to life and explain himself. "And why do you think he did it?"

She looked up to find Hong staring at her just as intently. "Ms. Caruso, are you prepared to keep working with the FBI?"

"Yes," she answered without hesitation, but then added more slowly, "as long as the FBI realizes that when the Senate inquiries start, my time might not be my own."

"That's acceptable," Hong said, again as if weighty discussions about the matter had already been held at his headquarters.

"So if I'm on the team . . . ?" Caruso prompted, hardly believing what she was hearing and saying. If she'd thought this conversation had been bizarre to begin with, it had now crossed into surreal territory.

"Do you know how to read a military personnel jacket?"

Caruso picked up Varik's sheet again, saw nothing of particular note on it. "What am I missing?"

"It's what Colonel Varik is missing. Namely, suitable accomplishments that justify his rank and the length of time he's spent at it. The lack of detail suggests that his career accomplishments have been in classified areas."

"Sounds reasonable," Caruso said.

"It *is* reasonable," Agent Hong told her, a man unused to being questioned.

"But what does it mean?"

"That is what we are working to uncover, Ms. Caruso. According to the Air Force, Colonel Varik is attached to the 16th Special Operations Wing at Hurlburt Field in Florida, but is currently assigned to the Air Force Office of Special Investigations, Detachment 804, operating out of Vandenberg AFB."

Vandenberg? Caruso folded her hands on her desk, hoping that she was betraying nothing of her surprise. Farren had visited Vandenberg the day before he died. And Vandenberg was the base Dr. Rey had been trying to contact, looking for Captain Mitchell Webber.

"You say that as if there's something wrong with those assignments," she said.

"Not strictly wrong, but unusual," Hong explained. "Air Force officers do cross train. No doubt there are many reasons why a Special Forces airman might want to learn criminal investigatory techniques, especially in support of counterterrorism missions."

"But?" Caruso asked.

"Colonel Varik has not undertaken AFOSI training at Andrews, as required."

"So, putting that together with Varik's classified past, you believe he's involved in a classified project at Vandenberg, having nothing to do with the Office of Special Investigations, or Special Operations."

Hong nodded, twice. "Varik is a man out of place."

Caruso tapped her finger on Varik's sheet. "Bottom line, Agent Hong."

"Three other people are out of place with him."

"A conspiracy?"

"Possibly."

"Who are the other three?" Caruso consciously made her face relax into the same expression of bland indifference Hong wore. She had an awful premonition that one of those three names was going to be Kai Teller.

But he wasn't the first on Hong's list.

"Do you know General Dwight Salyard?" Hong asked.

The name was vaguely familiar to Caruso. "I believe he's at Vandenberg. Launch director? Something like that."

"Something like that. He's assigned to Space and Missile

Command Systems, Detachment 9. They maintain the launch facilities at Vandenberg."

"But you're about to tell me his military career is as mysteriously blank as Colonel Varik's, right?"

Caruso saw Hong's eyes widen just for an instant, in appreciation, perhaps. But she hadn't gotten to her present position without being able to read people. FBI agents just took a little longer.

"Precisely," he confirmed.

"You said there are two more people out of place."

"Captain Mitchell Webber."

Webber as potential conspirator startled Caruso. "Doctor Rey's friend?"

"More than that, we believe. They lived together for several years."

"And he's at Vandenberg."

Hong nodded. "For no reason that's supported by his file. He, too, is involved with the Special Operations Command, and is currently based at Hill AFB in Utah. His military record is also curiously devoid of accomplishment."

Caruso suddenly realized what Hong was trying to establish. "This conspiracy within the Air Force that you think is directed at NASA, it's operating out of Vandenberg?"

"At this stage, Ms. Caruso, I'd be interested in hearing what you believe."

Caruso accepted the challenge. "Well, what do we know? Doctor Farren heard something that made him think someone might be trying to sabotage the shuttle mission. He told Kai Teller, who didn't believe him. He probably tried telling other people he knew. They didn't believe him. So he told someone at Vandenberg."

"Doctor Farren met with General Salyard on the afternoon of April fourth."

"And you say Varik killed him the next day."

"Varik and Webber were both present in Vandenberg on the fourth."

"That's right," Caruso said as she sought to weave all these new facts together. "Webber was on the Freefall Red Team out of Vandenberg to recover the *Soyuz* in the Mojave."

"Which brings us to the fourth person who is out of place."

"Doctor Rey," Caruso guessed. If Hong had been going to name Teller, he would already have done so. "But Agent Hong, I've met her, I've read her file, and—"

Hong cut her off. "Ms. Caruso, the FBI believes that a criminal conspiracy exists, led by General Salyard. We do not know how many people are involved, but we include Colonel Varik, Captain Webber, and Doctor Rey among them."

Apparently, Caruso thought, as Hong continued, what she believed was no longer important.

"The FBI questioned Doctor Rey two days ago in Colorado Springs. She was in the company of Captain Webber. Both of them refused to answer our questions. The FBI now believes that Doctor Rey was specifically chosen and groomed for her position on the most recent shuttle flight to be in place to deliberately sabotage the shuttle and the station, on behalf of that conspiracy."

"No . . ." Caruso said in disbelief. And then she realized what else she'd have to say. "Unless you're suggesting that . . . that Doctor Rey's employer is somehow mixed up in all this."

Hong shook his head, once. "Mister Teller's companies derive most of their income from Air Force contracts. The FBI believes General Salyard, or someone operating under his direction, applied pressure on Teller to select Doctor

Rey to be the payload specialist for the LRV mission. If anything, Teller is a pawn."

Caruso considered Hong's theory. "A conspiracy . . . against NASA . . . coming from the Air Force . . ." How many times had she herself railed against the Air Force? But she'd never suspected anything like this.

"Or, more likely, Air Force personnel," Hong amended.

"But *why?*" That was the big question Caruso couldn't fathom. She stared out at the rain and the clouds, saw the faintest glimmer of an answer. "Unless . . ."

"Please continue," Hong said.

"What if it's not a conspiracy directed at NASA— because that makes no sense. But a conspiracy directed against something NASA is *doing?*" Caruso tried and failed to think of just what NASA was doing that would excite such enmity.

"To answer that, we are relying on your expertise."

Caruso nodded. "Of course . . ." She looked at Hong, recalling what she had said earlier, about being involved in work greater than any one person. "What's the next step?"

"We look for connections. What scientific experiments were under way on the station. Which contractors were involved. What was the value of the work being done. That information will come from NASA. In the meantime, the FBI is looking into General Salyard's personal finances, his recent travels, and the same for Captain Webber, Colonel Varik, and Doctor Rey."

"Personal finances?" Caruso asked. "You think whatever's going on is about money?"

"It is always about money, Ms. Caruso. Government contracts and contractor fraud go hand in hand. Somewhere, we will find the evidence that will explain how someone might profit from 'inconveniencing' the shuttle and the station. And that will give us our motive."

Hong got to his feet, reached forward and took Varik's sheet from Caruso's desk, slipped it back into his briefcase. "I'll expect the breakdown on experiments, contractors, and value this afternoon."

Caruso stood, as well. "Certainly."

Hong nodded, once. "Ms. Caruso." He left.

For a few moments, Caruso remained in the silence of her office, contemplating the likelihood that a cancer had been growing within her operation and she had completely missed it.

Somehow, at some level she couldn't quite see yet, for some reason that remained unclear to her, Caruso knew the FBI had to be wrong about the conclusions they had reached. Conspiracies were for other government agencies. Not NASA.

All her instincts told her Hong and his colleagues were being led astray by their focus on money as the motive. *There's a lot of idealism here,* she had told him. That was where she would look for the motive, and the answer. Beliefs had always cost more lives than any drive for profits. In times of peace or war.

Caruso had another realization. If what had happened to the shuttle and the station wasn't an act of criminals, someone *had* declared war on NASA.

Just as Kai tried to tell me, she thought. *Well, better late than never.*

It was time NASA began fighting back.

17

GENERAL SALYARD WALKED SWIFTLY through Hangar 27, past the shrouded form of the SOV *Eagle,* twin to the *Falcon* that was already mated to its Venturestar booster and on a secure pad. Security curtains around the advanced-concept spacecraft properly shielded its revolutionary airframe from Vandenberg's engine technicians, and its extraordinary engine from the airframe team. The best place to stop rumors was before they could begin.

He quickly rounded the Space Operations Vehicle simulator, whose hydraulic pistons were hissing softly as Lieutenant Colonel Christa Bowden, in the flight-deck compartment concealed within, worked to perfect the docking maneuvers she would carry out as part of next month's mission.

But the general's attention was not on what would happen weeks from now. He was responding to an alert from Major Freeman Lowell in Operations. Something so critical Lowell would not relay it over Salyard's encrypted cell phone—only on the secure blue line in Salyard's office, or in person.

Salyard entered the temporary offices constructed at the back of the hangar, where he had first met Captain Webber, and continued down the narrow corridor, looking straight ahead so the hidden cameras and weapon detectors could more easily identify his face and scan him.

At the end of the corridor, he opened one of the few flimsy, hollow-wood doors in the office block that was without a central pane of glass. He heard the lock unclick an instant before he touched the doorknob. It clicked again when he closed the door behind him.

The small room he had entered held only an elevator, whose polished steel doors were already open and waiting.

Salyard stepped in. The moment the elevator doors slid closed, the general placed his right hand on the biometric scanning screen, making sure to press his palm against the positioning posts that separated his fingers. The brief sparkle of a swiftly moving red laser beam accompanied the measurement, and confirmation, of his hand's dimensions. Other sensors confirmed body temperature and pulse rate, to ensure his severed hand could not be used to breach security. Seconds later, the elevator began its descent.

Two hundred feet beneath Vandenberg's newest complex of hangars, the steel elevator doors opened into hidden and unsuspected territory: the foyer of the United States Space Force Central Command.

Salyard strode across the polished terrazzo floor of the double-story entry hall, feeling pride as his footsteps carried him over the five-foot-wide bronze disk holding the engraved emblem of the USSF: a silver eagle clutching a golden bolt of lightning, soaring protectively above the Earth. Ringing the emblem, its motto, proposed twenty years ago by General Abraham Salyard: AB ASTRA OMNIA VICTORIA. *From the stars, total victory.*

Dwight Salyard was doubly proud; to serve his country, and to continue the path his own father had blazed.

The guards in their blue berets saluted him as he passed through the wide double doors leading out to the glass-walled balcony that separated Central Command's glass-walled row of Operations staging offices from the mission-control centers one story below. Each of four mission controls in the cavernous theater was screened from the others. Each facility had an independent series of tiered Evans consoles and huge twenty-foot display screens on the far, double-story wall.

The elevated Operations level ran the full width of the theater balcony. From here, command personnel were able to keep track of up to four separate missions, though, presently, only two mission control elements were operational. One was staffed on a permanent basis to monitor the USSF's on-orbit assets. The other was staffed at a standby level to monitor the *Falcon* during its hold for launch.

In Salyard's tenure as Commander, USSF, there had only been one period in which three mission control elements had been simultaneously operational. But it would not be long before all four elements would be continuously staffed and Central Command would warrant its nickname: Olympus. For that, the general thought, as he gazed down upon the airmen of the USSF, was exactly what they would soon become—gods in the heavens throwing their thunderbolts at any mortal foolish enough to threaten the United States.

From Salyard's left, Major Lowell hurried out of one of the staging offices. "General, I have that information at my workstation."

Salyard followed the short, balding officer back through a sliding glass door into his dimly lit and noticeably quiet, glass-walled enclosure, home to five consoles and five somber-faced airmen seated at workstations monitoring satellite communications. The enclosure's light level had been reduced to make it easier to read the large but distant screens of the four mission controls on the floor below.

Next to the viewing wall, Lowell stood beside his own console so Salyard would have clear access to what was on the major's computer screen—a digital photostat of a legal document.

It was a Federal arrest warrant naming Daniel Varik as a suspect in the murder of Edward Farren.

"It entered the system yesterday," Lowell said. "Our ongoing automated search brought it up ten minutes ago. But because it's a sealed warrant, it looks like they're planning on sitting on it for a while."

"They? You mean, the FBI?"

Lowell nodded. "That tactic usually means they're looking for co-conspirators."

It was a brilliant move, and Salyard knew Teller deserved acknowledgment of such. Not only had the CEO of Teller Technologies sent the FBI against Salyard's Space Force, the man had also kept his own company completely out of the conflict, or believed he had. But the winner in that particular contest was a foregone conclusion, Salyard knew. *And it won't be Teller. It's just a matter of how quickly I can make the federal charges go away.* The logical first step for rapid containment of this attack would be to move Varik out of the FBI's reach.

"Do we know where Colonel Varik is?" he asked Lowell.

"He's in the SOV simulator, General."

"I'll talk to him. Keep him on base for now, and, in the meantime, take Vandenberg to Threatcon Charlie. Make sure everyone knows it's a drill. But no noncontractor civilians are allowed on base without signed authorization, and that means FBI agents, should any show up at the gate."

"Understood, General."

"As soon as you're done with that, I want orders drafted for Colonel Varik, sending him to . . . let's say, South Korea. The orders must originate from Special Operations Command, and I want you to backdate them by at least a week. Then, set up a chain of documentation, and when the FBI finally do make their inquiries, let them know that our own office of Special Investigations is scrutinizing the colonel for the same charges as part of a larger criminal matter, and the Air Force claims jurisdiction."

"All bases covered, General."

"That's the idea."

Before leaving to brief Varik, Salyard paused, remembering his duty as a leader. "And, Major, thank you for bringing this to my attention so promptly. You've helped defuse what might have been a major disservice to the Project."

Lowell straightened his shoulders. "Thank you, General."

"Carry on," Salyard said. He began to walk back to the glass doors and the balcony, already mulling over a list of operatives he could send against Teller in Varik's place. That the owner of TTI still had to die was even less in question than before. The man possessed no more secrets that his death could conceal. The taped conversation from the runway at Patrick Air Force Base, between Teller and Derek Frame, had told Salyard all he needed to know: Kai Teller was aware of what was on the Moon; TTI's rover had recovered proof; and Dr. Corazon Rey had returned that proof to Earth.

Which is why she now joined her employer on the target list.

Salyard turned right on the thickly carpeted balcony, the direction that would take him back to the double doors connecting Operations to the foyer and the elevator. As he did so, to his left, the main display screens in one of the unused facilities on the floor below switched on.

The general's first quick glance suggested to him that some kind of test was being run. A second glance stopped him in his tracks.

A moment later, Lowell rushed out of his office to stand against the floor-to-ceiling wall of glass that overlooked the lower levels. The major placed his hands on the glass as he stared in shock at the image on the twenty-foot display, which, according to the codes that Salyard saw running at its lower edge, originated from the Overwhelmingly Large Telescope Array in Utah.

Other officers spilled out of their staging offices, their faces blank with shared shock as they gaped at a high-resolution, adaptive optics, computer-enhanced photograph of an object very familiar to General Salyard and everyone who worked for him in the United States Space Force.

The *Tai Ping*. The Chinese space station.

Like most Chinese nomenclature, the station's name had many meanings, most of them having to do with peace and security, with a connotation that those conditions arose from strength. And now, Salyard thought, every sense and instinct on high alert, it seemed the *Tai Ping* was every bit as mutable as the meanings of its name.

Because the Chinese station had changed configuration.

Every six months for the past two years, the Chinese Space Agency had launched one major component, building an X-shaped assemblage of cylinders unlike any other in space. The first two cylinders had been linked end to end. The next two had been joined at their intersection, side to side. But unlike the Russian space station, *Mir,* or the ISS, the *Tai Ping* had no solar arrays, and China would neither confirm nor deny to outsiders that the new station was powered by a small nuclear reactor. Though that, Salyard believed, was the only possible explanation.

Now the configuration showed a second X shape in place of one of the cylindrical components. Salyard knew at once what he was seeing.

One of the cylinders had been a shroud, and now that shroud had opened to reveal the real on–orbit component that had been protected inside.

The newly revealed object was a *Shenzhou* spacecraft, joined to a lunar lander, identical to the one Varik and Webber had photographed in the Red Cobra 8 installation. The Chinese had finished building their moonship *on orbit.*

"Those bastards . . ."

Major Lowell was beside him. "General, now we know why they don't have a booster on the pad. They've got to know we can see it. They've got to know we know what they're doing."

"They do know, Major," Salyard said. "And they're telling us they don't care. Because it's too late. They're going to the Moon. And they're going *now."* Almost forty years since America had won the last race to the Moon, the general knew his country had just entered another, with even greater stakes.

Salyard shook off the unfamiliar weight of defeat, the image of his elaborate flowcharts falling like the crumbling blocks of an ancient abandoned city. Every meticulous plan he had put together over the past two days, the past two years, useless now.

Because strategy no longer mattered. Only time did.

General Salyard issued new orders.

18

"WHY ARE WE always saying good-bye?"

Webber kept his hands on the steering wheel of the black Intrepid Bailey had rented for him. He kept his eyes fixed on the entrance to the short-term parking lot at the Colorado Springs Airport, with its amazing view of snow-capped mountains. He and Cory had been here for an hour.

"Because we're not," Webber said.

"We're about to."

Cory's silence was almost physical, her way of trying to get him to say something more. But Webber was tired. They had stayed up half the night with Bailey and Hubert, waiting for Teller to return Cory's multiple calls. The industrialist had finally phoned back to Bailey's cell phone at four in the morning, from his plane, to make the arrangements for this morning.

"You want to know why I went to work for Kai Teller?" Cory asked.

Webber watched a car enter the lot, tracked it as it drove off to the side and took the first open parking space the driver came to. He judged it not a threat. "All right, why did you?"

"Number one, it was the kind of job I'd never want."

"Coming from you . . . I guess that makes perfect sense."

"I'm serious, Mitchell. Even the thought of getting into the shuttle made me feel sick. I mean, the idea of being in space, that's okay. That sounded sort of fun. But to put on a spacesuit, get strapped into a chair, have someone light the fuse on a gazillion pounds of explosives? Voluntarily?"

"So why'd you do it?"

"Because you would have."

Webber had to look at her then.

She stared back at him as if daring him to question her. He did. "I give up. I don't get it."

"Every day, you do stuff like that. Stuff you can't talk about. Because of, you know, Opsex—"

"Opsec."

"Right. But for me, what we went through in Antarctica, the Harrier, the Blackbird, the—" She hunched forward and dropped her voice to a low stage whisper. "—Nevada Rain . . . you know better than anyone that kind of stuff was a first for me."

"So?"

"I learned I could do it . . . change. I thought maybe it was time I tried something new again. It worked for us the last time."

Webber hesitated. In a way she was right. "Is that why you took off to Houston without me?"

"You were getting ready to go to Utah, remember?"

"Yeah, but we could've worked something out."

"That's not what you said a year ago."

"As a matter of fact, Cory, I did. And as I recall, there was a proposal in there, too."

"When? Oh, right, that one. In my experience, all proposals from naked men are suspect, until repeated clothed."

Webber smiled without wanting to. "But I did ask," he said.

"No, Mitchell. You told me. There's a difference."

Webber's hands tightened on the steering wheel. "Are you saying, everything we went through . . . was because I didn't ask you the right way?"

"I'm not arguing semantics. You said what you felt was right. You told me we were going to Utah. I didn't seem to have a say in the matter."

It was times like these that Webber understood why he enjoyed his profession. No ambiguities. No diplomacy. No searching for the right word or worrying about nuance and shading. He was told what to do, and he did it. Action, pure and simple. And decisive. Free-falling through clouds toward a freezing reservoir in the middle of China was an easier assignment than talking to Cory any day. But sometimes, he knew, the easy way wasn't the best way. Or the most rewarding.

"If that's the case," Webber said carefully, "if that's the way I made you feel, then I'm sorry, and all I can say is that it wasn't what I was thinking. It wasn't what I meant."

Cory reached out to put her hand on his. "It took you a year to figure this out?"

Webber was motionless. "You make me feel bad enough to apologize to you. And now you make me feel bad for apologizing." He stared straight ahead at the lot entrance, seeing nothing and everything. "You know, maybe the reason I'm so confused all the time is because *you* don't know what you want."

"You know something, Mitchell. You are absolutely hopeless."

Webber turned to her, anger rising. "What?!"

Then Cory suddenly pulled his face down to hers and kissed him so deeply and so thoroughly it was as if the past year had never happened.

When she let him breathe again, Webber felt light-headed, dizzy.

"What took you so long?" was all he could say.

"You," Cory said.

Webber tried to read the numbers on his watch. He had no real idea how much time had passed. "And you're getting on a plane in thirty minutes."

"It's that good-bye thing we have."

The air in the enclosed car was charged, electric. A haze of mist half covered the windshield. Webber turned the key so he could open his power window. "We should know better."

"Better than what?"

Webber checked his watch. "Thirty minutes from now you're getting on a plane with Teller and staying put with him until we can figure out who's after you, and why." He steeled himself for the confusion and hurt that he knew he would see on her face. "And I've got to report for duty. This isn't the time to start anything."

"I agree," Cory said slowly. "But we started a long time ago."

This time the silence between them lasted more than a minute. Cory broke it first.

"Mitchell, you know what your problem is?"

Webber forced the words from himself as if he were pulling a tooth, trading a short burst of pain for the end of a long course of it. "Your boss will be landing in fifteen minutes. Let's get this over with."

"What if it already is?" Cory said.

They left the car in mutual silence and frustration.

• • • •

The worst thing about Mitchell Webber, Cory knew, was that he was right about things far more times than he deserved. Half the times she'd disagreed or argued with him, it wasn't because he was wrong, but because she didn't want him to get cocky about being right. She'd always liked him better when he was kept off balance.

But this time, she was the one who had been thrown for a loop.

I'm the one who's hopeless, she thought as she watched Webber scan the terminal alcove they waited in.

Kai Teller's plane had landed almost half an hour ago, but the airport's security guards wouldn't let her or Webber out on the tarmac until the jet and its pilots had been cleared through security.

Cory felt miserable. She wished she and Webber had waited in the car. He—and she—were tensing up each time someone new stepped around the corner from the fast-food concession about fifty feet away in the main area of the terminal. Stress like that wasn't good for anyone, and the truly awful background music they were piping into this small corner of the airport wasn't helping. Nor was the old, cooked-onion smell that permeated the sit-down restaurant in which they sat.

"Look, Mitchell," she finally said, after almost twenty minutes of awkward stillness between them. "I don't ever want to do this again."

"Do what?" he asked, without even looking at her, as if he couldn't wait to unload her on Teller.

"Say good-bye without knowing when we'll see each other again."

"A year from now," Webber said. "We'll make it a tradition."

Because he was at least still talking to her, Cory took her

chance to tell him something she'd not had a chance to yet. "There was another reason I took the job in Houston. Besides you, I mean. It was something I knew I could do when the job was over."

Webber shrugged, his typically taciturn way of telling her to continue.

"They always have a press conference, you know? Up in the shuttle. You've seen them. All the astronauts float in a bunch and take questions."

"Yeah," Webber said, still intent on his sentry duty.

"The photos go around the world. They get students across the country to watch on NASA TV. So, I thought, if I got a chance to be in one of those press conferences, get my picture all over the world, I could do it in my Earthguard T-shirt. I mean, it's not as if they could send me home early, and it's the one place they couldn't drag me off the podium."

Webber turned around and looked at her, frowning. "Earthguard? You're still associated with those environmentalist whackos?"

Cory lifted her crutch, thinking Webber was lucky he wasn't in range. "The environmentalist *activists* who do twice the job politically correct Greenpeace ever did."

"Right," Webber said. Then he turned back to keep watch.

"It was a good plan," Cory said to the back of his brown leather jacket. Without Earthguard and its protest about nuclear weapons at the South Pole, she'd never have sailed to Antarctica, where she and her brother had reconnected with Webber.

The glass door to the tarmac suddenly opened and Kai Teller materialized in the doorway, unmistakable in his loose white shirt and blue jeans. Someone looking like a cross between a uniformed pilot and a bodyguard was right behind him.

"Cory!" Teller said as he walked toward her, arms outspread, smile blinding. "No, no—don't get up!"

But Cory was already half on her feet without using her crutch when Teller suddenly embraced her.

She flinched and he instantly stepped back in concern.

"My back," she said.

"Sorry, but . . . I am so glad to see you. So glad you're unhurt. Relatively."

Cory was suddenly aware of a tall presence beside them. So was Teller.

"Kai Teller," Cory said. "Mitchell Webber."

The two men shook hands and Cory could see they were both set at ten on the Richter scale of testosterone, sizing each other up.

"Captain Webber, thank you so much for . . . helping Cory. Why don't we go talk in my jet?" Teller took Cory's crutch and handed it to Webber, then put her arm through his own.

Cory saw Webber's face darken and she spoke up quickly. "Good idea." She limped off with her employer, without another glance at Webber.

The wind was gusting across the tarmac, not conducive to conversation, and Cory found herself pressed against Teller just to keep upright. He pulled her closer to him to steady her as she made her way up the small, fold-down staircase into the Gulfstream. Webber followed, then Teller's pilot, who quickly retired to the cockpit.

The plane was an oasis of soft muted color and textures; the luxuriously comfortable chairs were covered in soft leather. Trying hard not to think about the doomed calves and lambs and piglets and kids, Cory took the seat that Teller swiveled out for her. She'd learned, no matter what

Webber thought, that activism, to be effective, sometimes demanded difficult decisions of its followers. This was neither the time nor the place to point out that meat was murder.

"Very nice," Webber said as he looked around the passenger cabin, running his hand over the leather upholstery.

Teller acknowledged the compliment with a nod as he offered him a seat next to Cory, then asked if either of them would like a drink, even water. Webber shook his head.

Cory asked for coffee. Teller slid open a cherrywood panel to reveal an espresso machine built into the bulkhead. He put a delicate bone china demitasse under a spigot, pressed a button, and after some clunking and whirring, a double stream of frothed coffee filled the tiny cup.

Feeling quite perverse, Cory thanked Teller far more politely than she had ever thanked Webber for anything.

Teller sat down across from Webber, not from her. It was, Cory felt, as if her employer wanted Webber to know that she was more than a prize to be fought over, she had graduated to property being staked out.

"So, Cory ... I have to ask ... ," Teller said, almost apologetically.

Cory nodded, reached into the pocket of her Eddie Bauer canvas jacket, gave the small metal sample case to Teller.

He hesitated before opening it, but not for long. He stared at the fingers inside as if he were staring at the largest diamond in the world.

"You knew what you were bringing back," Webber said. Cory could hear the edge in his voice. He was spoiling for a fight.

"I *suspected,* Captain Webber. I didn't know. And I certainly didn't imagine . . . human remains. That's not what our information suggested at all."

"What information?" Cory and Webber asked at the same time.

Teller's cool amusement was matched by Webber's hot annoyance. "Let me ask each of you the same question," he said. "Did either of you ever see a movie called *Capricorn One?*"

Webber shrugged. But Cory thought the title familiar. "The faked Mars landing?"

"That's the one," Teller said. "It's an old film. Supposedly inspired by the modern folklore maintaining the Apollo lunar landings took place in a movie studio."

"The Japanese rover disproved that," Webber said flatly.

"There was never anything to disprove. The evidence for the landings has always been overwhelming. Beyond questioning. Those who argued otherwise, well," Teller lifted an eyebrow, "I've always suspected they're more on a par with the Flat Earth Society than people who really believed in what they were saying."

"So what's an old movie have to do with what's in that case?" Webber asked. Cory noted the suspicion still in his voice.

"Let me begin by saying that NASA didn't fake the Moon landings. But for many years, there have been all sorts of intriguing stories coming out of Russia that suggested the Soviets might have actually tried to do exactly that."

"Seriously?" Webber asked.

"Well, that's the question, isn't it?" Teller weighed the sample case in his hand. "The Soviet Union's been gone for almost twenty years, but historians are still discovering its secrets. For the first decade, the Russian Aviation and Space Agency denied the Soviets were ever even in a race for the

Moon. Then the details started coming out of the massive effort they had put into it. The L–3 Program."

Cory couldn't be sure what was behind Webber's unusually solemn expression as he asked, "Why do you think they lost the race?"

Teller gave him a half-smile. "They weren't capitalists. They didn't understand about efficiencies in design and manufacture. If there is one term that defined the monolithic Soviet approach to technology, it's 'brute force.' Their boosters were monsters."

"And they kept blowing up," Webber said. Cory wondered when, and how, Webber had become an expert on Russian space technology of the 1960s. Not that he'd ever tell her anyway.

"They did, indeed, Captain," Teller agreed. "Because they were never tested properly. The American approach was incremental. Build the smallest part of an engine, test it, refine it, combine it with the next component, test it again. Test test test. Then, when something went wrong, it was usually only *one* thing. Identifiable and easy to correct."

"Except for the Apollo capsule fire," Webber said.

Cory watched as Teller studied Webber. "Is this a subject that interests you?"

Webber shrugged off the question in a way that Cory knew meant he was lying. He'd never been able to lie to her. "Yeah, I'm interested in it."

But Teller appeared to accept the statement at face value. "Then you know the Apollo fire was an aberration of NASA's approach. It happens. In fact, it's almost inevitable. The system works well; the politicians want it to work better; the engineers push it a bit here, cut corners a bit there, until the process is continuing to work more from luck than from rational design. That's when luck runs out, hubris steps in, and the Apollo capsule catches fire, or the *Challenger* blows up, or the *Columbia* disintegrates, and everyone puts on the brakes and goes back to the solid, basic approach they should never have abandoned."

Teller put the sample case on the tray built into the wide arm of his seat. "The Soviets, on the other hand, they didn't have a solid, basic approach to fall back on. What they did have was at least two different engineering teams working on their lunar program, and the politics of the time kept those two teams from cooperating, or even talking with each other about what they were doing. So right away, you've halved the effort you can put into the project. And then, when time got tight, they built their boosters from untested components and fired them off. Meaning, when their boosters exploded, spectacularly, the Soviets had almost no way to determine which of a hundred different things might have gone wrong.

"In the meantime, NASA's slow, methodical, step-by-step approach became the tortoise that overcame the hare."

"So, if I follow you," Webber said, and Cory still had no idea what he was fishing for, just that he *was* fishing, "the Soviets realized they were going to lose the race to the Moon, and decided to fake a landing?"

Teller nodded. "That's the theory. In fact, there's reason to believe that's how the legend of the faked Apollo landings grew in America. The Soviets were successful in soft-landing probes on the Moon. They even deployed *lunokhods*—remote-controlled rovers. That's how I found out about the story of the Soviet fake landing, how it might have been true."

Cory saw an opportunity to join in. "Right. I remember you told me your engineers studied the old Soviet rovers." She spoke to Webber. "Kai told me they actually had successful sample return missions as far back as the early seventies." She noted Webber's flinch at her use of her employer's first name. *Well, he can't have everything his way,* she thought. *I'm no one's property but my own.*

If Teller had noticed any undercurrent between his guests, he chose not to say so. He merely added detail to her statement. "Three missions, as a matter of fact," he said. "In 1970, '72, and '76. Their rover missions and their sample-return missions were separate, but both were successful."

"Successful, *after* they lost the big race," Webber said, as if that were significant.

Teller didn't appear to know what Webber meant— Cory certainly didn't—because her employer continued on as if Webber hadn't spoken at all. "Anyway, Captain, when my people heard the stories, I was already committed to launching the first commercial lunar-sample-return mission. So, when it came time to choose a landing spot, I spent a considerable amount of money buying information from some old-timer Russian rocket scientists. To a man, they were quite embarrassed by the whole thing, but they did eventually tell me where on the Moon a Soviet lunar landing *might* have been faked—*if* it had been faked—by sending a robotic lander for the world to track, while the lunar cosmonauts remained in a Moscow television studio.

"I was going to the Moon anyway, so I figured, why not land at those coordinates? At the very least, I'd still get my hundred million dollars' worth of Moon rocks." He picked up Cory's sample case and brandished it, before putting it down again on his seat tray. "And at best, I uncover a stunning piece of untold history, get *two* hundred million dollars' worth of publicity, and some actual lunar artifacts to sell."

Something Bailey's husband had said floated into Cory's

mind. "Wouldn't any artifacts belong to the Russian government?" she asked.

Teller smiled at her. "You don't think they'd be eager to sell them for hard currency, do you? I'd pick up a good salvage fee."

Webber checked his watch again.

Cory gave him a sidelong glance, perplexed more than curious. He'd told her he didn't have to catch his plane at Peterson Air Force Base until noon, so something else had to be making him jumpy. And as much as she wished she could take the credit for that, she didn't think she was the cause, nor was the argument they'd had.

"So, Mister Teller," Webber began.

"Kai, please," Teller said.

Webber's quick acceptance of the invitation was casual, and rang incredibly false to Cory. *What was Mitchell after?* But once again, Teller did not pick up on it.

"Kai," Webber said. "Why do you think someone wanted to blow up the space station to keep those fingers from getting back to Earth?"

Teller leaned forward as if he couldn't have heard Webber right. "I beg your pardon?"

"It's Cory's point, and it's a pretty good one," Webber said, as if she had never raised a good one in her life. "The explosions that hit the station and the shuttle happened at the precise moment she completed her part of the LRV mission."

Teller hesitated, seeming confused, but Cory knew her employer was never confused. So it wasn't just Mitchell who was flying under false colors. "That's true, I suppose."

"Don't suppose," Webber said. "Here's your eyewitness. Talk to her about it."

Teller looked at Cory inquiringly. "Something new, Cory?"

"Just what I told you from the station," Cory said truthfully. "Bette Norman pulled a knife on me and I swear she was ready to kill me if I didn't let her get the samples. And those thugs the other morning, the ones I told you about on the phone. They definitely wanted to take me somewhere, and Mitchell is convinced they wanted to kill him."

Teller studied them both, before coming to some decision. "I do have some new information of my own that might help."

"We're listening," Webber said.

"Completely off the record, mind you," Teller cautioned.

"We brought you that sample case," Webber pointed out. "This whole thing's off the record."

"Fair enough," Teller agreed. "The FBI is investigating what happened to the station."

"Is that your news?" Cory said, disappointed. She'd been hoping for much more. "They've already hauled us in for questioning."

"Both of you?" Teller asked.

"Me, mostly. Captain America made a pain of himself, so they took him in just for spite."

"What did they ask you?" Teller asked Cory.

"You name it," Cory told him. "Who would want to destroy the station? Did I suspect any of the astronauts? Were you in collusion with the Russian mafia?" Cory stopped, looked at Teller. "Did the FBI pull you in, too?"

"They haven't gotten to me yet. But I have been flying back and forth a considerable amount. Between Houston and the Cape. Sorting this all out."

"But you know about the FBI investigation," Webber said.

"I believe I started it. You know Tovah Caruso?"

Webber nodded. "Chief administrator of NASA."

"When all this began," Teller said, "before we even knew if any of the astronauts would come back, I told her about a consultant I'd used on occasion who had concerns that someone might want to sabotage the mission."

"Who?" Webber asked.

"A retired engineer, used to work for NASA." Teller looked from Cory to Webber as he said the name. "Ed Farren?"

Cory had never heard of him. Neither, it seemed, had Webber.

"Shortly after the shuttle was lost, Doctor Farren died. Under questionable circumstances."

"How questionable?" Webber asked.

"As it turns out, he was murdered," Teller said. "A very sophisticated operation, too." He poked his finger behind his ear. "A small pinprick in the fold of his ear. A neurotoxin that mimicked heart failure. If the coroner had not been told by the FBI to investigate every possibility, it would never have been caught."

Webber had become very still and quiet, which signified to Cory that he was focused specifically on some idea he wanted to keep all to himself.

"Any suspects?" he asked.

"The name I've heard," Teller said, "is Daniel Varik."

"Varik," Webber repeated with apparent disinterest. And though it was obvious to Cory that Webber knew the name, Teller gave no sign of noticing that recognition.

"I have no idea who Varik is or what he does," Teller said, "but he apparently is the one the FBI is interested in."

"What are your security arrangements like?" Webber asked out of the blue.

"You're worried about Cory. I understand," Teller said.

He glanced at Cory, who couldn't help bristling at the antediluvian nature of all this protection–of–fair–maiden business. Even if it was warranted. "After everything you've told me, I'm worried, too."

"You can protect her?" Webber asked.

"I guarantee it," Teller said.

"How?" Webber asked. *He's so predictable,* Cory thought. *Mitchell always wants details. But at least it's not just my word he questions.*

"The same protection I have, Captain." Teller nodded toward the flight cabin. "Bodyguards. This plane. My estate in Maui."

The mention of Maui took Cory by surprise. "Does anyone have any idea how long this is going to go on?" she asked. She was not going to be imprisoned in some faraway castle just so the dragons couldn't eat her.

"I suppose that will be up to the FBI," Teller answered.

"Maybe not," Webber said.

Cory was more convinced than ever that Webber knew something he wasn't sharing. At any other time, in any other circumstances, she knew she would have called him on it, prodded him unmercifully until he confessed what he was trying to keep secret. But not this time. Not with things the way they were between them. She also knew that for once he wasn't keeping something just from her, he was keeping it from Teller. And it could be for good reason.

For one of the few times in her life, she decided to give Webber the benefit of the doubt. Bailey would be proud of her. Even if it was too late for her and Mitchell, and she hoped it wasn't, she was making progress.

Teller suddenly became more perceptive. "Captain, do you have additional information?"

"No," Webber said unhelpfully. "Wish I did." He checked

his watch for a third time. "I have to go." He stood up.

Teller stood, as well. Cory tried to, winced, and ended up taking Teller's hand again. It felt surprisingly smooth compared to Webber's calluses and scars.

For an appalling, thrilling moment, Cory had the feeling Webber was about to pull her away from Teller, but then he asked if anyone had a pen.

Teller handed him something the size of a large toothpick that he took from the side of a paper-thin Palm Pilot.

Webber took a business card from his pocket. Cory recognized it from last night's hotel. He scribbled a number on the back, gave the card to Cory.

"This is Willie's number at work. Not a direct line, but the switchboard can be lied to. And you know Willie. She's really good about tracking people down." He smiled as if he was making a joke, but the smile didn't reach his eyes. "Me and just about anyone."

Cory wasn't sure what Webber was trying to tell her, but she thanked him for the card. "Is there any way I can reach you?"

"I'll be at the same place for a while." He turned to Teller, shook his hand. "Good meeting you. I hope things work out."

"Thank you, Captain. I'm sure they will."

Then Webber nodded toward Cory as if she weren't in the plane. "Can I have a moment?"

"Certainly," Teller said. He picked up the sample case and moved forward to the flight cabin.

"A moment?" Cory asked.

Webber took her hand, squeezed it, and Cory understood it wasn't a romantic gesture. It was a warning.

Webber leaned close, his breath warm in her ear as he whispered, "Daniel Varik's at Vandenberg. He's an Air Force colonel."

Then Webber stepped back, didn't take his eyes from Cory's.

"Outstanding," she said.

"You be careful," Webber said quietly. "And you make sure Teller's careful."

All Cory wanted to say and couldn't was, "What about you? Do you have to work with Varik? Do you know what he does at Vandenberg?"

But Webber's face had gone blank again, and Cory knew she was looking at the brick wall of operational security.

She squeezed Webber's hand back, leaned forward to whisper herself. "Tell me something, please. Is there any chance the Air Force is behind what happened up there?"

Webber met her eyes directly. "I honestly don't know. But I will find out."

He tried to move away, but Cory wouldn't let go of his hand. "If they are, they destroyed the shuttle. Tried to destroy the station. Killed eight people."

"I'll be careful, too," Webber promised. Then she felt his hand leave hers, and she was filled with the sudden fear that this was truly their last good-bye.

"Mitchell . . ."

So quickly, she wasn't even sure it happened, he drew a finger across her cheek. "Tradition."

Teller returned to the cabin so soon after Webber's broad-shouldered form disappeared out the cabin door, that Cory wondered if he had been watching, perhaps on a hidden camera.

"Nice fellow," he said easily. "Where's his new assignment? Vandenberg?"

Cory made a noncommittal noise. She knew Teller was capable of making his own confirmation; he didn't need hers. Besides, he probably already knew.

"Any luggage?" he asked.

"Just me and my crutch," Cory said. She had even stopped carrying a purse during her year in Houston. If something didn't fit in her pockets, she no longer saw the need of carrying it.

"Well, let's do something about that," Teller told her. "We'll go shopping. In Los Angeles."

"Why not?" Cory said as she slowly eased herself down again in the soft leather chair.

Teller stood over her, with the admonishing look of a concerned parent. "Everything's going to work out, you know."

Cory nodded, even as she realized how much Teller had in common with Webber.

He couldn't lie to her, either.

19

WEBBER BECAME AWARE of the helicopter following him when he was still half an hour away from Peterson Air Force Base.

The Intrepid had a sunroof with a tinted window. At stoplights, he was able to glance up to confirm the helo's presence.

It was black, of course. Almost any helicopter seen in silhouette against a bright sky or clouds appeared black, so its color told him nothing about it. But from its rounded nose and the length of its tail, even at its present altitude he could identify it as a Pave Hawk. Which meant it was Air Force. Which meant he was in trouble.

At least Cory is safe. Webber held on to that thought as he rapidly ran through his current options. Teller looked like a man who was used to taking care of himself, and his pilot had been carrying a gun in a shoulder holster beneath his uniform jacket, implying that the TTI employee had duties other than flying. From the clusters of antennae Webber had noted on the Gulfstream, the jet was loaded with every state-of-the-art flying instrument, from GPS to satellite FDR, as well as the latest in TCAS and GPWS—Traffic Alert and Collision Avoidance Systems, and Ground Proximity Warning Systems. Planes outfitted so thoroughly often also had the advanced autopilot ability, shared by most commercial airliners and the space shuttle, to land themselves at Category 3B airports without a pilot at the controls. That meant Teller would never be more than an hour away from a safe landing anywhere in the United States and Canada, with or without a functioning flight crew.

It was simple for Webber to extrapolate from the level of safeguards on the plane to picture a fleet of armored cars and a phalanx of armed bodyguards serving TTI.

As for Teller himself, and the way he had been looking at Cory, as if she were destined to become his newest possession, Webber didn't want to think about that. He knew that despite the connection he'd felt again with Cory in those last few moments in the plane, he had no claim to her. Not after the past year. And certainly not after these past few days.

But at least she was safe.

Unlike him.

At a traffic light intersection, Webber pulled into a self-serve Exxon station and stopped the car at a gas pump beneath a rain and snow shelter. He opened the door, listened carefully for any sound that didn't come from the street traffic, and could just make out the helicopter's engine and rotor noise fading away.

He surveyed the terrain as if he were behind enemy lines. There was no chance for emergency extraction by Fulton skyhook here, as there had been in China. He was on his own.

Webber walked to the sales kiosk, staying beneath the shelter and out of sight from the air, to pay cash for the gas.

He was determined not to leave any record of his presence, or to alert whoever might be monitoring the banking system for any use of his ATM card.

He judged that if he took off his leather jacket, changing his visual profile from black leather to a white T-shirt, and timed his move for after the helo's next pass, he could sprint over to a small strip mall next door to the gas station. There was a Chinese restaurant in it, from which he could call a cab.

Then Webber realized his evasive tactics would work even better if he could convince someone to drive his car from the gas station and draw off the helicopter.

He had around eighty dollars in cash. He hoped it would be enough.

The pale-faced cashier on the other side of the payment kiosk window looked to be a high-school student, with stringy brown hair and a nasty patch of acne ineptly concealed under a thick coating of colored cream. Webber decided the cashier's age might make things easier. "Hi," he said with a friendly smile. "Is there a mechanic around?"

"Sorry, mister, just gas."

Webber took his roll of bills from his pocket. "Do you know anything about cars?"

The kid shrugged. "I guess."

"I just rented that car and it's got a strange shimmy or something. Do you want to take a look at it?"

The kid started to shake his head, but Webber held up the cash. "I'm in a real hurry. I'm going to have to call Hertz, but it's going to take forever to explain what's wrong. I don't know the first thing about cars."

The kid looked at the money, then shouted back to someone in the food-mart half of the kiosk to take over the register and came out to look at Webber's car.

Webber gave him the keys, stayed outside the car so the kid wouldn't feel he was about to be kidnapped, and told him to start it.

Webber could just make out the distant rumble of the helo as the ignition caught. The timing of his diversion was going to work out just fine.

"Sounds okay," the young cashier said.

"Now it does," Webber said. "But take it around the block, see what the wheel does."

The kid gave him a suspicious look. "I shouldn't," he said.

"I'll stay right here," Webber told him. Through the open driver's window, he handed the kid twenty dollars. "You come back and tell me what you think."

With money in hand, the kid ran out of arguments and suspicion.

"Why not go around two blocks," Webber said. "You can't feel it till you get it up around thirty for a minute or so."

The kid clearly couldn't make sense of what Webber was asking him to do, but he wasn't about to back out now. "Okay," he said uncertainly.

Webber could hear the helo over the car's engine. From the intensity of the sound, he estimated it was about five hundred feet overhead, which meant this was going to be perfect. "See you in a few minutes," he said, then stepped away from the car.

The kid put the Intrepid into drive, pulled out from under the shelter, and just as he turned toward the street, he suddenly jammed on the brakes and brought the car to a screeching stop.

An instant later, a huge blast of wind hit Webber, stinging him with bits of grit kicked up from the gas station's pavement.

The helicopter was landing in the food-mart parking lot, in front of Webber's car, clearing the telephone poles and power lines by less than ten feet. But it still sounded distant. Webber had been mistaken in his identification of it. It wasn't a standard Air Force Pave Hawk. It was a KH-60R Star Hawk, in full hushed mode, just like the one he had flown on to recover Cory.

Even while the helo was still settling, two airmen in flight suits leapt out of the Star Hawk and ran toward the Intrepid, in the heat of the moment taking the kid at the wheel for Webber. Puzzled the airmen hadn't drawn their sidearms, but seeing the teenager was not in danger, Webber ducked suddenly behind the gas pumps, threw off his jacket, and started to walk slowly toward the strip mall, planning to start running the moment he was out of sight of the helo.

But his plans soon changed as a dark brown Crown Victoria jumped the parking lot curb, skidded to a stop in front of him, and two men in rumpled business suits stumbled from the car, one reaching inside his jacket.

The Intrepid was now Webber's fastest means of escape. He looked back to see the kid, out of the car, pointing right at him. And one of the airmen already running in his direction.

Webber's decision was simple. Two unarmed airmen were easier to take out on the way to regaining his car.

His glance swept back to the men in suits. He heard the man with his hand in his jacket shout, "Captain Webber! FBI!"

Webber changed tactics again. If the Air Force was the enemy, then the FBI could be the best way to evade the airmen. He held his position.

Then the man took his hand from his jacket and brandished a folded sheet of blue paper. "You are under arrest!"

Before Webber could reply, an airman behind him shouted, "Captain Webber! This way!"

Webber saw both airmen pointing toward the open side hatch of the Star Hawk.

"Don't even think about it!" one of the FBI agents shouted.

Now both men from the Crown Victoria had drawn guns, and fast as he was and as much as he wanted to, Webber knew he couldn't outrun bullets.

"Drop your weapons now!" That command had come from one of the two airmen, now charging toward the FBI agents with drawn .45s.

Webber couldn't believe it. He was about to be caught in a firefight between the FBI and the Air Force. But for what reason?

Then the FBI agents were on him, one of them spinning him around so he could slap on handcuffs.

"The Air Force has jurisdiction!" an airman shouted, close enough now that Webber could see he was a master sergeant, last name McGraw. McGraw's partner was the same rank, his last name, Duburg.

Webber didn't make it easy for the FBI agent behind him, struggling to keep him off balance.

The other agent faced down the airmen with his gun drawn. "Back down now or we arrest you for obstruction!"

The airmen didn't budge. McGraw had the deeper voice and he bellowed, "You leave, or we arrest you for interfering in an investigation vital to national security."

Sergeant Duburg caught Webber's eye. "Captain, we have orders from General Salyard to bring you in."

Webber knew that was a message. They were letting him know that there was no Air Force investigation—or some other officer would have given the orders. These airmen were attempting to keep him from the FBI.

That was good enough for Webber. Now he knew which side to go with.

He gave up his false struggle against the FBI agent behind him, spun around to crack his elbow into the man's face, dropping him instantly.

The second agent turned at the sound of the first agent's moan, got Webber's fist in his nose and staggered back with a howl of pain.

Sergeant McGraw deftly relieved the agent of his gun, and let him fall to the pavement unassisted.

Webber quickly looked around the gas station. Cars had sprawled to a stop at the intersection. Onlookers crowded the sidewalks. The inevitable sirens were already rising above the soft rush of the spinning helo rotors.

Duburg stepped up to Webber. "Captain Webber, despite the uniform, I'm Lieutenant Colonel Andrus, USSF. General Salyard sends his compliments and requests you get your ass aboard that bird ASAP, sir."

Webber took two seconds to retrieve his leather jacket, then joined the airmen as they ran toward the Star Hawk. "Did the general know I was catching a flight back to Vandenberg at noon?" He waved to the kid, staring at him from beside the Intrepid, mouth open.

"Something's come up," Andrus said. "He's got us all jumping through hoops. There's an F-35 standing by at Peterson to get you back to Van faster than you know what."

Webber scrambled into the Star Hawk, and the helo lifted off before the hatch was shut.

"An F-35?" Webber asked as he found a side seat and strapped in. It was the country's newest, unclassified production combat aircraft, also known as the Joint Strike Fighter.

"Whatever the general has in mind for you, sir, he wants you there yesterday."

• • •

With its classified speed topping out just under Mach 2, Webber brought his F–35 in to land at Vandenberg thirty-two minutes after leaving Peterson Air Force Base.

He was instructed to park the plane at the end of the runway for the ground crew to deal with. He was out of the cockpit and into a Humvee in less than a minute, and the driver burned rubber getting him to their destination—Hangar 27.

The guards at the personnel entrance were ready for him and waved him through. Inside, General Salyard was already waiting with three other officers in flight suits. Webber knew Varik, but not the others.

"Captain Webber reporting as ordered, General."

Salyard pointed to the side and started walking. Webber and the other three followed briskly.

"I understand Andrus led a cavalry charge to get you here." The general's comment sounded casual, but Webber caught the charged tension in him and the others. This wasn't Salyard the politician before him. It was Salyard the warfighter.

The general waved a hand at the others. "These are your fellow crew. Varik you know. He's mission commander."

The word "mission" jumped out at Webber. He had no idea what Salyard had in mind, other than it seemed critical.

Salyard pointed to a serious young woman with a cap of short blond hair. "Lieutenant Colonel Christa Bowden, SOV pilot."

The term "SOV" electrified Webber. Whatever the mission was, it involved a Space Operations Vehicle. It could only mean he was going into space. Now, not two years from now. Salyard had invited him into the USSF to become exactly what Bowden was.

The third member of the crew was a rail-thin Hispanic who was the only one to smile at Webber as Salyard introduced him. "And your mission specialist, Captain Philo Rodriguez."

Webber restrained himself from asking any questions. Things were moving so quickly, there was such urgency in the air, he had no doubt he'd know everything he needed to know in minutes.

In the meantime, he continued to follow Salyard as the general led the crew away from the SOV flight simulator and around the black security curtains. When they were on the other side, away from the main personnel entrance, Webber could see that the arrangement of the curtains was exactly what he had guessed. There was one large object hidden behind them, but split into two separate working areas, so the technicians on one side could not see the other.

Then Salyard came to a stop facing the curtains. He raised his hand, giving a signal to someone unseen.

Webber heard powerful motors start and the loud, hollow clanking of metal chains. Eighty feet overhead on the hangar's ceiling, guide tracks moved as the security curtains were pulled aside.

"Captain Webber, your ride is currently on the pad. But this is the same class, same generation."

As the black curtains slowly moved apart, the wedge-shaped cross section of the craft was revealed, raised about ten feet from the hangar floor on a dense network of metal scaffolding that was threaded with stairways and work areas. But Webber looked past the distraction of the supporting framework to take in the craft itself.

To his eye, the sweep of its dull-finished black hull made it resemble some creature from an alien sea. It had the compact silhouette of a manta, but without the wide wings. It seemed to be in motion just sitting there, like something alive, something captured.

"This is the SOV *Eagle,*" Salyard said with obvious pride. "Once known as the military space plane, at least five generations removed from those original plans."

Webber whistled. The black curtains were still moving, more of the vehicle was being uncovered. Now he could see it did have two pairs of wings, one large pair aft, a smaller pair coming off the nose. Twin rear stabilizers distinguished the blocky aft section.

"After the boost phase, the vehicle has an overall length of sixty feet. Main fuselage width is twenty feet. Rear wingspan, fifty-eight feet. Forward wingspan, twenty-three feet." Salyard started walking toward the nose of the vehicle, and it was unlike any spaceframe or airframe Webber was familiar with.

Side to side, the SOV was the same width at the nose as it was at the tail. It was tapered only in height, with the leading edge of the craft about one foot thick, and the rear about twelve feet.

There were no visible windows or portholes, though there seemed to be an access hatch on the side, about midway.

Salyard continued with his descriptive detail. "It is covered with rigid ceramic cloth, over heat-resistant tiles, over a titanium frame. It is capable of descending from orbit, engaging in hypersonic transatmospheric flight, and then skipping out of the atmosphere back to orbit."

Webber understood the general was informing him that the vehicle could serve as a bomber.

"It is also capable of supporting a crew of four for up to sixty days on orbit, a crew of eight for thirty days, or any variation in between.

"It launches shrouded on a Venturestar reusable launch

vehicle, and with appropriate boosters, can attain geosynchronous orbit. Additional block boosters and consumables are prepositioned in orbit, providing for expanded mission time if required."

Salyard looked at Webber. "And that is about all the time we have for your briefing, Captain. Any questions?"

Webber had thousands. He asked one. "Is this a training mission, General?"

"This is as real as it gets, Captain."

"Then I am confused, General. I'm not qualified to fly an SOV, and if Colonel Bowden is . . . I don't know what my role on the mission is supposed to be."

"You won't be flying *Falcon,* Captain. That is Colonel Bowden's territory. You'll be flying the *Kitty Hawk,* and it's already on orbit, waiting for you."

"Kitty Hawk?" Webber asked, wondering how he was expected to fly something, let alone a spacecraft, he had never trained on. "What is that, General?"

"It is a United States Space Force Lunar Expeditionary Vehicle. In three hours, you and your crew are launching in *Falcon.* And in three days, you are landing *Kitty Hawk* on the Moon."

BLUE MOON

T MINUS 3 HOURS

1

"**HERE'S HOW IT'S** going to play out," Salyard said.

In a blindingly lit white room, Webber stood spread-eagled as one technician measured his arms and legs and a second scraped at the dark hair on his chest with a dry disposable razor to clear patches for medical sensors. Less than thirty minutes had passed since Salyard had given Webber his orders, and Webber still hadn't processed the information, still couldn't quite believe any of this was real.

Part of him half expected to discover that what was happening was a high-pressure simulation, a rite of passage for all new recruits in the USSF. They'd suit him up, strap him in, and then at the last second, announce it had all been a drill.

But Salyard gave no indication that he was anything but serious.

"For the launch, for the rendezvous, for the three-day flight to the Moon, even for the first hour of descent, you're going to be flying fat, dumb, and happy."

Webber knew the pilot's term. It meant a flight was strictly autopilot, no surprises.

"Hard to believe," Webber said. He flinched as the medical tech in a white jumpsuit stuck a cold biomedical lead to his chest.

"Not really. Ninety-nine point nine percent of all spaceflights are automated or robotic. Strictly speaking, even the shuttle doesn't need a pilot. It launches on its own. The pilots may like to take the stick for the last few S-curves and final approach, but the computers are still running in the background. In fact, the only action a crew member *has* to take is to physically pull the controls that lower the landing gear, and deploy the drag chute. Everything else is fully automated. And, I assure you, Captain, there's never been a case where the data show the computers would have done anything but land perfectly."

"Don't tell the astronauts that," Webber said. The second tech who had gone over and around him with a tape measure had finally finished and scurried away.

"Like most flights, the pilots are there for times when something goes wrong," Salyard said. "Or in your case, when we need to do something the computers can't handle."

For Webber, that was the big question that still hadn't been answered. He knew he'd be expected to land a vehicle called *Kitty Hawk* on the lunar surface, but no one had yet explained why that task had fallen to him. "What is it that I'll be doing on this landing, General?"

"The hardest part. The one part we can't program. Landing in difficult terrain—an area called Rimae Tannhauser. You're going to have to contend with craters, boulders, uneven surfaces." Salyard paused as if preparing to cross a point of no return. He said to the medical technician, "Excuse us, please."

The tech left at once.

"You are also going to have to contend with debris, Captain."

Here it comes, Webber thought. *We're going where Teller's rover has already gone before.*

"May I ask the nature of the debris, General?"

Salyard pursed his lips for a moment, hesitating. Indecision in such a high-ranking officer was unusual to Webber. "Have you ever heard of something called Project A-119?"

"The name isn't familiar, General."

"It was a questionable operation the Air Force had, back in the late fifties. They wanted to launch an ICBM to deliver a nuclear warhead to the Moon."

Webber had never heard of such a project. It sounded faintly ridiculous. "Was there a particular reason for wanting to do that?"

"At the time, no," Salyard said. "Oh, they had a group of scientists create justifications for doing it. Carl Sagan was one of them. But they finally admitted it was just sabre rattling. Showing off for the Soviets. In the end, they didn't implement it."

Webber had caught Salyard's odd turn of phrase, decided the general had chosen it for a reason, and called him on it.

"You said, 'at the time,' there was no reason to do it. Did that change at all, General?"

"You pay attention," Salyard said approvingly. "The last Apollo landing on the Moon was seventeen."

"December 1972," Webber added.

Salyard raised an eyebrow as if surprised Webber knew the date. But he continued without comment. "However, it was not the last *American* landing on the Moon."

For all that Webber had been expecting to hear something like this, he was still taken aback to hear it stated so plainly. "Then someone's done an outstanding job of preserving the secret."

For a fleeting moment, Salyard smiled. "That's the Air Force. But the mission itself wasn't outstanding."

Webber understood. "You mentioned debris."

Salyard nodded. "It was called Project Hammer. In the mid-seventies, the Department of Energy discovered pretty much by accident that a manufacturing flaw had been introduced into the control chips of an entire series of Krytron switches."

Webber knew those switches intimately. "They're the timing triggers for nuclear warheads." Their function was to ensure the simultaneous arrival—at every detonation point around the noncritical shell of plutonium—of the electrical signals triggering the explosives that compressed the shell into a critical mass. If the timing was off, even by microseconds, the explosives would not detonate uniformly, and nuclear detonation could not take place.

Salyard nodded again. "When that hit the fan, around the summer of 1977, we were looking at the possibility that more than ninety percent of the warheads in our inventory were duds."

The significance of that revelation was more shocking to Webber than a suppressed, secret Moon landing. If the Soviet Union had ever suspected America no longer possessed a nuclear deterrent, the balance of power in the world would have been altered overnight.

"So the Air Force decided to test a nuclear weapon on the Moon?" he asked. It was Cory's worst nightmare, and he hoped she'd never hear about it.

"It makes more sense when you think about it," Salyard said. "The engineers needed an aboveground test of a battle-ready weapon. But the test ban treaty limited us to underground detonations, and forced strict limits on the size of the yield, which wouldn't have done us any good for the weapons we needed to check out. The responsible parties faced three choices. One was completely unacceptable: initiating a crash program to replace every Krytron trigger on every warhead in our arsenal. It would have taken fourteen months, and no one believed we could keep what we were doing from the Soviets, which would have opened the door to nuclear blackmail.

"The second choice wasn't much better. Deliberately breaking the test ban treaty and detonating a warhead in the atmosphere. The National Security Council debated staging it as an accident, or trying to disguise it as a meteor explosion, but the political fallout was judged to be too dangerous. In those days, if you recall, China was still conducting atmospheric tests and needed to be reined in. And the Soviets would have gone back to their superbomb tests in a minute. So the third choice was taking a warhead to the Moon and detonating it there, where no one on Earth could detect it."

"And that was simpler?" Webber asked.

"We already knew how to go to the Moon, Captain. The Air Force had command and service modules from the White Lightning project ready to fly. Grumman built an upgraded lunar lander based on the Apollo designs in ten months and were damned pleased to do it. The big difference between Project Hammer and an Apollo mission was that there was no way we could hide building and launching a new Saturn V rocket. So, we took three launches to get everything into orbit. One launch for the command and service module. One for the lander. And one for the booster stage that sent the spacecraft from Earth orbit to the Moon. Even in 1978 there was enough space activity to disguise three extra launches."

"But something must have gone wrong," Webber said, knowing something always did.

"It did. The lander crashed on touchdown. We're still not certain what happened. Telemetry showed a main-engine malfunction thirty seconds before the lander reached the surface. Either the propellant tanks blew and the lander broke up at an altitude of nine hundred feet, or the lander simply lost power and dropped from that height. The bottom line is, right now, on the Moon, there are the bodies of an Air Force astronaut, the wreckage of a lunar module, and a one-kiloton nuclear warhead."

Webber thought he had the connection he'd been looking for. "And Kai Teller found it," he said.

But this time, Salyard shook his head. "*We* found it, Captain. The Air Force has piggybacked onto every Moon survey mission for years. Clementine in '94. Lunar Prospector in '98. The ESA's SMART-1. Japan's Selene probe. We come in, offer computer expertise and free equipment for the chance to test various procedures, and then we basically hijack the entire data stream. Whenever images are returned from the approximate area that we believe the '78 lander crashed in, we get to see the data first. Last year, the effort finally paid off. We found the crash site. That's one of the reasons why the government is finally beginning to fund NASA's requests for new crewed lunar-landing missions."

"No one else noticed the wreckage?"

"Not at first. We, of course, altered the images before they were released, erasing the debris field."

But Webber had heard another of the general's revealing turns of phrase. "Not at first," he repeated.

Salyard frowned, and Webber finally realized he was looking at the general's way of displaying anger. "Somehow, Teller got hold of the raw data. He saw the debris field, sent his own rover for it. In the meantime, the same images made their way to China. That debris field is where we believe the first Chinese lunar landing is to take place, very soon."

Webber suddenly understood the purpose of the mission. "We're the clean-up squad."

"The ultimate Freefall mission," Salyard said, in confirmation. "We were able to shut down Teller's communications with his rover, so we didn't have to contend with any video signals it might have sent back. But we're not going to be able to do a thing about a Chinese landing. So before they get there, we have to get to Rimae Tannhauser, and we have to sanitize the site."

In the world of military euphemisms, Webber knew the term 'sanitize' could have many different meanings, some of them sinister. "For this mission, what is our definition of 'sanitize,' General?"

"We have to get the warhead out of there. That's the primary mission goal. The country can live with the revelation of a failed, secret mission to the Moon. Everyone responsible is retired or dead. It will be an embarrassment, but we'll live through it. Finding the warhead, though, that's completely different."

Webber remembered what he and Varik had discussed when he had questioned the presence of weapons on the SOV simulator. "It's a violation of the Outer Space Treaty of 1967."

"A flagrant one," Salyard agreed. "And worse, it opens the door for the Chinese to proceed with their own plans to test weapons on the Moon."

That was revelation number three for Webber. "That wasn't a cover story?" In his first meeting with Salyard, the general had explained the supposedly real purpose of his and Varik's incursion into Red Cobra 8 as a foray to determine the status of China's plans to test energy weapons on the Moon. But even that story had been a cloak of misdirection and deception.

"Not at all, Captain. When you've spent more time with us, you'll realize that those in the Project have a need to know everything related to our mission. So we all share in the information the Project requires."

"Understood, General."

Salyard checked his watch. "We need to get you prepped and suited up. What time did you eat last?"

Webber looked up at the blazing fluorescent lights that lined the ceiling, trying to remember that far back. To a different world. "This morning, Colorado time."

"Well, we're just like NASA in that respect. Preflight enemas, no charge." Salyard clapped his hand on Webber's shoulder. "You're going to be in your pressure suit for approximately ten hours. No plumbing. Get used to it."

"Yes, General," Webber said. For all the space training he'd undertaken, he'd never flown in space. There were bound to be some surprises he'd have to take in stride. "Anything else I should know?"

Salyard actually gave that question some thought, and for a brief, crazy moment, Webber speculated about what else the general could tell him that could top what he'd already said. But the general's answer was short and prosaic.

"Varik and Bowden are veterans. They know the SOV, so you just follow their lead. Rodriguez is a rookie like you. It's his first flight. But his role doesn't start until you land at the crash site. He's the tech who has to deal with the warhead. And as for you . . . after you dock with the *Kitty Hawk,* you'll have three days to familiarize yourself with the craft. You will be able to run training simulations, so that's where I expect you to spend the flight."

Three days, Webber thought. *To learn to fly a spacecraft.*

"I see that look," Salyard said, "and I understand what

you must be feeling. But your record tells me you already have the flight experience you need to handle the lander. Especially your helicopter training. I have full confidence in you, Captain. Otherwise, you wouldn't be on this mission."

Webber glanced over to the far side of the prep room to see three technicians waiting patiently. One held a folded orange flight pressure suit, another a helmet, boots, and gloves. The third tech had a white bag in her hand. Webber didn't linger on thoughts of what was in the bag. "One last question, General?"

Salyard nodded.

"Who was first choice for this mission?" The timing was such that Webber knew something else had gone wrong.

"Four brave men who died in the KC–135 crash two days ago."

With that, it all made sense to Webber. "Thank you, General."

"I'll talk to you on the pad." Salyard shook his hand, waved over the technicians, then left.

The briefing had been critical for Webber's understanding. Not only for what the general had told him in words, but for what he'd said between the lines.

Webber considered the facts in evidence now. Cory's employer had known about the crash site of an American mission, not a possible faked Soviet landing. The general's Space Force had known that Teller's rover had been sent to the Moon to reveal the crash site, and so had jammed its communications.

How far did Webber have to stretch those three facts to know who had sabotaged the shuttle and the station to prevent any debris from the crash site returning to Earth and Teller's control?

The answer, Webber knew, was not far at all.

The FBI believed Colonel Varik had murdered one of

Teller's consultants who had stumbled on evidence of the sabotage plot. And General Salyard directed Varik's every move.

It no longer mattered to Webber that he was working for the United States Space Force.

All he could think was that he was working for the enemy.

It was a situation he could not let stand.

In the corridor outside the astronaut prep room, Salyard encountered Major Lowell. The major had been up for days now, and looked it. The dark circles ringing his protruding pale-blue eyes were masklike, startling.

"General," Lowell said in greeting. His fingers were gripped so tightly on the manila folder he carried, it was as if the major feared the thick file would escape if released. "How's Captain Webber?"

Salyard smiled, pleased to share his satisfaction. "Excited enough that he believed the Project Hammer cover story." In reality, Project Hammer had been conceived in 1978 as a means to test an experimental enhanced radiation nuclear weapon on the Moon, but, like A-119, had never been carried out. There was, however, enough of a paper trail to provide cover for what some industrious researcher might suspect after the crash site had been sanitized.

"Are you certain, General?" Lowell asked nervously.

Salyard understood, but didn't appreciate the implication of the question. "Why shouldn't I be?"

Lowell held up the unmarked file. "These are the surveillance reports on Teller. Early this morning, he landed at Colorado Springs Airport. Captain Webber was seen escorting Doctor Rey onto Teller's plane. They remained onboard for approximately twenty minutes, and then Captain Webber left."

Salyard felt a sudden rush of adrenaline as once again he had to change strategy on the fly. "Webber and Rey? With Teller?"

"We knew Webber and Rey had a history."

"I don't care about their past, Major. We know from that physicist at the Air Force Academy that Rey brought back human remains from the LRV. And we know from Teller's conversation at Patrick that *he* knows Rey brought something back. So if Rey is now *with* Teller, we must assume that she has given those remains to him." Salyard frowned.

"Where are Teller and Rey now?" he asked.

"Teller's pilot filed a flight plan for D.C., then changed it after takeoff to go to Los Angeles."

Salyard nodded, not surprised. "He knows he's being tracked. Los Angeles will just be a refueling stop. He's going to be heading for his estate in Maui. That's where we can take him out. And Doctor Rey with him."

"Understood, General," Lowell said. "What about Captain Webber's involvement in all this?"

"He obviously sanctioned Rey's turning over the samples to Teller. And that makes him a traitor to the Project. And to his country."

Lowell swallowed. "Your orders, General?"

Salyard's answer was a simple "None."

Lowell seemed puzzled.

"We still need someone to land at the crash site," Salyard said, by way of explanation. "But after that . . ." He let his voice trail off, seeing no need to continue the thought aloud.

The situation concerning Webber was obvious to him, and in a few minutes would be obvious to Colonel Varik as well.

Once Webber reached the Moon, he would not be coming back.

2

THREE HOURS LATER, the *Falcon* rose to the heavens from Vandenberg, a night-black blade slicing into the reddening sky, held aloft by a hilt of incandescent fire.

Beneath it, the curve of the Earth grew more pronounced, the crisp shoreline of California, the wave-textured blue of the Pacific and the crimson brilliance of the clouds pure and intense as distracting detail disappeared.

Beyond the thundering craft, the arc of the sky grew richer, the blue of dusk deepening to indigo.

But within the cramped and windowless craft, Mitch Webber kept his attention only on the display screens he could make out between the forward seats of Varik and Bowden, the colors on those screens smearing in doubled reflections within his helmet's visor. Webber was a pilot first and by nature. To be strapped into a machine that took flight solely by the grace of computers was unnatural and unnerving.

Colonel Varik's midwestern twang came over Webber's snug headset. "This is *Earlybird* at one hundred eight nautical miles, showing go for EOI. CenCom, do you copy?"

The response from Central Command was immediate and crisply devoid of static or echo, digitally processed and cleaned by the decryption circuits in the comm system. The two hours Webber had spent on his back in this cabin, waiting for liftoff, had been a nonstop technical briefing on the *Falcon* and its capabilities. Unlike NASA's crewed missions, the communications between USSF space vehicles and their Central Command were immune to interception.

"Copy that, Earlybird. You are go for EOI."

The shaking of the crew module was beginning to diminish, but Webber still felt himself jammed into his acceleration seat by a giant's fist. At an altitude at which a space shuttle would already be shut down and on orbit, the engines of the *Falcon's* Venturestar RLV—Reusable Launch Vehicle—were still firing, the craft still rising.

Webber watched the countdown on the middle screen. The voice of Central Command kept pace.

". . . five . . . four . . . three . . . two . . ."

Whatever the voice said next, Webber didn't hear it because the cabin and his helmet rang with a sharp explosion.

Instinctively his hands jumped forward as if there might actually be controls within reach that he could use.

But his hands fell back as once again he was pressed even more violently into his seat, and his conscious mind finally caught up with his instincts and he realized what had happened.

Sixteen explosive bolts had detonated to instantly separate the *Falcon* from the Venturestar's booster. At the same time, two sets of RCS—reaction control system—thrusters had fired. One set on the Venturestar punched down its blunt nose more rapidly than if it had just been allowed to coast on momentum, making the flattened cone-shaped booster drop sharply away from the wide wedge of the *Falcon* and its still–attached second-stage ELB—Expendable Launch Booster. The second set of RCS thrusters was on the *Falcon* itself, and kicked it up and away from the dull black ceramic–tiled bulk of the Venturestar.

Only one point five seconds later, when the separated components of the craft were already three hundred feet apart, the engines of the *Falcon*'s expendable launch booster fired, their explosive plumes safely missing the Venturestar, which had already rolled like a breaching whale to begin its computer-guided glide path to an automated landing at a Vandenberg runway.

Now the sleek SOV accelerated again, adding another 800 mph to its velocity, keeping each astronaut within locked in his or her seat, unable to move under the force of 5.2 gs, punishing compared to the 3.2 gs experienced by shuttle crews.

The voice of Central Command kept up a soothing litany of numbers, but Webber heard little of it through the rushing thunder of his heartbeat. His eyes hurt. His chest might as well have been encased in concrete. He felt saliva digging into the back of his throat and he could not swallow.

The suffocating pressure lasted for 344 seconds, and through it all, the only coherent thought in Webber's mind was, *I am not in control.*

And then, as if he were in nothing more than a roller-coaster car that had suddenly topped the crest of an infinite hill, the pressure vanished, and as he gulped in a deep breath of relief, he felt himself fall gently *up* from his seat.

In space, the elongated, sharp-edged rhomboid of the now silent expendable launch booster gently tumbled from the flat dorsal hull of the *Falcon* and began its own long fall toward the Earth, one it would never complete because atmospheric friction would reduce it to ash before it came within twenty miles of the ocean.

In the *Falcon's* crew module, the sudden silence was a physical sensation, as was the apparent lack of motion.

Webber had the unusual experience of feeling himself tremble in his pressurized flight suit in all directions. Beside him, Captain Rodriguez raised a gloved hand in a thumbs-up position. Seconds later, Webber's stomach rebelled and for a terrorizing moment he pictured himself vomiting inside his helmet. But the promethazine patch he had been given after his enema seemed to be easing his symptoms. The feeling of nausea didn't leave him, but the sudden urge to vomit did.

"This is *Earlybird*," Varik radioed, "at eleven minutes into flight, now on transfer orbit. Commencing longitudinal roll maneuvers in three . . . two . . . one . . . mark."

Despite himself, Webber tensed, expecting to be slammed back into his seat. But instead, all he heard were distant thumps and hisses, and his seat and restraints tugged gently against him as the crew module began to rotate.

"Halfway there," Varik said for the benefit of his crew.

More thumps and hisses that Webber now knew were the SOV's RCS thrusters making their minute adjustments to the *Falcon's* angle of flight under the control of its pilot, Lieutenant-Colonel Christa Bowden. Then the slight movement of the cabin stopped once more. All was still again, the only sound the faint whisper of air circulating through his helmet.

"And we are on the wire," Bowden said.

Webber forced himself to relax. The *Falcon* was now in a coast phase. In five minutes, plus or minus a second or two to be decided by the onboard computers, the SOV's exo-atmospheric engine would fire for the first time and send the craft into its geostationary orbit, for rendezvous with the *Kitty Hawk* Lunar Expeditionary Vehicle.

It still perplexed Webber that during his briefing no one had answered his completely reasonable queries about the logic of parking a lunar vehicle in such a high, and thus fuel-expensive, orbit. For that matter, no one had even been able to tell him why the USSF would preposition a lunar vehicle in the first place. Unless a lunar mission had been planned for much longer than the year General Salyard had admitted to.

But that would suggest Salyard had known the crash-site coordinates of the Project Hammer lunar module much longer as well, and that didn't seem reasonable. With all the general thought was at stake here, wouldn't he have authorized this mission immediately upon receiving that information?

Which, to Webber, raised another possibility: The United States Space Force had other reasons for going to the Moon.

OVER THE PACIFIC

Cory Rey stared straight ahead as the TTI corporate Gulfstream V began its descent, and stopped trying to make sense of all that was happening. The one glimpse she had taken through the passenger window beside her had revealed only blue water, stretching to infinity, no hint of land in sight. It triggered memories of her first flight with Mitchell. Unpleasant then, and unpleasant now.

This flight, from Kahului Airport on Maui where Kai Teller kept an estate, had taken just under three hours, flying almost exactly due south to the equator. In all that time, she'd glimpsed only a few jagged reef islands, none of them with obvious signs of human habitation. But it was still more than she'd seen of Maui, whose airport had simply been a refueling stop, just as Los Angeles had been. Teller had left the plane at both airports, but only for a few minutes each time, and his change in mood made it easy for Cory to see that something had happened to cancel his decision about shopping in Los Angeles and staying in Maui. Instead they were headed for a new destination— Jarvis Island.

But Teller hadn't volunteered a reason for his change in plans, and she saw no point in asking. No matter where he was taking her, it was all the same to her.

"It's worth seeing from the air," Teller said as he leaned against Cory's seatback and pointed out the window.

Cory kept her eyes straight ahead on the cherrywood cabinetry she faced. "Maybe when we're closer."

Teller gave her a quizzical look. "You flew in the shuttle. Walked in space. Came down in a *Soyuz* of all things. And now you're saying you have trouble with flying?"

"I have trouble with landing where there's no land. Been there. Done that. Still have nightmares."

"Oh, there's land," Teller said. "Coming up just about ... now."

Cory sighed, knew she couldn't resist. She risked a quick look. And saw a brilliant-green emerald set within translucent turquoise.

The island itself was small, a mile wide, perhaps two miles across at low tide. Its encircling coral reef was a shimmering blue-green halo, inset again by a thin ring of bright, white sand. The tightly-matted clumps of dense inland vegetation were those of tropical jungle.

"Now, tell me what's wrong with that," Teller said.

But Cory was a scientist. Whether or not she thought something was beautiful had nothing at all to do with her observations of its attributes. "There's no point of land down there higher than ten meters. So you can't possibly collect enough rainfall to support that ecosystem."

"I don't need rainfall. See those platforms?" He pointed ahead.

About a quarter mile from the island's northwest-facing shore, Cory saw what appeared to be two large drilling rigs, huge and intricate assemblages of pipes and metal, all painted white, blinding and new in the equatorial sun. Then she realized that what she thought was a tower for a drill was really a rocket booster encased in a gridwork support structure. Webber would know what kind of rocket it was. She only noted that it seemed small.

"You have your own sea launch capability," she said in surprise.

"Soon enough," Teller agreed. "But the other platform, see the underwater pipe?"

Cory turned her attention to the neighboring platform, which had no tower. She could see that beneath the incredibly clear water a long pipe stretched from the platform to the island. It ran through an opening in the surrounding reef, then emerged on the beach and disappeared into the jungle.

"Desalinization?" she asked.

"Solar powered," Teller said with satisfaction. "Non-polluting. Virtually no maintenance. Turned a dead patch of equatorial rock into a paradise."

"I can see that. But why?"

"Because I could. The technology is there. The technology for a hundred different modern marvels exists all around us, on drawing boards, in scientists' minds, engineers' dreams, even in patents no one will exploit. And all it takes is someone with the will—"

"And the money," Cory added.

Teller nodded, not offended. "And the resources, yes, to make those dreams and those marvels real. I took a handful of dreamers who had plans for this island, I gave them the resources, and together we have terraformed it, just as humans will someday terraform Mars."

Cory was impressed, even inspired, but having sold a little snake oil in her day, she also sensed she was getting the version of the story deemed fit for public consumption. For people like Kai Teller, dreams were only a starting point. Somewhere in that verdant paradise of his was an ulterior motive.

She guessed it was the launch platform.

"So who owns this island, really?" she asked. "Doctor No?"

Teller only smiled, and wagged a finger at her, leaving Cory with something new to think about. The absence of answers was often another form of deception.

The pilot's voice clicked on over the intercom. *"Mister Teller, Doctor Rey, we're on our final approach. Please be sure your seat belts are fastened."*

As Teller slipped into the seat beside Cory and snapped his seat belt closed, Cory took a last look at the island before the jet's course swung it out of view. "We're on our final approach to what?" she asked. Her stomach fluttered. She saw no sign of a runway. Only a handful of tan-colored prefab buildings a few hundred yards up from where the water pipe hit the beach, and beside them a small, circular area marked with a giant white H in a circle, indicating a helicopter landing pad.

"I'll let you be surprised," Teller said. He leaned closer to Cory to look out the window beside her. She was very aware of him brushing her arm, so close to her side, the warmth of his body. "Jarvis Island is an unincorporated territory of the U.S. government."

Cory wanted to move away, not because she was troubled by his close presence, but because she wasn't, and that didn't feel right. Not when Mitchell was so far away, and there was still so much that was unsaid and unsettled between them. She could still feel the touch of his hand on her cheek.

"What's an unincorporated territory?" Cory asked. She made a move to sit back in her seat, slightly shifting away from him, hoping he'd settle in his own seat, too. But the movement made her back twinge. She ignored it and pushed back more, breaking contact with him.

Teller gave no sign he'd noticed her discomfort. "It means no one wants it," he explained. "Fish and Wildlife used to administer it for the Department of the Interior. It was a National Wildlife Reserve. Had a few birds. Some scrub. Not enough of anything to register any damage when that giant tsunami from Antarctica came through a few years back. Mixed history like all the small South Pacific islands—it was a guano mine in the 1800s. Annexed in 1858 by the United States, who left about twenty years later. Then annexed by the British about ten years after that, but they never did anything with it. We got it back in 1935, but moved out after the war, then came back to build a weather station for International Geophysical Year in '58. Only to leave again . . . This putting you to sleep yet?"

Cory shook her head, eyes fixed on the view out the window, wondering how there could still be pockets of real estate like this: countries making claims and counterclaims, but not caring enough to do anything about them. The wind-chopped surface of the water was streaming past now, only a few hundred feet beneath them. What were they going to land on? The TTI jet didn't have pontoons. She clutched the arms of her chair. The plane was only a hundred feet or so above the water now, still descending as the reef and beach flashed by.

An instant later, the reef and beach were replaced by the mottled brown-and-white surface of a paved runway, bounded on the side she could see by dense jungle growth. Cory gasped and looked quickly past Teller—who was enjoying her reaction—to the other side of the plane, where she saw more jungle vegetation streaming by those small windows, as well. She pressed her face against her window, looked up, could just glimpse blue sky above.

"I confess," Teller laughed. "Just call me Doctor No."

The Gulfstream braked slowly and smoothly, so Cory knew the hidden runway had to be considerably longer than the jet required.

"You're right, you know," Teller said as the plane slowed. "I didn't just transform this island for the sheer aesthetic joy of it, though that was a pleasant spin-off."

"The launch facility."

Teller nodded. "Space is going commercial, Cory. The biggest obstacle we're facing is government interference."

Cory gave him a sharp look. "You mean, petty regulations about safety and responsibility and keeping million-pound boosters full of rocket fuel from flying over populated areas in case something goes wrong? How unreasonable of the government."

Teller made a show of holding up his hands as if to ward off an attack. "I don't have a problem with safety regulations. No responsible business does. I spent three and half million dollars creating an environmental impact statement for this island, determining what a desalinization plant and associated facility would mean to it."

" 'Associated facility'? You mean the government doesn't *know* about your launch platform?"

Teller shrugged. "The Coast Guard visits once a year

to show the flag. So far, they . . . uh, haven't noticed."

"Of course not. Because you made the launch platform look just like the desalinization plant." Cory didn't know whether to be impressed or appalled. "So what kind of antispace obstacles is the government putting up these days? I mean, they're letting those X-Prize companies launch tourists into space."

Teller dismissed the space tourist industry with disdain. "For a hundred grand, you get your astronaut wings for taking a suborbital flight higher than sixty-two miles, and you get to take some pretty pictures for the family photo album. As long as the rockets don't blow up and the companies pay their taxes, the government doesn't care about tourist flights."

The TTI corporate jet rocked to a gentle stop. Cory glanced out and saw they were parked next to the circular helipad, which made no sense at all because from the air the pad had been surrounded by jungle.

The pilot came out of the cockpit, nodded to his two passengers, then opened the side hatch.

"So what does the government care about?" Cory asked as she and Teller stood and stretched their legs.

He flicked a glance at her. "Remember the Japanese rover?"

"Little *Niju,* on the Moon." It was the only Japanese rover Cory knew about.

"It failed."

"Really?" Cory said. "The photo of the old bleached flag made the front page of every newspaper in the world."

A rush of moist tropical air filled the Gulfstream's passenger cabin and Teller turned his face into it, closing his eyes briefly, then opening them again. "And then what happened?"

Cory was also distracted by the scent of things growing. Not least because the mere fact that she could smell them meant that the incredible sinus congestion that had plagued her in space was finally gone.

"This is what happened," Teller said when she didn't answer him. "Just when the Japanese sent up the first commands to have the rover circle the landing site and take pictures from different angles, it stopped working."

Cory was getting impatient to feel ground beneath her feet again, but Teller was making no move to leave his plane. "It *had* been up there for half a year."

"Exactly my point. Once it got through the first lunar night, that thing was rated to last two years."

"Space equipment never fails?"

"All the time," Teller said as he finally began moving forward to the passenger hatch. Then he paused and gestured to her to go ahead of him. "Especially when it gets in the government's way." He held up the small metal sample case containing the fingers from the Moon. It hadn't been out of his reach for the entire flight. Not that she blamed him. But what did a faked Soviet Moon landing have to do with government interference in Kai Teller's plans for commercial space missions?

Now beside the open door, Cory saw the top of a roll-up stairway. But her urgency to leave had lessened. She turned around to face her host. "Are you suggesting that the U.S. government doesn't just suspect the faked Russian crash site exists, they *know* about it?"

Teller looked hard at her. "If I tell you, are you ready to commit?" he asked her. "Are you ready to be in this all the way?"

Cory felt her temper flare. How dare he ask her that? "Listen, I made that decision when I smuggled your sample cylinder from the station."

"Mister Teller, Doctor Rey?" The pilot was on the

ground before the open hatch. "We're ready for you now." The copilot was with him now, too.

"Just a minute," Teller said. He drew Cory to one side, where no one else could hear. "Sure, you made that decision, but you didn't smuggle that sample off for me. You did it for yourself."

"I didn't know if I could trust you!"

"What about now?"

"I'm here, aren't I?"

"That's not the answer I need, Cory. I'll protect you from whoever's after you, until Webber or my people sort out what's happening. But if you want to be part of the process, you're going to have to do better."

Cory suddenly felt sure that Teller had brought her here for more than her safety. He wanted something from her.

She made her decision.

"Okay. Do I understand you? No. Do I think I'll agree with everything you might say to me? No, again. But do I trust you? Yes. Absolutely."

Teller moved closer, as if she had opened the door to something more.

"And the reason I trust you so absolutely," Cory added, "is because if you lie to me, or use me, my ex-SEAL ex-boyfriend will be on your case, not me. So, what's the deal?"

Teller stepped back. "I know what Webber's new assignment is, Cory. I found out in Maui. I know where he's going."

"Where?"

"Same place you are," Teller said. "The Moon."

3

THE TRANSFER TO geosynchronous orbit took five uneventful hours, and as far as Webber could tell, an inordinate amount of fuel.

When he'd heard the fuel numbers Bowden reported to CenCom, and compared them to the fuel capacity figures he had been briefed on, Webber hadn't understood how the *Falcon* had enough fuel to continue to the Moon, let alone break orbit for a return to Earth. When he'd queried Bowden, her answer had been to the point.

"It's an Air Force tradition, Captain. Comes out of decades of flying long-distance missions in planes that don't have enough fuel capacity. We just factor in refueling in flight."

Webber recalled Salyard's mention of prepositioned supplies. Now he realized the general had been referring to fuel supplies as well as air, water, and the usual consumables.

"Compared to NASA's, our approach has given us a tremendous launch capability," Bowden had gone on to tell him. "They're desperate to perfect a heavy-lift, single-stage-to-orbit spacecraft that's completely reusable. But the trade-offs involved strictly limit the size of the payload they can launch. For the Air Force, and the Space Force, we just keep adding boosters and launches. The mission is the goal, not the means."

Webber had thanked her for the background, but had refrained from remarking how much the Air Force approach reminded him of what Teller had called the Soviet Union's chief technological downfall—a reliance on brute force.

Webber's nausea was fading, but still present. He took off the snug Snoopy cap that held his commset in place, to rub his face and his eyes. Under USSF flight rules, after the *Falcon* had passed an orbital altitude of 480 nautical miles and, presumably, the threat of sudden attack, the crew could remove their gloves and helmets and unstrap from their seats. On a different mission profile, they would also have been permitted to remove their pressure suits. But since the suits would be required again on docking with the *Kitty Hawk,* it was more efficient to keep them on.

Fortunately, there wasn't anything for Webber to do at this stage of the mission, and no one seemed interested in conversation.

Unlike most of his other missions, there wasn't a great deal of camaraderie or banter among this group. Considering they had never served as a team before or bonded through intense training, it wasn't unusual that there might be some distance between them all. But Webber was finding the lack of interaction odd.

After everyone in the crew removed helmets and gloves, Varik had activated the sequence that retracted a flush-mounted plate in the forward hull, making it slide up and back along the *Falcon*'s sharply sloping nose to uncover two forward-facing viewports. It would be their first naked-eye

view of space, and the crew's reaction had surprised
Webber. There wasn't one.

They'd been treated to a view of the half-Moon almost
directly before them, about the same size as it was viewed
from the ground, but rich with all the crisp detail invisible
from within Earth's atmosphere, and missing from the
computer-generated illusions of the flight simulator in
Hangar 27.

Webber had been transfixed by the sight, even forgetting, momentarily, his knotted stomach. But after taking
only a few seconds to look ahead at their eventual destination, Colonel Varik returned to reading his on-orbit
checklists and Captain Rodriguez busied himself digging
through the ration packs. The packs were stowed in a
Velcro-sealed pouch on the back of Christa Bowden's
flight seat.

"I guess you've taken this flight before," Webber said as
he floated behind Varik's seat. With only five feet of clearance between the deck and the ceiling of the passenger
cabin, Webber was discovering that floating went a long
way to prevent the feeling of being cramped.

"This part of it," Varik said. He looked up and Webber
saw the colonel's taut face reflected against the half-Moon
in one of the steep and slanted viewports.

"Does it ever get routine?" Webber asked.

Varik looked to his checklists again. "Yes."

Webber said little else during the transition. Nor did the
others. Even communication with Central Command was
almost nonexistent, reduced to the occasional exchange of
acronyms and codes. At this distance from Earth, the
encrypted signals that passed between the *Falcon* and the
ground were configured to appear as nothing more than
standard message traffic among the U.S. military network.
No space buffs or amateur satellite hunters would notice or

be able to trace those signals. And the space-black finish of the *Falcon*'s ceramic hull and its radar-absorbing properties kept the craft invisible to optical astronomers and deep-space radar as well.

As long as everything remains routine, Webber thought. He wondered what the plan was for when routine no longer applied to what they were planning to do.

At Orbit Transfer Burn plus 312 minutes, a slow chime sounded in the cabin. The proximity alert lacked the high-pitched warble that would indicate an unexpected threat. Webber recognized the chime as the docking acquisition signal.

"Here we go, people," Bowden announced. "Strap in and prepare for docking." Then she and Varik ran each other through their checklists, confirming that the computer settings displayed on the console screens were correct.

Webber was beginning to see exactly why Bowden's title was "flight supervisor" first, and "pilot" second. The *Falcon* was capable of flying itself.

After two minutes, the proximity chime changed to a tone, and Varik switched it off.

"Twenty klicks, closing on the wire," Bowden said.

Webber heard a slight drop in the level of random speaker noise in his commset that let him know Varik was receiving a response on a voice loop not connected to Webber's own channels. Most likely it was confirmation from Central Command.

At five kilometers, Bowden toggled on the docking lights, and Varik called for target acquisition lights.

Now in his helmet once again, Webber peered ahead, trying to glimpse his first view of the *Kitty Hawk* in space.

He saw nothing.

At two kilometers from rendezvous, Bowden announced

another confirmation that *Falcon* was on the wire, but this time Webber caught no indication of a response from the ground for Varik.

Then a star flickered.

For a moment, Webber didn't register the image. Stars flickered all the time. He corrected himself, *but not in space.* He trained his eyes on the dark patch of nothing where the flicker had originated.

He saw it again. Now there were four of them, flashing in random patterns, once every few seconds.

"Target acquired," Bowden said. "Eight hundred meters."

The docking lights of the *Falcon,* impossible to see from behind their source in the absence of atmospheric backscatter, finally played across the *Kitty Hawk.*

But the target was not the *Kitty Hawk.*

It was a Milstar satellite. Enormous. Like part of a locomotive that had been split in two and spread apart, all hard angles and foil-covered boxes, stretched aloft between two vast blue wings of solar arrays.

Is that how they hide their assets? Webber asked himself. How often had the media reported yet another launch of an unidentified military satellite, "believed" to be a Milstar or a spy satellite? And hadn't General Salyard himself suggested that the USSF had been building its on-orbit forces in full view of the world, without requiring the prodigious effort of hiding multiple secret spacecraft launches?

"Looks just like a Milstar," Webber shared with the others over the cabin voice loop. He couldn't help but be impressed.

Varik replied, "That's because it is a Milstar. Look past it."

Webber did so, then realized that for the solar wings to be working, they should be rotated to face directly into sunlight, which would render them blindingly bright. But they weren't. Instead, they were angled sideways to the sun, so they reflected as little light as possible.

But the docking light beams that bounced off the arrays revealed something else. The dark shape of a long cylinder rising from behind the Milstar's midpoint on the side facing away from the Earth.

As the *Falcon* drew closer and the angle of the docking lights changed against the panels, even more became visible. Webber stared in fascination at what lay beyond the Milstar, hidden by the satellite everyone in the world expected to be there and thought nothing of, and which no enemy could yet reach.

The structure appeared to be as long as the International Space Station. But unlike the ISS, all of its modules were stacked in a single line, and there was no intersecting truss to support football-field-size solar arrays.

As the *Falcon* slowly glided past the Milstar, uncovering more and more of the hidden structure behind it, Webber saw at the very end of the massive complex, four long corrugated black vanes with the appearance of battle ribbons flying from a standard raised high. Clearly, they were thermal control panels—mechanisms for dumping excess energy, not creating it. No source of power was apparent.

Nor was the *Kitty Hawk*.

Not that anyone was talking about either of them.

"Am I allowed to ask what that is?" Webber finally asked.

"You're allowed to *ask*," Varik said. It was the closest thing to humor Webber had heard the colonel attempt. He decided to respond in kind.

"In that case, is anyone allowed to answer?"

After a long pause during which Webber heard the

Falcon's RCS thrusters fire and felt the craft spin precisely as the stacked black modules slid away from the viewports, Varik said simply, "Bowden, you're on."

Bowden promptly began to give Webber a new briefing, even though she was the *Falcon*'s pilot and responsible for the current approach. It seemed the docking procedure was completely computer-controlled as well.

"We are docking with a USSF MOL Type Four, designation Geosynchronous Staging Platform Three, also called G-SAP," Bowden said, pronouncing the acronym *gee-sap*. "It is a habitable space station, providing access to on-orbit resupply and refueling facilities for the USSF fleet of three-stage SOVs."

Simultaneously with Bowden's rapid-fire description, Webber parsed its military terseness. MOL could only stand for Manned Orbiting Laboratory, an Air Force manned-spaceflight program from the '60s, which he thought had been canceled long ago. Obviously, though, it had gone "black," because the designation "Type Four" implied it was now in its fourth generation. Also, the fact that this particular MOL was called a "geosynchronous" platform suggested there were other platforms in nongeosynchronous orbits, and it had become necessary to distinguish between them. That the platform had been numbered "three" wasn't as informative. It could mean there were at least two others, but three could also be the platform's model number.

Most tellingly, though, was the fact that Bowden had called it a "habitable" space station. That implied it wasn't crewed now, but it most likely had been in the past.

"Can I ask how long it's been up here?" Webber tried.

Varik spoke up this time. "The first Air Force MOL went up in 1975, a year after the last Skylab crew. The first MOLs had limited lifetimes, longest one lasted twenty-seven months. The new ones, like this G-SAP, they've got a demonstrated on-orbit lifetime that's much longer."

"Anything else?" Varik asked, even though he hadn't actually answered Webber's last question.

Webber decided to accept the open invitation, see how advanced the Space Force program really was. "Sure. Colonel, have you been to the Moon before?"

"I haven't," Varik said. "But the *Kitty Hawk* has."

"With astronauts aboard?" Webber asked, disappointed that such a great adventure had been undertaken without the world knowing, but not surprised by it at all.

But Varik had not finished.

"Captain Webber," he said, "if this mission goes as planned, you will return to the Earth as the thirty-first human to have walked on the Moon."

"Not counting the one who died in Project Hammer," Bowden added.

Now Webber was more than surprised. He was astounded. Because of the math. Twelve Apollo astronauts had walked on the Moon. There were four astronauts in this spacecraft ready to do the same. For the total to reach thirty-one, that meant that the United States Space Force had sent fifteen additional astronauts to the Moon. Fifteen. In secret.

"Why so many?" Webber now knew why Salyard had good reason to keep the *Kitty Hawk* in such a high orbit. It saved fuel for all the round-trips it had made to the Moon, without having to keep escaping from low Earth orbit.

The *Falcon* shuddered, and was still. The star field beyond the viewports no longer moved to indicate the craft was turning.

"That, Captain Webber," Varik said, "is something you *don't* need to know until we get back."

Bowden turned off the docking lights. "And we're docked," she said.

Webber was impressed when Varik and Bowden both unlocked their restraints and floated free from their seats, and when, beside him, Rodriguez did the same. Docking was obviously so simple, it did not even require shutdown procedures. No wonder Varik considered spaceflight routine.

"Don't we have to report we're here?" Webber asked. There had been much less contact with Central Command in the last hour of this flight.

"We're in the Milstar shadow," Bowden said.

"So . . . the satellite part is real?" Webber asked.

"Fully functional, Captain. Provides visual and radar cover. But the radio interference from its transmissions blocks out anything we can send for about a radius of twenty klicks. We report to CenCom when we enter the station and use its hardwired systems to transmit directly through the Milstar."

Rodriguez spun around and dove behind Webber's seat to the deck hatch in the floor at the back of the cabin. "Beginning manual check of the docking hatch," he said.

As Varik and Bowden floated past him, Webber unlocked his restraints but held on to his seat to keep from drifting into their way.

A series of lights on a small control panel by the hatch glowed green. "Green, green, green, green," Rodriguez confirmed. "We are go for interior hatch open."

"Proceed," Varik ordered.

Rodriguez braced one hand on a loop restraint, then grabbed the hatch lever and pulled. The hatch opened smoothly, no indication of there being a pressure difference between the cabin and whatever was on the other side. Airlock or station module, Webber didn't know.

Rodriguez then slipped headfirst through the open hatch, but only traveled about three feet before he stopped. Webber guessed that was the distance between the floor of the *Falcon*'s flight deck and the exterior hatch on the spacecraft's hull. The roof access hatch he had seen on the *Eagle* in Hangar 27 was used as launch-pad access only.

For a few moments, Webber could hear Rodriguez's breathing on the voice loop, then once again the captain announced, "Green, green, green, green. We are go for exterior open."

"Proceed," Varik said again.

Preparing, just in case the atmosphere suddenly rushed from the cabin, Webber tightened his grip on a loose strap from his chair. The point of wearing the bright orange pressure suits for this part of the mission was not lost on him. If the MOL wasn't crewed on a regular basis, it was entirely possible that environmental failures could occur.

On this occasion, however, only a few tumbling particles of what looked to be loose insulation puffed through the open hatch past Rodriguez, and then simply floated by innocuously. Pressure had been equalized between the SOV and the MOL.

Rodriguez floated back out of the hatch and spun around to orient himself to the cabin's relative up and down. "Hatch is open and ready, Colonel."

"Thank you, Captain," Varik said, then pushed one hand against the ceiling and dropped effortlessly through the hatch, boots first.

He's done that a hundred times, Webber thought. It was just too perfect and practiced a move.

Bowden went next, arms first like a high-diver. Webber knew he was the low man on this mission and waited for Rodriguez to go next. But the Air Force captain pointed to the hatch. "You're next, Captain."

Webber thanked him, floated down to the hatch, grabbed the sides, and then wriggled through, banging his boot on the edge.

Emerging from the open hatch in the MOL, he suffered another stomach-wrenching bout of vertigo as his senses suddenly told him the new cabin he'd entered was upside down.

He hit the surface that was oriented as the floor, absorbing the impact with his arms before his helmet could make contact. Then he pushed up and spun so he was aligned as Varik and Bowden were, boots down, helmets up toward the *Falcon,* just as Rodriguez dropped smoothly through the hatch as Varik had, boots first.

Then each of the three moved off to do something specific, and Varik told Webber to stay clear of all controls and wait while they secured the station.

Webber took the opportunity to examine his surroundings, being careful not to move his head, giving his stomach time to settle down.

The station was older than he expected it to be. Most of the four surfaces in the roughly eight-by-twenty-foot cabin were dull brushed metal, saving on paint or other fuel-expensive coverings. Exposed pipes and wiring conduits were extensively labeled with stenciled codes. His eye followed a major bundle of thick wires, held together by plastic ties and attached to a fabric air duct that ran the length of the module. The wires appeared to be afterthoughts, since they awkwardly overlapped storage-locker doors and otherwise cluttered the layout.

Somehow, Webber thought, taking in the outdated style of the warning signs and the colors of the wires and the look of the lockers, it was as if the module were a holdover from the early eighties, when the space shuttles were new. The cabin's interior didn't come close to matching the sleek functionality of the *Falcon*'s flight deck.

Finally Varik pushed himself away from the console he'd been working at and floated toward Webber. At the same time, Rodriguez closed the hatch leading back to the *Falcon* and Bowden kicked off to dive through a hatch leading to another module.

"Captain," Varik said, "quick orientation." He pointed to the red band that ran across the deck beneath their boots. Every few feet, a white triangle was painted on it, each pointing in the same direction. "Red is station down. Triangles indicate the direction of Milstar and the Earth to port. The Moon and points beyond are starboard."

"Stars are to starboard," Webber confirmed. The system had been designed by a sailor.

Varik didn't seem to register the connection. "We are currently in docking module one. This is the module you will return to on any alarm, sealing hatches on your way. Immediately to port is the habitat module. Food, water, head, sleeping compartments. Next two modules down are supplies and storage, and that's where the stack ends. There is no interior access to Milstar."

"Got it," Webber said.

"Immediately to starboard is the operations module with communications center and signal processing. Next module up is service. Don't touch anything. Next module up is propulsion. Same rule. Next up are docking modules two, three, and four. The *Kitty Hawk* is docked at four. Questions?"

Webber wondered why Varik had bothered to point out the living arrangements. "How long will we be here before ... ." Webber couldn't help himself, he smiled as he said his next words. "... before we go to the Moon?"

Varik rattled off more details, as if they were commonplace. "Just as on the ground, we have two lunar launch windows each twenty-four-hour period—when the plane of our orbit intersects the plane of the orbit we need to establish around the Moon. Based on the lighting requirements we will need on site, we have mission-critical launch windows over the next three days. Current plan is to run you through at least a day of drills while the *Kitty Hawk* is docked. We will then have our pick of four launch windows. No weather concerns."

"Very good," Webber said, as if there were anything else he could say to a mission commander who had just given him his orders.

Varik gave a brusque nod, looked over to Rodriguez. "Captain, have you secured life support?"

Rodriguez pushed up on a wide rocker switch, and a board of lights switched on. Among them Webber could see old CRT displays showing lines of green type, like something from a computer museum.

"Life support is secure, sir," Rodriguez confirmed.

"Helmets off, gentlemen." Varik unsealed his visor and tugged it open to equalize pressure between his suit and the MOL's atmosphere. Then he unsealed his neck ring and lifted his helmet.

Webber did the same, felt his ears pop and his nausea return as he smelled at least ten years' worth of stale sweat and sour food. He coughed, trying not to gag.

"It'll get better as the filters work on the air," Varik said. "We'll take a meal break for thirty minutes, then get up to the *Kitty Hawk*."

Spinning as he tried to unfasten his boots, Webber hoped it wouldn't take him the full thirty-minute break to get out of his pressure suit. Not that he was hungry. But just as he braced himself and came to a triumphant stop with his right boot in hand, everything changed again.

Christa Bowden came floating down from the operations module, helmet off, face pale, cheeks flushed.

"Colonel! I made contact with CenCom. We have new orders from General Salyard."

Varik reached out to catch Bowden's arm, bringing her to a stop in the center of the cabin. "Go ahead."

Bowden's eyes met Webber's. She looked to Varik, uncertain.

Varik spoke impatiently. "If the orders affect the mission, then we all have a need to know. Go ahead."

"Sir, we are to launch on the first available window, coming up in three hours."

If Varik was surprised, he hid it well. But he didn't bother suppressing his annoyance. "Did the general say why?"

Again Bowden glanced at Webber, but this time she didn't hesitate.

"We're going to have company."

4

"**THE CHINESE DID WHAT?!**" Tovah Caruso asked in surprise.

On her desktop computer screen displaying the teleconference link from the Johnson Space Center, Flight Director Leo Milankou repeated the news relayed from the Pentagon. "They launched from their space station! A *Shenzhou* and a lander, along with an orbital booster that they've already dropped. About one hour ago."

Caruso couldn't have been happier. "Have they made an announcement?"

"Not yet. But they've got a press conference scheduled for six A.M. local time. Guess they want to give the news to a billion or so of their fellow countrymen first."

"What do you think?" Caruso asked, hoping for a positive answer. "Are they going for a landing?"

"Definitely," Milankou said, and his smile was as broad as hers. "We figure they've had the lander up there for at least four months. Plenty of time to test it. This is showtime."

"Great," Caruso said. "This is just what those idiots in . . ." She suddenly remembered who was sitting across from her desk, amended her statement. "This is just what the politicians need to give them a swift kick. Nothing like seeing the Red Star flag raised on the Moon and hearing 'The East Is Red' coming from on high."

Special Agent Hong cleared his throat in irritation.

Caruso sighed. Her unexpected reprieve had been all too brief. "Leo, I have to go. To a meeting. But get Public Affairs to put out the word. NASA congratulates the People's Republic of China on this bold undertaking and welcomes them into the community of lunar explorers. This profound shared experience can only make the bonds between our countries stronger . . . and so on. Same thing we did for their first crewed launch, and their space station, but a lot bigger."

"They're already on it," Milankou confirmed.

"We'll talk later," Caruso said, and touched the key that disconnected the link. She looked at Hong and felt the thrill of elation leave her as if she were deflating. "Sorry, Agent Hong."

"I am surprised at your reaction," the somber FBI agent said.

Not as surprised as I am that you just said something off topic, Caruso thought. "Space travel is probably the most important human endeavor of the twenty-first century," she said instead. "As a shared international experience, instead of being the great leveler, it's the great uplifter."

Hong looked spectacularly unimpressed by the sentiment. "I've always thought of it as a needless extravagance."

You would, Caruso thought darkly, but she had faced the same in Congress and the Senate each year when she made the pilgrimage, hat in hand for the fiscal crumbs that kept NASA almost alive and functioning. She decided to treat Hong like the senator from a certain great state where creationism was considered a science and money spent on space programs was no different from cash thrown into a bonfire.

"The time for arguing that the space program is an extravagance is long gone," Caruso said evenly. "America is already a space-based culture and there's no going back. Our communications, our agriculture, our entertainment delivery systems, our emergency response capabilities, and our national defense are as firmly wedded to space assets as they are to electricity."

"You're talking about satellites," Hong said. "I'm talking about the space station and going to the Moon and Mars."

Caruso kept her temper under control. "So let's talk about GM, Ford, all the Japanese car manufacturers—they stay in business by making affordable, appealing cars for the public. But you know what else they do? They build one-off racing cars that cost millions. And concept cars. And they sponsor student contests to build contraptions that can cross the country on a gallon of gas. And not one of those programs makes financial sense. There's no money in it at all. But you know what else those programs accomplish?"

Hong offered the predictable answer. "Publicity. They make all their money back on free hype."

"That's only half of it. Those special projects are company engines. They're irresistible magnets for the best and brightest minds in their fields. They're like lightning rods pulling in ideas, huge flashes of inspiration and energy coalescing into one place and time. They free engineers to think about things outside the bounds of 'affordable' and 'appealing.' They give scientists permission to explore a wild new idea—without, I may add, worrying about talking five hundred middle managers into agreeing to take a risk. The bottom line is that the money car manufacturers spend on those open-ended, experimental programs is insignificant to what they spend on practical matters. But the payoff? Well, it's an army of creative personnel filled with new ideas and approaches. And sometimes, one of those ideas becomes a breakthrough that turns out to have an application no one ever anticipated. Then the entire industry benefits."

Caruso was just getting warmed up. Agent Hong didn't stand a chance. "And speaking of satellites, the first satellite this country sent up did nothing except put us into second place to the Russians. But fifty years later, even you have to agree that our country couldn't get by without satellites.

"So that's why we need a space station and reusable launch vehicles and an outpost on the Moon *and* an expedition to Mars. Because all those wild, useless, uplifting, inspiring mad dreams are what will bring forth the best of our scientists and our engineers. And what's more, they will define our society fifty years from now as surely as our first satellite gave us the technological achievements we depend on today.

"This country has lots of companies that can handle the commercialization of space. But for the commercialization of space to grow, what this country desperately needs is an engine. That's what NASA needs to be. A lightning rod. Not the post office. And not business as usual."

Hong interrupted her. "Does that speech work in appropriations hearings?"

Caruso switched hats. "I'll let you know if I still have this job in the summer," she said, taking comfort from the knowledge that if she wanted to, she could physically toss her insufferable visitor out of her office. "You were saying something about this conspiracy you've uncovered?" That had been the topic under discussion when Milankou had called in with the happy news about the Chinese lunar mission.

"There's been a leak," Hong said.

Caruso sensed an accusation lurking beneath that statement. "I've discussed it with no one but you. How bad a leak?"

"Three of the suspects have vanished. Varik, Webber, and Rey."

"Can you call in General Salyard?"

"Not until we determine if he's leading the conspiracy, or another link in the chain, taking his orders from someone else."

Obviously there was something more Hong had to tell her, but he was waiting to see if she might reveal something first.

But Caruso had nothing to reveal. "Is there any way I can help you?"

She watched Hong decide to overcome his reluctance. "What do you know about the relationship between Kai Teller and Corazon Rey?"

Caruso was surprised that she felt a tiny pang of jealousy. "I wasn't aware they had a relationship, other than their professional one. Is it important?"

"We have reason to believe Captain Webber delivered Doctor Rey to Mister Teller."

"Delivered?" Caruso asked. "You make it sound as if she was in a body bag."

"He escorted her to Mister Teller's jet. Then he left, and she remained onboard. The jet is currently believed to be en route to Maui."

Caruso felt more than a pang of jealousy at that news. Teller's sprawling home overlooking the wilds of Maui's northwest shore was a corner of paradise. "He does have a home there."

"The question is," Hong said, "why would two of the conspirators be in contact with one of the people against whom they are conspiring?"

The question is, How should I know? Caruso thought. "Maybe they're not conspirators. Maybe Teller doesn't realize they're conspiring against him. Maybe your information is incorrect."

"We have photographs."

"This is your world, not mine. Enlighten me."

"All three of them are involved."

Caruso shook her head emphatically. "No. That I will not believe. Kai Teller's as dedicated to the space program as anyone I know. And he doesn't have it in him to kill innocent people."

"But as you pointed out in our last meeting," Hong said, "if the mission profile had been followed, then no loss of life would have occurred."

Primed to protest, Caruso hesitated. Kai was sharp. He wasn't above stacking the deck to ensure a good deal. But to send explosives to the station? "There's still the problem of motive," she argued. "He spent a hundred million dollars on his lunar sample return mission. He's rich. His company's successful. I'm sure there will be some insurance money to help cushion the loss, but why would he take all the risks you're suggesting to attack his own company? And for that matter, didn't he get this whole investigation started by telling me about Farren? That's what made me go to the FBI."

The stolid-faced agent regarded her impassively. "Those are valid observations currently under consideration. But when we add the actions of the Russian Aviation and Space Agency to the mix, the conspiracy does take on a larger perspective."

Caruso sighed. "So you're back to that? That what happened was some kind of Russian mafia shakedown?"

"We don't know, Ms. Caruso."

Caruso heard the unspoken question in that statement.

"Well, neither do I, Agent Hong."

Hong gazed at her, still emotionless. "There are two reasons why that might be true." Then, before she could reply, he stood up, briefcase in hand. "Good day, Ms. Caruso. We'll be in touch."

As swiftly as that, he was gone, leaving her with a blank computer screen, the model of the Space Shuttle *Constitution,* and the realization that she knew two reasons the FBI would be investigating to explain why she had not been able to tell them what Teller was up to.

Either she truly didn't know anything, or she was part of the mysterious conspiracy herself.

TTI LAUNCH CENTER / JARVIS ISLAND

Moonlight flowed like silver honey across the gentle sea. Slow-moving whitecaps glowed blue against dark water. Pale clouds like ghosts wreathed the stars. The soft pulse of distant breakers defined the silence of the night and the perfection of the island.

Cory didn't want to be here. Neither did she want to leave. And right now, she couldn't decide who was to blame for her conflict. Mitchell Webber for bringing her to this point in her life. Or Kai Teller for making it possible.

She stood on the rustic wooden veranda of the TTI corporate lodge on Jarvis Island, staring out at the sea, wondering if she'd ever be able to sleep easily again. It was late, the same hour as Hawaii, but her body was still on some mixed-up combination of Colorado time and NASA's Greenwich Mean Time, senses still spinning from all that had happened this past week.

"Whenever I come here," Teller said unexpectedly but quietly behind her, "I always wonder how I can ever leave."

Cory felt guilty. Here she was in paradise, while Webber was in Vandenberg, with Daniel Varik, murderer.

Or on some impossible mission to the Moon, as if that could be true.

Teller leaned against the railing, facing her, a glistening balloon glass of white wine in each hand. He offered her one.

When in Rome, she thought. She took it.

Teller had the good taste not to propose a toast. He simply turned around, and like her, gazed out at the Moon and the night and the ocean, in companionable silence.

Help, Cory thought. This was all manipulation, but he was doing it so well.

She gulped down a mouthful of wine, realizing too late that it was really quite remarkable.

"Penny for your thoughts?" Teller asked.

They'd bankrupt you, Cory thought. She took another sip of wine, savoring it this time. Then she looked at her host. Like her, he had changed into what all his staff wore here: a colorful Hawaiian-print shirt and loose white trousers, Teva sandals. Cory's outfit was courtesy of one of the women who worked here, who was almost her size. The welcome experience of putting on fresh, cool, and clean clothes had been restorative. So was the wine and the moonlight.

"Confusion," Cory said truthfully. "Pure and total. About everything."

Teller's face was transformed by a smile, one side lit by the half-Moon, the other by the warm lights from the veranda windows, from the comfortable rooms within.

"Define 'everything,' " he said.

Cory spoke aloud the mystery she had been unraveling since Teller escorted her from his jet this afternoon. "You wanted to tell the world the truth about the faked Russian landing, right?"

"It's interesting, don't you think? Maybe not an impor-

tant historical occurrence, but certainly a fascinating foot-
note."

"Then why not tell them?" Cory asked.

"No evidence."

"Come on, that's not the way it works. You've got the
fingers from the first sample. People know you. You're not a
crackpot. You go on the talk shows, give press conferences,
and state your case, and then you say you're going to go
looking for more evidence."

"They won't let me, Cory."

Cory studied him, wondering who "they" were. "What
do you mean?"

"Communications with my rover failed."

"But the rover still worked. Its computers were smart
enough to . . ." Cory broke off in sudden understanding.
"Someone shut them down. . . . The government. No . . .
the Air Force. They run the satellites."

Teller nodded. "I knew you'd figure it out. That's
another reason I hired you."

Cory discovered her hands were shaking. She set her
wineglass down carefully on the flat railing of the balcony.
"The Air Force went after the shuttle and the station? To
stop those samples from coming back?"

"A group within the Air Force," Teller said. "Secret,
and highly compartmentalized. The United States Space
Force."

Cory's stomach twisted. "They killed people to keep the
secret of a fake Russian landing?"

And the moment she uttered those words, she knew
how false they were.

"Oh my God," she murmured as she looked up at Teller.
"It wasn't a faked landing. It was *real*."

Teller nodded again, his eyes never leaving her. "One of
the greatest secrets of the twentieth century."

Cory leaned against the railing, feeling breathless. "That's . . . staggering."

"More than that, Cory. It's potentially destabilizing." Teller picked up her wineglass and handed it back to her. "Do you know what's at stake here?"

Cory thought it was self-evident. "The truth," she said.

"More than that. National pride."

But Cory didn't see where that fit in. "So the Russians sent a guy to the Moon. How does that—"

Teller's expression had answered her question. It wasn't just the greatest secret of the twentieth century. It was the greatest secret in history.

"The Russians got there *first?*" Cory felt gooseflesh crawl up her arms, her back, her scalp.

Teller looked up at the Moon, where thin glowing clouds framed it. "There is that possibility. *Apollo Eleven* lifted off from Kennedy at eight thirty-two A.M., Wednesday, July 16, 1969. It landed on the Moon on July 20, 1969, at four-seventeen P.M., Eastern Daylight Time."

His recitation of times and dates like the lines of a favorite poem made Cory realize how important this subject was to him, how much he knew. "Is there any way to know the Russian launch and landing times?"

"The primary launch took place July 13, three days before Apollo, at three-fourteen A.M., Baikonur local time. Two other launches took place during the preceding ten days, to get all the elements into orbit."

Cory searched for the hidden meaning in his story. "But still, if it launched from Baikonur, there has to be a record."

"There is. The launch payload was called *Zond* 15. The fifteenth Soviet lunar probe."

Cory had it. "An unmanned probe."

"According to the official records."

"But you believe it was manned."

"You saw the bones yourself, Cory."

But Cory wasn't yet ready to fully accept something so big. "Those bones . . . they are evidence, sure. But only of someone unknown to history, dying on the Moon. They could also be from an unpublicized experiment involving cadaver parts that was conducted there, just like the cadaver experiments on the shuttle."

Teller shook his head. "The *Zond* probes were modified *Soyuz* capsules, and *Soyuz* capsules were built to carry cosmonauts to the Moon."

Cory imagined what Webber would say. "Circumstantial at best."

"What if I tell you there is also a tape. A voice transmission, in Russian, confirming lunar orbit insertion, on July 17. Apollo was still two days away."

Cory's skepticism notched up and she ran with it. "The bones are real, I give you that. But a voice tape? That's got to be the easiest thing in the world to fake."

"No question. That's why I don't make it public. I believe it's legitimate. But I'm aware my belief isn't enough. I want photographs of the Russian lander. I want wreckage from the crash, if there was one. I want scientific instruments. I want the mission patch from the cosmonaut's spacesuit."

"And then you'll end the secrecy and tell the world?"

"Exactly. And then I'll tell the world."

Cory put her wineglass back on the railing. "That's where Mitchell's going, isn't it?" she said, finally believing it. "He's joined the Space Force and they're sending him to the Russian crash site and . . . he's going to pick up the pieces and sweep it under the rug so the world will be safe for democracy. Just because . . ."

"Cory," Teller said unexpectedly, "my rover is still operational."

Cory stared at him. "Right now? At the crash site?"

Teller nodded. "A region called Rimae Tannhauser. The rover's in low-power mode so no one can detect it. And what the Space Force doesn't know is that it has a secondary communications channel."

"Well, let's go turn it on and get those pictures on television!" Cory was filled with fresh hope, energy.

But Teller wasn't as enthusiastic. "You're forgetting pictures can also be faked. These days, as easily as an audiotape. If I activate the rover now, in twenty minutes, the Space Force will jam its signal and that will be that. We'll have twenty minutes of low-resolution video that some twelve-year-old *Star Wars* fan could have whipped up on his home computer."

Cory realized Teller had already thought this through. "But you do have a plan, right?"

"I do. When the Space Force mission arrives, we switch on the rover's camera, and we catch them in the act of destroying the evidence, in their Space Force suits, probably with their landing module in the screen. That they can't accuse us of faking. Especially when we go public with the fingers."

His plan was breathtaking, flawless. The whole world would see them changing history. "Kai, I have to be part of this."

"Are you certain?" Teller asked.

Cory knew what he was asking her. "You mean, because Mitchell will be part of that team." Everything in her life came back to this somehow: that she and Mitchell were always on the wrong side of the issues, and each other.

"You know, Kai, whenever it's a question of the right, decent, smart thing to do, Mitchell always starts talking about 'chain of command' and 'they have their reasons' and 'the good of the country comes first.' "

"These days, it's hard to argue with sentiments like that," Teller said gently.

"But when those sentiments are used as the excuse to lie to the public, to shelter criminals, to allow politicians to evade responsibility *and* prosecution . . ." Cory couldn't finish, recalling the cruelties of her parents' lifetime of struggle. They'd been crushed by their adopted country's uncaring bureaucrats, whose refusal to look beyond rules and regulations had denied them America's promise of justice and equality.

Cory felt Teller's hand touch her shoulder, the gesture of a friend.

"I guess I'm just sick to death of the government lying," she said. "Trading lives for secrets that should be exposed."

Teller didn't try to touch her again. All he said was, "I understand."

"So . . . so tell me, what happened with *Zond* 15?" she asked, looking for distraction from her feelings of conflict. Despite what she had just said to Teller, she wasn't sure Webber could really do such a terrible thing, even if he was under orders. *Because he'd be erasing history,* she thought. *Even worse—he'll be erasing the truth. And what could justify that?*

Teller accepted her change in mood without comment. "Well, what nobody argues about is that the *Zond* crashed on the Moon."

Cory took the opening he had provided. "What *do* they argue about?"

"When it crashed. There are no unequivocally accepted data. At the time of Apollo, Jodrell Bank Observatory said the *Zond* crashed July 21, a few hours before the Apollo lander took off from the Moon. But when Russia finally went public with their Moon program back in the nineties, their official records showed they sent commands to the *Zond* to fire its rockets and crash on July 20, twelve hours *before* the Apollo lander even set down on the Moon."

Cory took refuge in examining the details of Teller's

hobby mystery. "Could there have been a delay in the probe carrying out its commands? Or maybe illegible handwriting—on the part of whoever maintained the log of launch activities. A transcription error? Translation error? There could be lots of reasons for the discrepancy."

"No errors," Teller said. "Two different crash times because . . ." He held up two fingers. ". . . two different crashes."

"Why two?"

"The Russian mission architecture was similar to ours. Apollo consisted of a combined command module and service module docked with a separate lunar lander. The service module got them to the Moon and back. The lander took them down to the lunar surface and up. And the command module reentered the atmosphere and brought the astronauts all the way home.

"The Russians had their *Soyuz* to act as the combined service and command module to take two cosmonauts to the Moon and back. Then they had a one-man lander to take one of those cosmonauts to the surface."

"And back?" Cory asked.

"That was the plan."

"*Was* the plan." Her question was obvious enough that she didn't have to ask it.

"Here's my theory."

Cory was suddenly reminded of Bailey's husband and his theories, and hoped she wasn't about to be subjected to flying saucers and little green men again.

She wasn't. It was worse.

"Everyone knows the United States and the Soviet Union were involved in a desperate race to be the first on the Moon. And that the race wasn't even. But most people don't know that, for most of it, it was pretty easy to call who the winner was going to be."

Cory took a wild guess where he was going. "The Russians."

Teller nodded. "They beat us to most of the major milestones required for building the technical expertise for a lunar mission. First lunar flyby. First lunar impact. First soft lunar landing. First man in space. First man to orbit the Earth. First spacewalk. Bing, bing, bing."

Cory wasn't completely ignorant of the space race. "First woman in space, too, I believe."

Teller smiled. "I forgot who I was talking to."

"So all those firsts," Cory said, "and they didn't beat us to the one that mattered most. Why?"

"Two ways to win a race," Teller answered. "First way is to be faster than the other guy. Second way?"

Cory had spent enough time with Webber to know the way he would answer that question. "Make the other guy slower."

Teller nodded. "I believe that when the United States determined it could no longer beat the Russians to the Moon solely by technical expertise, we undertook missions of sabotage."

"NASA spies?" Cory said in disbelief. "Rocket scientists going undercover with Walther PPKs and Aston Martins with ejection seats? Not even I buy that, Kai."

"I'm not saying NASA had a clue what was going on. It's a civilian agency. The race was military. You don't think the military establishment of the late sixties had the will to take on the Soviets? The CIA certainly did. And back then they were joined at the hip to NASA."

Cory paused. *In for a penny, in for a pound,* she thought. "So what did they do?"

"Made the Soviets slower," Teller said. "Remember, our Apollo program hinged on the Saturn V booster. It was big enough and powerful enough to get our astronauts and their modules to the Moon. The Russian lunar mission hinged on their giant booster, too. The N-1. It could have taken them to Mars. And those boosters kept blowing up. Including one on June 14, 1969. And one on July 13. And *those,* I'm convinced, were their manned lunar missions."

"And *we* blew them up?"

"Somehow, yes. Industrial sabotage. A sniper sending a fifty-caliber explosive shell into a fuel truck. Any booster is a bomb waiting to go off. And when those N-1s went off, it was like a small nuclear warhead. The Russians had to cover up the losses of their top scientists and generals by holding back the reports of their deaths, saying they all died of car accidents and failed operations and heart attacks over the next six months."

Cory still didn't buy it. "Is it possible that the Russians just didn't build good rockets? Like you told Mitchell?"

"Webber was testing me, Cory. All those leading questions about the Russian boosters blowing up. I knew what he was doing: asking if I knew about the American sabotage of the Russian space program. So I just gave him the party line. Monolithic Soviet engineering, poor organization, no capitalist drive for excellence. Because the truth is, if there's one thing the Russians do well in space, it's build boosters. Hell, the main rocket the U.S. Air Force uses these days, the Atlas V, that's built around Russian rocket engines. Nobody does them better."

"You're serious about all this?"

"It fits the facts. The smoking gun's been missing for a long time, but that's only because the U.S. government has maintained strict control over the crime scene."

"The Moon," Cory said. "Creating obstacles for the commercialization of space."

Now it was Teller's turn to get worked up. "The

American government's half-assed policy on space exploration, its parsimonious treatment of NASA, the barely concealed contempt that government officials constantly display
toward anyone who espouses the value of space science and
exploration and all the benefits that accrue from those pur-
suits, can only have one of two explanations. Either the government is made up of blind, self-serving anti-intellectuals
who can't see further than four years into the future . . ."

"I didn't know you could speak my language," Cory
said lightly. It was odd to be on the receiving end for once.

". . . or," Teller continued, "they've got some terrible
secret they want to keep hidden for as long as they can."

Cory wasn't completely convinced by his argument and
had no way to check his facts, but she no longer doubted
his conviction.

"That's why we have to do this thing," Teller said. "And
that's why we have to do it right. No loose ends. No circumstantial evidence. I've put a rover on the Moon, at the
Russian crash site, under the government's nose, and I
intend to use it to tell the truth to the world. Let the chips
fall where they may."

He looked at her, full of urgency. Cory felt the seduc-
tive, dangerous force of his compelling personality, his will.
"I need you to do this for me, Cory. I need you at the control station. And I need you to be able to keep going when
the government says they're shutting us down and threatening to throw us into an oubliette."

"I'll do it," she heard herself say.

They stared at each other now as if one of them was
about to say something more, do something more. The
night was suddenly very real and dark around them.

Then the door from the lodge opened beside them, and
the night gave way to warm amber light.

It was Derek Frame, agitated, clipboard in hand.

"Mister Teller, Cory, I . . ." He looked down at the clipboard as if he couldn't quite believe it existed.

"Derek . . . ?" Teller said. "What's happened?"

"It's . . . it's the Chinese, Mister Teller. Their space station . . . it's not a space station. They . . . they just broke orbit and they launched for the Moon."

"Orbital inclination?" Teller asked.

Frame handed over the clipboard. Cory could see a printed sheet on top, covered in dense numbers. "Barring course corrections, they're dead on the lunar ecliptic. On track for Tranquility."

Teller flipped through the sheets on the clipboard as if he were on the verge of panic. "You're certain it's manned?"

"No word from the Chinese news agencies, Mister Teller. But a new crew docked with the station two weeks ago. We're assuming that means they're on their way."

"This is terrible," Teller said as he ran his finger over a row of numbers.

As far as Cory could determine, there was only one reason why Teller would be so concerned about a Chinese lunar mission—their destination. "Kai, if the Chinese are heading for the Russian crash site, too, doesn't that make things better? Now it's not just up to us to get the truth out. The taikonauts will do it, too."

Teller's only response was to brusquely order her to wait where she was until he returned. Then he rushed off with Frame.

Left alone on the veranda, freed from whatever moonlight madness had nearly swept over her, Cory came to her own inescapable conclusion. Teller had another purpose for going to the Moon, and it had nothing to do with making the truth known.

She would have to do that, herself.

5

JUST ANOTHER SIMULATION, Webber told himself.

He had finished the preflight checklist with Captain Rodriguez in the seat behind him, and was trying to convince himself he was simply another pilot in another simulator for another round of training. He was not taking risks. He was not making history. He would activate a few controls, and the computers would do the work.

Except that when Webber moved his gloved hand away from the flight console, it did not settle back to his pilot's seat.

He was in free fall. The one condition a simulator could not duplicate for more than thirty seconds at a time. The one condition that shattered his illusion, and his concentration.

Mitch Webber knew without question he was in the pilot's seat of a spacecraft 22,500 miles above the Earth, orbiting at almost 6,000 mph. And in less than ten minutes, he would initiate the firing sequence that would send this very real spacecraft to the actual Moon.

The only part of his mind-control exercise that was the same in both scenarios, was the fact that he would not be making history in either case. At least, not any history he could ever talk about.

Varik was beside him, in the commander's seat of the Lunar Expeditionary Vehicle cabin, which was much more constricted than the *Falcon*'s flight deck. The colonel was checking the positions of the overhead circuit switches, reading out their positions from the flight manual checklist displayed on the large computer screen on the console before him.

Like Webber and the other astronauts in the cabin, Varik was sealed in a dull white pressurized flight suit, complete with helmet and gloves. The suits were the inner, life-support layers of what they would wear on the Moon. The lighter, orange pressure suits had been left behind in the *Falcon,* which was still docked with Geo-synchronous Staging Platform Three, awaiting the crew's return.

"LTG Master Alarm . . . close," Varik said.

Christa Bowden's voice joined the loop as she repeated the switch status from her position behind Varik. "LTG Master Alarm, close." The two of them were both serving as flight supervisors on this launch, with Varik taking over the technical settings Webber had not yet studied.

"ACS pressure . . . on," Varik said.

Again, Bowden confirmed the setting.

"RCS system A, B-2 quads . . . auto."

The statement and response became a background chant to Webber, as if he were listening to medieval monks reciting biblical lessons in an unknown tongue. *Someday,* he thought, *space travel will be that old, and this LEV will be seen as a primitive curiosity, little more than a Conestoga wagon or a sailboat of papyrus.* He smiled at the thought. It was something Cory might say. He shut out thoughts of her and Teller. There'd be time for that when he got back.

Varik and Bowden had finished their checklists. The flight console was fully lit. The two main screens angling up from the curved control console—one for Varik, one for Webber—were green, no caution windows or alerts flashing.

At the bottom of each screen, Webber saw the running countdown. Four minutes to G-SAP separation. Five to trans-lunar insertion.

Varik toggled on the main S-band commlink to check the computer display, looking for confirmation that the transmissions would be correctly routed through the Milstar while they were still in its EM shadow. Then he spoke: "This is *Fastbreak* to Central Command. We are go for separation at two hundred seconds . . . mark."

"*Fastbreak, this is Salyard at CenCom. We confirm you are go.*"

Unlike Webber, Varik did not seem surprised by the voice that had replied. "Good to hear from you, General. Any word on our friends?"

"*Chinese news agencies still haven't said anything. But some European bureaus are just beginning to report that China has launched a lunar probe from their space station.*"

Varik gave a short, sharp laugh. "Hasn't anyone noticed the station isn't there anymore?"

"*As a matter of fact, it is. Seems the Chinese have been planning this a long time. Put their lunar craft and fuel on orbit inside modules that looked like space station components. Those components are still there.*"

"Do we know that it *is* a manned landing attempt, General?"

"*We have picked up encrypted voice communication from*

the Chinese craft. Our radar scans make it consistent with a combined Shenzhou III *capsule and two-man lander. A lunar flyby or lunar orbit mission is possible, but the analysts say unlikely. "*

"Any idea where they're headed?" Varik asked.

"That's why the analysts believe this is a landing mission. Their trajectory puts them on track for Landing Site One, and all other points on that orbit."

Webber wondered why Salyard had added the reference to all other points on the orbit. The fact that a third party had entered the race didn't necessarily change the urgency of this mission. But if, indeed, the Chinese had no knowledge of the Project Hammer crash site, then any other place they landed on the Moon was to the Space Force's advantage.

"Understood, General," Varik replied, as if Salyard had said something more than what Webber had heard. Then, before Varik could continue, Lieutenant-Colonel Bowden interrupted. "Excuse me, General, Colonel, we're coming up on two minutes to separation."

"In that case, how's your LEV pilot working out?" Salyard asked.

Webber was puzzled by the serious undercurrent in Salyard's tone.

Varik turned in his seat to look at Webber, gave him a thumbs-up sign. "He's holding up pretty well for a squid, General."

Varik had used the Air Force term for a sailor. Webber returned the thumbs-up.

"Ready to go to the Moon, Captain Webber?"

"At this point I'm ready to walk there, General." Webber kept his eyes on the computer countdown now, slipped his hands around the flight controllers.

"Good man, Captain. CenCom wants you to stand by for

some updated course corrections we'll have ready for you in about two hours."

Webber watched the numbers roll past. Sixty seconds to separation. Two minutes to ignition. He was about to light off a 380,000-pounds-of-thrust firecracker and the last thing he needed to hear was that he might be pointing it in the wrong direction. "May I ask why, General?"

"The Chinese might not know they're in a race, Captain. Earth's gravity will cause their velocity to decrease for the first half of their coast to the Moon, and we'd like yours to increase. So we can turn their six-hour lead into a deficit."

"Understood, General." Webber kept his doubts to himself. Traveling to the Moon faster than the flight plan, even by six hours, would require using more fuel for increased velocity, and even more fuel for braking the LEV in lunar orbit. The net result would be less fuel for returning home.

"Twenty seconds to separation," Bowden announced.

Varik prepared to shut down communications. "General, we're about to disconnect the main umbilical. We will resume communications at the end of TLI burn. *Fastbreak* out."

"Godspeed," Salyard said, then Varik toggled the main switch and Webber heard the background hiss in his commset cut out.

"Coming up on ten seconds," Bowden advised.

"Umbilical disconnect," Rodriguez confirmed as Webber felt a vibration twang through the cabin.

"Internal power," Varik said.

Bowden began the countdown from five.

Webber took a breath, kept his attention on the situation display in the middle of his screen. A wireframe model of the ungainly *Kitty Hawk* floated in a wireframe box representing G-SAP docking module four.

On Bowden saying, "One," the cabin shook slightly as the docking clamps released.

Webber carefully moved the translational controller to the left, and felt himself sway slightly to the right as he finally took control of the *Kitty Hawk,* and prepared to set his course. For the Moon.

From space, there was little to see of the moment of separation. The joined modules of Geosynchronous Staging Platform Three formed a long black silhouette against space, noticeable only because of the stars it blocked.

Then, in total silence, one module appeared to break apart from the others, to be left behind. But it was the LEV *Kitty Hawk,* sliding easily from its docking module, appearing to hang in space as G-SAP III and its anchoring Milstar satellite swung slowly away.

At fifteen seconds after separation, small quick lights flashed on the LEV, and the two-stage lunar-landing craft began to rotate, aligning its longitudinal axis with its movement around the distant Earth.

At fifty-five seconds after separation, G-SAP III was a safe fifteen hundred feet away. Five seconds after that, the *Kitty Hawk*'s main engine ignited in a silent, purple-white bell of radiance, and the blocky, faceted craft began to accelerate, leaving Earth orbit entirely, on a course to where the Moon would be in seventy hours.

USSF CENCOM / VANDENBERG AFB

At 284 seconds elapsed time, looking down into Mission Control, Element Three, General Salyard watched the main screen as the optical feed from OWL continuously updated. It showed a tiny point of light wink out, vanishing in the rippling pixels of the computer-enhanced image.

"That's visual confirm on engine shutdown," Major Lowell said, beside Salyard. The two of them were standing side by side at the glass wall on the upper level of the underground Central Command facility.

According to the telemetry readings on the side screen, the main engine burn had lasted 284 seconds, and during that time, though the *Kitty Hawk* was not observable by naked eye on Earth, its rocket fire could have been picked up by sensitive ground-based telescopes. But now, it was a ghost, observable by no one, and no technology, traveling at 23,500 mph—6.5 miles per second.

Salyard patted the shorter man's back. "Three days, and it's all over."

Lowell's response was almost apologetic. "Except for Teller."

"A loose end. He won't be with us long. And with nothing left on the Moon to point to, the evidence Rey gave him is worthless. If it ever shows up in anyone else's hands, it's easily debunked once we explain how easy it is to fake radiation exposure."

"Then it is over," Lowell said, and his relief sounded even greater than Salyard's.

The doors to Lowell's staging office slid open and a young lieutenant approached with a message slip. "Pardon me, General," she said as she gave the message to Lowell. "This came in for you, Major." She left as quickly as she arrived.

Lowell read the message, tense again. "The FBI's at the gate."

Salyard showed no concern. He had already set his defenses against this attack in place. "Have Sergeant Tucker explain that Varik is on his way to South Korea, and that I will fill them in personally once the Threatcon drill is over."

"They don't want Varik," Lowell said, apprehensive, as if troubled that events were somehow spinning out of control. He handed the slip to Salyard. "They want you."

NASA HEADQUARTERS / WASHINGTON, D.C.

Tovah Caruso looked at the flashing update on her computer screen, and might as well have heard bells toll.

Her aide had just confirmed a meeting for her, Monday morning, at the White House. No doubt that undated resignation letter she had signed on the first day she had served as NASA's chief administrator was already waiting for her there, already filled in with Monday's date. At least the president had the decency to tell her she was fired to her face, and was giving her the weekend to clean out her office.

Caruso ignored all the other calendar entries that followed the White House meeting. She even ignored all the entries remaining for today. She had fifty-six hours remaining to her at NASA. It would be a shame to waste them.

She turned her attention back to the pad of yellow legal paper she had been writing on.

Six names were there. The ones of interest to the FBI. Salyard. Varik. Webber. Rey. Teller. And hers.

Lines ran between them as Hong had described the suspected connections. Cory Rey's name was in the center, because that's where the FBI claimed it belonged. The link to all the others.

Certainly, Caruso could see the logic of connecting Rey to Teller, to her, and, of course, to Webber. But the link to Salyard and Varik, that just didn't hold up.

If all these people were involved in some unnamed conspiracy, then Caruso knew there was still a missing connection. She ruled out any higher-ranking official to whom Salyard might be reporting. A link solely to the general was not a link to the group as a whole. If there was an unseen puppet master above the general, then the principle of plausible deniability was in full effect.

She tapped the tip of her pen in the center of the page, in the center of the names. There had to be another name that deserved to go there, right in the middle of everyone and everything, so obvious that Caruso knew that when she finally thought of it, she would wonder how she could have missed it for so long.

She tried to create sense connections. She pictured Doctor Rey in her blue astronaut jumpsuit. She pictured Teller in his white shirt and jeans, how she had first seen him in the ISS Flight Control Room on the day this had all begun. She remembered the flight from Washington, the meeting with the team who had worked out how to get a spacesuit to Rey, how to boost the station's orbit. She remembered Milankou in the FCR, the tension, the confusion when Milankou and Teller had spoken at the same time to answer her question about . . .

Caruso sat back in her chair, wondering how she could have missed it for so long.

She hit the intercom switch on her phone.

She asked to be put through to Space Command and the missing name—Major Wilhemina Bailey.

6

MITCH WEBBER DIDN'T HAVE TIME to contemplate either the wonder of space travel, or the tedium of it.

Each free moment he had was spent with feet looped under the restraining straps at his pilot station, as Varik and Bowden alternately subjected him to training drills. When the commander and SOV pilot weren't putting him through his paces, they retreated to the back of the circular cabin where four cloth panels arranged like circular shower curtains provided visual privacy and a dark environment for sleeping.

The other space rookie, Rodriguez, spent most of his time reading or looking out the windows.

This trip was completely unlike any NASA expedition. NASA astronauts were very aware they were explorers supported by taxpayer funds. Almost every minute of their time in space was tightly scheduled, every task productive.

But there were no explorers on the *Kitty Hawk.* She was a troop transport, and the only mission to be accomplished was the one at the end of the trip. So there were no experiments to run, no photographs to take. Like every other soldier throughout time, all the crew of this ship had to do was await the call to action.

Except for Webber. He had the other half of what every soldier had to contend with. Drills.

Fortunately, after a few hours of initial confusion over the layout of the flight controls, Webber became comfortable with the fly-by-wire system. The movements he put into the controllers had no direct effect on the lunar-landing craft's thrusters and orientation. Instead, his inputs were interpreted by a suite of three computers which ensured he couldn't inadvertently turn the LEV on its side, or descend too quickly.

Bowden's explanation was that the autopilot system was designed so that should the day come when a lunar site was visited on a regular basis, once a clear landing area had been established, the LEV could land on full automatic. Only the uncertainty of the terrain they were headed for on this trip, Bowden pointed out, made Webber a necessary member of the crew.

Webber decided he'd take that observation as somewhat of a compliment. But he paid more attention to the fact that Varik had taken over from Bowden in the middle of their conversation, as if she might have been saying something he wasn't supposed to hear.

"How are you feeling about all of this?" Varik had asked when Bowden had floated back to her privacy cocoon.

"Good to go," Webber answered. "The controls are close to the F-35."

"That's a fighter. I've flown it. It's nothing like this."

Webber saw where the confusion lay. "I meant the Marine version." Each service had a slightly different variant of the Joint Strike Fighter's main design. "That has vertical takeoff and landing capabilities, like a Harrier. You can rock the stick all you want, but the thing will just float to a landing."

Varik didn't like being corrected. "Not on rocks, it won't. Let's work on aborts."

Webber was ready for more, but he did have a question about the conditions under which he would be permitted to abort a landing attempt. He understood that the mission was critical. As of the last position fix, the *Kitty Hawk* would be following the Chinese moonship into orbit by two hours, though CenCom was working on the specifics for another engine burn to shave the Chinese lead even more. But after all this effort to beat the Chinese, in case they did intend to land at the Project Hammer crash site, Webber had to know which was more important.

"If fuel is low, do I commit to a no-return landing so we can at least bury the nuke where the Chinese taikonauts can't find it? Or do I put the crew ahead of the mission and go back to orbit without landing?"

Webber waited for Varik to give him the rundown of the mission's rules, most likely ending with the colonel's assuming responsibility for calling for a landing or an abort to orbit.

But the colonel didn't.

"As long as you set us down intact," Varik said, "we've got thirty days of consumables to hold us through to a rescue mission."

"We've got another LEV?"

Varik assumed the blank expression Webber knew so well.

"Right," Webber said. "We have rescue capability. Good enough for me."

"Let's practice aborts," Varik said.

For Webber, the tedium of space travel began again.

TTI LAUNCH CENTER / JARVIS ISLAND

Cory awoke that afternoon without knowing what time it was, and she wasn't quite sure of the day. Her small guest room had a shower and a coffeemaker, and she almost felt human when she limped out into the brilliant sunshine and saw the rich tropical foliage that surrounded the lodge.

Someone had hung a note on her door, inviting her to the flight center whenever she woke up. She walked to it now, an expert on her crutch, following the small signs that were at every turn of the dirt and gravel path.

The route took her by the helicopter pad she had seen yesterday, when they had landed. It also gave her a chance to see how Teller had arranged the trick with the disappearing runway.

It was covered by a huge expanse of camouflage netting.

Cory stood on the mottled brown pavement, and decided the color scheme was something that had been designed to work with the pattern of the overhead netting and the random twists of green and brown fabric woven through it. She would guess that from the air, or from satellites, photographs of Jarvis Island wouldn't reveal any runway at all. Unless the photos were taken in those few minutes when the cantilevered arms she saw along one side of the runway angled back to clear the netting.

She wondered why Teller had gone to such incredible lengths to disguise a runway. It gave the island a feeling of being more a fortress than a terraforming experiment or sea-launch facility.

But that was the least of the questions she was considering today, so she kept walking.

From the outside, the flight center building looked little different from the lodge. It had rough-hewn wooden walls, a corrugated tin roof, and a wide and welcoming veranda.

But once Cory stepped inside, it was as if she were back at NASA, with painted walls, bright lights, modern office furniture, and the artificial breeze of air-conditioning.

A technician in the requisite white trousers and colorful shirt greeted Cory by name and escorted her to the flight control room. Cory wondered if Teller was setting up his own cult. Or maybe he just owned a Hawaiian shirt factory.

The flight control room had a keypad lock on the door, which Cory thought was another sign of overkill in the middle of the Pacific. Inside, the room was much smaller than anything at NASA. There was a conference table and whiteboard to one side, a small kitchen area and refrigerator to the other, and in the middle three large workstations, each covered with multiple monitors, a mix of old-fashioned CRTs and inch-thick LCD screens mounted on swinging arms.

Derek Frame was scowling in front of a monitor that displayed some sort of a spreadsheet, and didn't notice her entrance. Teller was at another of the stations, and he brightened as he saw her. She guessed whatever had captured his attention was under control again, and she was back on his map.

"Cory! Just in time!" He gave her a quick hug, mindful of her back. "We're about to find out if our rover's still alive."

Somehow, Cory thought Teller's mood indicated he wasn't worried about a negative determination.

He pulled up a rolling office chair for her, cloth-covered this time, and took her crutch to lean it at the side of the workstation.

"Recognize those?" he asked as he pushed her up to a large monitor in front of which was a standard computer keyboard and two teleoperation hand controllers.

"Is this how you run the rover?" she asked. The controls

looked new, no traditional buildup of grease stains and dirt trapped in the plastic grooves.

"No," Teller said, "this is how *you* will run the rover."

"*If* the rover's still alive," she said.

"Let's find out." Teller instructed Frame to send an inquiry.

Cory wasn't sure what he was doing. "If you send a signal, aren't you letting the Air Force——" She corrected herself. "——the Space Force know the rover's still there and operational?"

"Slow and steady, Cory," Teller said. "Just like the tortoise. We've been sending short, coded signals over the past twenty-four hours. Only two minutes' worth of total transmission time, so it's nothing intelligible to anyone but our rover."

"How does it signal back?" Cory asked.

"A burst transmission, compressed and encrypted. We time it so it comes in just as whatever communications satellite is handy passes within a few degrees of the Moon. That way, if anyone notices it, it seems like a spurious satellite signal." He glanced over at Frame. "How are we doing?"

"Satellite coming up in two minutes," the big man said, then looked over at Teller and realized Cory was present. He gave her a subdued greeting, and went back to his monitor.

"Is everything okay with Derek?" Cory asked. The time she and Frame had spent in Huntsville had been the highlight of her year of astronaut training. He was usually the loudest one in the bar.

"We're making history here," Teller said. "I think we're all feeling the pressure."

A reasonable answer, Cory thought, *if only it were true.* She wasn't as gullible today.

She pointed to the hand controllers. "Okay if I try these out?"

"Sure," Teller said. He hit a few keys on the keyboard, and a three-dimensional animation of the LRV appeared on the monitor in front of her.

It was a fairly standard rover—a six-wheeled platform, about four feet long, two feet across, with its flat top made of photovoltaic cells—until one counted all the options. A telescoping stalk at one end contained the widely separated twin camera lenses that provided three-dimensional imaging capability. At the other end, a double-hinged robotic arm ended in a cross-shaped "hand," each component serving a different purpose. Two were grippers, a third was a high-speed vibrational cutter for chipping off rock samples, and the fourth was a microscopic-lens camera for detailed examination of samples.

Cory slipped her hands into the controllers, made some experimental movements to have the simulated rover on her screen turn in a circle, and noticed the lag in response. "Is this a shared network?" she asked.

"It is a *lunar* simulation," Teller said. "One-way light time to the Moon is about one point two seconds."

Cory was embarrassed she had overlooked such an obvious fact of physics. "So when I send a command, it takes two and a half seconds to get a confirm."

"Einstein wins again," Teller said. He pointed to one of the LCD monitors. "This is where we should pick up the burst transmission. Ten seconds."

"What kind of data will it send?" Cory asked.

"Keep watching."

A few seconds later, Derek Frame called out, "Got it!" and the handful of other Hawaiian-shirted technicians in the room applauded. "Decompressing and decrypting," Frame continued. "And . . . there it is!"

A low-resolution picture suddenly appeared on the display, and there was no doubt it showed a rock-strewn terrain, very similar to images Cory remembered from the Apollo photographs.

"Still alive," Teller said.

"Except," Cory said, "where are the Russians?"

Teller traced his finger over what Cory had thought was a boulder to the side of the screen. "We're missing an indication of scale," Teller said, "but from the depth of field in the image, I'd say this object is close to the lens, about fourteen . . . sixteen inches across. And see how spherical it is?"

"Right," Cory said. "Like a white bowling ball."

"Try a space helmet," Teller said. "The rover retraced its tracks and it's right in the middle of the landing site. I'll bet you ten kilos of lunar rocks we're looking at the body of the first man to walk on the Moon. And I guarantee you, his name isn't Neil Armstrong."

COLORADO SPRINGS

Tovah Caruso tuned out the wailing infants, and instead concentrated on the odd plaque she had noticed on the wall in Major Bailey's brown-and-silver-striped dining room.

It was a small rectangle of highly polished oak, inset with a brass plate engraved with a simple inscription. *In recognition of a significant accomplishment.* Nothing else.

But hanging beside that plaque, another clue to indicate exactly how significant that accomplishment had been: a photograph of Major Bailey, together with a woman who was more than likely her sister or close relative, and an older man and woman, perhaps her parents, all standing proudly with the president of the United States, in the Oval Office no less.

Caruso heard footsteps behind her, turned to see

Bailey's husband, Dominic Hubert. The dual wailing sirens from the nursery down the hallway were winding down.

"Sorry about that, ma'am," Hubert said.

"Sorry I rang the doorbell," Caruso replied. "And please, call me Tovah."

Hubert grinned, and his pale freckled cheeks became apples. "Sure, Tovah. Can I get you some tea? Herbal?"

"Yes, please."

Hubert ducked into the kitchen. Caruso studied the dining room's other photos and certificates and plaques. Now the crying had stopped completely, and she turned to see Major Bailey tiptoe out of the hallway. She was still in her uniform blouse and slacks, though she was in stocking feet.

"Little devils," Bailey said, and she shook hands with Caruso.

"Angels, I'd bet," Caruso said. "Thank you for seeing me."

Bailey smiled, apparently holding no grudge from the sharp words Caruso had used before Rey and Lazhenko had returned from the station. "Half of me's being polite, the other half is very curious."

They sat down in the cozy living room, and Caruso felt comfortable at once. This was a home that felt lived in, newspapers scattered, baby toys in piles. She could see an old-fashioned white-enamel refrigerator through the kitchen doorway, and it was covered with Post-it notes, a calendar, and photos and comic strips clipped from magazines and newspapers.

"That's an intriguing plaque you have on your wall," Caruso said, "beside the picture of the president."

Bailey smiled again, but didn't speak.

"My husband was a test pilot," Caruso said, understanding Bailey's silence. "He had one like that. He was very proud of it. I never knew what it was for, but I was proud of it, too."

Bailey's smile faded as she picked up on what Caruso wasn't saying. "Your husband . . . ," she began to ask.

But Caruso gave a small shake of her head. "Eight years ago."

"I'm very sorry."

"He did what he was born to do. Not too many of us get that opportunity."

"No, ma'am," Bailey said.

"She said to call her Tovah," Hubert said as he came from the kitchen with a tray of steaming tea mugs.

"Tovah," Bailey said. Then they talked about tea and what cookies to have with it and how long the twins were liable to sleep, while Bailey and her husband waited for their guest to get to the point of her unusual visit.

Caruso didn't make them wait long.

"On Monday, I'm going to see the president, and he's going to shake my hand and then fire me." She held up a hand to keep Bailey and Hubert from interrupting with unnecessary sympathy. "So I'm here as a private citizen, not NASA, understood?"

Bailey and Hubert accepted that, but cautiously.

Then Caruso told them everything she knew about the FBI's investigation into the loss of the shuttle and the damage to the station, starting with the murder of Ed Farren, and ending with Special Agent Hong's announcement that the conspiracy included Doctor Rey and Kai Teller and perhaps even the Russian mafia.

Caruso appreciated that Bailey and Hubert looked as stunned by those revelations as she had been.

Bailey was the first to speak. "Doctor Rey could not be part of anything like that. Absolutely, one hundred percent, not possible."

"I agree," Caruso said.

"And the only way Captain Webber might be involved," Bailey went on, "is if . . . he's part of some investigation, or something he's involved with has been misconstrued by the FBI."

"I don't know Webber as well as you do," Caruso said, "but that's my sense of him, too."

Hubert gave her a perceptive look. "My sense is that you want to know something. Something you think Willie can tell you."

Caruso nodded. "What happened on the station was too well coordinated to be an accident. It was a deliberate attack for a distinct purpose. And what the FBI can't figure out is what the motive for that attack might be."

Caruso knew she was onto something right away because she saw that blank, operational security look come to Major Bailey. She continued, "My best guess is that it has something to do with the samples that came back from the LRV."

"Ma'am," Bailey said formally, "Doctor Rey said she was unable to recover any samples."

"I heard that," Caruso said. "But now, what I need to hear, is what she and Kai Teller discussed."

Bailey shook her head. "I can't . . ."

"And I need to know what she told you when she thought she wasn't going to make it back."

Hubert looked at his wife, and Caruso knew she had come to the right place.

"She's in real trouble, Major Bailey," Caruso said. "So is Captain Webber. Eight astronauts and one engineer have already died. And I know in my gut it all has to do with what she said to you. And whatever that was, I'm sure, has something to do with what came back from the Moon."

Hubert took his wife's hand, squeezed it.

"This isn't a military matter, Major," Caruso said emphatically. "I would understand the constraints on you if it were. This is about friends. This is about the civilian space program. If you know something that can help Doctor Rey and Captain Webber, that can help your country, it's the right thing to say what you know."

Bailey looked at her husband and asked a question with her eyes.

Hubert nodded. And Caruso knew she'd made her case.

"Fingers," Bailey said. "That's what came back from the Moon. Human fingers that had been exposed to unfiltered solar radiation for close to forty years."

"But no one ever died on . . . forty years?"

"We thought it might have been an experiment," Hubert said. "Like on the shuttle. Maybe the Apollo astronauts took cadaver parts with them to see what the effects of vacuum exposure would be."

Caruso shook her head. "They did a bunch of crazy, classified experiments in the old days. But body parts to the Moon? That never happened."

"Maybe on a Russian *lunokhod?*" Hubert asked.

"We can put bodies in vacuum chambers on Earth. So can the Russians. If human remains came back from the Moon, someone had to have died up there. But who? And why is that worth blowing up the space shuttle and . . ." Caruso faltered, stricken to realize she knew what would make blowing up the shuttle worthwhile.

"It's a Russian," she blurted out. "A Russian cosmonaut died on the Moon. It's the only secret worth killing for. It's the only reason that explains what the FBI calls a conspiracy."

Bailey and Hubert exchanged glances, then looked back at her.

"But . . . why don't we know about it?" Hubert asked.

"From forty years ago, it would have to have been a Soviet mission that put a cosmonaut on the Moon. Those guys are selling secrets right and left. They would've told someone by now."

"I work with the Russians," Caruso said slowly. "It would all depend on who the cosmonaut was, why he was there." There was one condition she knew of, that would make the secret even more dangerous. "When he was there. Forty years? You're certain about that?"

"It was an estimate," Hubert said. "Based on gamma–ray trails in the bone."

Caruso was feeling shellshocked. "If the remains date back to '68 or the first half of '69 . . . that's the height of the space race. Something like that, it could change everything."

There was a long silence, broken by Bailey.

"It wasn't a space race," she said quietly. "It was a space war."

Caruso went on alert. That wasn't an idle comment.

"Major Bailey," Caruso said, "what do you know about what happened back then?"

"Ma'am," Bailey said in a tired voice, "I think you'd better talk with my father. He was there."

7

20:00 GMT, SUNDAY, APRIL 13

MITCH WEBBER SPUN SLOWLY in circles in the center of the flight deck of the *Kitty Hawk,* recalling how, years ago, when the Air Force had wanted to begin the funding process for a space-based war vehicle, they'd begun with the truth. Their new, hoped-for weapons platform was proudly called the Military Space Plane.

But then reality had descended on them. Since weapons were banned in space, and the idea of orbiting fighters and bombers made citizens nervous and politicians too eager to ask probing questions, the MSP underwent a public relations makeover. Emerging on the other side, it was reborn, bland and innocuous, as the Space Operations Vehicle.

The same change in designation clearly applied to the suit Webber was attempting to put on, the one his crewmates called an EMS—Expeditionary Mobility Suit. To Webber's trained eye, it was Lunar Combat Armor, the only designation that explained its many unusual features. Not the least of which was its exterior covering. The mottled pixel print of the outer layer of his suit was nothing less than a variation of the Army's three-color disruptive urban combat pattern, with a darker gray in place of white.

Then there was its other major innovation, the one that put it far ahead of NASA's current models and nearly all other suits Webber had trained in: its implementation of Distributed Life-Support Modules.

A traditional spacesuit, whether designed for EVAs in Earth orbit, or for walking on the Moon, housed all the vital life-support systems in one large unit worn on the astronaut's back. But in the Space Force's EMS model, that one unit had become eight.

The eight miniaturized life-support modules attached to the EMS in several locations: across the upper back, the upper chest, behind the triceps of each arm, on the sides of each thigh, and behind the calves. Operating together, the DLSMs could provide up to six full hours of oxygen, cooling, and communications. And, in the event of catastrophic damage—that is, suit punctures—any one of the eight, each of varying size and capacity, could provide at least a thirty-minute blow-out window of survival to keep an astronaut supplied with oxygen.

The EMS had also half the thickness of other suits Webber had worn, and the slanted visor of its armored helmet featured a Heads Up situational computer display, which he could operate by voice command.

The final telling detail, Webber thought, that supported his label of Lunar Combat Armor, were the holsters, not that his crewmates had called them that. But that had to be the function of several of the pockets built into the camouflaged outer covering. So far, Webber had seen no sign of the weapons that might go into them.

And that's a good thing, he thought. Three days of four strangers sharing this small cabin had made conditions tight enough. Bowden and Rodriguez, especially, had almost stopped talking to him, confirming his suspicions of his presence being superfluous. His only real conversations now were with Varik, and even those were limited strictly to topics related to the mission.

Webber was fully into his EMS an hour before the scheduled burn for Lunar Orbit Insertion. Flight rules called for all crew to be suited up during landing, with helmets sealed, in case a hard touchdown caused a depressurization event.

Webber adjusted his foot restraints to allow for the added thickness of his lunar boots. Fortunately, his EMS, like Bowden's, was classified as a pilot's spacesuit, and so had uninsulated inner gloves. The extremely thin gloves would make handling flight controls easier, but Webber and Bowden would have to don thicker pairs in two situations: a depressurization event or exit from the LEV for the lunar surface. The lunar suit's inclusion of the special adaptation for pilots was another sign to Webber that the Space Force, and the Air Force, had been flying in space for a considerable time.

At one half hour before the LOI burn, he was in position, Colonel Varik at his side, even though this time Webber was certain he could handle the checklist on his own.

At twenty minutes before burn, all four members of the crew were waiting for contact with CenCom.

Precisely as scheduled, Salyard came on. He had the latest update on the Chinese mission. "*According to the Deep Space Tracking Network, you are now one hour, twenty-three minutes ahead of the Chinese mission.*"

Webber's crewmates reacted positively to that news. Webber didn't. He'd done the fuel calculations. Although the additional engine burns Central Command had programmed for them had increased their speed toward the

Moon, they now would have to use even more fuel to slow down and enter orbit. And more peculiar than that, his math had convinced him the safety margin for landing was nonexistent. There was a new risk facing them. They might not have enough fuel for liftoff and return to Earth.

Three days ago, at the beginning of his simulation training, Webber had practiced landing techniques with the general's assurance that he would have a five-minute reserve for hovering. That reserve was gone. Now he'd have to come in and choose a safe landing area on the first attempt. There would be no second chances.

"Colonel Varik," Salyard continued, *"do you foresee any difficulty in completing the mission in that one hour, twenty-three minute window?"*

"None at all, General."

To say that his mission commander was being overly optimistic was a gross understatement. But while Salyard was on the loop, Webber refrained from questioning Varik.

"Then Godspeed, Kitty Hawk," Salyard concluded. *"I will next talk to you when you have landed. CenCom out."*

Webber watched the countdown readout in the main display screen. Nineteen minutes to go. He turned his head in his wide helmet to look at Varik. "Colonel, how confident are you that the Hammer nuke is going to be that easy to find, and recover? What if the casing's cracked? Or if it's punched into ten feet of lunar dust?"

Varik didn't bother looking back at him, as if his observations, like his presence, were of no consequence on this flight. "We have orbital photographs, Captain. What we're after is intact, and in the open."

"Ah," Webber said. It was a logical answer.

But all he could think was that this mission was a repeat of Red Cobra 8. Varik and the general knew something he didn't. And he was in harm's way again. A pawn.

COLORADO SPRINGS

Tovah Caruso pressed the phone closer to her ear, so she could hear Leo Milankou over the twins' renewed and lusty duet. "What do you mean, there's a second mission?" she said.

As she strained to hear Milankou's explanation, she smiled apologetically at Randolph Bailey, who sat across from her in his daughter's living room, waiting patiently. The moment he had arrived, the phone had rung and set off the small life-forms down the hall. If these interruptions ever stopped, Caruso was counting on him being as forthcoming as his daughter.

"We're using the Deep Space Tracking Network to follow the Chinese mission," Milankou said. *"And they kept getting what they thought were doubled readings, slightly out of phase. But one of those readings just started a Lunar Orbit Insertion burn, about an hour and half ahead of the Chinese mission. So it's got to be a second mission."*

"No one's taking credit?" Caruso asked. She looked up as Bailey and Hubert came back to the living room, each patting a hiccuping baby slung over one shoulder.

"China announced their mission. No one else is saying anything."

"Any chance it's a backup to the Chinese mission? You know, they're doubling the odds that one or the other will make it back?"

"Trajectory's going through what they thought were those doubled readings to see if they can come up with a good origin for the second mission. But right now? Everything points to its having been launched from geosynchronous orbit."

"Well, that's just crazy," Caruso said, perplexed. "Keep at it, Leo. And let me know what you come up with."

"Will do," Milankou said, then hung up.

Caruso switched off the cordless phone and looked around for a place to put it, finally settling on a stack of home decor magazines. She smiled again at Randolph. "Sorry for the interruption."

"Did I hear right?" Hubert asked. "There are *two* Moon missions under way?" He slowly rocked back and forth in the wooden rocking chair, keeping his infant son, or daughter, in practiced, constant motion. The baby's gurgling rose and fell with each rock of the chair.

Bailey's eyes narrowed as she looked sharply at her husband. "You weren't supposed to be listening." She patted her baby's back vigorously and Caruso heard a loud belch.

"Oh, leave the boy alone, Wilhemina," Randolph Bailey told his daughter. "If Ms. Caruso wanted to keep a secret, she could've taken that phone into the can."

"Dad!"

"It's true," Randolph said. He smiled conspiratorially at Caruso. "Don't you say that's true?"

The senior Bailey was a knockout, with a courtly charm that was hard to resist. Seventy-five, slim and dapper, with a fringe of short gray hair and a startlingly white mustache and goatee highlighting blue-black skin. With the jaunty beret and quilted, Nehru-style jacket he wore, Bailey's father reminded Caruso of painters she had seen in Paris, working at easels along the Seine.

"Absolutely true," Caruso agreed, falling under his spell. "It's not as if anyone can hide a trip to the Moon." She noticed Bailey's skeptical expression, decided to let it go; children always misjudged their parents. "Colonel Bailey," she said to Bailey's father.

"You call me Randolph." He smiled at his daughter. "My girl's the brass in the family now."

"All right, Randolph. Again, I have to thank you for coming to see me."

Randolph patted his daughter's hand. "Any excuse to see my grandkids."

Bailey shifted her now-quiet bundle to her other shoulder, gave her father a stern look. "Dad, I think Tovah has some things to discuss with you other than the twins."

Randolph nodded, became serious. "I understand, Wilhemina."

Caruso had already decided on her approach to the senior Bailey. The same one that had succeeded with his daughter: straightforward and to the point.

"Randolph . . . while we were waiting for you to arrive, your daughter told me about a story you had told her. About being called into the Johnson White House on a Sunday night in 1967."

"That's true. Only, it was a Saturday night. February twenty-fifth."

"You remember it that clearly?"

"As I'm sure my girl told you, it was the photographs, mostly. And the fact that Jim Webb—he had your job back then—he was getting ready to put out the first report on the two-oh-four fire. And he wasn't willing to call for a major overhaul."

"The two-oh-four fire," Caruso said. "*Apollo One.*"

"That was the production number of the command module. They didn't call it *Apollo One* till after the widows lobbied for it. Doesn't matter what you call it. Still three good men who died who didn't have to."

Caruso agreed; she felt the same way. "Your daughter told me that the man you met with that night, he called the space race a space war?"

Randolph nodded again.

"And that you suspected he was going to authorize sabotage of the Russian space program, to buy us time to redesign Apollo?"

"Didn't 'suspect' anything. The man good as said that's what he was going to do. My job was to get the president to hang tough with Jim Webb. The man from State said if I could get the command module redesigned, he'd get me all the time I needed."

"Do you know what kind of sabotage took place?"

Randolph stroked his goatee, gave her a measured look. "Tell you what. Before I start telling you what went on back then, suppose you tell me what's going on right now."

He was right. Sharing went both ways. "I'll do my best," Caruso said. "The main thing is—despite the recent . . . trouble . . . with the shuttle and the station—we did bring back lunar samples. They included human remains, and I believe there's a chance that they're from a Russian cosmonaut who died on the Moon. Around the time of the first Apollo missions."

Randolph seemed in the moment to age ten years before Caruso's eyes. His erect posture slumped. "You're the chief administrator of NASA and even *you* don't know." Caruso wasn't sure if he was talking to her, or to himself.

"Know what?"

"They beat us, Ms. Caruso."

Caruso stared at him. Hubert's chair stopped rocking and Bailey leaned forward, intent on her father, as if this part of her father's story was new to her, too. "The Russians beat the Americans to the Moon?"

"Damn right. But at least we managed to bring our boys back."

"May I ask how you know this?"

"I heard the transmissions the poor guy sent back. Last thing we heard, he was go for landing, a couple of hours before the *Eagle* was ready to descend."

Caruso didn't know what else to say. "They beat us by *hours?*"

"Oh, it was tight, I tell you. We were sending commando teams in to blow up their boosters. Slowed them down, but didn't stop them. They wanted to get to the Moon worse than we did, I'd say. I think that's why the Russian kid tried it."

"Tried what?" Caruso asked in the silence that filled the room.

"A one-way trip. I think that's why they never said anything about it, too. You see, it was a suicide mission."

Then Bailey's father finished his story, and Caruso got the strong feeling that he was relieved to finally be sharing it with people who could understand it.

"The Russians were all set to go in the same launch window as *Apollo Eleven.* But we blew up their booster. So they did a crazy multiple launch, stripped down the weight. Their mission profile called for two cosmonauts, with one landing and one staying on orbit. But all they sent was the one poor guy. Almost no consumables. And no fuel for the ride home."

"You heard all this?" Caruso asked for confirmation. "At NASA?"

"Ms. Caruso, I was crammed into the Batcave—a dark little hellhole back of the big screens in Mission Control. Had my finger on a kill switch the whole time Armstrong and Aldrin were on the Moon. They never knew it, but that cosmonaut had set down somewhere near them. We didn't know if he had landed safely or not, but we were set to cut communications, just in case this stranger turned up, scared the holy crap out of our boys."

Bailey was staring at her father. So was Hubert. But neither questioned him.

Caruso rubbed at the back of her neck, felt a tension

headache coming on like she hadn't felt in years. "Randolph, do you have any idea why after all these years, no one's ever talked about this?"

"I always figured the Russians didn't want to 'fess up to a desperate mission that didn't work. And for us, we really did win, ma'am. President Kennedy set the ground rules. Send a man to the Moon *and* return him safely to Earth. That cosmonaut might have made it to the Moon first, *if* he didn't die on impact. But our boys came home. The way I see it, that's the win right there. And no one with the clearance to have been in on the affair would be in any hurry to take that win away from us."

Caruso took a moment to compose herself. Randolph's story did fit the facts. Except for one small point.

Someone *was* willing to try to take the win away from the country by revealing the truth of what had happened. And someone else was willing to kill to keep that truth hidden.

Caruso had no choice but to admit that the long-ago space war was still being waged.

Only this time the combatants weren't two superpowers. The war had been reduced to a battle between two individuals, one civilian and one military. Kai Teller and General Dwight Salyard.

And this time, the whole world would lose.

8

MITCH WEBBER TOOK OVER from the computers at 5,000 feet, and deployed the LEV's landing legs.

If he looked dead ahead, through the main viewports, he saw the lunar horizon straight and level. If he looked down, through the angled window rising up from the deck between the pilot's and commander's stations, he could see the gray-black terrain slip by, like the frozen surface of a dirty sea peppered with raindrops that would never smooth or fade.

But somehow, what his senses could not convince him of, was that he was looking at the billion-year-old terrain of the Moon. The actual Moon.

It was easier to believe that this was all a dream, that he was back in free fall over China, in the grip of some flash of hallucinatory fugue in the split second before realizing his parachute would not open.

That was easier to accept than what he was doing and what he was about to do.

But he still flew the *Kitty Hawk* perfectly.

At 4,000 feet, he saw what had to be the crash site.

"We're overshooting," he told Varik. "See down there?"

A series of distinct cylinders were laid out in parallel on the lunar surface, a few of them partially buried. Perhaps from impact, he decided. But as he prepared to adjust the craft's angle of descent, he was suddenly struck by how large the cylinders must be to be so clear from this altitude. Then he realized it wasn't debris from a wreck he saw. It was something that had been constructed, at least twice the size of the ISS.

Just as in China, Varik seemed to know something about what was beneath them. "That's not what we're after," the colonel said.

"If it's not the crash site, then what the hell is down there?" Webber asked. This mission's failure was not going to be on his head.

Varik's answer was sharp and angry—the tension had become that strong. "It's *our* base, Webber. Where *we* test our weapons."

"What?" Webber forced himself to concentrate on flying. He couldn't believe what he had just heard. "Tranquility Base?" was all he could think to say.

"The name gets changed every funding cycle. It was Horizon first. Then Touchdown. Blue Moon, even," Varik said. "Right now, we're calling it Area One."

"We have people down there?" Webber still couldn't wrap his mind around the revelation.

"Once a year, Webber. We go down, deliver equipment, swap out components. The rest of the time, it's automated."

And illegal, Webber thought. *No wonder they had so much equipment prepositioned.* "Why?" he asked, a world of confusion in the one simple word.

Varik's reply was more like a growl than an answer, as if

the colonel could no longer control his contempt for Webber. "Because we're America. And, whatever it takes, we're going to win. Now stay with the coordinates."

Webber kept his eyes moving between the altitude readout and the lower window, both hands on the controllers, to bring the craft down smoothly. But he couldn't let go of what he had seen.

"Three thousand feet," Varik said.

That won't be everything, Webber thought. Not based on his experience with Varik and Salyard. *There's going to be something else they're not telling me—for a reason.*

"Twenty-five hundred."

As Varik continued to respond only to give him the altitude, Webber was shaken by the hot surge of anger that was more than cabin fever.

At eight hundred feet, Varik was first to see the crash site, called it out by a steep crater wall.

A moment later, Webber saw it, too. A white-and-silver lunar module lay on its side, surrounded by glittering wreckage, everything half-buried by dark rocks.

But Webber gave no more than a glance to the site. He channeled his anger, attention focused solely on his job: selecting the smoothest terrain within walking distance.

He angled back on the controllers, bringing the *Kitty Hawk* in at a steeper angle.

"What're you doing?" Varik demanded. "You're bringing us in short."

"I'm steering clear of those boulders," Webber said. From the multitude of crisp black shadows near the crashed lander, he could see there were no clear areas near it at all.

At five hundred feet, he had thirty seconds of fuel left. If he didn't land by then, he knew he would have no choice but to abort to orbit, or let Varik make the decision to strand everyone on the Moon for the next thirty days, awaiting rescue.

Then again, Webber thought with perverse satisfaction, *we could camp out in Area One.*

The *Kitty Hawk* kept descending, Webber keeping its speed just above the threshold that would trigger the computers to take over. At twenty seconds of fuel and two hundred feet, he saw two possible places to set down. One was a suitably smooth stretch of terrain, but angled. The other was flatter, but strewn with small rocks.

He only had a heartbeat to decide, went with his instincts.

He passed up the smooth but angled site for the rocky one.

"One hundred feet," Varik read out. "Fifteen seconds."

Webber throttled up to slow their descent.

"You're taking us right into those rocks," Varik warned.

"They're uniform," Webber said. "Look at the texture of the shadows."

Varik pointed to the smooth slope. "Over there! No rocks!"

Webber did not change course. Fifty feet. Eight seconds. "Look at the angle, Colonel. If the ground's soft, we fall over."

"Brace yourself!" Varik shouted, and his angry voice echoed in Webber's helmet.

"Twenty feet," Webber said. The screen showed four seconds of fuel remaining. He could do this.

"Ten feet . . . eight . . . five . . ."

The fuel warning alert began to chime. Three feet from the ground, the computers were about to abort to orbit.

"Override that!" Webber shouted. "Contact light!"

The sensors hanging down from the landing legs' foot-pads had brushed the ground.

Webber instantly released the controllers to shut off the main engine and slapped the abort cancel switch because Varik was too slow.

The *Kitty Hawk* dropped three feet, with unearthly slowness.

Webber heard crunching noises through the deck, felt the lander shift to the side, angling slightly. But then it held, no more than five degrees off the horizontal.

"We're down," Webber said, and refrained from adding "no thanks to you" for Varik. "Anyone have anything momentous to say?"

Varik disconnected his flight harness. "We have one hour, twenty-three minutes to sanitize this site. Let's move."

Not quite as stirring as "The Eagle has landed," Webber thought. *But it'll do.*

And then it finally sank in.

He wasn't dreaming.

He was on the Moon.

And his only thought was, *I wish I could share this with Cory.*

TTI LAUNCH CENTER / JARVIS ISLAND

"They'll have landed by now," Teller said.

Cory snapped out of her reverie on the veranda of the flight center building. She had been thinking about Webber, and San Diego: that almost magic year before she had gone for astronaut training. How much more unprofessional could she be?

"We should go inside," Teller said. He offered her his hand, and between it and her crutch, she got up from the chaise lounge with what she thought was all the grace of a pregnant hippo.

She took a moment to fully shake off her thoughts of Webber, gave Teller a questioning look.

He smiled. "Yes?"

"Why do you really have this island?" she asked.

"Doesn't everyone dream of owning one?"

"With a disappearing runway? A secret launch pad?"

"Scouts' motto," Teller said. "Be prepared."

"For what? Invasion?"

Teller lost his smile. "Cory, I can't wait for the government to come to its senses. I'm going into space now. Starting my own program. If I can continue to do business with NASA, fine. Or work with the European Space Agency, or Japan's or . . . or even China's, I'm ready, willing, and able. But the real breakthroughs are going to come from one person with a vision. And hokey as it seems, I intend to be that person."

"Even if you have to fight?" Cory asked. Even if he was still not being completely truthful with her about what he was up to on the Moon, Teller was wearing her down. She had almost bought his argument that the United States government didn't want private industry in space. And that part of that might be because they didn't want anyone to find out what happened on the Moon forty years ago. Though, if Teller succeeded, that was a battle they were going to lose today. She had less difficulty believing that the government didn't want anyone else to have the surveillance ability they had. She agreed with Teller that when everyone had equal access to surveillance, everyone would be equal.

"Name one visionary who didn't have to fight." He opened the door that led inside. "Let's go fire the first shots."

Cory hobbled inside, heading for the center room.

A minute later, after Teller had input the proper code

into the door's electronic keypad, Cory was back in the wheeled office chair, hands in the two controllers, ready to take charge of Teller's lunar rover.

Derek Frame was at his workstation, calculating the next window of opportunity for receiving images from the Moon. Teller served as cheerleader to all the technicians in the room.

"Thirty seconds," Frame announced.

That was when Teller changed the conditions.

"All right, this time keep the transmission open. I'm guessing they can't jam us without jamming their precious Moon expedition." He turned to a young man by a stack of digital video recorders. "Are you ready to capture?"

"Standing by," the young man said.

"Then start them now."

Each recorder was brought on line.

"Ten seconds," Frame said.

Cory watched Teller watching the blank monitor. His passion for space was unquestionable. But the real secret lay in whatever else it was that drove him. Maybe this would be the day she'd learn that secret.

"Here it comes," Derek Frame said. "Live from the Moon . . . heeerrree's rover!"

The LCD screen in front of Cory changed to show a slightly higher resolution image of the burst image that had been transmitted the day before, and now the spherical object was definitely recognizable as a helmet. Cory moved the controllers precisely, and almost three seconds later, the image on the screen began to pan.

"I have control," she said.

Teller stood behind her. "Go as wide-angle as possible, then do a three-sixty. Their lander has to be there someplace."

Cory began to make the camera adjustments, and the excitement of what she was involved in eclipsed, momentarily, her concern over Teller's motives and her conflict about Webber's, without her even realizing it.

Not only am I on the Moon, Cory thought. *I'm going to be there with Mitchell.*

USSF CENTRAL COMMAND / VANDENBERG AFB

General Dwight Salyard considered himself under siege, and for good reason.

The FBI agents who had been turned away at the gates of Vandenberg two days ago, had pressed their case to the Bureau's top level, which had, in turn, applied pressure to the Department of the Air Force.

Because of his position, Salyard could be certain he would never be charged with any crime, but he knew he could not escape the FBI's interrogation. For the time being, he had argued to Air Force Intelligence that he was currently pursuing a vital project of supreme importance to national security. Because of his reputation, his word had been accepted. For the time being.

But the implication was ominous. As soon as his mission was completed, or as soon as the Threatcon Charlie drill at Vandenberg had been concluded, Salyard would have to make himself available to the FBI for questioning about the destruction of the shuttle and the sabotage of the space station.

Salyard would do it, of course. His own commanding officer in the Pentagon must be protected at all cost. But he'd damn well make certain that Kai Teller of TTI paid in full for the petty distractions he had put into motion.

In the meantime, he had more appropriate duties to consider. He was in Mission Control, Element Three, no longer looking down through the glass wall, but on the floor itself, ready to share every moment of the adventure underway.

Webber had landed the *Kitty Hawk* flawlessly, almost an hour and a half ahead of the Chinese mission. That left Salyard's team ample time to sanitize the Russian crash site, *and* deal with Webber. At least the most critical part of current USSF operations was going well.

On this shift, Major Lowell was serving as the mission communications officer, and Salyard could hear his constant conversation with everyone in the LEV. Except Webber, of course. Webber was the only member of Salyard's team who had not been told what the rest of the mission would entail.

Lowell turned away from his console, his hand over his slender microphone, looking for Salyard. "General, they are preparing to depressurize *Kitty Hawk* and go EVA."

"Very good," Salyard said. "Carry on."

Lowell faced his console once more as the main display screen on the back wall suddenly flickered into life.

Salyard stared at the screen, puzzled. If the astronauts had not left the LEV, their helmet-mounted video feeds should not yet have started. He walked up behind Lowell. "Did someone start up ahead of time?"

Lowell seemed as puzzled as he was. "I'm checking that now, General." He adjusted the Ku-band controls on his console, but the main screen was filled with static. "That's odd. It's an encrypted signal."

"That's SOP," Salyard said.

"Yes, General, but it's not our encryption protocol."

"Could anyone have changed their settings?"

"Not without reprogramming. I'll check to see if anyone's transmitting."

"Do that," Salyard said with growing misgivings. "And

if that signal's not ours, then throw it over to the NSA. I want it decrypted."

Lowell looked back at Salyard, apprehensive. "Do you think there's another camera transmitting from the site, General?"

Salyard wouldn't put that past Teller. But fortunately, the situation was almost under control. The crew had their orders. "If there is, Major, it won't be transmitting for long."

US SPACECOM / CHEYENNE MOUNTAIN AIR FORCE STATION

Major Bailey knew her life was a series of contradictions. She loved her job, but she loved her husband and her babies. She loved every minute in the Mountain. But she loved being home in her house. And she could think of nothing more rewarding than inventing and testing new ways of reconfiguring the country's vast constellations of observational satellites, just as she could immerse herself in recipe experimentation in her kitchen. She guessed that simply meant she loved everything her life had to offer, and she took part in everything with equal joy.

Tonight was no exception. A special project had come to her desk. She was to turn portions of her orbital listening posts away from Earth for the next three days and listen in on all the transmissions from the Chinese lunar mission. The transmissions were encrypted, but to the assets she employed, that only introduced a few seconds' delay as the signals were reprocessed.

Bailey was especially grateful for the challenge, because she craved the distraction. Like everything else that was important in her life, she loved her father, and she was proud of all he had done in his career. But what he had confessed of America's actions during the sixties had upset her. If America was anything, it was a country that played by the rules. Sending commando teams into another country to blow up rockets and kill civilians? Just to win a politically inspired technological challenge . . . that wasn't the country that she knew, or believed she served. She could only hope that those dark days remained in the past where they belonged, and she trusted in Tovah Caruso to do what was right—see that the truth finally came out.

Bailey put her father's revelations into a separate compartment in her mind and shut its door firmly. She still felt bad for having betrayed Doctor Rey's trust, telling Caruso about the lunar samples. But she'd be talking with the doctor again sometime, and she was sure they could work it out. Nothing was forever. Not between friends.

An hour into her shift, Bailey was pleased to pick up the first transmissions from the Moon. Her decryption process took only fourteen seconds to lock on to the protocols being used by the Chinese Space Agency. Soon the quiet murmur of Chinese taikonauts talking with their mission control ran in the background murmur of her cavernous monitoring room. In another section of the Mountain, she knew translators would already be creating live, English-language tapes, and written transcripts of all that was being said.

A few minutes after her latest technological triumph, one of Bailey's technicians came to her with a new report. An encrypted video signal, also from the Moon.

Bailey made the assumption that it was a visual transmission from the Chinese mission, and used the same techniques to isolate, enhance, and decrypt the signal. Soon the jumbled signal on the main screen began to smooth out.

Bailey felt the thrill of discovery all firsthand explorers shared. She was going to see new glimpses of the Moon from orbit, or even the inside of the Chinese spacecraft.

Decryption of the video signal took longer than the audio, fully a minute before the moving images coalesced into something comprehensible.

And completely unexpected.

The background murmur in Bailey's sanctum became a roar as her staff realized what they were seeing.

American astronauts had returned to the Moon.

In secret.

9

THE *KITTY HAWK* DID NOT HAVE an airlock, and when Colonel Varik depressurized the cabin, Webber's lunar suit stiffened around him as the air within it expanded in the absence of outside pressure.

The very real sensation was disconcerting to Webber, juxtaposed as it was with his dreamlike movements in a gravitational field only one-sixth as strong as that of Earth.

He'd now spent more than three days in microgravity, and that had affected his perception of the Moon's pull, making it feel stronger than it should. But it wasn't so much the lightness of being that felt alien to Webber, it was the change in the time and duration of his movements.

As Varik and Bowden and Rodriguez assembled their equipment by the open hatch, Webber hung back, held out his arm, then let it drop.

It fell as if it were passing through honey.

He tried jumping, just a small hop, pushing only with his feet, and failed to rise off the flight deck. Gravity might be different on the Moon, but inertia remained the same. With his feet burdened by inflexible Moon boots, he wasn't generating enough force to achieve liftoff.

So, as Varik slid a heavy box out to Rodriguez, Webber bent his knees and gave jumping another try.

This time, he did leave the deck, though his leap was only about as high as he might have managed on Earth, given the extra hundred and fifty pounds of his spacesuit. But on this second attempt, his fall back to the deck occurred, noticeably more slowly.

Webber concentrated on committing the sensation to memory. After this mission, especially after he had dealt with Salyard and Varik, this opportunity would never come his way again.

Then Varik's voice hissed over his helmet speakers. "Webber, you're up."

The colonel was standing by the open hatch, through which Webber glimpsed the lunar surface beyond. He could see Rodriguez already bounding away, around the slope, in the direction of the crash site. "One small step and all that crap," Varik said.

Webber didn't even try to comprehend how someone could regard such a moment with cynicism. No matter how many times it had been experienced. *Nor,* he added to himself, *this mission in particular.*

He bent down to duck through the hatch, then straightened up on the small platform outside and finally saw the Moon. *Saw* the *Moon.*

As only a handful of others had seen it before, in all of human history.

Words fell away from him as wonder spread within him, bringing with it the contentment of an achievement surpassing anything else he had ever done.

"Move it, Webber," Varik said. "We're on the clock."

"Right, right," Webber acknowledged, startled, unused to being out of step on a mission.

He grabbed the railing, turned around, and began to descend the metal rungs attached to the landing leg. The *Kitty Hawk* was larger than the original Apollo lunar modules, but it was still basically an ungainly, faceted cylinder, with its crew cabin on top of its lower descent stage. A ladder, another, humbler invention of humankind, was still required to set foot on the Moon.

Bowden gave him the warning when he was two rungs from the bottom. "Hold on and drop down," she advised.

Webber took the suggestion, and almost tripped as his boots hit the concave landing pad at an awkward angle. Human reflexes had evolved to react to full-gravity falls. But on the Moon, falls had easy landings.

Webber held his breath as he stepped off the footpad and onto the lunar surface. A shiver ran down his spine as he felt the slight give of the powdery covering, even heard the crunch of it through his boots. He stepped back and looked down in awe, seeing his footprints, knowing all the ones he left here would remain unchanged for thousands, perhaps millions of years.

"Let's move those boxes," Varik said.

The colonel moved rapidly down the ladder, as if well accustomed to lunar gravity, and Webber automatically stepped back from the LEV to stay out of his way, inadvertently treading on a group of ragged rocks. He threw out his arms for balance as his boots began to slip.

He was falling backward, yet so slowly he was also able to keep himself bouncing along, though each bounce propelled him farther away from the LEV.

"Don't fight it," Bowden called out to him. "Fall and brace with your arms."

Again Webber followed her suggestion and stopped struggling. From an upright position, his body fell so gradually that Webber had time to place both his hands behind him to protect his suit from contact with the ground.

"Now push," Bowden said.

Webber pushed off with both hands and, with surprisingly little effort, he was back on his feet. He felt like a human version of an inflated, anchored, punching doll.

"You'll get the hang of it," Bowden said, not unkindly.

"While you carry crates," Varik added.

Webber felt rebellious. Maybe Varik was bored by his surroundings, but he could never be. On his return to the *Kitty Hawk* and Varik and Bowden, Webber tried something he'd always wanted to try, and never dreamed he could. The old hop-and-skip stride he had seen the Apollo astronauts use. Once he had his rhythm, the bounding movement felt completely natural.

Stopping was another matter, though. He couldn't. Until he collided with the ladder.

"You've just exhausted your learning curve," Varik said. He pointed to two metal containers, shaped like soldiers' footlockers, stacked on top of each other by the ladder. Webber had last seen them stowed in the *Falcon*. "Those are yours, Webber."

The colonel checked the time readout on the computer control panel attached to his right forearm. "We've got one hour." He picked up a large cylindrical container, about a foot across and two feet tall, and moved off with his own version of the skip, in the same direction that Rodriguez had taken, toward the wreckage hidden on the other side of the slope.

Bowden picked up a second cylindrical container, then cautioned Webber, "Go down on one knee. It'll make it easier to get up with the crates."

Webber's first attempt was a failure. He couldn't get back on his feet. The crates were much heavier than he had estimated. "I thought these were empty," he said on his second, more successful try. "For debris."

"No time to take it away," Bowden said, then bounded away, her cylinder safely in hand.

Webber was soon behind her, awkwardly hopping and skipping forward, bearing both of the crates. Despite the lesser gravity, he was breathing hard as he rounded the slope and finally saw the crash site for himself.

It was not what they had told him it would be.

TTI LAUNCH CENTER / JARVIS ISLAND

"Are they wearing *camouflage?*" Cory asked as she watched the strangely outfitted astronauts gather around the crashed lander.

"Looks like it," Teller said.

A fourth astronaut hopped into range of the camera and stopped clumsily. After a moment, he dropped the two metal crates he had been carrying. He must have said something, too, because the other three astronauts turned to him.

"Should I zoom in?" Cory asked.

"Not yet. Another minute or two to establish the entire site, then we'll go in on name tags and faces." Teller turned to the technician operating the digital recorders. "Are you getting this?"

"Yes, sir. Multiple copies."

The astronauts stood in place. Occasionally, one of them made a halfhearted attempt to gesture.

"They're not doing anything," Cory said. "I can always zoom back if something happens."

"Okay," Teller agreed. "Use the zoom and see if we can get images of these people that will help identify them."

"Let's try Mister Butterfingers," Cory said. She moved her controllers to center the fourth astronaut in the center of the video display, then pushed in.

He was in the shade of the nearby slope, so his gold visor was not in place.

Cory tweaked the camera angle so the slow zoom pushed right in on the astronaut's face. And in the same instant her eyes told her he might be familiar, her heart confirmed it.

Mitchell. On the Moon with her.

USSF CENCOM / VANDENBERG AFB

The rolling hash of visual static that marred the main screen in Mission Control, Element Three, suddenly crackled into crisp imagery.

Four astronauts standing by what had to be the crashed lander.

"General, those are our people," Major Lowell said. "Check the camouflage patterns and their suits."

But Salyard did not share the major's enthusiasm. His face darkened with outrage. How could he have been outmaneuvered again? By a civilian.

"Ask yourself where that video is coming from, Major."

"Oh my God . . ." Lowell said as he realized the answer to the general's question. "Teller's rover is still operational."

"Shut it down," Salyard said. "Shut it down now!"

US SPACECOM / CHEYENNE MOUNTAIN AIR FORCE STATION

Major Bailey had lived in the world of military secrets and hidden histories long enough that she knew exactly what she was seeing on the main screen.

The video images her team had decrypted were not connected to the Chinese lunar mission.

This was the crash site her father had described.

The astronauts were on a classified mission.

As the camera pushed in on the last astronaut to join

the group, she was not surprised to recognize Captain Mitchell Webber.

And she knew the video signal could only be coming from Kai Teller's rover.

Bailey eyed the four phones at the side of her console. Gold for initiating Flash Alerts, red for receiving them, green for internal calls, and a particularly ugly gray one for everything else.

She looked again at the live images from the Moon.

She picked up the gray phone.

She told the sergeant on the switchboard that Spacecom needed to speak with the chief administrator of NASA in sixty seconds.

Then she waited, simultaneously watching both the video and her watch.

At fifty-five seconds, the gray phone rang.

RIMAE TANNHAUSER

Webber skidded to a stop when he rounded the slope and found the others by the wreckage of the crashed spacecraft. It was like nothing ever built by NASA, with a large hammer-and-sickle icon peeling away from its silver metal, with the Cyrillic initials CCCP on a faded painted rectangle by its open hatch. The words, *Slava Rossii,* were still discernible beside it.

"It's a Russian lander," Webber said. He let the crates fall from his gloves and they tumbled slowly to the lunar ground.

Everything Salyard had told him about Project Hammer and the Air Force astronaut who had died in 1978 had been an outright lie.

No, more than that. *Everything* Salyard had told him had been lies. The Russian lander was obviously not a modified Apollo lunar module. The ascent stage was a large metal sphere like a diving bell, with scooped indentations for the windows and hatch. The crumpled descent stage, what was left of it, was like a gigantic robotic spider, legs twisted in all directions.

The terrain told him more about the Russian cosmonaut's last moments. The exterior crater wall was scarred by gouges. The Russian pilot had come in too quickly, and unlike Webber, had chosen the smooth slope instead of the flat but rocky surface. The lander had hit hard, the uneven strain buckling one of its legs. Then the whole craft had rolled three hundred feet at least, cracking open, spilling everything.

"What's going on, Varik?" Now that the secret was out in the open, he saw no reason for Salyard's crew to lie to him again about their mission.

Neither did Varik. "Exactly what it looks like, Webber. This is the crash site of the Russian lunar mission that might have landed before Armstrong and Aldrin. We don't know if it's true, and we don't care. For the good of the country, we're going to sanitize it."

Then Webber saw the body. Far enough away from the lander that it was obvious the cosmonaut had survived, at least for a few minutes, maybe hours.

"How are you going to sanitize *this?*" Webber demanded.

Varik turned away from Webber, to Rodriguez. "Captain, set the timer."

"How long?" Rodriguez asked.

Varik checked his time readout. "The Chinese will be landing in forty-eight minutes. That should do nicely."

Webber took a step forward. "No! You can't!" He finally knew what they had not told him. They were going to do more than change history. They were going to erase it.

Varik pulled a tool of some sort from a pocket on his

leg. "Thanks for getting us down in one piece, Captain. But now, you are more trouble than you've ever been worth."

I was right about those pockets, Webber thought.

Varik aimed his weapon.

USSF CENCOM / VANDENBERG AFB

"I have it locked!" Major Lowell called out.

"Now!" Salyard said in fury.

Lowell threw the switch as on the video display Varik raised his HVG—High Vacuum Gun.

The video image dissolved into static, as the signal from the rover was jammed once more.

TTI LAUNCH CENTER / JARVIS ISLAND

"No!" Cory jumped to her feet and cried out, her back seizing up in sharp, agonizing pain, as she saw what was obviously a weapon being aimed at Webber.

Then the image dissolved.

"They're jamming it again!" Teller said. He looked at the recorder technician. "But you got it? You got enough?"

The technician nodded. "You'll own Salyard now," he said gleefully.

Cory leaned against the workstation, dizzy with the realization of what Teller had been keeping from her. "What do you mean, 'own'? Is that what all this was for? Blackmailing Salyard? Not exposing him?"

"This is real life, Cory. If I expose him, then he's gone, and the Space Force with him. But between what you brought back and what we have on disk, I can control him. Not only will my company thrive, but I'll be setting the direction for space exploration for the next twenty years."

He'd said it himself—Dr. No! But she hadn't listened to her own instincts. Too busy thinking that she could out-smart him, when he'd managed to manipulate everyone, including NASA and the military. *But Mitchell . . .* Well, that was her fault alone. She'd dragged him into this all by herself.

"We won, Cory," Teller said. "And it's all thanks to you."

US SPACECOM / CHEYENNE MOUNTAIN AIR FORCE STATION

One minute into her conversation with Tovah Caruso, describing exactly what was in progress on the Moon, Bailey saw the video image fade just as one astronaut pointed what seemed to be a weapon at Webber.

"Hold on, Tovah," Bailey said, breaking off abruptly. Then she called out to her team. "Okay, what happened to the signal?"

The answer came back in seconds. "It's being jammed, Major."

"From where?"

The answer took an eternity. Ten seconds. "Air Force circuits on the Milstar system. They're blasting microwaves in the Earth–Moon corridor."

Bailey relaxed infinitesimally. Some problems had easy solutions.

"Shut down Milstar," she ordered. "Every satellite offline now! I want that video signal back."

Bailey uncovered the gray phone again and spoke rapidly. "Tovah, don't talk, just listen. Since I'm going to be court-martialed anyway, can you call a press conference and hook the video feed I'm going to send you into NASA TV?"

NASA's chief administrator was as quick as she was. "I'm with you, Major. Give me five minutes."

The video signal was back in three.

10

WEBBER FLEW THROUGH vacuum seeking cover from whatever Varik aimed at him.

He saw something flash by his helmet, but heard nothing.

He lunged behind a large boulder, nearly toppling over as he skidded to a stop in a cloud of black dust. Then he crouched low, holding still, ears straining for any change in the flow of his suit's oxygen. For any sign of puncture. Nothing. All was normal.

"Smart move, Webber," Varik said over his speakers. "Now sit down and stay out of the way."

Webber understood how disadvantageous his position was. Varik could be running toward him now, and he wouldn't hear the approach. Varik could be standing five feet away from the boulder, waiting for him to look over it.

He cast his gaze around, looking for any sort of improvised weapon, found only a fist-size rock, but he grabbed it anyway, and clutched it so the sharpest edge faced out.

Then he noticed that the computer readout display on

his right forearm was reflective. He angled it out from behind the boulder, used it as a mirror.

Varik, Rodriguez, and Bowden were gathered around the two cylindrical containers from the *Kitty Hawk*. Joined together, Webber had no doubt those containers held a nuclear explosive that would vaporize this site and all its evidence.

Stopping them was his only mission now.

He just had to figure out how.

TTI LAUNCH CENTER / JARVIS ISLAND

"It's back!" Cory said as the video from the rover returned to the screen.

Teller looked confused, as if he had not anticipated this development. "They must have stopped jamming. But why?"

"Who cares?" Cory said as she slipped her hands into the rover controllers again. "Where's Mitchell?"

She could only see three astronauts now. They were doing something to two cylindrical containers that, to Cory, were all too recognizable to someone who had been an antinuclear weapons activist since she'd been in high school.

She zoomed the rover's camera in, just as one of the astronauts lifted a cone-shaped object from one of the containers.

"Those are nukes!" Cory said. "They've got nuclear bombs on the Moon!"

US SPACECOM / CHEYENNE MOUNTAIN AIR FORCE STATION

Bailey nearly choked as she recognized what the camera was pushing in on.

It was a W-71 tactical nuclear warhead.

"People," she called out to her team, "I don't care what

it takes, get me voice communications to those astronauts ASAP. Find their frequencies, get me a transmitter with the power I need, then turn me loose."

USSF CENCOM / VANDENBERG AFB

As the camera pushed in on the W-71, Salyard stared into defeat. There was no more reason for anger at the enemy. Or pride in his mission.

Everything was lost. His father's dreams. What he himself had built.

But at least he could spare the country a loss as catastrophic as his own.

He reached into his jacket, brought out the small red card with the detonation code for the warhead now on the Moon.

"Major Lowell," he said calmly. "When you see that Colonel Varik has set the timer on the warhead, please transmit this sequence."

He handed the card to the major.

"This will set off the warhead at once," Lowell said.

"That's right," Salyard agreed. "Whoever that dead Russian bastard up there is, he isn't going to take the Moon from us."

But Lowell stood up and in front of every technician in Mission Control, Element Three, he committed his first act of insubordination.

"Those are our people, General. They deserve better than that."

Salyard's eyes flashed with menace. "Don't you understand? Apollo was our triumph. NASA squandered it. But we can keep the dream alive. *We* can, Major. The United States Space Force. We can regain the respect this country has lost. Control space, and we can control the world."

Lowell crumpled the small red card and dropped it at the general's feet. "My duty is not to control the world. It's to defend my country—from enemies, foreign and domestic."

"The world's not like that anymore," Salyard said. "I gave you an order."

Lowell shook his head, more in sadness, Salyard thought with fury, than in defiance. "No one here will accept an order to kill our own people. Stand down, General."

Salyard looked at the determined faces of the others in the room, saw no sign of support, saw the end, accepted it as befit a warrior facing impossible odds. He stepped closer to Lowell, who had the grace to flinch, whispered softly, "You can't stop this, Major. I was given my orders. Tomorrow, they'll be yours."

But Lowell wasn't there yet. "Stand down."

Salyard turned and left, able to leave the field only because though his part in it was over, the war continued.

There were those in the Pentagon who would see to that.

TTI LAUNCH CENTER / JARVIS ISLAND

"There he is!" Cory said with joy. She had been panning the rover's camera back and forth, desperate, fearful.

She felt giddy with relief as she zoomed in on Webber, huddled down behind a boulder, watching the three other astronauts work with the warhead.

He's not with them, Cory thought, elated. *They tried to hurt him because he knows what they're doing, and he wants to stop them. I have to help him. But how?*

And then she laughed out loud, startling herself and everyone else in the room. Including Teller, who stared at her. "What's so funny?"

Cory's hands were a blur in motion as she twisted the

rover controls, switching them from "camera" to "drive."

"The oldest trick in the book!"

"Not with my rover," Teller said.

But Cory was on a mission of her own. She kept one hand in a controller, pushing the rover on. With the other hand, she swept up her crutch and expertly swung it around to jab Teller in his midsection.

When he doubled over with a strangled gasp of surprise, she flipped the crutch up so the padded armrest slammed into his chin.

The clash of his teeth made Cory wince, but Teller hit the floor with a satisfying thud.

Defiant, she looked around at the other members of Teller's staff, wondering what their next move was going to be, and how she could fend them all off.

Derek Frame stepped around Teller's still form, came to her chair.

Cory tightened the grip on her crutch. "Something you want to say?" she asked.

"They've got nukes on the Moon, Cory. You gotta stop them."

RIMAE TANNHAUSER

Webber realized disadvantages worked both ways. If he couldn't hear them, then they couldn't hear him.

The only strategy he had left was an all-out frontal assault, to take out Varik and his weapon first.

He'd feel a lot better about his plan if he could think of a way to create a diversion, but—

A sudden cloud of sparkling dust was rising from the ground, over by the cosmonaut's body. Webber's first thought was that a dust devil had sprung up, but he quickly ruled that out—the Moon had no atmosphere.

But it was his heaven-sent diversion. The TTI rover.

Driving straight for Varik and his crew, its robot arm thrashing.

US SPACECOM / CHEYENNE MOUNTAIN AIR FORCE STATION

As soon as the little robot started to haul across the lunar dust, Bailey let out a cheer.

From almost a half mile beneath Cheyenne Mountain, she knew *exactly* what was happening a quarter million miles from Earth: It was the cavalry riding to the rescue! And the charge was led by Cory Rey.

RIMAE TANNHAUSER

Webber waited for the first one to notice the intruder and point it out to the others.

Bowden. She gestured frantically to the rover as it closed on them, at all of five or six miles an hour.

Varik and Rodriguez bounced to their feet, Varik reaching for his weapon again.

Webber seized his opportunity, angling first to come in opposite the rover, then charging straight for Varik's back.

US SPACECOM / CHEYENNE MOUNTAIN AIR FORCE STATION

Bailey's gray phone rang. She picked it up without looking at it.

"Are you watching NASA TV?" Tovah Caruso asked.

"I surely am," Bailey said, her eyes never leaving the jerky video image from the rover as it trundled toward the three astronauts, even as Webber closed in on them from the rear. "Time to get the word out and make sure the whole country tunes in."

Those two are *a dream team,* she thought, *even on two separate planets.*

RIMAE TANNHAUSER

Webber had no time or inclination to refine his plan. He just went with brute force and slammed his outstretched hands against the back of Varik's helmet as hard as he could, hoping that the impact would slam Varik's skull against his visor—the one unpadded, unyielding surface inside his suit.

Bowden and Rodriguez leapt away in surprise and the rover kicked up more dust as it changed direction to give chase.

Webber took Bowden's earlier advice and surrendered to his fall. He stopped on Varik's back, knelt beside the man, and rolled him over.

Blood streamed from Varik's nose and there was a blotch of it on the inside of his visor. Webber's strategy had worked.

Then Varik lifted the weapon still clutched in his hand.

Webber pushed the weapon aside and raised the rock he carried and brought it down as hard and as fast as he could onto Varik's visor, sharp point first.

Varik's eyes widened as the first chip appeared in the outer, protective visor. He struggled now to raise his weapon like a club.

But Webber had given Varik all the chances he deserved. He brought the point of the rock down again. The protective visor broke apart. Webber struck again, and with that next blow, Varik's inner visor disintegrated in a sudden puff of ice crystals and spinning shards of polycarbonate. Webber's vision misted as a great cloud of boiling blood erupted from Varik's bleeding nose, gaping mouth, and eyes.

The colonel died so quickly, his body didn't even move.

Webber breathed hard as he slowly bounced to his feet, stood over the body of his enemy, looked at the rock in his hand. To come all this way, with all this technology, and to fight with rocks. What did it matter that humans had come to a new world if they brought with them all that was wrong with the old?

He threw the rock away. Stepped back from Varik's body.

And in that instant missed the worst of the blow from the folded tripod in Bowden's hand. A little something from the Russian's lander, Webber thought as he spun around, saw what had happened. He raised his arm to block a second blow, aimed at his visor.

But the second blow was more powerful and he stumbled as Bowden pressed him backward, making him trip over Varik's body. Webber raised both his arms in a futile attempt to ward off Bowden's imminent, fatal blow.

And then Bowden's arms flew out and the tripod whirled away from her and Bowden herself twisted madly as the rover jammed its vibrational cutter into the small of her back, slicing sideways through all the layers of her suit.

Bowden was dead before her body could complete its fall to the lunar surface, forever still, but for the slow bubbling of frozen blood rising like magma from the long puncture in her suit.

Webber bounced to his feet again, looked around for Rodriguez, found him sprawled in the lunar dust, his helmet dark, frosted with blood, a jagged tear in his suit as well, over his chest.

Webber looked at the rover, leaned closer to its camera.

"Cory?" he mouthed silently.

Two and a half seconds later, the robotic arm bobbed up and down.

Two hundred and fifty thousand miles apart from Corazon Rey, Webber could not escape their connection.

They were a team.

11

MITCH WEBBER WAS at peace on the Moon. A battle that ten days ago he had never known existed, had been fought and won here. And whatever happened next, because of what Cory had been able to have the rover accomplish, Webber knew its camera had been working. That meant there would be a record of all this. If the world hadn't seen it as it happened, they would soon enough.

But before Webber left, he knew there was still more of the story to tell.

He found the body of the cosmonaut.

Lying faceup, as if to watch the Earth for eternity.

The Russian's body was frozen, but there was no sign of ebullism. He had died in his suit, no indication of suffocation. Webber guessed he had suffered internal injuries from the crash. The only damage to his suit was on the glove of his right hand, where the rover had carved away its samples.

Webber brushed dust off the cosmonaut's name badge: BELYAYEV.

Webber would never forget it, and he knew millions of others would join him in that promise.

Beside Belyayev, Webber saw a dark green case with Cyrillic writing he couldn't decipher. But when he opened the case, he knew at once why no one had ever spoken of this mission, even forty years later.

Inside was a Russian-made *Volta* shoulder-launched missile, modified for use in vacuum—modified to bring down the *Apollo 11* lunar lander as it passed over this site almost forty years earlier.

Whoever had given their orders to Belyayev, whether the Soviet Politburo or some secret cabal operating in the shadows, Webber knew they had sent that cosmonaut here with one purpose in mind: If the Russians could not be first on the Moon, then neither could the Americans.

He didn't want to think about what that decision had cost the men who had made it, or what it had cost Belyayev to accept those orders.

Instead, Webber chose to focus on the fact that the weapon was still sealed in its case, even though Belyayev had possessed enough strength to walk from the wreckage to this sheltered position.

Belyayev had journeyed to the Moon. Perhaps the cosmonaut had even been here first. But because he had not deployed his weapon, Webber wanted to believe he had left hatred behind him. Whatever role history ultimately gave this cosmonaut, Webber wanted to be sure that he was first known as a man of peace.

There was something else Belyayev had brought with him.

Webber pulled it from the tube and unfurled it.

It was still bright red and gold, and like the Apollo flags had a locking arm to keep it eternally aloft on a world without air and wind.

Webber stared at that design for a long time. It was reviled in places, mourned in others, but whatever its past, this explorer and his accomplishment were part of it.

Webber stood over the body of Belyayev. As a soldier, Webber's decision had already been made. As a human being, no other decision was possible.

With the rover's camera eye watching, Captain Mitchell Webber, USN, raised the Hammer and Sickle flag of the Union of Soviet Socialist Republics on the Moon.

Then he saluted the man who had brought it, who had died for the effort, and who, like the others, had in the end come in peace for all mankind.

The war was over.

The Chinese taikonauts landed twenty minutes later.

Their lander looked identical to the mock-up Webber had seen in Red Cobra 8, less than two weeks earlier. Though here, against the impenetrable black of endless space, the unusual metal pontoons on its descent stage glowed with a pale purple light that was not the radiance of rocket fuel.

The lander hovered for long minutes as well, as if fuel consumption were of no concern to its crew. And when, at last, the Chinese lander touched down on the Moon, it did so without any spray of dust or other indication of rocket exhaust. How the craft flew was unknown to its closest human witness—Webber.

A few minutes later, two taikonauts emerged, and Webber shook their hands, not knowing which surprised them more: the newly planted Soviet flag, or his being there to welcome them.

But even if they'd been expecting to find the crashed Russian lander, maybe even had had some plans to score a propaganda victory with it, that no longer mattered.

Because, somehow, miraculously, Major Bailey had already made contact with him through his suit radio, and he knew the recordings that Cory had made possible were on every channel, being played nonstop.

In a world without lies, blackmail is impossible.

The Moon truly belonged to everyone now, as it had from the beginning.

But all Mitchell Webber wanted was to go home.

12

WEBBER RETURNED TO EARTH the thirty-second of thirty-four human beings to walk on the Moon, wondering about that number and the day they would stop counting such things. Number 500? Number 1,000? 10,000? Because that day would come, he knew, when the Moon would simply become another place. It was the way of things.

But for now, this day was bright and the California desert air was hot and the sky was blinding blue, and to have been to the Moon was still something that mattered.

He moved carefully down the stairway from the Space Shuttle *Endeavour*, determined to stay upright in full gravity, to finish this mission under his own power. At last, he stepped onto the runway, back to Earth, his white NASA sneakers on Edwards' gray-black asphalt. He closed his eyes, remembering gray boots against gray dust.

Nothing he had achieved, none of his accomplishments, would last longer or matter more than his footprints on the Moon.

They were a thousand permanent testaments to what

he'd done five days ago, the decision he had made. A thousand reasons why his country might never forgive him.

But he also remembered the words never spoken by President Nixon, words written for the astronauts of *Apollo 11* in case their mission had ended in tragedy instead of triumph; a eulogy the current president had delivered to the nation and made his own after the events of last Sunday, events witnessed by millions who knew at last that the first man to walk on the Moon had also been the first to die there.

"In ancient days, people looked at stars and saw their heroes in the constellations. In modern times, we do much the same, but our heroes are epic figures of flesh and blood. For every human being who looks up at the Moon in the nights to come will know that there is some corner of another world that is forever humankind."

Those words had also been an acknowledgment, not just for Belyayev, but for all who came before him. The unknown pioneers, driven—by whatever the motives of their times and places—to be the first.

In his dreamlike state, Webber felt hands take hold of his elbow as white-jumpsuited technicians guided him and the other four of the orbiter's crew across the tarmac to a blue NASA van. He swung his gaze slowly around the runway, glanced back at the *Endeavour*'s blinding-white form, only minutes removed from space, heat-rippled air dancing around it, its grace and power stilled for now, but not forever.

There was still a station to repair. Worlds to be explored. Heroes to be buried. Whatever new form NASA took after this, whatever remained of the United States Space Force, the mission and the dream would continue, and, Webber hoped, only good men and women would lead the way.

Unlike other shuttle landings, there was no public-address stage, no microphones, no press. Only thirty-two

technicians in white jumpsuits from the Orbiter Processing
team, with a smaller group of older men in Air Force blue,
and a handful of civilians. Those technicians who weren't
already at work on the *Endeavour* were standing by the van,
waiting for the astronauts to reach them, as if this moment
required something more than the usual clamor of congratulations, because so much had changed in the last five
days, the past and the future among them.

One development that promised to change the future
even more, in ways still unimaginable, was the new Chinese
lander's unique propulsion system. All during his return to
low Earth orbit as the sole passenger of the SOV *Falcon*,
right up to his spacewalk rendezvous with *Endeavour*,
Webber had been bombarded nonstop with questions about
what he'd seen of that lander.

But now the questions directed at the shuttle crew, himself included, addressed more mundane matters as they
neared the NASA van where a woman in a NASA windbreaker stood ready with a clipboard to check in each passenger.

But the voices merely came and went unanswered, as
Webber saw two women waiting by the van, there to speak
to him before he disappeared into the debriefing session
that would probably take weeks, ending only, at best, with
his signature on an agreement of nondisclosure; at worst,
on court-martial papers.

Tovah Caruso and—

Webber stopped walking, swaying as he tugged his
elbow free of the technician beside him, and then was
nearly knocked off his feet by the force of Cory's fierce
embrace. His journey had come full circle.

"How come nothing you do can be normal?" Cory's
voice was muffled, her face buried in his chest.

"I blame this girl I know."

She drew back, stared up at him. "Just tell me you're okay."

Clumsy for more than one reason, he drew her close again. "Now I am." When he next opened his eyes, Caruso was beside them.

"Captain Webber," she said, "welcome back to Earth. Welcome home."

A new and shockingly strong wave of emotion unexpectedly robbed Webber of his ability to speak. Something about the juxtaposition of the words "Earth" and "home." Everything was different now. He felt different now. He wondered what other surprises awaited him.

Webber fumbled with a pocket of his blue NASA flight suit and drew forth the clear plastic sample bag he had refused to let the *Endeavour* crew seal in the case with the other lunar material he'd returned with.

Inside the small bag was a circle of cloth, stitched decades ago, lovingly with pride, red silk forming a resplendent draped flag, linking the small blue disk of earth to the silver disk of the Moon. The dark dust of that new world still clung to each thread.

Webber held the mission patch out to Caruso. "I thought . . . for his family."

Caruso took the patch from him, held it for a moment, reverently, then handed it back. "His name was Pavel Belyayev. Turns out there are some relatives, and I think you'll be the one giving this to them. You're quite the hero in Russia, you know."

"Just the thing to advance my career at home."

"You're a hero here, too," Cory said with a catch in her voice.

Webber turned their praise aside. "I raised the Hammer and Sickle on the Moon. If Belyayev was there first, I changed the results of the space race."

"No. Armstrong and Aldrin were the first to land and come back," Caruso said. "You just made sure the whole story could be told, whatever the consequences."

"That makes me a whistle-blower, not a hero."

"It's one thing to be first, Mitchell," Cory said with heartfelt pride. "But it's better to do the right thing. That's what this country knows more than any other."

Webber looked down at Cory. "Flag waving? From you?"

Cory put her arm through his. "Yeah, well, blame this guy I know."

"Excuse me, Administrator Caruso?" It was the woman with the NASA jacket and the clipboard. "We're waiting on Captain Webber. He's the last one to board. We have to get him to medical."

"In a minute." Caruso looked from Webber to Cory, and whatever she was thinking of saying, she didn't. Instead, she walked toward the NASA van by herself. They were alone again.

This time when Webber finally released her, Cory was the one who couldn't breathe. The van to take him to the medics was waiting. And somewhere on the base, so were his interrogators. "I'm not saying good-bye," he said. "This won't take that long."

Cory gave him her best skeptical look. "Mitchell, they took nukes to the Moon. It's going to take forever to understand that insanity." She looked up, past him, to the sky. "Makes you wonder what else they're hiding up there."

Webber kept his face impassive, even as he saw the look on her face that told him she knew he had another secret. He hoped she'd changed as much as he had, that now she could accept that there would always be some secrets better kept. *Blue Moon.*

He tensed as Cory started to say something, to protest,

to rail against the system that he served. But, then—Webber caught his breath—she simply sighed, and took his hand.

"No good-byes," she agreed. "Because I'm not going anywhere."

Webber picked her up and hugged her, thinking of the future—their future.

"That's what you think," he said.

AFTER PRODUCING more than 12,000 pages of testimony, the Senate investigation of the ISS/Constitution disaster identified 986 design deficiencies in the space station and orbiter serious enough to be likely contributors to the unanticipated chain reaction that claimed eight lives and one shuttle, and damaged the space station.

The primary cause of those tragic events, however, was officially ruled "unknown." Additionally, no connection could be found between the disaster and the covert efforts of a rogue U.S. Air Force faction to destroy evidence of the Russian lunar landing before the Chinese could recover it. The Secretary of the Air Force and the Joint Chiefs of Staff were appropriately shocked and appalled that such a misuse of government funds and military hardware could go unnoticed. To put the taxpayers' minds at ease, a full DoD investigation was also convened, though the results, the committee chairman said with regrets, remained classified in the interests of national security.

Tovah Caruso kept her job under the president who had appointed her, and the next. Kai Teller kept his company, though he was forced to sell his Jarvis Island launch facility to the Air Force, and never funded another private lunar mission. Lieutenant-General Dwight Salyard, who was, according to those with a need to know, following orders, retired with an extra star, and the promise to never write his memoirs. With Daniel Varik *unavailable for questioning, the final determination of Ed Farren's death remained "heart attack."*

The Chinese lunar lander's unique method of propulsion was eventually identified as the Holy Grail of space exploration—a reactionless drive. The electrostatic thruster required no propellant, a consumable that accounted for more than ninety percent of the American space shuttle's mass at launch. It required access only to a source of energy that could be as simple as sunlight falling on photo-arrays, or a small nuclear reactor.

While China's engineers had labored to create the first new breakthrough in rocket propulsion since gunpowder, in the United States, electrostatic thrust devices were the domain of wild-eyed hobbyists who flew flimsy contraptions of tinfoil and balsa wood with no moving parts, only long extension cords. But most galling of all to the NASA engineers seeking to derive the principles of the Chinese breakthrough by poring over the video recordings made by Cory's rover, it appeared the new drive was based on a U.S. patent granted back in 2001. The final insult was that the patent had been filed by NASA. For reasons that had never been made clear, funding had not been available to pursue the revolutionary concept.

That denial of support led Tovah Caruso to suspect the hand of yet another government agency at work, developing the drive in secret, only to be surpassed by China. The thought reawakened her bittersweet dream of what the American space program might be if all its research efforts were allowed to be combined, instead of parceled out clandestinely.

Within two years, the International Space Station was repaired and upgraded and leased to a consortium of aerospace companies. Although tempted to gut NASA's other programs to pay all costs, Congress and the Senate didn't, their decision aided by China's surprise announcement of plans to establish by the end of the decade a permanent observatory outpost near the ice deposits at the Moon's north pole.

With politics once again fueling the fires of competition, the

House Appropriations Committee began bipartisan work in earnest with NASA to refocus on its abandoned vision for space exploration and devise a realistic way to pay for an American Mars landing within ten years. If science itself wasn't important to the politicians, beating the Chinese was. But whatever the motive for such exploration, the American people, and the world, would benefit from that competition for years to come.

Following the transfer of secret testimony from the Pentagon to the Russian government, the Russian Aviation and Space Agency underwent a management upheaval and, to cover certain accounting discrepancies discovered at the time, began supplying extra Soyuz lifeboats to the ISS at no extra charge, ensuring that six astronauts and cosmonauts could be onboard at all times. Plaques for Pavel Belyayev and Anatoly Rushkin were placed on the Wall of Heroes at the Kremlin, beside the burial vault of Yuri Gagarin, the first human in space. Commander Yuri Lazhenko, his wife, son, and daughter, moved to Cocoa Beach.

Mitch Webber and Cory Rey traveled to Russia as guests of the Russian people and were awarded the Medal of Service to the Russian State, first class—the country's highest civilian honor. They also were given plaques, which this time stated exactly what they'd done.

Major Wilhemina Bailey began an informal investigation of her own, looked through a few old files, and talked with certain retired officers. Some of her findings were quite startling to her, and she did not share them with her husband. The next time Professor Tripurasundari Shiourie raised the question of Roswell, Bailey had to wear her best poker face and say she could not discuss it.

Other than the SOV Falcon and the LEV Kitty Hawk, no other assets of the United States Space Force—or even the force's existence—were disclosed to the public. The MOL follow-ons linked to the Milstar communications satellites remained classified. The twenty-year-old weapons-testing facility on the Moon, once code-named Blue Moon, now known as Area 1, wasn't even mentioned in the classified DoD hearings.

But already bought and paid for, it did not go to waste.

Less than a year following the ISS/Constitution disaster, the facility's new owners—the United States Navy, on a mostly fact-finding and survey operation—made the first return mission to Area 1.

During their five-day stay, the naval team took a few minutes to plant another American flag on the Moon. It was larger than the old Soviet flag Webber had placed at the Russian crash site, and was made of ceramic cloth with permanent dyes guaranteed to withstand unfiltered sunlight for more than a century without fading.

And there was no danger of the new flag falling over in the exhaust of the Navy lander when the expedition returned to Earth.

Tovah Caruso's suspicions were confirmed. Another government agency was suppressing NASA's work.

The Navy lander's engines required no propellant.

ACKNOWLEDGMENTS

Once again we have been privileged to receive insights and information from those who work in the reality we turn into fiction. In particular, at Johnson Space Center, we are deeply indebted to William Foster, who generously arranged for us to see firsthand many of the settings in this novel, from the ISS training mock-up to the "batcave," as well as to try our hands in the space shuttle flight simulator. Foster's notes on an early draft of this book were invaluable, and we trust he and his colleagues will forgive us where we have simplified complex procedures for dramatic reasons.

At Kennedy Space Center, we must also thank Jeff Lauffer for his enthusiastic support, and especially for arranging our tour of the magnificent spacecraft *Atlantis*.

Closer to home, we have benefited from the boundless store of technical knowledge and the artistic talent of Michael Okuda, who not only created the emblem of the USSF and the diagrams in this book, but provided welcome notes on shuttle and station technology and operations. Michael and Denise Okuda both were instrumental in opening the doors of NASA to us, and Denise's organizational skills ensured all of us went through those doors on time and on budget.

This is our twenty-third book to be published by

Pocket Books, which we hope gives some indication of the high regard we have for our publishing team, and how much we appreciate their efforts on our behalf. For this novel, we are fortunate to have had the expertise of two editors—also known as the reader's first line of defense—John Ordover and Margaret Clark. John's sweeping story sense and enthusiasm launched this book on the proper course, and Margaret's unflagging support and professionalism brought us to a safe and solid landing. We are also indebted to Scott Shannon for always being in our corner, and to Louise Burke for her insightful guidance.

As always, our agent, Martin Shapiro of Shapiro-Lichtman, has smoothly steered us through the shoals of the publishing business, freeing us to concentrate on writing—no writer could ask for more.

In regard to certain technical matters referred to in this book, we know that NASA's current plan to retire the shuttle fleet by 2010 means there will never be a *Constitution*. But we could not bring ourselves to describe the destruction of an existing shuttle, so we reached back to the past and selected the name originally chosen for the very first shuttle, which was subsequently renamed *Enterprise*.

As for the reality of a so-called reactionless drive, we invite readers to investigate U.S. Patent #6,411,493 assigned to NASA. The technology described in this patent dates back to the 1920s and has created an international community of amateur experimenters who routinely build balsawood and tinfoil constructions called "lifters," which float without need of moving parts or propellant. Some investigators claim the lifters work because they generate an "ionic wind," which means they can only operate in an atmosphere. Others claim to have observed the lifter effect in vacuum chambers, suggesting that a different phenomenon is at work. Unfortunately, despite NASA's interest in patenting the technology, to date the agency has yet to publish the results of any peer-reviewed experiment that would either prove or disprove that lifters are something more than a wind generator. Given the simplicity of the required experiment, it's understandable why some people believe the experiment has indeed been run, and that positive results ensured that further investigation would be conducted by labs that never publish their results in anything other than highly classified military journals.

Finally, the eulogy prepared for the *Apollo 11* astronauts in the event of disaster was written by President Nixon's speechwriter at the time, William Safire.

We are thankful that the eulogy was not needed, and that Neil Armstrong and Buzz Aldrin returned safely home as the first humans to walk on the Moon.

Any opinions to the contrary are fiction, as is this book.

—J&G Reeves-Stevens
Los Angeles, November 2004